# Tempted by Love

## The Steeles at Silver Island
## A Love in Bloom Novel

## Melissa Foster

ISBN: 978-1948868501
ISBN: 1948868504

This is a work of fiction. The events and characters described herein are imaginary and are not intended to refer to specific places or living persons. The opinions expressed in this manuscript are solely the opinions of the author and do not represent the opinions or thoughts of the publisher. The author has represented and warranted full ownership and/or legal right to publish all the materials in this book.

TEMPTED BY LOVE
All Rights Reserved.
Copyright © 2020 Melissa Foster
V1.0
7.17.20

This book may not be reproduced, transmitted, or stored in whole or in part by any means, including graphic, electronic, or mechanical without the express written consent of the publisher except in the case of brief quotations embodied in critical articles and reviews.

Cover Design: Elizabeth Mackey Designs
Cover Photography: Wander Aguiar Photography

PRINTED IN THE UNITED STATES OF AMERICA

# A Note from Melissa

Jack "Jock" Steele had the world at his fingertips until he suffered a devastating loss that forever changed him. I knew the minute I met him that he needed a woman who was strong and compassionate, and Daphne Zablonski is his perfect match. But I also knew he needed her daughter, Hadley, to convince him to find his way back to the life he wanted to live and the future he deserved. What I hadn't realized was just how much Daphne and Hadley needed him. *Tempted by Love* is an emotionally captivating story about a man who has lost it all and carries a torturous secret, a divorced single mother who has everything to lose, and the little girl who helps them heal. I hope you enjoy it as much as I have. If this is your first Love in Bloom novel, all Love in Bloom stories are written to be enjoyed as stand-alone novels or as part of the larger series. Dive right in and enjoy the fun, sexy ride. For more information on Love in Bloom titles, visit www.MelissaFoster.com.

Avid readers of my Love in Bloom series will remember Jock and Daphne from the Bayside Summers series and may have also seen them in *A Little Bit Wicked*, the first book in The Wickeds: Dark Knights at Bayside.

I have included a Steele family tree and a map of Silver Island in the front matter of this book for your reference.

I have more steamy love stories coming soon. Be sure to sign up for my newsletter so you don't miss them.
www.MelissaFoster.com/Newsletter

## FREE Love in Bloom Reader Goodies

If you love funny, sexy, and deeply emotional love stories, be sure to check out the rest of the Love in Bloom big-family romance collection and download your free reader goodies, including publication schedules, series checklists, family trees, and more!
www.MelissaFoster.com/RG

Bookmark my freebies page for periodic first-in-series free ebooks and other great offers!
www.MelissaFoster.com/LIBFree

# STEELE FAMILY TREE

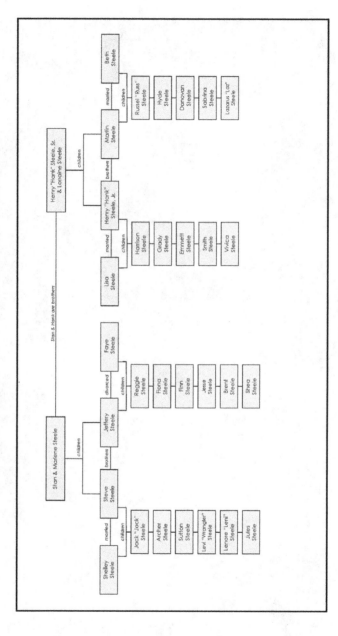

**Stan & Marlene Steele**

Children:

**Shelley Steele** married **Steve Steele**
Children: Jack "Jock" Steele, Archer Steele, Sutton Steele, Levi "Wrangler" Steele, Lenore "Leni" Steele, Jules Steele

Steve Steele and Jeffery Steele are brothers

**Jeffery Steele** divorced **Faye Steele**
Children: Reggie Steele, Fiona Steele, Finn Steele, Jesse Steele, Brent Steele, Shea Steele

Stan & Hank are brothers

**Henry "Hank" Steele, Sr. & Lorraine Steele**

Children:

**Lisa Steele** married **Henry "Hank" Steele, Jr.**
Children: Harrison Steele, Grady Steele, Emmett Steele, Smith Steele, Vivica Steele

Henry "Hank" Steele, Jr. and Martin Steele are brothers

**Martin Steele** married **Beth Steele**
Children: Russel "Russ" Steele, Hyde Steele, Donovan Steele, Sabrina Steele, Lazarus "Laz" Steele

New York Times Bestselling Author
# MELISSA FOSTER

# SILVER ISLAND

Wildlife Refuge

Rock Harbor

Seaport

Fisherman's Wharf

Brighton Park

Seaport Primary

Rock Bottom Bar & Grill

Trista's    Happy End

Silver Island Airport

Rock Harbor Primary

Lovers Cove

Top of the Island Winery

The Bistro

Silver Monument

Silver Island Community College

Silver House

Majestic Park

Brighton Bluffs

The Sweet Barista

Scoops

Silver Island High

Silver Harbor

Sunset Beach

Silver Haven Primary

Marina

Fortune's Landing

Silver Haven

Chaffee

Fortune's Cove

Bellamy Island

Cuddlefish Cove

# Chapter One

DAPHNE ZABLONSKI WAS running late *again*. Her entire life had been running just south of *on time* since her daughter, Hadley, was born nearly three years ago. Luckily, the friends she and Hadley were meeting for breakfast were very understanding, as were her bosses, Drake and Rick Savage and Dean Masters, the owners of Bayside Resort, where she worked as the office administrator. She only had to walk next door for breakfast, which was great, but first she had to get out the door, and she couldn't shake the feeling she was forgetting something. *Hadley's backpack, bird, lunch, snacks, water bottle...?*

She glanced at her honey-haired daughter sitting on the floor by the coffee table playing with her favorite toy, a stuffed bird given to her by Dean's brother Jett. Jett was one of only a handful of people her little girl gifted with a smile. Hadley withheld her adorable toothy grins as if she had only a limited supply, which sometimes saddened, and often worried, Daphne. Hadley's latest obsession, for whom she had an endless supply of smiles, was Jack "Jock" Steele, who was quite possibly the most gorgeous man Daphne had ever set her eyes on, and equally mysterious. When Hadley wasn't around, Jock came across as an intriguing gentleman who knew far more about etiquette than Daphne probably ever would. But all that disappeared the minute he set eyes on her little girl. While Hadley would give her baby teeth to be in Jock's arms, Jock cringed every time she was near him.

*Story of my life.*

Being a single mother was hard enough. Having to dodge emotionally unavailable hot guys because of her daughter's penchant for them made it even more difficult.

"Go now?" Hadley turned serious blue eyes to Daphne. "See my baby?"

Rick and his wife, Desiree, had recently had a baby boy, Aaron, and Hadley was madly in love with him.

"Not yet, chickadee. Mommy needs to figure out what I'm forgetting." *And make sure the coast is clear.*

She and Hadley lived above the resort's main office. Jock had rented a cottage there for the next few months, and Hadley made a beeline for the tall, darkly handsome *cringer* every time she saw him. Daphne had to time their exits carefully, or she'd be forced to endure that beautiful man looking like he wanted to bolt at the sight of her precious little girl.

She hurried to the window for her morning spying mission. Although Jock rarely came out at night, mornings were a different story. Sometimes he sat outside with his laptop, writing, she assumed, but other times he went running with her bosses. Daphne didn't know much about Jock's current life, although she knew he was from Silver Island, near Martha's Vineyard, had written a bestselling book when he was in college, and then he had spent a decade taking care of Harvey Fine, an aging philanthropist. Harvey was Daphne's friend Tegan's great-uncle. He had passed away last summer, and from what Tegan had said, the loss had torn Jock up. He'd taken off to travel and had returned a few months ago to help Tegan with her late uncle's amphitheater business.

Daphne peered past the array of cottages flanking the recreation center to the glorious view of Cape Cod Bay and allowed her gaze to linger there for a few seconds, hoping it would calm her quickening pulse. But just as it had since Jock had moved in, her stupid heart beat faster as she shifted her gaze to cottage number three. She felt like a stalker, noting that there were no lights on and there was no movement in the yard. If Jock was going running this morning, he'd meet up with Rick or Dean. Daphne glanced toward the inn where Rick and Desiree lived and then in the direction of Dean's cottage and breathed a sigh of relief. The coast was clear.

Hadley pushed to her feet in her bright-yellow shorts and cute white shirt with tiny pink bows all over it and toddled to the door. "Go *now?*"

"Yes!" Daphne hurried to the foyer, shouldered her purse and Hadley's backpack, and pulled the door open. As Hadley toddled out with bare feet, Daphne groaned, realizing what she'd forgotten. "Hold on, Had. We forgot your shoes."

"*No* wait." Hadley plopped onto her butt on the top step.

"*Hadley,*" Daphne said in her best warning voice, causing Hadley to huff out a breath. Daphne peeked inside and snagged her daughter's sandals from the foyer.

She hated that their mornings were always rushed. It seemed no matter how early they got up, they still ran behind. But she'd figured out a few time-saving tricks, like putting Hadley's backpack in the car *before* meeting her friends for breakfast so she wouldn't have to trudge back upstairs with her little curmudgeon, which could cost them an additional ten minutes. Longer if her newly potty-trained princess needed to go to the bathroom, because Hadley insisted on stripping naked every time she used the potty. But family and friends were important to Daphne, and she'd rather give Hadley the fun of a quick breakfast with friends who cherished her as much as Daphne did and allow her to spend a few minutes loving up baby Aaron than just send her off to daycare as if that were the most significant part of their day.

"*Now*, Mommy?" Hadley asked as Daphne shut the door.

"Yes. *Go*." She locked the door as Hadley slid down the steps on her bottom, making a singsong "Ah*haahha*" noise as she went.

Daphne followed her down and pushed open the door that led into the resort offices. There was another set of steps that led from Daphne's bedroom balcony to the ground below, but the steps were too steep for Hadley, so they almost always used the office entrance.

She nudged Hadley along. "Come on, baby. We're late." They hurried past her desk, and Daphne unlocked the front door and pushed it open. A wave of dry heat held the promise of another summer scorcher.

Hadley rushed out the door, turning around on her belly to slide down the front steps.

"Wait for me," Daphne said as she locked the office door.

"*Huwwy*." Hadley popped up to her feet in the grass, immediately hopping from one foot to the other. "Pokey! Pokey! Pokey!"

"Sit down on the step. Let's put on your sandals."

"I do it!" Hadley plunked down in the grass. "Pokey legs!" She rocked on her butt from side to side.

"Sit on the steps, honey."

Hadley shook her head, lips pursed, brows furrowed.

"Suit yourself." Daphne handed her the sandals. There were only so many battles a mother could fight, and pokey grass on her daughter's legs was *not* one of them.

The offices were located across the gravel road from the tennis courts and pool, which were busy all summer long and would come to life in another hour or two. Daphne always parked in front of the office, so she wouldn't need to worry about Hadley darting out in front of cars. Feeling the seconds ticking by like minutes, she opened her car door and leaned in to tuck her purse under the seat. She glanced out the driver's-side window at her little slice of heaven—two wooden chairs and a small table tucked beneath the umbrella of a large tree where she sat and read every night. An anticipatory thrill moved through her. Her days were so busy, by the time Hadley went to bed, she craved the simple, quiet spot.

"Okay, little miss. Ready?" She turned around and found Hadley's stuffed bird lying on the ground and her daughter running across the grass toward Jock. He was coming out of his cottage with Rick and Jett, all three of them shirtless. Daphne's pulse raced, bringing beads of sweat to her skin, as Jock looked over—and froze.

*No, no, no!*

Daphne picked up Hadley's bird, hoping to distract her daughter with it, and ran after her. "*Hadley!* Come back! I have your bird!"

Jock's gaze shot past Hadley to Daphne. *Look away. Please look away.* She didn't know if she was hoping he would look away or if she was telling herself to, but she was powerless to break their connection, and he continued staring, turning her into a tingly, anxious mess. She'd always been a curvy girl, and she was still carrying a good fifteen pounds of the weight she'd gained during her pregnancy. Her breasts felt like water balloons, her thighs rubbed together, and her belly jiggled with every step. She felt like she was moving in slow motion as his eyes drifted down her body, spreading heat like wildfire in their wake.

"*Dock! Dock!*" Hadley yelled, running faster.

Her daughter's pleas snapped her back to reality, and as Rick stepped forward and swooped Hadley into his arms, Daphne swore Jock took a few steps back. *Ugh!* She must be delirious to have been lost in a man who couldn't even look at her daughter.

Hadley pushed at Rick's chest, tears streaking her face as she reached grabby hands toward Jock. "*Dock! My Dock!*"

"I've got you." Rick rubbed Hadley's back, trying to coax her into calming down. He was as sweet with her as he was with his new baby boy.

"I'm sorry," Daphne panted out, sweat dripping between her breasts, as she reached for her daughter.

"It's okay. I've got her. Catch your breath," Rick said.

Jock turned an apologetic gaze to Daphne and said, "Sorry, Daph."

"Here, give Hadley to me," Jett suggested. "She loves Uncle Jett." Jett had been Hadley's pre-Jock obsession.

As Rick tried to hand her over, Hadley wailed, "*Dock!*"

Daphne's heart broke for her daughter as Jock's jaw tightened. This was *exactly* what she'd hoped to avoid.

"Sorry, Hadley," Jock said with a regretful expression. "I'll meet you guys down by the water." He headed for the path that led down the dunes.

"Dock! *Peese!*" Hadley cried, arms outstretched.

Daphne wanted to shake Jock and give him a piece of her

mind, but Hadley needed her, so she retracted her mama claws and reached for her daughter. "Come here, baby. Sorry, you guys," she said, trying to ignore the pitying look in Rick's eyes.

"Daphne, don't take it personally," Rick said. "Jock doesn't go anywhere near Aaron."

"Yeah? Well, that stinks. What kind of a friend does that?" She patted Hadley's back and said, "It's okay, sweetie. Let's go have some of Desiree's breakfast goodies."

"*Dock…*" Hadley whimpered, tucking her face in the crook of Daphne's neck.

Daphne stroked her back. "Shh. It's okay, baby. Hold your bird." She handed Hadley her bird, and Hadley clutched it against her chest.

"Daph," Jett said cautiously. "Jock's a good man. He's just uncomfortable around little kids."

Jett had always been good to Hadley, bringing her presents and lavishing her with attention. Daphne trusted his judgment, but he and Jock had gotten close these last few months, and sometimes friendship had a way of overshadowing deficits.

"Well, this is *my* little kid, and she's hurt and confused." Daphne brushed Hadley's tear-soaked hair from her cheek and lowered her voice to say, "He doesn't need to *like* her, but that was…" She shook her head and shut her mouth before anything too harsh came out.

"I get it," Jett said as she started walking toward the inn. "But you can't judge a man until you've walked in his shoes. I thought the soles of my shoes were worn thin, but they're nothing compared to his."

His words gave her pause, and she stopped walking. Jett wasn't one to refer to the broken fences that had kept him from his family for many years and had only recently been rebuilt.

She met his gaze, hoping he'd say more, but he just shrugged and said, "That's all I can tell you."

"*Hungy*, Mommy," Hadley said softly.

Daphne glanced at Rick, hoping he'd give more of an explanation.

"I don't know what's going on with him," Rick said. "But I know Jock's not a mean-spirited person or a child hater."

She didn't know how to respond, so she said, "I'll keep that in mind." She pressed a kiss to Hadley's forehead. "Say goodbye to Rick and Jett."

"Bye," Hadley said in a craggy voice.

"See you soon, sweetie," Jett said.

Rick cocked a grin and said, "Hey, Had. Don't eat all of Desiree's chocolate-filled croissants. Save one for me."

Hadley lifted serious eyes to Rick, his attempt at lightening the mood having no effect, and said, "*'Kay*."

Daphne mulled over Jett's words as she carried Hadley across the grass. A cool breeze swept up the dunes, and she turned her face toward it, catching sight of Jock on the beach below, pacing by the water's edge. Her stomach knotted.

He had become part of their friend group through Tegan. Daphne didn't go out with her friends often, but when she did, if Jock was there, he was never standoffish toward anyone except Hadley, which was why Daphne worried he simply disliked her daughter. But given what Jett and Rick had said, she wondered if there was more to it.

"Dock!" Hadley pointed at Jock.

Daphne silently chided herself for not walking farther away from the dunes where Hadley couldn't see him.

"*Dett*." Hadley accentuated her word with a shake of her hand. "*Wick!*"

Relieved the sight of Jock hadn't brought more tears, Daphne tried not to let Jock's behavior get the better of her, and in her best happy-mommy voice, she said, "They're going running, and we're going to see Aaron and eat breakfast."

"My baby!" Hadley wriggled from Daphne's arms and ran toward the white picket fence surrounding the side yard of the old Victorian inn. Summer House and the accompanying cottages were owned by Desiree and her half sister, Violet, who had left last week to travel overseas with her husband.

Dean's wife, Emery, came out of the kitchen door cradling Aaron in her arms, and Cosmos, Desiree's scruffy pooch, darted past her, causing Hadley to squeal. Hadley crouched and pushed her hand through the fence. Cosmos licked her fingers, and when Hadley pushed her cheek against the fence, he licked that, too. A glorious smile split her daughter's pudgy cheeks, and sweet giggles tumbled out. Music to Daphne's ears.

"How about we go in and see him?" Daphne opened the gate, and Hadley toddled in.

"Morning, girls," Emery called out as Hadley raced by her chasing Cosmos. Emery taught yoga at the inn. She was about four and a half months pregnant, and she'd just started to show, but she still looked hot in her yoga pants and yellow tank top, with her long light-brown hair pinned up in a ponytail. "Girlfriend, why do you look like you're ready to kill someone on such a gorgeous morning?"

"Don't ask," Daphne said, admiring Aaron. "Good morning, little man. Hadley was so excited to see him, and now look at her, chasing after Cosmos." If only it was that easy to distract herself from a certain resort resident. Cosmos and Hadley began running around the table, and Daphne said, "Hadley, play with Cosmos *away* from the table, please."

Hadley ran toward the fence on the far side of the yard, and Cosmos bounded after her just as the other girls came out of the house with breakfast. Their friendly greetings brought Daphne's tension down a notch.

"I wish I had that much energy in the mornings," Desiree said as she set a tray of croissants and fruit on the table. She looked beautiful in a floral nursing top and tan shorts, her blond hair tumbling over her shoulders in loose waves.

Chloe set a tray of bacon and eggs on the table and said, "I have that much energy in the mornings. But Justin and I do our best to use it up."

The girls laughed.

Chloe was a tall, slender blonde. She was the administrator for an assisted living facility, and she'd recently suffered a frightening sexual harassment situation with her boss. It had been harrowing for her and her fiancé, Justin Wicked, an artist and a member of the Dark Knights motorcycle club. Thankfully, they were past that now, and Daphne was glad her friends' lives were finally getting back to normal.

"It sounds like you and Justin are on the same page as me and Dean." Emery nuzzled Aaron and said, "Pregnancy hormones are the *best*."

Tegan set a pot of coffee and a carafe of orange juice on the table and said, "There are no pregnancy hormones over here, but I'm still like the Energizer Bunny."

Daphne was happy for her friends, but now that they were all coupled off, her lack of a love life seemed magnified. As she dished breakfast onto a plate for Hadley and began cutting the fruit for her, she said, "You guys have fun with that while I'm over here buying stock in Energizer batteries. My battery-operated boyfriend has been the only action I've gotten since my divorce. After three years of exclusivity, I'd say my BOB and I are pretty much on the marriage track." She glanced at Hadley, knowing she should call her over to eat, but Hadley listened to *everything* these days, so she let her play for a few more minutes and filled a plate for herself.

"We've all been there," Emery said.

"Mm-hm," Chloe said. "Well, not *three* years, but a long time."

"Your time will come," Desiree said, pouring coffee for everyone.

Emery handed Aaron to Desiree and plucked a piece of fruit from the tray. "You're a smart, gorgeous mama, Daphne. The right man is probably just around the corner."

Daphne bit into a piece of bacon and said, "Package deals are not exactly the going trend, and I don't have time to meet a guy, much less date one."

"What about Everett?" Desiree asked. Everett Adler was a music teacher at the local high school who ran the offices of Bayside Resort on the weekends. "You two have a lot in common. He's divorced with a little boy, and you both work at Bayside."

"I forgot he was divorced," Emery said. "He's really cute, and his little boy is adorable."

"Everett is great, but it's not like that between us. He doesn't make me all tingly." The trouble was, nobody made her body tingle like Jock did, which was ridiculous. Besides, when she was around him without Hadley, she usually became too flustered to speak.

"I can't be the only one who has noticed the way Jock looks at you." Tegan tore off a piece of a chocolate croissant and popped it into her mouth.

Daphne sipped her juice and said, "Yeah, like a mess of a mom who can't control her toddler."

"More like a guy who wants to sink his teeth into your *honey bun*," Chloe said with a smirk.

Daphne gave her a deadpan look.

"What? There's serious sizzle between you two," Chloe said. "He's always checking you out."

There were times like this morning when he was *looking* at her, but probably not seeing much more than the woman who couldn't control her little girl. Then there were the rare occasions when their eyes had briefly met across a room and she'd thought that maybe she'd seen a spark of interest. But he'd only done it when Hadley wasn't with her, and she'd quickly realized he'd probably just been making sure her daughter didn't pop up. If not for Hadley, he probably wouldn't ever even notice her. It didn't matter anyway. She didn't want a man who didn't want her daughter. She'd been down that painful route with Hadley's father.

"If not for his fear of Hadley, I don't think he'd even notice me."

"Why not?" Emery asked. "Look at you. You're curvaceous and beautiful."

Daphne scoffed and grabbed her belly roll. "*This* does not create inescapable lust like you guys have with your guys."

"Oh, *please*." Emery waved her hand dismissively. "Dean thinks motherhood is sexy—all phases of it."

"Dean would say women with three legs were sexy if you had that many, too," Daphne teased. Her friends' significant others were madly in love with them, and Daphne wanted that, too. But she needed more. She wanted someone who adored every part of her, including her daughter.

"Remember when we went to help Tegan with her amphitheater a few months ago and Jock was there making breakfast?" Chloe asked. That was when Jett and Tegan had been dating only a few weeks, before Jett had moved back to the Cape to live with her. He'd traveled all the time, and Tegan had missed him terribly. She'd also been trying to get new programs for the amphitheater up and running. Chloe had gathered the troops, and they'd all taken the day off to help Tegan with her work and distract her from missing Jett.

"Of course," Daphne said. "I'll never forget our Absentee Boyfriend Damage Control mission."

"Then you remember that when Jock put a plate of bacon on the table, you said you were going to skip it because it went straight to your hips," Chloe reminded her.

Tegan's eyes widened and she said, "I remember that. Jock gave her one of those lusty looks and said with a figure like hers, she shouldn't worry about it."

"Because with a body like mine, what's another pound or two?" Daphne sighed. "Look, I appreciate your support, but I know I'm not every guy's cup of tea, and that's okay. I have child-bearing hips, a thick waist, meaty thighs, and my arms jiggle, but I *like* myself, and I like food too much to want to change. Especially for a man."

"But *that's* what we're saying," Chloe exclaimed. "You're beautiful exactly as you are, and guys definitely check you out. Jock included. He was leering at you the whole time at Gavin and Harper's wedding. Justin even made a comment about it."

"Oh, please. The only one Jock lit up for at that wedding was Tara, that blond photographer. Remember the way she hugged him?" Daphne would never forget it, because she'd been a teeny-tiny bit jealous.

"Didn't she say they were old friends?" Emery asked.

Daphne rolled her eyes. "Like nobody sleeps with their old friends?"

"I think you're wrong. I haven't seen Jock look at anyone else the way he looks at you," Chloe insisted. "I think that man knows true goodness when he sees it."

"We can agree to disagree on that point, but it wouldn't matter if he did. He got on my last nerve this morning," Daphne admitted. "Hadley took off running toward him, like she always does, and he froze. You guys know how he is with her—and don't try to pretend otherwise. I always try to avoid him when I have Hadley, but I swear she has a built-in homing device specifically for the big, *cringing*, frustratingly hot pain in my butt. He practically bolted while Hadley cried for him. It was heartbreaking. You know, when I met him at Gavin's birthday party last year, I said he must be pretty special for Hadley to have attached herself to him that night the way she had. Jock said her radar was *off*, and I have to agree. My poor daughter has got the worst man radar." *And clearly since I think he's hot, I have the same problem.* "I have to find a way to help her or she's going to spend her whole life chasing unavailable men. I don't know if it's because my ex isn't in our lives, or because I'm doing something wrong, or what."

"Hadley does *not* have bad radar. I think it's just the opposite. She *loves* Jett, and he's the best man I know," Tegan said. "Remember when we were painting your apartment, and I was telling you guys about me and Jett getting together? Everyone else said he'd never settle down, but, Daphne, you told me that you thought there was a great guy under all the cold-shouldering he used to do. You said you wouldn't blame me for falling for him. Well, you were right, so I think Hadley is spot-on with her male radar. I've known Jock for a *long* time, and beneath all of his cold-shouldering toward little ones lies a great man, too."

"*And* you're an amazing mom, Daphne," Desiree said as she began nursing Aaron. "Don't ever doubt that. You're not doing something wrong just because Hadley runs to Jock. He won't come near Aaron, either. He said he's uncomfortable around babies, and I don't think that's all that strange. Not everyone is good with kids."

"I know. I get the whole not being good with kids thing. But it's not easy to watch my little girl begging for his attention and having her tiny heart broken. Jett said something this morning that made me think there's more to Jock's aversion to kids than just disliking them." Daphne bit into a croissant and looked at Tegan. "Do you know if there is?"

All eyes turned to Tegan, and she said, "He doesn't dislike children." She lowered her eyes and pushed food around on her plate.

"Spill it, chick," Emery said.

Tegan's brows knitted. "Okay, *yes*. There's more to it, but it's not my story to tell. He didn't even tell me about it until I'd known him for a few years."

"I respect your loyalty, but *Daphne* is our girl," Chloe said firmly.

"I know. I'm sorry, Daph, but I can't breach his trust," Tegan said. "What I can tell you is that I think he's still having a hard time with Harvey's death, which is understandable. Imagine caring for someone twenty-four-seven for your entire adult life, and then suddenly they're gone and you're alone."

"It's been a *year*," Daphne said carefully. "I haven't dealt with losing someone I loved, but you seem okay and he was your relative."

"I am okay, but I didn't live with my great-uncle day in and day out for years on end. You have to understand, Jock left his entire life behind when he came to live with Harvey. His world revolved around my uncle because of his poor health, and despite their age difference, they were best friends. Jock's starting over. He was a *brilliant* writer, but he hasn't written in more than a decade. I was hoping that all the traveling he did would help him find his muse and work through his troubles. But I don't think it did because he put all that time into helping me with the theater, which I love, but it tells me he's not putting words on the page."

"That's the other thing I'm wondering about. When your uncle ran the theater, it was solely a children's theater. You said Harvey went to nearly every show, and Jock had to be with him, right?" Daphne asked.

"I know what you're getting at," Tegan said. "You want to know how Jock could be around all those kids and not freeze up or walk away. I asked him about that a few weeks ago, and he said the kids were there for the shows and for Harvey. They never tried to connect with Jock. He said he felt invisible to them. But I know firsthand that he created those barriers. He was standoffish during the shows and made it clear that he was there for Harvey and nothing would take his attention away from him. Believe me, plenty of single moms tried to change that. I saw it when I visited, and I used to tease him about it. Harvey did, too. But it was like Jock had blinders on. I'm sorry he has a tough time with young kids, and I can't imagine how hard it is to see him react that way to Hadley, but he's a *good* man and he's worth being patient with."

"It's not like that between us. I was just curious, but I appreciate your insight." Daphne saw Hadley toddling toward Aaron and Desiree. She hurried around the table and said, "I have to get Had's hands washed before she gets puppy germs all over Aaron."

She scooped up her daughter and took her inside to wash her hands. When they came back out, Hadley went straight to Desiree and stroked Aaron's head as Desiree nursed him. "I love my baby."

"Aaron loves you, too, sweetie," Desiree said. Her love of Hadley was as tangible as her love for her own son.

"I kiss him?" Hadley asked.

"She's so precious," Chloe said quietly.

Desiree nodded. "Yes, you can kiss him."

Hadley kissed Aaron's head, and Daphne's heart melted. Hadley's gushing over the baby was bittersweet. Daphne had always wanted a big family. But the way her life was going, there would be no siblings in Hadley's world for a very long time, if ever.

"*Awwon* eating?" Hadley asked.

"He is. Do you want some breakfast?" Desiree asked.

Hadley scowled, vehemently shaking her head. "I big *guul*."

"She thinks you want to nurse her." Daphne patted the chair beside her and said, "You are a big girl, and Mommy's got your breakfast right here. We need to eat pretty quickly to get to school."

Daphne had heard horror stories about children crying when they were dropped off at preschool. She'd decided early on to call daycare *school* in the hopes that when Hadley started preschool next week, she wouldn't be one of those crying children.

"I'm totally stealing your use of *school* when Aaron gets

bigger," Desiree said as Hadley climbed onto the chair beside Daphne.

"Let's hope it works," Daphne said.

They chatted as they ate, and Daphne tried to keep up, but her thoughts kept trickling back to Jock's continual dismissal of her daughter and Tegan's private knowledge of whatever was behind it.

"Hello?" Chloe waved her hand in front of Daphne.

"Sorry. I must have zoned out." She blinked several times to clear her head and glanced at Hadley, who was devouring blueberries.

"We're all getting together for a bonfire on the beach Friday night. Can you make it?" Chloe asked.

"Let me check my very busy social calendar." Daphne laughed and said, "Oh yeah, I *don't have one*. Of course Hadley and I can make it."

"Good." Chloe finished her juice and said, "I was also wondering if you had any thoughts on where we should hold the next book club meeting."

Daphne and Chloe ran an online erotic romance book club with members all over the world. Although most of the discussions took place on the forum, every month a member was chosen at random to select the next month's book and the location of the in-person meeting. Members who couldn't make it to the meeting were invited to join them via video chat. Daphne, Chloe, Tegan, and a handful of other members from the Cape got together for their own monthly meetings. This month a member in Nebraska had chosen the book *His Surrender* and a location that was near her home.

"How about Nauset Light Beach?" Daphne suggested. Her parents had a standing date with Hadley the nights of Daphne's monthly book club meetings, and even though they kept her overnight every few weeks, they were always eager for more.

Chloe nodded. "Sounds good to me. What do you think, Tegan?"

"Yes, perfect. I just started reading this month's book." A shimmer of excitement flared in Tegan's eyes. "Have you started it yet?"

"Yes," Chloe and Daphne said in unison.

"Talk about being thrown right into the fire. I'd let that sexy chef"—Chloe glanced at Hadley—"*lick my muffins* any day."

"I like muffins," Hadley said around a mouthful of eggs.

Daphne stifled a laugh as she wiped Hadley's mouth. "That's because you're my mini me." But unlike her daughter, Daphne smiled often. She'd been through enough with her ex-husband to realize how precious good times and close friends were, and to appreciate them all.

Desiree cradled Aaron in her lap as she fixed her nursing bra and said, "I can't read those books without turning bright red."

"Why do you think I hide in my chair and read at night when it's dark out and nobody can see my face?" Daphne said. When she and Chloe had first started the book club, they'd planned to read all types of romance. Daphne had never even read erotic romance until a member had chosen an erotic book. It had taken some time to get comfortable with the raw sexuality in erotic romance novels, but once she had, it hadn't taken much for her to allow herself to fantasize about being one of the heroines. Now erotic romances were all their book club read, and she couldn't get enough of them.

"We all know why you read those books. To rev you up for that *boyfriend* you've had for three years," Emery said with a wink.

There was some truth to that. Her life was so focused on work and taking care of Hadley, she couldn't remember the last time a living, breathing man had made her feel *wanted*. Not that she'd ever be brave enough to be as open, passionate, and dirty with a real man as the heroines in her books were, but fictional boyfriends knew all the right things to say and do to make a woman feel safe enough to want to let go. To make *her* want to let go too.

"I don't know how you guys keep track of all those members," Desiree said, drawing Daphne back to the conversation.

"Daphne is a pro at keeping track of people and what they need," Chloe said. "We share the answering of posts on the forum, but Daphne does the heavy lifting when it comes to handling the online discussion questions each month, coordinating in-person meetings and Skype sessions, and coming up with ways to keep the forum fresh and exciting for new and existing members. She amazes me."

"You do just as much, Chloe, and planning meetings and coming up with ideas for discussions are what I love doing the most."

Before taking the job at Bayside, Daphne had worked at other resorts where she'd handled events, and she missed it desperately. She'd thought the book club might fill that longing, but as much as she enjoyed it, she still missed real event planning. Now that Hadley was getting bigger, she had more time to think about her future—*their* future—and the things she wanted for them. Like a small home of their own someplace where there were other children for Hadley to play with and a job where she had new, exciting things to look forward to. When Daphne had taken the job at the resort, events had been on her bosses' agenda for a year or two out, but it had been two years and she was still waiting. Her mother had been urging her to talk with them about the event ideas for the resort she'd been jotting down and tucking away. Maybe it was time to feel out the situation. What better way than to ask her bosses' wives?

"Can I get your opinions about something?" Daphne asked.

"Of course," Emery said.

"Ever since Desiree and Rick's wedding here at Summer House and Harper and Gavin's wedding on Silver Island, I've been *really* missing event planning. I'm thinking about asking the guys how they'd feel about hosting weddings and other events at the resort. We get calls about it all the time. I've turned down two people just this week. Do you think they'd be open to the idea?"

"You're already so busy," Chloe said.

Daphne shrugged. "I know, but I love planning events. They're fun for me."

Chloe shook her head. "I hate to tell you this, but Serena said that Drake's time is stretched so thin between the resort and his music shops, I doubt he has anything left to give." Drake's wife, Serena, was Chloe's younger sister. In addition to co-owning Bayside Resort, Drake owned a chain of music shops along the East Coast. He and Serena were away for the next few weeks setting up a new shop in another state.

"And with Aaron, I want Rick to work less, not more," Desiree said. "I'm sorry, Daphne."

"Me too, with Dean," Emery agreed. "He's already splitting time between the resort and his landscaping business. I think the guys really like how low-key the business is. It's manageable for them, and they've worked hard to get here. *You've* worked hard to get it there. Maybe you can do smaller events for the renters? Like game nights?"

"Maybe," Daphne said, feeling deflated. "We'd better get going or I'll be late for work again. Finish up, Had."

Hadley pushed her finger through the top of her croissant. When she pulled it out, it was covered in chocolate. "*Wick* want *dis?*" She sucked the chocolate off.

Emery stifled a laugh and said, "Oh boy. You are going to have your hands full when she's a teenager."

"Tell me about it." Daphne hoped Hadley would grow up to be less shy about sex and her body than she was but still have enough respect for herself to demand it from others. She had no idea how to teach that to her, but she was due a trip to the library and it never hurt to do a little research. She wiped Hadley's hands and said, "Are you ready to go to school?"

Hadley nodded, climbing off her chair as she said, "Kiss my baby bye-bye."

Daphne watched her toddle around the table, kiss Aaron's head, and tell him she loved him. The girls mooned over her. Hadley might not be a smiley child, but she was loving, thoughtful, and kind. Maybe it shouldn't bother Daphne that Jock didn't stick around long enough to appreciate those things about her, but it did. The same way it bothered her that the one man she should stay away from was the only man who made her body go up in flames.

# Chapter Two

*ANOTHER DAY SHOT to hell.*

How many days did that make it? Three hundred and sixty-five torturous days and as many unbearable nights? For ten years?

*No. Not ten.* The time Jock had spent with Harvey had been anything but a waste.

He tried to focus on the heavy bag as he beat it to smithereens, blocking out the din of the boxing club and the self-loathing permeating his mind, but the morning had been replaying in his head like a bad movie all damn day. He couldn't escape the sounds of Hadley's cries or the hurt and anger in Daphne's eyes as he'd stood there without saying a word like a fucking prick when that adorable little girl had come running toward him. He'd been pounding the heavy bag for forty minutes, and still Hadley's pleas brought back the sounds of his baby's weak cries and the crushing feeling in his chest when his son had taken his last breath.

He punched the bag harder. Sweat dripped down his face, burning his eyes as memories of the car accident slammed into him. The crash had stolen Jock's girlfriend, Kayla, and their son. It had driven a wedge between him and his twin brother,

Archer, Kayla's best friend since childhood, and had sent Jock spiraling into a depression he was sure would be his end. He gritted his teeth, punching faster, harder, pushing past muscle fatigue, past the clenching in his gut, struggling to find his limit so he could push past that, too. He'd hit the damn bag until he dropped if he had to. He *should* be able to put his horrific past behind him and move forward by now, to pick up that sweet little girl and earn that pretty smile along with her beautiful mother's respect. Daphne probably hated his fucking guts, and he didn't blame her. But she and her daughter were two of the reasons he'd come back to the Cape to try to work through his hellish past instead of trying to settle down in some other part of the country. Come hell or high water, he was going to find his way clear of this—or die trying.

Brock "the Beast" Garner stepped beside him, watching him go at the bag. At six four and about two thirty, with thick blond hair and chiseled features, Brock lived up to his nickname. He was a local boxing champion and the owner of Cape Boxing, the club where Jock had been trying to find his salvation for the past few months.

Jock dragged his forearm across his sweaty brow and said, "Hey, man. How's it going?"

"Seems like it's going a lot better for me than it is for you." He flashed a friendly smile that turned him from a beast to a gentle giant. "I haven't seen you going at it this hard for a while. What's happening in that head of yours?"

"Just trying to calm the chaos." Jock wasn't one to air his dirty laundry. Jett and Tegan knew what he'd been through, as had Harvey, but beyond that, he kept his shit locked down tight. Or rather he *had*, until he'd lost Harvey. Now the ghosts of his past were rattling their chains, trying to break free from the dungeon in which he'd buried them, and he had no fucking clue how to stop them.

"Woman trouble?" Brock asked.

*If only.* Jock hadn't had a relationship with a woman since the accident. He swallowed hard, pushing back the memories before he dredged that awful shit up, too. "Yeah, you know how it is," he said. It wasn't a total lie. Daphne was a woman, and she definitely created chaos in his mind.

"Can't say that I do." Brock eyed his raven-haired wife, Cree, sauntering over from the boxing ring. At first glance, Cree, dressed in head to toe black, from her tank top to her combat boots, with colorful tattoos snaking up her arms and neck, appeared to be the polar opposite of clean-cut Brock. She definitely had a tough side, but she was the kindhearted pixie to Brock's gentle giant.

"Guess not," Jock said as Cree reached for Brock's hand and Brock leaned in for a kiss. He tried to ignore the wave of jealousy he'd felt lately when he saw happy couples. That new, uncomfortable sensation had started shortly after he'd met Daphne. It was just one of the differences he'd discovered in himself since Harvey's death.

Jock had been a writer and a caretaker, and he'd been phenomenal at both. But he hadn't written a word in more than a decade, and while he'd loved caring for Harvey, he wasn't a caretaker at heart. The problem was, he was floundering. He had no idea *who* he was anymore. Harvey had left him a fortune on the condition he publish another book, and Jock knew it was Harvey's way of pushing him to get back to living a *real* life. Harvey had badgered him to bridge the gap with his family, whom he saw only a couple of times each year for a few hours, to get out with people his own age, and to live the life Jock's baby boy never got the chance to. Jock didn't give a rat's ass about the inheritance. He'd made good money off his book, and Harvey had paid him handsomely. He'd lived a very frugal life and had enough money tucked away to last several years. But Harvey had saved him from falling off the face of the earth. He'd become his family, his prankster buddy, and his closest friend, and Jock wanted to make him proud. He had spent a year trying to write. The trouble was, he had no idea how to find his muse or his way back to his family, much less ever have another relationship with a woman.

"Hey, Jock. See the gorgeous girl with long, light-brown hair standing by the ring?" Cree pointed to a tall, fit woman wearing spandex and pretending she wasn't watching them in the mirror as she drank from a water bottle. "She just started working out here and she was asking about you. I know you like your privacy, so I didn't say anything other than you've worked out here for a while."

Cree was always trying to set him up. He'd told her dozens of times that he wasn't looking to become involved with anyone, but that hadn't stopped her yet, so he'd learned evasion tactics. "Thanks, but I'm actually on my way out."

"I could introduce you for another time," she suggested hopefully.

Jock shook his head. "You're one persistent woman."

"She believes everyone should be in love." Brock hugged Cree against his side and said, "She's not wrong, you know. The right woman can calm that battlefield in your head."

"I'm good, thanks." Jock held out his gloved hands and said, "But you can get these off for me if you're itching to help."

"I've got it." As Cree took off his gloves, she said, "You should come to Undercover one night and hear me and Brock sing."

Undercover was a local nightclub, and Jock had heard both Cree and Brock sing there before. Cree had the voice of an angel and she was in negotiations with a music label to cut her first album, and Brock sang a cappella with two other boxers.

"I'll think about it."

"If you give me a heads-up, I can let her know when you'll be there," she said cheerfully, handing him the gloves.

"I'd really like to fly under the radar if you don't mind," Jock said as casually as he could, hoping she wouldn't push him any further.

"Leave the guy alone, babe. He doesn't want to be set up with every woman in here." Brock swatted her butt, and she walked away giggling. "Sorry, Jock."

"No worries. You two make love look easy. That's a good thing." Jock had loved Kayla like a close friend, and they'd had fun together, but he'd never experienced the kind of love Brock and Cree had. The kind that lit a guy up from the inside out. His thoughts drifted to Daphne, but he knew better than to allow himself to play in that sandbox. The last thing she needed was a fucked-up guy like him in her life. He grabbed his bag from the bench and shoved his gloves in it. "I'm taking off. See you around."

"Hope you find the remedy for that storm in your head."

"Thanks, man. Me too."

Jock headed outside feeling a little less agitated than he had when he'd arrived. The brisk evening air cooled his sweaty skin. As he climbed into his Range Rover and headed for the resort, his thoughts returned to Daphne and Hadley. Rick had told him that Hadley had stopped crying after a minute or two that morning, but that didn't soothe the ache that had been his constant companion ever since he'd walked away.

He stopped at a convenience store for a Powerade, and as he walked by a display of roses that he must have passed a hundred times, he paused, thinking about buying one for Daphne as a token of apology. He had no idea if she even liked roses, but didn't most women? Aw hell, roses signified much more than an apology. Harvey's craggy voice whispered through his mind. *The way to a woman's heart is knowing her favorite things.*

Jock and Daphne had been at enough of the same gatherings and outings with their friends that he knew she loved three things, and Hadley topped that list. The other two were bacon and muffins—all kinds of muffins, from what he could tell. When Daphne saw muffins, her eyes brightened the way other women's eyes did when they saw diamonds. And she did this nervous thing every time, taking a small step back from the table, her beautiful baby blues shifting around her, as if she wanted to make sure everyone else got their muffins first. He thought about the other things he'd noticed about her, like the way she read rag magazines sometimes when Hadley was playing in the yard or on the beach, and how she tucked them away whenever someone walked by, like she didn't want anyone knowing she read them. He wondered what other guilty pleasures she had.

He couldn't exactly bring her a pound of bacon, though he did enjoy watching her eat it. Watching Daphne and her voluptuous curves do anything was *his* guilty pleasure.

"Excuse me," an older man said, jerking Jock back to reality.

He realized he was blocking the aisle and said, "Sorry." He stepped aside and went in search of muffins. There were too many choices—chocolate chip, blueberry, and apple crumble. He grabbed a box of each and snagged a few other things he thought she'd enjoy, hoping the gesture would help ease the pain he'd caused. By the time he went to get his drink, he thought the apology gifts just might do the trick.

As he drove to the resort, every mile took his guilt deeper. This wasn't the first time he'd had that reaction to Hadley, or the *tenth*, and he knew it wouldn't be the last. He was a pretty in-control guy, except when it came to the flood of horrific memories that accompanied the look or touch of a baby or small child turning to him for protection or care. He gritted his teeth, gripping the steering wheel tighter. What the hell was wrong with him? He knew how it felt when his own child had suffered, and he hated that he'd caused Hadley and Daphne any grief at all, much less time and time again. There were no two ways about it. He needed to fix this shit or get the hell away from them. He eyed the bag with his purchases, anger and frustration coiling inside him like a viper readying to strike. This was a ridiculous gesture. As if muffins or magazines could ease the pain of her child hurting? Or wipe away the memory of his asinine, though visceral, reactions? He was a fucking idiot. He threw his hand across the passenger seat with a *roar* of anger, sending the bag flying against the dashboard, and his purchases tumbled out.

*Fucking muffins.*

Food couldn't fix this.

He wasn't sure anything could.

His gut knotted as he turned into the resort. His headlights flashed over Daphne curled up on a chair beside the office with her legs tucked beneath her. Her beautiful blond hair curtained her face as she looked at a laptop balanced on her legs, a slice of pizza hanging from her fingertips. The familiar jolt of adrenaline that always accompanied the sight of Daphne flooded his body with awareness.

He'd never forget the first time he'd seen her at their friend Gavin's birthday party last summer. The shy beauty hadn't known he'd spotted her stealing glances at him, her cheeks pinking up each time she'd looked over. He'd been stealing his own furtive glances, drinking in her sweet curves and innocent eyes. Their gazes had collided for only a moment, and he'd been struck by the surge of electricity and longing that had consumed him. It had been forever since he'd felt anything even close to desire, and with one simple glance, crimson staining her cheeks, Daphne had ignited passion he'd never felt before. In the space of a single breath, her image had been etched into his mind. At the time, he'd been vaguely aware of Rick and his brother, Drake, on their knees, trying to coax a smile from a wispy-haired little girl in a pink dress. He'd been about to go introduce himself to Daphne when that little girl had toddled over and wrapped her arms around his leg, blinking the same wide blue eyes up at him as the ones that had mesmerized him moments earlier. Tegan had come to his rescue, reaching for the little girl, but she'd clung tighter to Jock, leaning away from Tegan, her cheeks puffed out in anger. And then she'd flashed the cutest grin up at Jock, and his fucking muscles had corded tight. Daphne had nervously approached him and said he must be a pretty special man to win over her little girl.

*Her little girl.* The realization had hit him like a brick in the face.

Daphne was even sexier and more precious up close. He'd known then that he would be in deep trouble if he didn't break the spell she had him under. He'd thought he'd known just how to squash it, and he'd told her that her daughter's radar was *off.* He'd been blunt, thinking she'd storm away, but instead it had earned the most enticing smile he'd ever seen, and it was that shy and somehow also seductive smile that he conjured late at night, luring him into the world of dark desires she'd awakened. Daphne Zablonski had become his *wonderwall*, the person he was drawn to when they were out with their friends and thought about in the hundreds of hours in between. The one he knew enough to keep his distance from.

Daphne looked up from her laptop, and Jock realized his foot was still on the brake and he'd been staring at her for far too long. She shaded her eyes from his headlights, leaning forward like she was trying to make out who he was. He could continue driving and hide away in his cottage, but she was the last person he wanted to hide from. If ever there was a time for him to man up and face the music, it was now.

He pulled into a parking space and cut the engine.

DAPHNE'S NERVES PINGED to life as Jock stepped from his SUV in a pair of gray sweatpants and a dark tank top, holding a bottled drink in one hand.

*Holy mother of all things hot and muscled.*

Lots of women loved men in suits, but Daphne had a thing for men in sweatpants and tank tops, and Jock was one exceptional-looking man. Moonlight illuminated him from behind, casting shadows over his face and making his broad shoulders and athletic frame seem bigger than life. Butterflies took flight in her stomach as he walked toward her. Once again she found herself wishing she could look away, but she was riveted to his silhouette.

He stopped a few feet from where she sat, the porchlight revealing his dark, troubled eyes. Had he thought she was someone else? Her nerves prickled, and then it dawned on her that he might be looking for Hadley, despite the late hour. As much as that bothered her, she'd been thinking about what Tegan had said all day. She felt bad that he'd lost Harvey after all those years together, and she could definitely relate to the whole walking in someone else's shoes thing that Jett had mentioned. When she'd been newly divorced, exhausted, juggling a baby, and trying to find a job, she used to wish people could spend a few hours in her life so they'd know how much determination and energy it had taken to simply get ready for the day, much less leave her daughter even just for an interview, worrying every second about her. Maybe Jock deserved to be cut a little slack, too.

"You're safe," she said more casually than she felt. "My daughter's upstairs fast asleep." She motioned to the baby monitor beside the chair.

"I wasn't...It's not that." He closed the distance between them and sat in the chair beside her. He set a Powerade in the grass and began wringing his hands, the muscles in his jaw clenching. "The way I act around Hadley, it's not her, Daph."

Part of Daphne wanted to ease whatever had him looking so troubled, but the mother in her needed to know more. "If it's not her, then what is it? Because it sure feels personal."

His eyes flicked up to hers. "It's *not*. I can't tell you how sorry I am for the way I react to her."

The honesty in his voice softened her a little, but it wasn't quite enough. "*Why* do you cringe when you see her? She's just a little girl."

"I know she is, and it's not fair. As I said, it's not her. It's *me.*" He leaned his elbows on his knees, shifting his attention to his wringing hands, and said, "Some things happened a long time ago that messed me up pretty badly." He was quiet for a beat, his pain weighing heavily in the air around him. He lifted troubled eyes to hers and said, "I thought I had moved on from it, but I guess I didn't realize how much it still affected me until Harvey passed away and I no longer had him to worry about day in and day out."

She wanted to ask what had happened, but the rawness of his grief was palpable, and Daphne understood grief. She'd grieved for her failed marriage and for her daughter who would not have a daddy, and it had taken a long time before she could talk about all the hurtful pieces. At least this time Jock wasn't avoiding her as he had that morning and all the times before. He was opening up, and knowing he was having such a hard time made her want to help him find his way to a better place. Tegan had said he was looking for answers. She didn't know what Jock's questions were, but maybe helping him would give her the answers she needed, too.

Before she could respond, he said, "I'm sorry. I interrupted your dinner."

"What?" She followed his gaze to the slice of half-eaten pizza she'd forgotten she was holding, and that reminded her that while he was sitting there looking studly, her hair was pinned up in a messy bun, she had no makeup on, and she wore one of her biggest, comfiest sweatshirts. With her luck, she probably had pizza in her teeth, too. *Way to add to his hot-mess-of-a-mother image of you.* "Oh, no, it's fine. I got busy with book club stuff and forgot I was even eating." She waved the half-eaten slice. "I was almost done."

"Almost done?" He glanced at the pizza box. "But that's

only your first piece."

"I'm not very hungry." She was *starving*, but she wasn't about to tell him that. She set her laptop on the table, trying not to think about what was going through his head, like the fact that nobody got to be her size by eating *one* slice of pizza. "Have some, really. Go ahead. Dive in—feed all those muscles" rushed from her lungs. *Feed all those muscles?* Her cheeks flamed. *Why* did she invite him to eat with her? All that vulnerability of his must have turned her brain to mush.

He laughed softly and said, "You're so damn cute, you should come with a warning label."

*Cute? Warning label?* What did that even mean? *Cute* was for Hadley. But it wasn't like he'd call her *sexy*. No one had *ever* called her sexy except her girlfriends, and they practically had to, like sisters.

"I'll tell you what," he said, reaching for a slice. "I'll *feed my muscles* if you promise to eat more than one piece. You've got to keep your energy up to chase after your daughter."

"Mm-hm." She nibbled on her slice, and he finished his in four bites, watching her the whole time, making her even more self-conscious.

He opened his Powerade and said, "Want some?"

"No, thank you. I have lemonade." She reached for her cup in the grass on the other side of her chair as he took a drink. Even his Adam's apple sliding up and down his neck was sexy.

He ate another slice of pizza as she ate the last bite of hers. He took another drink, his eyes trained on her as he lowered the bottle to the grass and licked his lips. "Ready for more?"

"Oh, *yes*." Her words came out embarrassingly breathless, and she felt her cheeks burn again.

He chuckled, shaking his head as he handed her a slice of

pizza, and said, "Forget the warning label. You should come with an ice pack."

She narrowed her eyes, hurt burrowing deep inside her. "Is it *that* painful to eat with me that you have to ice your eyes or something?"

His brow furrowed, and he lowered the slice he was about to bite into. He leaned closer and said, "No, Daphne," in a deathly serious tone. "It's not my *eyes* I'm worried about."

*Oh. My. God.* He had to be kidding, didn't he? She shoved the pizza in her mouth, earning the sexiest grin and a shake of his head along with a rumbly laugh. They ate in silence. He openly watched her, and she nervously looked away, but her eyes were drawn right back to him every time.

She scrambled for something to say to ease the tension humming between them. When she finished eating, she said, "You mentioned Harvey. Tegan said you took care of him for a long time."

"Twenty-four-seven for a decade, give or take. I was pretty lost when we first met, and by the end we were as close as friends could be." He reached for another slice of pizza and lifted his brows in silent offering.

"No thanks. I've had enough."

"I'm not sure I know the meaning of *enough*."

His dark eyes remained trained on her as he took a bite, eating almost half the slice, and licked the corner of his mouth. Daphne's mind went straight to the gutter, thinking about all the other things he could do with that tongue. She gulped her lemonade, vowing not to watch him eat *ever* again, and hunted for a safe topic that her sex-starved mind couldn't twist into a fantasy.

"You must miss Harvey a lot," she said as she set her glass

on the table, trying not to look at Jock's mouth. But she liked getting to know him, and *holy hotness*, she liked his handsome face and pillowy lips too much not to look at him.

"I do miss him. He could be a pain in the ass sometimes, but I sure loved him. He enjoyed getting under my skin." He smiled, as if he were reliving a memory.

"How so?"

"He was an eccentric retired actor, and a hell of a prankster. He'd fake his death every few weeks, sending me into a panic."

"Oh my goodness! That's awful," she said with a laugh.

"*That* was Harvey. He once hired a guy to act like a burglar, and of course I had no idea, so I protected Harvey. That prank didn't end well for the other guy." He shook his head and said, "Then there was the time he pretended to choke in a restaurant, and when I got behind him to do the Heimlich, he started yelling, 'Help! This guy is trying to kill me.'"

Daphne laughed. "I'm sorry. I'm sure that was embarrassing, but he sounds hysterical."

"He was a riot."

"Tegan told me he gave you your nickname. Does your family call you Jock, too?"

"No. They call me Jack. When I first started working with Harvey, he called me Jock as a joke, giving me shit because I was athletic. I made the mistake of telling him never to do it again, and from that moment on, he not only called me Jock, but he also introduced me as Jock to everyone."

"It sounds like he knew how to take a prank to the next level. Which name do you prefer?"

"Definitely Jock. Not only does it hold fewer bad memories, but Harvey taught me more than you could ever imagine. I'd like to make him proud, get back to writing…" His expression turned thoughtful, and he said, "Honestly, now that he's gone, I'm floundering a little, trying to figure out who I am without him in my life."

"That has to be hard. I'm already worrying about the day Hadley will go off to college or get her own apartment. Your situation is a lot worse than an empty nest."

"Yeah," he said softly. "Well, that's a hard subject. Let's talk about you, Daph. You mentioned a book club. Is that the same book club Tegan is part of?"

"Yes. Chloe and I run it."

As she took a drink, he said, "I hadn't pegged you for an erotic romance reader. How erotic do you like it? Red rooms, whips and chains?"

She choked, spewing lemonade all over his sweatpants. "*Ohmygosh!* I'm sorry." She grabbed a handful of napkins and started wiping his lap, blushing fiercely and rambling like an idiot, but she was unable to stop. "They're just books. I didn't write them." *Wipe, wipe, pat.* "It wasn't always erotic. We were reading regular romance, but—" He put his hand on her wrist, making a guttural noise as he moved it away from his crotch.

"Oh my God!" It came out sounding as mortified as she felt. She turned away, crossing her arms over her middle. "I'm sorry. I didn't try to. I didn't mean to. I didn't feel…" She snapped her mouth closed, because now that she was thinking about it, she *had* felt something. A very formidable *something.*

"Daphne, it's okay."

She shook her head, closing her eyes, hoping he'd go away. His body heat soaked into her back, and she squeezed her eyes closed.

He put a hand on her lower back, his breath warming her ear as he said, "You're used to being a mom, which means cleaning up messes."

"You must think I'm ridiculous," she said.

"Did it feel like that's what I thought?"

The air rushed from her lungs, and her eyes sprang open. He leaned into her line of vision, his eyes glittering with heat *and* amusement. "It's my fault. I was just trying to make you blush."

"Well, congratulations, Jock," she said with a nervous laugh, choosing *amusement* because she had never been very good at handling *heat*. And when it came to Jock Steele, she didn't trust that what *she* felt as an inferno might be nothing more than a flicker of a flame to any other woman. She'd already made enough of a fool out of herself tonight.

"You've managed to *completely* embarrass me." She put the dirty napkins in her empty glass and started gathering her things. "To answer your question, I'm not into whips or chains or anything like that. I barely know what to do *without* any accoutrements. I'm just a working mom trying to make it through each day with a little entertainment in the form of books. That's *all*."

"Daphne," he said, moving into her line of sight again. "I wasn't making fun of you."

"Great." *Pile more embarrassment onto the heap.* "Then my radar is just as far *off* as my daughter's."

A slow grin curved his lips. "Oh, Daphne. You *are* the perfect remedy for a hard night."

"Here we go again with sexual innuendos I'm not sure how to respond to." She flopped into her chair.

"Wow, *okay*." He sat down, trying to quell his laughter, and said, "That was *not* a sexual reference."

"No? Well, there's proof once again that I'm always the girl who is one step behind. You must be a glutton for punishment. *Why* are you still here?"

"Because you and I are not so different."

She rolled her eyes.

"I'm serious, Daph. I spent a decade taking care of a man who got sicker every year. My life was spent feeding him, bathing him, making sure his every need was taken care of, entertaining him, trying to give him reasons to smile, to laugh, to make it through one more day. He wasn't a kid, but I loved Harvey Fine like family, and when you love someone, you do anything and everything for them. My life revolved around him, much like yours revolves around Hadley."

His words hit her right in the heart. "Okay, you have a point."

"Having a friend who is grounded in reality and not part of a couple or all about nightclubs and hooking up, is refreshing. I love Tegan and Jett, and our other friends here, but let's face it: They're all paired off, and now their lives are about creating a new life together."

"You noticed, huh?" she said softly, surprised at how similar his thoughts were to her own.

"Yes, and I've also noticed that you're beautiful, smart, and funny. You're *real*, Daphne, and that makes you even more special. I'm proud to call you my friend."

A friend. *Friends* she could handle with a little more grace...as long as her overactive imagination and needy hormones didn't get out of control. She exhaled a calming breath.

"Better?" he asked.

She nodded. "Yes, thank you."

"Good. Now, *without* talking about red rooms, because

you'll just embarrass me, tell me about your book club."

She laughed, and then she took the opportunity he was giving her to regain control, telling him about the club, the forums, and the monthly meetings. "Since Chloe and I run the club, we split the administrative work like answering questions on forums and coordinating meetings."

"Doesn't that make the club feel more like work?"

"No. It actually makes it more enjoyable. I get to know the members better, and we get off topic and talk about life as much as we talk about books. One of my favorite things to do is come up with discussion questions about the books for the forum each month. I try to think outside the box, asking questions that go deeper than just *Would you date this guy?* or *Did you think the heroine handled such and such well?* I like to ask about *why* characters do things and pick out aspects of the hero's or heroine's personality to see if our members can tie it to their backstory. It's fun."

"Careful, words like *backstory* are turn-ons to writers."

She blushed again.

He laughed and said, "Sorry."

"No you're not." She swatted at his arm, and he dodged it.

"Yeah, you're right. I'm not. Do you enjoy reading other genres?"

"Yes. I *love* women's fiction, cozy mysteries, literary fiction. Just about anything except maybe scary stories."

The edge of his lips quirked up. "Guess that knocks my book out of the running."

"I knew you were a writer, but I didn't realize you wrote a scary book."

"I haven't written in years, so it doesn't much matter. Have you always been a reader?"

"Yes. My dad is the Eastham fire chief and my mom runs our family business, Putt This mini golf, which is also in Eastham. Before we were old enough to stay home alone, we would go to the mini golf after school with my mom, do our homework, and stay until closing time. My mom took us to the library every Saturday and we'd each check out a stack of books to read during the week." Jock was looking at her intently, listening to every word she said as if he were truly interested. Maybe it was just curiosity, since Jock was a writer, but it was nice that he seemed so attentive.

"You said *we*. Do you have brothers and sisters?"

"I have a twin brother, Sean, and an older sister, Renee. Sean's a firefighter, and Renee runs a boutique. How about you?"

He nodded. "I've got three sisters and two brothers." He was quiet for a moment before saying, "I'm a twin, too."

"Really? Brother or sister?"

Tension tightened his features as he said, "Brother."

"Do you and your twin finish each other's sentences? Sometimes Sean and I do. Although we're pretty much opposites. He's loud and outgoing, and all those books we got at the library? He never read his. He can barely sit still long enough to read a single page."

Jock's cell phone rang, and he said, "Excuse me." He pulled his phone out of his pocket, glanced at the screen, and silenced the call, shoving the phone back into his pocket. "I should probably take off, get showered. I'm sure I stink from boxing."

She wondered if the call was from a woman. He probably flirted with *lots* of women. Maybe he had a booty call tonight. Her stomach twisted uncomfortably at the thought.

"You definitely don't stink," she said as they both stood up.

He rolled his shoulders back, and it made him look even broader, bringing his muscular arms into focus. "How long have you boxed?"

"I learned when I was a kid. My father got sick of my brother and me hollering at each other and gave us boxing gloves, taught us a few things, and let us go at it. I boxed through college, then stopped when, um…when I was taking care of Harvey. I started again when I got back to the Cape a few months ago." He picked up his empty Powerade bottle and glanced at the table. "Do you want some help cleaning up?"

"No, I've got it."

"Thanks for sharing your dinner and hanging out. I had a great time, and I'm really sorry about how I am with Hadley. I hate that I made her cry. I'll do my best to handle those situations better, but I can't make any promises."

She was glad he wasn't brushing his issues with Hadley under the carpet. It took a lot of guts to face a mother whose child he'd hurt, and that gave her renewed respect for him. "It's okay. At least now I know there's a reason behind it, even if you don't want to talk about exactly what that reason is. It helps knowing you're aware and that you'll make an effort to try with her, even if you can't make any promises. You should know that I've been trying to keep her out of your way as much as I can."

He nodded, regret rising in his eyes. "You shouldn't have to, Daph." He glanced at his SUV and said, "I used to be better at this kind of thing. You can probably tell that after hanging out with Harvey for so long, I'm not used to forming close friendships with women other than Tegan, who's basically like a sister to me."

"I couldn't tell. I don't know what you mean."

He flashed that charming smile of his, and her traitorous

body tingled to life again. *Calm the heck down. Friends don't get tingly over friends!*

"I, uh…" He cleared his throat, shifting his feet. "I wasn't sure how to apologize for how I've reacted to Hadley, so on the way back from boxing I picked up a few things to give you as apology gifts."

Her heart fluttered at this thoughtfulness. *"Apology gifts? Now you've piqued my curiosity.* You didn't actually buy anything, did you?"

"Well…" He glanced at his vehicle again, and said, "I'll be right back."

She watched him walk away. He looked even more delicious now that she'd gotten to know him a little better. He leaned into the passenger side, ducking down, and she lost sight of him until he headed her way again carrying a paper grocery bag.

"Jock Steele, that's an awfully big package."

"*Shh.*" He lowered his voice and, with a playful look in his eyes, said, "We don't want to make the other guys around here jealous."

She laughed softly, liking his lighter side, and whispered, "I won't tell a soul."

His smile held just long enough for her to appreciate the way it softened his features before his expression turned serious again, and he said, "You deserve an awfully big apology, Daphne."

"Which you already gave me," she reminded him.

"Maybe so, but I noticed that you like muffins, and I thought you might like some for breakfast tomorrow."

"You *noticed?*" Why did that make her insides fluttery again? "I am a muffinaholic," she admitted. "Anything baked, really. Doughnuts, cake, blueberry-cream-cheese pastries from the bakery around the corner, too. I *love* sweets."

"Well, they love you, too, because they go to all the right places." He shifted the bag in his arm, eyes never leaving hers, and said, "And there's that blush I can't stop thinking about."

*Friends. Friends. Friends.*

"I couldn't decide what type of muffins to get you, so I got all three." He peered into the bag and his brow wrinkled. "They had a little trouble on the way over, so I hope you're not picky about them being all in one piece." He looked embarrassed, which made him even more intriguing—more real, honest, vulnerable, like her—as he pulled out a dented box of muffins and said, "Chocolate chip."

"*Mm.* Yummy."

He shook his head and said, "*Cute,*" under his breath as he put the box back in the bag and withdrew the others. "Blueberry, and apple crumble. Heavy on the crumble."

Some of the muffins were broken, and the transparent box tops were smeared with crumbs.

"I think I love you," she said with a giggle. "Apple crumble is my favorite."

"I'll remember that next time. I also noticed that you like to read gossip magazines."

"*Guilty,*" she whispered as he pulled two magazines from the bag. "I *love* those. How did you know that?"

"A gentleman never reveals his source." He put the magazines in the bag and withdrew a deck of cards and said, "I've seen you playing solitaire on a blanket on the grass while Hadley was playing with her toys."

Her pulse quickened. She didn't think he'd even noticed her, but he must have paid pretty close attention to have picked up on so many of her favorite things.

"And lastly, because I'm an ass, and Hadley doesn't deserve that." He pulled out a tiny stuffed owl. "I know she has a bird she loves, but they didn't have any birds."

Her heart stumbled. "*Jock…*"

"I know it's lame, but—"

"It's *not* lame. It's incredibly thoughtful. I can't believe you bought us gifts, or even noticed all those things about me. And the owl for Hadley?" She put her hand over her racing heart. "She loves her *stuffies*. Thank you. But you didn't have to do any of that."

"It doesn't even come close to making up for my behavior, but I'm glad you like them. Do you want me to carry these upstairs for you? You'll probably have your hands full with the rest of your things."

"Um…sure, thank you."

She gathered her belongings, getting more nervous by the second. She'd thought his apology had revealed the type of man he was, but the gifts? That sweet little owl he bought for Hadley? *Holy cow…*What was she supposed to make of all of this? As he followed her through the office and upstairs, her mind began playing tricks on her. What if he wanted to come inside? Did she want him to? Her hands were shaking. *No.* He wasn't here for that, not after everything he'd said and how apologetic he was. They were *friends*. He'd made that perfectly clear. She was just being silly.

When they reached the landing, his big body crowded her, making her even more nervous. She clung to her belongings, sure he could hear her heart thundering as he gazed into her eyes. Neither one said a word, and he leaned in, his lips a whisper away from hers. A hundred thoughts raced through her mind as she held her breath, readying for a kiss—and heaven help her, she *wanted* it. But he reached past her and opened the door. The air rushed from her lungs for the second time that night, and she felt like a complete idiot.

"I...*um*..." Embarrassed, she hurried inside and set her things on the table by the door. She was blushing and hoped he wouldn't notice that she was also sweating. "Thank you again."

She reached for the bag he was holding, and their fingers touched. He moved his fingers over hers, holding her gaze, and said, "Thank *you*, Daphne. I had a really good time tonight. Same time tomorrow evening?"

Was he asking her on a date? A friend date? She swallowed hard, trying desperately not to make more of his hopeful expression, of his fingers resting on hers, or of the gifts. Who was she kidding? She was trying not to make more of the whole frigging *night*.

"I'll bring my muffins," she said nervously.

He smirked. "I do like your muffins."

When she realized how he'd taken what she'd said, her eyes practically popped out of her head. "*The* muffins," she said urgently. "I'll bring *the* muffins."

"Great. See you then."

He started heading downstairs and stopped, turning back to say, "You should probably lock the office door."

"Oh, *right*. Geez. I usually do that when I come in for the night." She followed him back down, trying *not* to look at his butt, an impossible feat, since it was *right* there and ridiculously hot.

They passed through the door at the bottom of the stairs, and as they walked through the office, he glanced over his shoulder, catching her staring at his ass. Her eyes shot up to his, her entire body flaming with embarrassment.

"See you tomorrow." He laughed softly as he pushed through the door, mumbling, "So fucking cute."

Daphne shut and locked the door, leaning against it, her head spinning, wondering what the heck just happened. She felt as bewildered as the heroines in some of the romance novels she read. But this wasn't someone else's story. This was *her* life, and Jock was a man who felt so horrible about making her daughter cry, he'd bought her a glittery purple owl.

She headed up to her apartment thinking about the things Jock had revealed about himself—and the things he hadn't. When she carried the bag of gifts to the kitchen and emptied the contents onto the counter, she realized that by the time he'd left, he seemed a lot more at ease, as if their talk had lifted a weight off his shoulders. But there was no denying the haunted look in his eyes when he'd talked about his past. It was apparent that Jock could use a friend, not a sex-starved single mother wondering if he was going to try to kiss her.

She brought the cute stuffed owl into Hadley's bedroom and sat on the edge of her bed. She brushed Hadley's bangs from her forehead, feeling conflicted about having the urge to kiss Jock when he'd made her daughter so sad. She'd enjoyed laughing with him tonight, learning about him, and even *blushing* over his comments. Did that make her a bad mother? Did it make her selfish?

She looked at the owl's round, innocent eyes and pointed yellow beak. Hadley would love it. The gift was as unexpected as Jock's apology and as the vulnerable and flirtatious sides of him she'd seen tonight.

If talking could clear the way to revealing those parts of him, she wondered how magnificent of a man might appear if he ever set himself free from whatever else he was hiding.

# Chapter Three

VOICES FROM THE beach carried in the breeze through the windows of Jock's cottage late Wednesday afternoon, blowing his notes off the edge of his desk. He snagged the papers from the floor and set them beside his notebooks, placing his phone on top to keep them from drifting again. He held his finger down on the delete key, watching the words disappear for the hundredth time that day. He'd been trying to write for hours, with nothing more to show for it than a bunch of half-assed ideas scribbled in notebooks. If trying to keep his hands off Daphne didn't take him to an early grave, the blank page surely would. When he'd written his first novel, he'd been a wild college junior out partying half the time, and still the words had flowed like a river. Sitting down to the computer had been a joy. Scenes had played in his head like a movie, seamless and impactful. Before the accident, he'd been cocky, determined, and relentless in all of his pursuits. But that devastating night had plagued him with guilt and nightmares, shattering his life *and* his imagination.

He pushed to his feet, pacing the small cottage. The nightmares had subsided years ago, but he was sick of not being able to clear his head enough to reach the creative parts of his mind that had driven him through college. His father thought his writing suffered due to PTSD from losing Kayla and the baby, his mother thought it was a broken heart, and he was sure his siblings had their own theories, too. His parents' theories were probably right, at least when it came to his reaction to young children looking to him for protection or care, because he was okay *around* children in general, until they clung to him, like Hadley did, or wanted to be held. He couldn't hold young ones without seeing his dying son in his arms.

But there was more to the death of his muse and the chaos in his mind than the losses he'd suffered. There was the secret Kayla had shared the night she'd died, that she was in love with Archer, and Archer's seething proclamation—*She's gone because of you, and as far as I'm concerned, you're dead to me, too.* His chest constricted, but he couldn't allow himself to get caught up in that now. He needed to find a way to move forward and find his goddamn muse before he lost his fucking mind.

His phone *ding*ed with a text. He strode past the open patio door and snagged his phone from the desk. *Jules.* She'd called when he was with Daphne last night, and he hadn't called her back. He rarely put off returning his youngest sister's calls, but last night he'd been struggling with his desire to haul Daphne into his arms and kiss her until her entire body blushed. He'd been too damn confused to deal with Jules's overzealous personality. Jules was several years younger than Jock, and they'd always been close. She'd been diagnosed with a Wilms' tumor when she was three, and she'd had one kidney removed. Jock had sat by her bedside day and night until she was fully recovered. She'd cried when he'd gone away to college, and of all his siblings, she was the one who continually tried to get him to move back to the island.

He opened the text, which he realized she'd sent to each of his four other siblings as well. Jules was the queen of group texts. Archer never participated in them, which wasn't surprising, since Jock occasionally did, and even that was too much crossing paths for his twin. Though Jock wasn't a fan of drama, he loved his siblings and the group texts kept him up to date with things back home.

He read Jules's text. *Oooooh it's halfway here!* She added a musical note and a megaphone emoji.

Jock had no idea what she was talking about. The phone *ding*ed three times in rapid succession with messages from their siblings. His younger brother Levi, who lived in Harborside, Massachusetts, responded with *Should I be worried?*

Levi's twin sister, Leni, texted, *What am I missing?*

*Is it just me, or does it sound like she's drinking?* their sister Sutton asked.

Another text rolled in from Jules. *It's Bon Jovi!*

In addition to being the queen of group texts, Jules also thought herself to be a music aficionado. In reality, she was a bundle of energy, happier than anyone Jock had ever known with the exception of his mother, and she *always* got the lyrics to songs wrong.

Another text from Levi popped up. *It's WHOA and THERE*

Sutton, who had been an editor for a fashion magazine before taking a position as a reporter with a different arm of the same company, texted, *Woah.*

*Some editor you are*, Levi responded. *I've got three words for you—dictionary dot com.*

Jules texted three laughing emojis followed by *Ooooh living on a prayer*. Leni chimed in with *WHAT IS THIS ABOUT? I'm in a meeting.* Leni worked for their cousin Shea's public relations company. She was always busy.

Jules answered immediately. *Grandma Lenore's party! We're halfway done with the prep.*

Their maternal grandmother's birthday was three weeks from Saturday. Jock wasn't planning to attend, although as he and his siblings did every year at her request, he'd donated to the Windmeyer Institute for Cancer Research.

Another text from Sutton popped up. *I'll be there. My brain is numb from reading fashion article submissions for Laken while she's at a conference.* She added an emoji of a head exploding. Sutton's colleague Laken had taken over her editorial job and she was still getting her arms around the position. Sutton helped out when she was able.

Levi responded with *If only you knew a good writer.* A thinking emoji popped up.

Jock grumbled, "Bastard," muted the group text, and set his phone down. His gaze moved to the corner of the room, where the antique typewriter Harvey had left him sat atop a table by the bookshelves. That typewriter had belonged to Harvey's wife, Adele. It had been left to her by her father, who had been a gifted writer. Everything Harvey had ever given Jock had either been a joke or was meant to help him in some way. There had been no middle ground with Harvey. Jock had a storage unit full of things Harvey had given him over the years, some of which he hadn't touched since his first year with Harvey, when it had been all he could do to make it through each day. Maybe he'd get lucky and there'd be a little magic in the old typewriter. That was probably what Harvey had *wanted* him to believe, anyway. The damn thing would probably fall apart the minute he used it.

He grabbed one of his notebooks from the desk and read

the notes he'd taken about possible story lines. He mulled them over one by one, trying to flesh out something more than a handful of sentences, but they all sucked. When his phone rang, he was glad for the interruption. Jules's name appeared on the screen. He answered it as he looked out the patio doors at the water, sunlight shimmering off the surface. "Hey, Jules."

"I know you were reading our texts. I could hear you breathing like a text creeper. You and Archer, both. *Oh my God! Jack!* You should use that for the title of your next book. *Text Creeper.* That's an awesome horror title."

He laughed. "I'll take it under consideration."

"You totally should, and you'd better have a good reason for not calling me back last night, like you were busy getting your groove on with a beautiful woman or knee-deep in writing another book or something."

He grinned, missing her even more. "You're a pest."

"True, but you love me."

"That I do."

"So, which was it?"

"Actually, I was having pizza with a friend, and time got away from me. Sorry for not calling."

"A *woman* friend?"

Her anticipation flitted through the phone, but he knew better than to tell her anything that would get her hopes up about him being in a relationship. Especially with a single mother, no matter how much he'd enjoyed last night. He went for a change in subject instead. "What else is going on? Are *you* seeing anyone?"

"*Yes.* Haven't you heard? A royal prince is visiting the island. He asked me to go back to his country with him. I'm thinking about it, so you should come to Grandma's party and meet him."

He chuckled. "You and I both know you'll never leave the island." Jules and Archer were his only siblings who had stayed on the island. Jules was so enamored with island life, she talked as if she lived in paradise.

"*Boo* on you, Mr. Know-It-All. I want to see you," she said pleadingly. "I miss you, Jack."

"I was just there for a wedding." Gavin and Harper had gotten married a few months ago at the Silver House, a resort on the island. Jock had called his parents and Jules ahead of time to let them know he'd be attending the wedding. He'd known Jules would show up to see him at his parents' house, and he'd also known Archer would stay away. He'd visited for half an hour; then he'd taken off and come back to the Cape. That had been a difficult night for reasons other than the discomfort of being home. Daphne and Hadley had been at the wedding, too. Daphne had looked sexy and beautiful in a royal-blue dress that made her eyes look even bluer, and Hadley had been adorable in a pretty pink dress. It had been hell watching Daphne dance with her girlfriends. He'd seen her dance a handful of times while they were out with friends at Undercover, and guys were always checking out her gorgeous curves. The fact that she could barely look at him without blushing had made him even more aware of the other guys admiring her at the wedding, and he'd felt *protective* of her. If ever there was a time he had wanted to take a woman in his arms and dance, it would have been Daphne the night of the wedding. He fucking hated that he couldn't be near her because of his reaction to Hadley.

"The wedding was *months* ago. You have to come for Grandma's birthday. You didn't come last year, and all she does is cry about how much she misses her eldest grandson. It's heart-wrenching."

"You're not a very good liar."

She sighed. "*Fine!* Leni is bringing her friend Indi, who is super cute, and we want you to meet her."

"*Jules,*" he warned for the umpteenth time, and tried again to change the subject. "Is your shop doing well?" Jules owned Happy End, an eclectic gift shop.

"It's going great! I just started carrying a new brand of greeting cards, the Mad Truth. They're hilarious, and the designer lives on the Cape. You should track her down. Her name is Madigan Wicked. I bet she's cute because her cards…"

A dog barked outside, and Jock heard Daphne calling Hadley's name. As Jules went on about that designer and the upcoming events she was planning at the shop, Jack went to the front window and looked outside. Cosmos was running in circles in the grass beside the entrance to the pool, and Hadley was chasing him, giggling up a storm. Daphne was bent over, holding her side like she'd been laughing too hard or running too long and she was smiling brighter than the sun. He'd never met anyone who could face down a man twice her size, fiercely championing for her child, and then turn around and be as delicate and vulnerable as butterfly wings. The way she'd blushed last night, the spark of surprise in her eyes when he'd given her the gifts, and her nervous laughter, which had caused her to look away in embarrassment, had all tugged at something deep inside him that he didn't quite understand and had no interest in fighting. Though he knew he had to.

"Promise me you'll come to the party," Jules said, bringing him back to their conversation.

"I can't do that, Jules." He watched Daphne sweep Hadley

into her arms as she ran by and twirl her around. The joy in their faces filled him with happiness.

"I'm going to come to that resort and drag your butt back here. I'm not kidding."

"Jules, you know how things are." His family didn't know exactly what Archer had said to him in the hospital, but the rift between them had affected everyone. It had hit Jules especially hard because she always wanted everyone to be happy, and it slayed him that he couldn't make that happen for her, though he did his best to minimize the damage. He hadn't wanted their family to take *sides* when it came to his and Archer's feud, but inevitably, fine lines were hard to toe. That was another reason Jock had stayed away from the island. Archer had built his life there, and because of Jock, he'd lost out on sharing that life with Kayla. His brother didn't need to deal with a divided family, too.

"You're both stubborn asses, you know that?" Jules said angrily.

He couldn't argue with her there. "Sorry, sis," he said, watching Daphne and Hadley play with Cosmos. He could hear their laughter ever so faintly now, and it was a sound of beauty. He wondered if he was being selfish forming a friendship with a woman who had so much happiness in her life. He didn't want to dim her light, but he sure wanted to bask in it.

He spotted a group of guys walking out of the pool, checking Daphne out, and his muscles corded.

"I'm not going to let you out of this," Jules said.

"I know," he said through clenched teeth, eyeing the guys who were now chatting with Daphne. Jealousy gnawed at him as Daphne flashed her glorious smile, looking down every few seconds in that bashful way he adored. Hadley wrapped her arms around Daphne's leg, and Daphne lifted her into her arms. Even from that distance, he could tell Hadley was scowling. "*Attagirl.*"

"What?" Jules asked.

"Nothing, sorry. I've got to run, Jules. Love you." He ended the call and strode over to the door. But as he reached for it, reality hit like a brick in the face. His hands curled into fists, and he uttered a curse. If he opened that door, Hadley would come running. That would serve his purpose in sending a message to those guys, but he fucking knew what would happen next—and there was no way he was going to put Hadley or Daphne through that again.

DAPHNE GRABBED HADLEY'S favorite pink pajama short set out of her drawer, the one with white birds all over it, and said, "Come here, Had. Let me help you get undressed."

"I do it!" Hadley pushed her shorts and underwear down to her ankles, plopped onto her bottom, and kicked them off.

"Underwear," Daphne reminded her.

Hadley pulled her undies back on and tugged her T-shirt up her belly. She struggled and twisted, trying to get it off. Daphne reached over to help, but Hadley leaned out of her reach, insisting, "I do it!"

Daphne wished she could bottle up her daughter's enthusiasm for doing things herself so she could give her a big dose during those trying times when she didn't want to do anything at all. Like earlier tonight, when she'd refused to take a bath because her owl couldn't take one with her.

Hadley wiggled and twisted, her face pinched with determination. Daphne couldn't suppress her smile. She loved her stubborn little girl so much, she physically ached with it. It had been just the two of them since Hadley was only a week old, and even in the most trying times, Daphne wouldn't want to imagine her life without her daughter in it.

"Honey, please let me help you."

Hadley made a whiny noise, shaking her head vehemently, and continued struggling.

"*Had...*"

Hadley shook her head again. "*I* do it." She pulled one arm out of the sleeve so hard, it looked like an act of defiance, and then she tugged the other arm free, but as she tried to pull the shirt over her head, it got stuck. "Mommy, help!"

"You did such a good job," Daphne said as she took it off. She put the pajama shirt over Hadley's head, and Hadley put her elbows against her sides, her fingers pointing toward the ceiling as Daphne lined them up to the sleeves and said, "Ready?"

Hadley nodded, and together they counted, "One. Two. Three. *Takeoff!*" As they shouted *takeoff*, Hadley's arms shot up through the sleeves.

Daphne wrapped her arms around Hadley, both of them laughing. She'd come up with *rocket ship arms* when Hadley was a wiggling, giggling moving target of about two years old.

Hadley put her soft hands on Daphne's cheeks and said, "Love you, Mama," and plastered her lips to Daphne's.

"I love you too, baby girl." Daphne kissed her cheek and patted her bottom. "Now, off to brush your teeth."

As Daphne picked up the dirty clothes, Hadley grabbed her stuffed owl and bird and said, "I *bwush!*" She hurried out of the bedroom and down the hall toward the bathroom.

Daphne dropped the dirty clothes in the hamper, mentally ticking off her to-do list for the evening as she followed Hadley down the hall. *Laundry, empty dishwasher*—she stepped over a doll—*pick up toys*. She needed to read more of this month's book club selection so she could come up with discussion questions, too. *No hardship there.* Among those thoughts were her plans to see Jock, which she was trying not to get too excited about. She knew it wasn't a date, but *still*. He'd brought her apology gifts! That was a pretty darn special gesture, especially the owl, which had immediately become Hadley's favorite stuffed animal. Daphne had almost told Chloe about last night when she'd called earlier, but she'd decided to keep it to herself because any way she framed it, it sounded ridiculous to be so excited about becoming better friends with a guy. At the same time, she kind of liked having private time to get to know each other better without the pressure of anyone making it into something that it wasn't. Including *Daphne*.

Hadley was standing by the sink on her tiptoes, trying to reach her toothbrush with one hand, clutching her owl's head and bird's tail in the other. "I *bwush*!"

"You will—just let me put the toothpaste on first." As Daphne did that, she said, "What story do you want to read tonight?" She felt a little guilty hoping Hadley picked a short one so she wouldn't miss seeing Jock when he came by. Although they hadn't specified a time, she was antsy to get outside.

"*How Much Love You*."

"*Guess How Much I Love You*," Daphne corrected her. She handed Hadley the toothbrush.

Hadley snagged it and spread her arms out wide, beaming at

her. "*Dis* much!"

"That's right." She touched the tip of Hadley's nose and said, "Even *more* when you brush your *back* teeth as well as your front."

Hadley watched herself in the mirror as she brushed the heck out of her front teeth and took one swipe at her back teeth. She spit down her chin and onto the edge of the sink and bared her teeth, showing Daphne.

Daphne absently wiped the sink and picked up Hadley's toothbrush. "You did a great job. How about next time you stand on your stepstool when you spit?"

Hadley giggled.

"Open up."

Hadley opened her mouth, letting Daphne brush the rest of her teeth. Daphne filled Hadley's PAW Patrol cup with water, and while Hadley rinsed her teeth, Daphne rinsed the toothbrush. Hadley leaned over the sink, dribbling the water out of her mouth instead of spitting.

"*Keen.*" Hadley lifted proud, bright eyes and a spit-covered chin to Daphne.

"Perfect." She washed Hadley's face, and after Hadley used the potty, they headed back to her room.

Hadley climbed into bed and snuggled up to Daphne for a story with her stuffed toys. Hadley knew the story by heart, and every time Daphne turned the page, Hadley called or acted out the measure the nut-brown hares used to proclaim their love.

"Dis much!" Hadley threw her arms out to her sides. She pointed her toes when the rabbit stood on his and shouted, "To the *wiver!*" "*Wiver* and hills!" "Moon!" as Daphne read.

When Daphne finished reading the story, she set the book on the nightstand, and Hadley snuggled against her side with a sleepy yawn. This was Daphne's favorite time, when her daughter went from constant movement to snuggle bunny.

"Sing, Mommy. 'Eyes on You.'"

Daphne had been singing to the tune of Chase Rice's "Eyes on You" to Hadley for a long time. With a few different words, which Daphne inserted, Chase could have written it about her life.

She whisper-sang, "We've been to North Carolina, seen the big blue sky. Driven down the coast a time or two. Brewster, Eastham, Wellfleet. I can't remember much of what I've seen. I believe I've missed it every time, because of my love for you." As she sang the chorus, using Chase's lyrics about keeping her eyes on Hadley everywhere they went, her daughter gave in to sleep. Daphne continued singing for another few minutes, before quietly moving off the bed. Hadley stirred in her sleep, and Daphne brushed a kiss to her forehead, whispering, "'Night sweet girl. Mama loves you."

She turned on the baby monitor and closed the door most of the way as she left the room. She didn't have to stay with Hadley until she fell asleep, although she often did, simply because she liked to. It hadn't always been that way. Daphne and Hadley had *both* struggled through the Ferber method, which had taught Hadley to self-soothe and Daphne to let her. But it had paid off. Hadley had become a great sleeper.

She hurried down the hall to her bedroom, her pulse quickening as she pulled off her sweatshirt, leaving on the peach tank top she'd worn underneath. She rifled through her sweaters for one that would look good, but not like she was trying too hard. She tried on a black crewneck, but black wasn't really her color, so she tried a yellow one. It was too bright. She tried on several others, but they were too long, too short, too tight, or just too *something.* Frustrated, she gave up and wore her old favorite, a long-sleeve teal V-neck with threadbare elbows and a frayed hem. She'd had it forever, and she loved it because it didn't cling to her belly or boobs.

She hurried into the bathroom to brush her teeth and hair. She couldn't remember the last time she was this excited to spend time with a guy. Then again, she hadn't spent time alone with a man since her divorce. She was usually with Hadley or with her friends. And she'd never met anyone like Jock before. He was like a mysterious puzzle—a sinfully *hot*, funny, and flirtatious puzzle. She felt like she'd discovered a few of his outer pieces last night and a couple of random center pieces, but she needed to find the corners to anchor the rest in place.

Her stomach growled, and she realized she'd forgotten to eat dinner. As usual, she'd fed Hadley but hadn't thought to feed herself. Did she have time to eat before Jock showed up? She should have asked what time he wanted to meet, but her brain had taken off for a vacation in Lustville when they'd said good night. If he caught her eating again, he was going to think she ate *all* the time. *Ugh.* Did all girls go through this?

*I made it through giving birth. I can make it through a night with my body tingling.*

She shouldn't even be *thinking* about choosing between eating dinner and talking with a guy. Who cared if he saw her eating again? This *wasn't* a date, no matter how much he made her body tingle.

She set down her hairbrush and took a deep breath. It didn't matter what she wore, or if she was eating dinner when he arrived. She was a busy mom, and *this* was *her* life.

With a little more courage and a little less giddiness, she left the bathroom and her worries behind, slipped on a pair of flip-flops, grabbed the baby monitor, and headed into the kitchen to make herself a peanut butter and jelly sandwich. The sight of the muffins reminded her that she'd said she'd bring them. She and Hadley had shared an apple crumble and a chocolate-chip muffin for breakfast.

She put one of each kind of muffin on the plate with her sandwich and cut them in half. After checking on Hadley one last time, she gathered the baby monitor, the plate, her book, a notebook and pen in case she had ideas for book club discussion questions, snagged a bottle of water, and hurried quietly downstairs, hoping Jock wasn't there yet.

# Chapter Four

THE NERVOUSNESS DAPHNE had thought she'd left behind returned with a vengeance, clinging to her like a second skin as she stepped outside. Daphne made her way around to the side of the building, saying hello to a couple as they passed, the din of guests milling around the recreation center carried by the chilly evening air. She was relieved Jock wasn't there yet. But that relief was short-lived. What if he'd already come and gone? What if he decided not to show up?

Too nervous to eat her sandwich, she settled into a chair with her book and began reading. A few seconds later she checked the time and wondered what time it had been when he'd shown up last night. Having no idea, she set her phone down and tried reading again, but she couldn't concentrate. Would she seem overly anxious if she was waiting for him when he got there?

All the second-guessing was painful.

She was being ridiculous. They were just getting to know each other better as friends. She shouldn't be nervous. Returning her attention to her book, she began reading, but moments later she realized she'd read the same paragraph twice and still hadn't processed what she'd read. She decided to text Chloe to distract herself. But she'd have to text back and forth and she didn't want to be focused on her phone when Jock got there, since he was coming to hang out with her. That thought brought a reminder of the call he'd gotten last night. Had it been a booty call? She wondered about his private life. She knew firsthand how hard it was to find free time with Hadley around. It must have been the same when Jock was taking care of Harvey. But while she'd gone three years without being touched by a man, she'd had a child to care for and for a while she'd had the grief of her divorce to contend with. Surely Jock's personal life was far more active than hers. That opened up several paths of curiosity that she couldn't help but ponder...

The next time she looked at the phone, half an hour had passed. Maybe he wasn't going to show up after all. Disappointment pierced her, but it was quickly followed by annoyance. That would be just plain *rude*. She should have at least checked to see if his SUV was parked by his cottage. She set her book and phone down and pushed to her feet.

As she came around the corner of the building, she plowed into him with an *umph*. He caught her around the waist, holding her against his muscular, broad body. He wasn't *bodybuilder* hard. He was firm and huggable. *Lickable. Oh God!* Now she was thinking about licking him, catapulting her lonely girlie parts into a frenzy of delight, making her blush even harder.

"*Ah*, there's the sweetest blonde around," Jock said, snapping her from her embarrassing reverie. His dark eyes trailed down her face, lingering on her mouth just long enough to stoke that tingly fire inside. "You're not trying to skip out on me, are you, gorgeous?"

*Gorgeous?* "Um...No. I was just..."

"Looking for me?" His hand pressed a little firmer to her waist.

She swallowed hard, trying to hold his gaze so she didn't appear as nervous as she felt, but his stare was too intense. It was like he could *see* right through her facade, and she had to look away.

He dropped his hand and said, "No warning label, no ice pack. *Girl*, you are going to be the death of me."

Laughter bubbled out before she could stop it, and she went to sit down, grinning like a fool. "You must *really* like to make me blush."

"Ya think?" he teased. "Where were you really going?"

She was already blushing, so she went with the truth. "To see if your truck was by your cottage."

"So you *were* looking for me." He sat, too, stretching out his long jeans-clad legs. He looked incredibly handsome in a black long-sleeved shirt that molded to his chest.

Daphne pulled her knees up and wrapped her arms around them, trying to get her tingles under control. "*Yes*, but not in a stalkerish way or anything. We didn't plan on meeting at any particular time, and I thought maybe you were coming later or…"

"Or not coming at all?" he asked carefully.

"The thought *might* have crossed my mind. You could have been at the boxing club or something."

He turned his chair to face her and leaned his elbows on his knees, those all-seeing eyes trained on her as he said, "Or *something?*"

"I don't *know.* You're a good-looking guy. You could have been out on a date."

His brow furrowed. "That would make me a dick, since I

asked you to meet me here tonight."

"You said it, not me," she said lightly.

"I'd like to think I'm better than that. But the truth is, I thought about canceling but *not* about standing you up."

"*Oh…*" She couldn't hide her disappointment, but annoyance was right behind, as it had been moments earlier. "Most guys would just lie. Why are you telling me?"

"I'm not a very good liar. I saw those guys flirting with you this afternoon and I wondered if it was unfair of me to take up your night when you could be out with someone who doesn't have trouble with young kids."

She scoffed to hide her hurt. "You *are* a good liar after all. Nobody flirted with me today."

"Daph, you don't have to hide it. I'm not your jealous boyfriend. I saw you playing with Hadley by the pool when those guys were checking you out, and then I saw them flirting with you."

"By the pool?" She mentally chased through memories of the afternoon. "Oh my gosh, you're crazy. Those guys were *not* flirting with me. They were asking about places to go around here, like clubs. I told them about Undercover and I said Provincetown has a ton of clubs." Provincetown was an arts community at the tip of Cape Cod.

"And they probably asked where you go, right?"

She thought about the conversation she'd had with them. "Yes, actually, they did. I told them I went to Undercover." *Were they flirting?*

He arched a brow.

"*Pfft.* You're nuts," she said.

"And you're an intelligent woman. I can't believe you'd miss the cues."

"Cues?" She waved her hand dismissively, laughing. Those guys were hot. Not nearly as good-looking as Jock, but they definitely could have their pick of women. "Okay, crazy man. For your information, single moms are not exactly sought-after dates. Why did you show up instead of canceling, anyway? And just so you know, it bothers me that you were going to cancel, even if it was for a thoughtful reason."

"Well, don't let it bother you too much. I could lie and say I figured I've got enough strikes against me because of my reactions to Hadley and I showed up to get brownie points." Holding her gaze, he said, "But the truth is, I had a really good time last night, and I couldn't stay away."

"Oh," she said casually, and then she processed what he'd said and the way he was looking at her, like he *really* meant it, and a more shocked "*Oh*" slipped out.

"It surprised me, too." His lips lifted with a tentative smile. "In case you haven't noticed, I'm not exactly the kind of guy who seeks out intimate conversation. But there's something about you…"

More nervous laughter bubbled out. "It's my muffins. You must really like them."

He barked out a laugh, which made *her* laugh, and blush, and laugh some more.

"I'm never going to mention muffins again! Seriously, though, you *are* a crazy man," she said. "I have Hadley. My personal life is the book club, times like this, and an occasional night out with friends. You're usually there when we go, so you know I'm all about hanging out with our friends and not out looking to hook up with guys."

"You may not be looking, but they're looking at you, Daph, trust me."

"Whatever," she said. "You took care of Harvey. You know how hard it is to fit in a personal life when you have someone relying on you. How did you fit it in for all those years? And don't say you didn't, because I'm not that naive."

"I don't think you're naive at all. I was pretty broken when I first started working for Harvey, and that lasted a while. But as things got better, I met a few women that I'd get together with from time to time. There were nurses who came to stay with Harvey while I was out so I could go scratch that itch, so to speak."

Daphne told herself not to ask about the pretty blond photographer from Gavin and Harper's wedding. But she was dying to know if they'd gone out, and she couldn't hold back. "Like Tara?"

Confusion riddled his brow. "Tara?"

"The photographer from Gavin and Harper's wedding? The way she talked, it sounded like you two were pretty close."

"*Mouse?*" He laughed. "She's almost ten years younger than me. I've known Tara since she was in diapers."

"Sorry for asking. I just…" She wasn't good at lying either, so she said, "I wanted to know."

"It's okay, Daph. I like that you *wanted* to know."

Her thoughts stumbled, but she managed "Why did you call her Mouse?"

"Tara used to hide in the pantry during parties, nibbling on snacks. At some point her sister started calling her Mouse, and it stuck. Tara's a sweetheart. I love her like a sister, but there's nothing more between us. If we looked especially close, it's because she's my niece Joey's aunt. My younger brother Levi had a baby with Tara's older sister, Amelia. Joey will be eight this year. Amelia never wanted to be a mother, so Levi is raising

Joey alone."

"I know a little something about people like that," Daphne said softly. "Is Levi a good father?"

"He's the best, and Joey is an amazing kid."

She fidgeted with the hem of her sweater and said, "I know you don't want to talk about your past, but do you react to your niece the same way you react to Hadley?"

THE WORRY IN Daphne's eyes was almost enough to sidetrack Jock from the comment she'd made about knowing people like Amelia. He could deflect her question and ask about her comment instead, but there was something about Daphne that made him want to stop deflecting. She hadn't pushed him to tell her more than he was willing last night, and now she was looking at him with worry in her eyes, not accusations. He appreciated that, and she deserved an answer.

"It was the same at first," he admitted. "But it's better now."

"That's good."

He couldn't tell if she was relieved by his answer or if it made her more curious. He followed her gaze to the food on the table and said, "Is that your dinner?"

"Yeah. PB and J. Want half?" She picked up half the sandwich.

"Seriously, Daph? *That's* dinner?"

"Yes, and don't make fun of me," she said with a flair of confidence. "I have a very busy life, and even though it looks like food is the priority, it's not."

"Why would it look like food is the priority? I've seen you

eat pizza, peanut butter and jelly, and muffins. Those are hardly signs of a foodie."

"For other obvious reasons," she said, and shifted her eyes away.

"*Hey.*" It came out sharper than he'd meant it to, but it brought her eyes to his, and he said, "The only obvious thing about you is that you love your daughter enough to put your needs second. That, and the fact that you are absolutely *stunning*, and kind enough not to blow me off for the way I react to Hadley."

"*Jock*," she said softly. "You don't have to say stuff like that to me."

"Would you rather I lied?"

She rolled her eyes, blushing fiercely.

"Roll your eyes all you want. All I can tell you is that from the first second I saw you at Gavin's birthday party last summer, you have become my *wonderwall*."

"Is that something dirty?" she asked with a lift of her chin.

He chuckled. "You're so damn cute. No, it doesn't mean something dirty." He wasn't about to admit that she was the only woman whose image he conjured when he was lying in his bed late at night, or that those thoughts were definitely dirty. "Wonderwall has a few definitions, but for me, it's the person I can't stop thinking about."

"Well, in that case, I'm sure it's because you're wondering if you'll need your running shoes when you see me with Hadley. She loved the owl, by the way. She's sleeping with it. Thank you for thinking of her."

"I'm glad she likes it. I think about her a lot. And just so you know, you're wrong about the running shoes. I definitely have a thing for your *muffins*." He snagged half of a muffin from the plate and took a bite, loving the crimson staining her cheeks. "You'd better eat your dinner before I do." He'd probably go straight to hell for what he was about to say, but Daphne's sweetness was an aphrodisiac. He couldn't resist holding her gaze and saying, "I've got a ravenous appetite. Once I get started, I can *eat* all night long."

Her eyes widened and her jaw dropped. He grinned, and she shoved her sandwich in her mouth. She sat up taller and pointed at him. "Stop saying stuff like that just to make me blush."

*Think what you want, babe. It's probably better that way, because you make it impossible for me to hold back.* He finished his muffin and reached for another half.

Between bites of her sandwich, she said, "I'm sure you have to eat a lot to keep up those muscles. You must work out all the time."

"I box to clear my head. I'm trying to get back into writing, but the words aren't coming."

"Tegan mentioned that Harvey left you a large inheritance if you publish another book."

"He did." *Two million dollars, to be exact.* "But I don't want to write because of that. I have enough money. Writing is what I *do*. It's who I am."

"But you were a caregiver, too."

"Yes, but that was different. I was in a really bad place when I met Harvey. He gave me a purpose, something to focus on to help pull my head out of the darkness that had swallowed me up. He pushed me to get involved with his business, and as his health deteriorated, I *wanted* to take care of him. I learned to take care of him. Writing is different. It was like writing chose me, not the other way around. And now that Harvey's gone and the words won't come when I try to write, I don't know who I am. Which is totally messed up, because before all that bad shit happened, I was *unstoppable*."

He pushed to his feet and paced, adrenaline coursing through him. "I aced everything I did. Top grades, top fighter. I was a cocky asshole, but there was *nothing* I couldn't achieve. As a college junior I wrote a screenplay that poured from my fingertips like magic, and on the suggestion of a professor, I turned it into a novel that sold in less than thirty days for an *insane* amount of money. The sky was the limit, and I was a fucking rocket ship. The guy I am now? Floundering? Unsure? I don't know who the hell he is, but he's *not* the man I was meant to be, and I'll be damned if he's going to steal the rest of my life from me." He realized with a shock how much he'd shared. He'd been holding it in for so long, it felt like it had been ripped from his bones.

"Whatever happened must have been really horrible to take all of that away from you." Daphne was quiet for a beat. "*Jock...?*"

He lifted his eyes to hers, and *holy hell*, understanding slammed into him. He'd needed her to know that who she saw wasn't all that he really was. What was it about her that was doing this to him?

Relieved that he hadn't spewed the whole ugly truth, he sat down beside her. "That unstoppable guy who pursued and conquered? That's *me*, Daphne. But this is the first time in years I've actually felt him inside me. I wasn't even sure that guy still existed."

"What do you think changed? Why do you feel him now?"

"I don't know," he said, needing to keep a modicum of distance until he could figure himself out. But the way she was looking at him was deeper than just a woman seeking an answer. She looked at him like she cared, and *man*, he wanted to earn more of that, so he told her the truth. "Maybe I do know. Have you ever met someone and wanted them to see the best version of you?"

"I guess, yeah."

"I think that is what's happening to me, and that someone is *you*. You must have inspired that part of me to try to break free, because all that stuff I just said shocked the hell out of me, too."

Daphne inhaled a shaky breath, fidgeting with the hem of her sweater.

"I'm sorry. I didn't mean to make you nervous. It's been a long time since I've had a friend like you or felt anything like this. It's incredible to actually *feel* again. Thank you."

She let out a soft but cheery "*Yay for me*," raising her fist in the air.

God she was cute.

"It's been a long time since I've inspired anything in someone else," she said as she reached for her bottle of water.

"There you go missing those cues again."

She took a drink, avoiding his gaze, and as she set the water bottle on the table, she said, "If I can bring out that hidden part of you, then maybe I can coax some story ideas out of you, too. You write mystery, right?"

"Not exactly. I write horror."

Her brow furrowed and she leaned back, as if what he'd said was contagious. "*Horror? Really?*" She said *horror* like a curse and *really* with intrigue. "I don't read horror, so clue me in. What's it like?"

"It's pretty much the opposite of romance. The goal of horror is to terrify the reader."

"I figured that much. But what did you write about? I don't even know the title of your book."

"The title is *It Lies*, and the story opens twenty years after a group of college kids killed a woman and got away with it. In the first scene, high schoolers are having a séance in the graveyard where she's buried, and they unknowingly awaken her spirit. She goes on a vengeful warpath, killing each of the people who were involved in her death."

Daphne cringed. "That's horrible."

"That's the point."

"I *know*, but why would *you* want to think about that kind of thing? No wonder you can't write. If you experienced something so awful that your entire life changed, then maybe you need to write something happier."

"Daph, I'm not a romance writer."

"I don't mean romance. Couldn't you write literary fiction, or even a less-gruesome mystery?"

He shook his head. "They're not really my thing."

"Okay. Then let's brainstorm and see what we can come up with that's horrific." She grabbed a notebook, pen, and the other half of her sandwich. She took a bite and said, "You fuel your muscles. I fuel my brain."

He'd like to fuel her brain *and* her body with a lot more than a sandwich. "You don't have to help me with this. I'm sure I'll figure it out eventually."

"Like you figured out that other part of you was still in there?" She opened the notebook and said, "How long did *that* take?"

"Daph, you're sweet to offer, but I don't want to waste your time. You don't even like the genre."

"But I like you, and I want to help you." She took another

bite of her sandwich. "How about a story about a haunted inn? You could use Summer House for inspiration. And the ghosts kills...." She shook her head, brows knitted, and said, "Forget that. Too close to home." She tapped her pen on the notebook, and suddenly her eyes widened. "I know! A story about a stalker. He can be *really* creepy, but instead of killing the girl, he falls in love with her."

"That would be romance."

"You're right. You know what? I stink at this. But I have an idea!" She pushed to her feet and put the notebook and pen on the table. "I have just the thing to get your words flowing. I'll be right back."

He watched her hips sway as she hurried around the building.

She returned a minute later with Scrabble and a gorgeous grin. "Ta-da!"

"Daphne Zablonski, you just got even hotter. You're a Scrabble girl?"

"Heck yeah. We keep a few games in the office. Do you play?"

"No," he said as she sat down. "I *win*."

"Not tonight you won't," she said sassily.

"We'll see about that." He moved the table between them, and as they set up the game, he said, "Let's make it interesting. If I win, you have lunch with me tomorrow."

"Sorry, but I eat at my desk and work through lunch so I can pick up Hadley before five."

He made a mental note of that and said, "Okay. If you win, I'll make you dinner tomorrow night."

"You mean *when* I win." She moved her tiles around on the holder. "And on the off-chance I lose?"

"You'll have to enjoy the dinner I make." He picked his tiles and said, "What do you say? I'm an amazing cook."

"I say I need more friends like you." Her eyes flicked up to his. "But seriously, shouldn't you get something if you win?"

"I am. I get to have dinner with you. Cooking for one is no fun."

They played a few rounds, and she put down the word *grudge*. "How about that?" she asked excitedly. "Does 'grudge' spark any ideas for a story?"

*Yeah, the story of my life.* "Not right off the bat, but it was a great movie."

"I never saw it. I'm sure we'll come up with better words to inspire something in that head of yours." As he took his turn, she said, "Why did you go with horror, anyway?"

"That's an easy answer. My brother and I used to scare the crap out of each other *and* everyone else. My mom says we started doing it when we were really little. I don't remember all that far back. But when we were about eight, a sitter took us to the movies. She bought us popcorn and candy and went to watch a chick flick in another theater. We got bored, so we snuck out of the movie we were supposed to watch and into the theater that was showing *Halloween*. It scared the hell out of us, but we *loved* it. Unfortunately, we were too young to realize that movies didn't all end at the same time. When we came out of the theater an hour after the kid movie had ended, the police had just arrived. Our parents were there. They were frantic, and the sitter was in tears."

"Your mother must have been terrified that you were missing."

"She was. But the worst part is that we'd seen the ushers looking down every aisle with flashlights and we'd hidden because we thought they would kick us out for not being there with an adult. I still feel guilty about that."

"I'd lose my mind if Hadley was missing. I worry all the time about something happening to her."

Jock hadn't understood how terrifying it had been for his parents until the night of the accident. "We deserved the grounding we got. But that movie was what sparked my love of horror. After that we were always trying to up our pranks a notch. We were young, so we didn't do a great job of it, but we were creative. We'd rig up sheets with string and trick our younger sisters into thinking they were ghosts. One time we put ketchup all over ourselves and spread it on one of our father's saws. My brother lay down in the yard like he was cut, and I ran inside screaming that he was dying."

"*Geez!* You really took it far."

"Yeah, I had no idea about the fears parents had back then."

"What did your parents do?"

"They laughed at us. It was *ketchup*, and we did shit like that all the time. Somedays we'd do it several times in one afternoon." He chuckled with the memories. "We were such dorks. It took a few years, but we finally mastered pranks. My parents' pantry has all sorts of prank stuff hidden in it, like ghost-pepper extract and ipecac syrup."

"You guys are *awful*. Did you prank your friends?"

"Only the ones we liked. It was sort of a rite of passage into our group."

"Which brother was your prank partner?"

A familiar knot lodged in his gut. "Archer, my twin."

"It sounds like you guys are close."

*Not anymore.* He studied the board and put down the word *enemy*. "Your turn, blondie," he said as he scribbled down his points.

"Enemy is a great word for a horror story." She set down the word *yellow*. "All villains are enemies. How about doing a story that's related to *It Lies*? Could the girl whose spirit came back have an enemy in the spirit world that takes vengeance in the real world, like she did?"

"Look at you, getting into horror. That's an interesting idea."

She leaned across the table, waving her finger at the paper, and said, "Write it down so we don't forget. Maybe it'll help you think of something later."

"I know *exactly* what I'll be thinking about later," he said as he wrote down her idea.

"How badly you lost at Scrabble?" she asked playfully.

Their eyes caught, and he said, "Sure, we'll go with that." The sweet smile that earned made him want to haul her over the table and kiss her.

"If you had a dollar for every time you made me blush, you'd be a rich man."

"I'm a rich man because I get to *see* you blush."

She gave him a deadpan look. "Now you're just trying to throw me off my game, and it's *not* going to work." She broke a piece off a muffin and ate it. "It's your turn. And I'm going to have to start messing with your head so you can see how it feels."

Little did she know she already was.

She leaned her elbow on the table and rested her chin on her hand, batting her lashes, her alluring baby blues adorably nervous, as she said, "So, mysterious neighbor, tell me something I don't know about you."

He was pretty sure saying *I want you lying naked in my arms, writhing in fits of ecstasy as I make you come so hard you can't remember your own name* was not what she was talking about. His cock ached at the thought. He tried to clear his throat, but it sounded more like a growl.

Her eyes narrowed. She sat up with a seductive expression and pushed her chest out. "A *big*, tough man like you can't tell me *one* itty-bitty secret?"

She was killing him. "*Daphne*," he warned, wondering where this confident seductress had come from.

Heat rose on her cheeks, but a flash of victory shone in her eyes. "Let's see how long you can keep it up." She reached across the table, brushing her fingers over his hand, and said, "What's wrong, Jock? You can't compete?"

"*Fuuck.*" He flipped his hand over and trapped her fingers beneath his. Their eyes locked. Her breathing shallowed. Lust shimmered in her eyes, and she bit her lower lip, like she'd been caught in her own web of arousal. He'd fantasized about how she'd look when she was hot and bothered, but seeing her swamped with desire surpassed even his wildest dreams.

Her mouth opened, then shut quickly. She tugged her hand free and threw herself back in her chair. "Forget it! I bet a guy like you can keep it up all night."

"Damn right I can," he gritted out.

"I meant *talking*!" She buried her face in her hands and made a laughing-whimpering sound. "*Talking* Jock! Talking!"

He had to laugh because she was so damn adorable. "You *ruin* me, Daphne."

"Yeah, *right*. Like all that stuff didn't just backfire on me." She peeked out from between her fingers and said, "Truce?"

"I wasn't aware there was a war going on, but sure."

She pressed one hand to her chest, exhaling loudly. "I am

*not* used to playing those games."

"That makes you even more attractive." He grabbed her water bottle, opened it, and handed it to her. "Drink this before you combust."

"Would you *stop*?" She took it, guzzling the water. "I might not be able to knock you off your game, but I can still win at Scrabble."

She set the water bottle on the table, and he picked it up. "Do you mind?"

"Go for it." Her eyes lit up. "Does that mean it worked a little?"

*So damn cute.* "If you think eight inches is a little, then yes."

She turned beet red, grinning ear to ear, and said, "I hate you, Jock Steele. And just for that, I'm going to blow you away."

He arched a brow.

"In *Scrabble*!" She gave him an imploring look. "Focus on the game, will you? You make it so hard."

He laughed.

She looked up at the sky and groaned. "Please, God, just strike me down right now before I put another foot in my mouth."

"I've got something much tastier than feet."

"Jock!" She laughed so hard, tears spilled from her eyes. As she swiped at them, she pointed at him and said, "Do *not* say a word."

He held his hands up in surrender.

They played a few rounds without talking, sexual tension buzzing in the air as they shared furtive glances and stifled laughs. It was the most fantastic night Jock had ever experienced, and he didn't want it to end.

Daphne put down the word *hungry* and said, "Did you learn to cook when you took care of Harvey?"

"No. It was when I was a kid. You couldn't grow up with my mother and not learn how to cook."

He spelled *yes* on the board using the *y* in *hungry*, and she glowered at him. He winked and said, "*Ravenous.*"

"I'm *not* falling for that, and I'm not offering you more muffins, because that would just end in you making me blush again."

"Don't withhold your *muffins*," he pleaded. "That's just cruel."

"Fine. Eat my muffins if you must, but I am not reciprocating and eating your...*éclair.*" Laughter burst from her lips, and they both cracked up. "*Okay, okay, okay.*" She wrapped her arm around her middle and said, "I've got to stop. My stomach hurts from laughing."

"Oh, *man.* You're a blast."

"I'm glad I'm entertaining you. What were we talking about?"

"Your muffins," he said coyly.

She waggled her finger. "*No.* We were talking about your mother. Tell me about her. Is she that bad of a cook, or were you left to fend for yourself a lot?"

"She's a phenomenal cook, and every meal is an event. But it's not the food that reels you in. It's her."

Daphne studied her tiles and said, "What about her?"

"I don't know. *Everything.* My mother is one of the most beautiful women I know. She's funny and loving, and she's just the best mom a guy could ask for. You should see my father with her. They're still so in love, he's always pawing at her, kissing her, like he'd never get enough."

"That's nice. My dad loves my mom, but he's not overly affectionate."

"I don't think my father could stand not touching my mother. She's just…You can't help but be drawn to her, and when she's cooking, she's always telling stories. She sucks you into her world without even trying. I can remember playing basketball in the yard as a kid and coming in for a drink or a snack, and she'd say"—he softened his voice—"'Come on, Jackie, let's whip you up something to eat.' Two hours later, I'd have a full meal in my stomach that I'd helped prepare and I was sitting there mesmerized by one of her stories."

"She sounds wonderful." Daphne set down her word and said, "How often do you see her?"

"Not very often."

"Why not?"

He shrugged and took his turn.

As he reached for the last of the tiles, she said, "Come on, *Jackie*, you're not getting off that easy."

"What did you just call me?" *God, this woman…*

"You heard me. *Jackie, Jackie, Jackie*," she said in a singsong voice.

"Those are fighting words, girl."

"*Oooh*, I'm scared," she said sarcastically.

He pushed to his feet and reached for her. She darted away, knocking the board off the table. He ran after her and caught her around the waist, hauling her back against his chest. She was laughing hysterically, trying to wriggle free, and she felt so fucking good, he tightened his hold.

"*Stop!*" she said through her laughs. "You're tickling me."

He put his mouth beside her ear and said, "You think you can take me on, Zablonski?"

"You think you can take *me* on, Steele?" she challenged.

In her struggles, she thrust her ass back, pressing against his cock, making him hard as stone. "You're playing with fire, blondie."

"What's the matter? My hot muffins too much for you to handle?"

She shimmied and twisted, breaking free at the exact moment he let go, and tripped over her feet, taking them both down to the ground. She landed on top of him with her breasts in his face. Popping up on her hands, eyes wide as saucers, she said, "I guess I *can* take you on after all."

In one swift move, he shifted her onto her back and straddled her hips, holding her arms beside her head. She was panting and smiling so bright, she lit up the night. He wanted to take the kiss he'd been craving, to soak up her light until it blinded the angst of his past. But he knew better, so he said, "You're a dangerous woman, Daphne Zablonski."

"Dangerous to your *manhood*," she said snarkily.

"You have no idea how accurate you are."

"I meant your *pride*!" she said, looking sweet and sexy and far too tempting.

He forced himself to climb off her, and as he helped her to her feet, all that sweet light turned dark and electric. Her eyes brimmed with desire and his body throbbed with it. It took all of his control to step back, but the sizzling heat between them was like a cable pulling him toward her. He couldn't look away, didn't want to put more distance between them, and by the way her breathing hitched, he was pretty sure she felt the same.

"Daphne? Jock?" Emery's voice broke their spell.

Daphne stumbled away, fidgeting with her sweater, embarrassment staining her cheeks. "Emery, Dean. Hi. We were just playing…"

"Uh-huh," Emery said with an approving grin.

Dean, a mountain of a man with bulbous muscles and a Viking-like beard, locked eyes with Jock and said, "*Playing?*" All of Daphne's bosses were protective of her.

"Scrabble," Jock explained. "Careful taking on this one." Jock began picking up the tiles from the ground and said, "She kicked my ass."

"I read a lot. It helps," Daphne said, nervously picking up the Scrabble board and placing it in the box.

"Since you love erotic romance, I bet it was an *interesting* game," Emery teased.

"That's not *all* I read," Daphne said, frantically gathering her things.

Jock put the last of the tiles in the box and said, "It's getting late. I should take off. Daph, do you want help bringing your things inside?"

"No thanks," she said softly, her eyes briefly meeting his, then shifting away, but not before he registered the embarrassment, disappointment, and definite *interest* he'd seen in them.

"Hey, are you guys coming to the bonfire Friday night?" Dean asked.

"I'll be there," Daphne said. "Hadley loves our date nights."

"*Date* nights?" Jock asked.

Daphne looked a little sheepish, as if she was afraid to look for too long, and said, "Mommy-daughter dates. Hadley loves them because she gets to stay up late and play on the beach at night. She usually wears herself out and falls asleep on my lap sitting by the fire."

Why did that sound wonderful to a guy who couldn't even stick around when her kid hugged his leg?

"I can't wait to have Mommy-baby dates," Emery said, hugging Dean.

"Me too, doll." Dean kissed her cheek and said, "How about you, Jock? Will you be there?"

He didn't want to show up at the bonfire and ruin Daphne's and Hadley's fun. "I think I'd better skip it." He glanced at Daphne and said, "I had a great time. I haven't laughed this much since Harvey was alive. Thanks for the game, and I sure enjoyed your *muffins*." That earned another fierce blush. "I'll see y'all tomorrow."

As he headed home, tomorrow seemed much too far away.

# Chapter Five

"LET ME CHECK the dates to see if the cottage is free." Daphne cradled the phone against her shoulder Thursday morning as she typed on her computer. She'd been making stupid little mistakes all day, like typing in the wrong dates, as she did just now. For the life of her, she couldn't get out of her *Jock fog*, which was how she was referring to the new scatter-brained moments she'd been experiencing since last night. She'd wanted to kiss him so badly when they were lying in the grass, she could taste it, and if that wasn't bad enough, she'd made herself crazy wondering if he'd been serious about making her dinner. She didn't think he was, since they hadn't firmed up plans, but she'd liked the idea of it.

"I don't have cottage number nine available that weekend," she said into the phone. "But we just had a cancelation on cottage thirteen, which is a three-bedroom. It's a little more expensive, but it does have a water view. Would you like to reserve that one?"

"Let me check with my husband and get back to you on that," the woman said. "But I have another question. My sister just got engaged, and I'm helping her look for a venue on the Cape where we can hold an intimate wedding with about fifty guests. What is your availability next May?"

For the hundredth time since she'd begun working there, Daphne tried to mask her disappointment as she said, "I'm sorry. We don't host weddings, but I can give you numbers of local venues that do."

Daphne gave her the numbers of other event venues, and after she ended the call, she looked over her to-do list. At the top of the list was creating next week's event flyer. A company provided monthly booklets listing events that took place all over the Cape. When Daphne started working at the resort, she began making more personalized flyers for the guests. Every other week she put together lists of only the local events and sights, like Emery's yoga classes, the art gallery at Summer House, antique shops, Friday-night band concerts, movie nights at Preservation Hall in the middle of town, and other nearby events. As she pulled up last week's flyer, the idea of planning a small wedding nagged at her. She missed the thrill of working with excited brides and grooms, coordinating music, flowers, and decorations, making sure the happy couple was dazzled and pampered and that their dreams were not only met but *exceeded*.

Her cell phone rang, and her mother's name appeared on the screen. It was like Grand Central Station this morning.

"Hi, Mom," she said as she grabbed her events notebook.

"Hi, sweetheart. I know you're busy, but I just wanted to touch base about Hadley's birthday." Her parents doted on Hadley, and they were throwing her a birthday lunch on her birthday weekend, which was still a few weeks away. "Your father is arranging for the guys to bring the fire truck, and—"

"Mom, I told Daddy he didn't need to bring the fire truck. He should wait until next year or the year after, when Hadley's old enough to remember her first ride." Her father had made a tradition of taking each of his kids on a fire truck ride around the neighborhood with lights and sirens on their birthday. Daphne had been putting it off for Hadley because the loud noises had scared *her* when she was little, and she didn't want Hadley to be scared, too.

"I know, but your father has been dreaming of this day since Hadley was born. Let Pop Pop have his fun, honey."

"*Fine*, but I'm riding on the truck with her. It's scary up there."

"You can argue with your father about that. I wanted to tell you that last night Renee and I picked up the cutest cake topper of a bird that looks just like Hadley's favorite stuffy."

"She'll love that, but you might want to pick up an owl, too. A friend gave her one the other day and it's already become her new favorite."

"Was it from Jett? He's such a sweetheart."

"It wasn't Jett, Mom. It was Jock, one of Jett and Tegan's friends."

"Hadley is one lucky little girl to have so many people who love her. Once she learns the power of the female smile, you'll have your hands full."

"I already have my hands full."

"I know you do, baby. How did your talk go with your bosses about holding events?"

Daphne had forgotten she'd told her mother that she hoped to find the time to speak with them this week. "I haven't talked with them, but the girls seemed to think they wouldn't be open to the idea. I'm a little worried about bringing it up. I don't want them to think I'm bored."

"Honey, you *are* a little bored. You have to speak up for yourself. Wasn't that why they renovated the rec center? To hold events?"

"Yes, but they're so busy." Daphne was so thankful for everything her bosses had done for her, and she felt a little guilty for even wanting more. They'd been flexible with her schedule when Hadley had been sick, they let her work through lunch to pick her up by five, and they rented her the apartment upstairs for practically nothing. She had a lot to be thankful for, and she was a little nervous about jeopardizing that.

"Maybe they need a little nudge. They've got a gold mine in you, honey. They need to use the skills you have to offer, or you should find a job with a company who will."

"I'll think about it." Another call rang through, and Chloe's name flashed on the screen. "Mom, I've got another call and a ton of work to do. Can I call you later?"

"No need. I just wanted to touch base. Love you, honey. See you soon."

Daphne switched over to Chloe's call and said, "Hi."

"We missed you at breakfast."

"I know, sorry. It was a crazy morning. Hadley insisted on changing her clothes three times and finally decided on the first outfit she'd tried on, and we spent twenty minutes looking for her stuffed bird, which we found in a cabinet where she'd made it a nest out of socks."

"I love that little munchkin so much," Chloe said. "I thought maybe you were just too tired from your Scrabble date."

Daphne groaned. "I'm going to kill Emery."

"I can't believe you spent time alone with Jock and didn't tell me. *What* is going on? Emery said you two looked like you were about to tear each other's clothes off."

"She said that?" Daphne sank back in her chair, panic

blooming inside her. "That's all I need, for Dean and the guys to think I'm going to get naked in the yard."

"Relax, they'd probably cheer you on."

"*No*, they would *not*, and it's not like that anyway. Nothing is going on with me and Jock. We're friends." She thought about that for a second and said, "At least I *think* nothing is going on, but I don't really know for sure. It's all very confusing."

"Aw, Jock has you all flustered," she teased.

"Chloe, *stop*. This isn't funny. I don't know if we're just friends, or if the almost-kiss last night was real or in my head. And it doesn't matter because he can't be around Hadley—"

"Hold on! You had an *almost-kiss?*"

"I think so," she said nervously. "I mean, I wanted to kiss him, and it sure felt like he wanted to kiss me. But when he was on top of me, it felt like that, too, only we were laughing—"

"On *top* of you? Okay, slow down. Tell me everything. Let's see if I can decipher Jock's *man speak* for you."

Daphne told her about Jock's apology and the gifts he'd given her and Hadley, the way her heart had nearly leapt out of its chest when he'd leaned in to open her apartment door two nights ago, and about their hysterical wrestling match last night. "He wants to try to be better toward Hadley and, Chloe, he says the nicest things. He said I'm *stunning* and that he thinks about me all the time, but then he says things like it's been a long time since he's had a *friend* like me. So...*friends*, right?"

"Maybe he's hinting around the friends-with-benefits bush?"

"Um, no thank you. I could never do that. I have a little girl to think about."

"Hadley would never know. Why not consider it? Jett and

Tegan were friends with benefits, and now they're engaged."

"Because I'm not Tegan." She lowered her voice even though she was alone in the office and said, "I can't open myself up like that and show him my mom bod without a commitment. I haven't even been with a man since my ex. I'm sure I'd do everything wrong anyway."

"Daphne, your mom bod is gorgeous, and sex is like riding a bike."

"I fell off my two-wheeler so many times I had training wheels until I got my driver's license. And Jock doesn't strike me as a friends-with-benefits type of guy, either. He's too genuine for that."

Chloe laughed. "Genuine?"

"Real. Honest. I see it in his eyes, and I understand now why Tegan said he was worth being patient with. We laugh, and we talk, and…" She sighed. "I'm blowing it all out of proportion, aren't I? I've been reading board books so long, I think I've forgotten how to read guys."

"You have not, and you read enough romance to stock a bookstore. If you ask me, you're both tiptoeing around the chemistry we *all* see between you. And as far as Hadley goes, he said he'd try, right?"

"Maybe you're right about the chemistry, and he did say he'd try. But there's definitely something in his past that caused his reaction to Hadley and Aaron. He said it was horrible, but he hasn't told me exactly what *it* is."

"I'm sure he will."

"Maybe at some point. We're getting to know each other better, but I *really* like him, Chloe, and that's a little scary. When we all go out as a group, he's funny and charming, but he holds back *so* much compared to when it's just the two of us.

You know how Justin looks at you like you're all he sees?"

"I love that look," Chloe said.

"Well, Jock looks at *me* like that, but also like he doesn't know if he should kiss me or run away from me."

The office door opened, and a young couple walked in. Daphne stood up, smiling at them, and said, "Chloe, I have to run."

"Okay, we'll catch up soon."

She ended the call and said, "Hi, I'm Daphne. Welcome to Bayside Resort."

"Hi," the kind-eyed man said. "We're the Wilmots. We have a cottage rented for the weekend."

"Yes, Kerry and Michael, right?" Daphne made a point of greeting guests by their names to make them feel special.

"That's right," Kerry said, reaching for her husband's hand. "We were referred by our friends who stayed here last summer, Mark and Ally Galloway."

"I remember them well," Daphne said. "They played a lot of tennis, and Ally enjoyed the early-morning yoga classes at Summer House."

"You have a good memory," Kerry said. "She told me to check out the yoga classes."

"I'll give you a schedule right after we get you registered and set up with pool passes and a parking permit." Daphne handed her the registration paperwork.

As she finished checking them in, she told them about the facilities and pointed out the events flyers and booklets. She gave Kerry a pamphlet about Emery's yoga classes, a map of the property, and the appropriate passes. "You'll be in cottage number eleven. If you continue past the pool and follow the road to the left, you'll pass cottages three through eight, and wrap around to the back of the property. Your cottage is the second one on the right. It's one of my favorites. You have a view of the water and of the beautiful patio and garden designed and landscaped by one of the owners, Dean Masters. Dean's wife, Emery, teaches the yoga classes at Summer House."

"How lovely," Kerry said.

"Thank you, Daphne. You've been very informative," Michael said.

"That's what I'm here for. I'll be here tomorrow, too, and my coworker Everett will be here Saturday and Sunday. If you need anything at all, don't hesitate to ask."

She switched the phones to the answering service and walked outside with them. "The yoga classes are held at the inn next door." She pointed to Summer House. "If you decide to take yoga classes, you can sign up here with me or at their front desk." She motioned toward the pool and said, "In the packet you'll find the electronic key to open the gate for the pool and tennis courts. And that building at the end of the road is the recreation center. Feel free to use the games and the pool tables. If you need a full-service office, there are two in the building that are free for guests to use. We simply ask that you reserve them here first."

"Wow. I might never leave," Kerry said. "Thank you so much."

"Enjoy your stay." Daphne waited as they got into their car and waved as they drove away. She walked down the steps and tipped her face up to the sun, enjoying the warmth. She loved days like today, when the breeze was just strong enough to blow in through the office's screen door. But nothing beat standing outside in the sun. She watched the Wilmots turn by Jock's cottage and wondered what he was up to. His SUV was in the driveway, and she hoped he was writing.

When she turned to go back inside, she noticed someone bent over farther down the driveway and went to go make sure they were okay.

The man turned as she approached, and her heart skipped at the sight of Jock's handsome face. Their eyes locked, and heat skated down her chest. Oh yeah, they had chemistry all right.

"Hey, Daph."

"Hi." Her eyes drifted down his bare chest, and as her gaze moved lower, the heat pooling low in her belly turned to panic at the sight of blood dripping down his knee and shin. "What happened?"

"Hit and run."

"You got hit by a *car*?"

"No, a bike. I was out for a run, trying to clear my head, and he came around the corner too fast. He didn't see me."

"Oh my gosh! Are you hurt anywhere else? Was the biker okay?"

"He was fine—just a few scratches—and I'm fine, really. I caught myself with my hands. Well, most of myself, anyway."

"That's a *lot* of blood, Jock. You might need stitches." She took his arm, tugging him toward the office. "Come with me. I'll get you cleaned up."

"You don't have to."

"Are you kidding? I know how guys are. I have a brother. You think if you slap duct tape on it, it'll be fine. Trust me, it won't."

"Hey, don't knock duct tape," he said as they entered the office.

She pointed to her desk chair and said, "*Sit*. I'm going to get the first-aid kit."

She hurried into the storeroom for the first-aid kit, then went into the bathroom to get a wet washcloth. She grabbed two extras just in case, and a basin of water to rinse the cuts. When she came out, Jock was sitting with his back to her desk, his head resting on the back of the chair, eyes closed. Her fingers itched to touch his delicious-looking skin. What would it be like to run her fingers over his chest? To slide her tongue along his abs? A thrill darted through her, and she allowed her eyes to slide even lower. His black running shorts did little to hide the lust-inducing package she'd felt on her backside last night.

Jock's eyes opened, and a slow smile spread across his lips, jerking her back to the moment. *What* was wrong with her? He was bleeding and she was fantasizing about his...

She tried to push away those thoughts as she went to him, doing her best to pretend he *hadn't* caught her staring at his junk, and knelt in front of the chair to inspect his wounds. There were cuts and scrapes on his knee, a gash at the edge of his kneecap, and another beside his shinbone, which was also scraped up. Dirt and gravel were embedded in the cuts. "Oh, Jock," she said softly. "That has to hurt."

"Nah. It's just a few cuts."

"There's gravel and dirt in them. I need to get it all out." She looked up, meeting his dark eyes, and said, "I'm sorry for any pain I'm going to cause."

"There's nothing I can't handle," he said with a wink.

"Except an almost-three-year-old wrapped around your leg," she teased, immediately feeling bad for doing so.

"Low blow, blondie."

"Sorry. That wasn't funny. I was just trying to take your mind off your cuts."

"My mind hasn't been on my cuts since I saw you walking toward me outside."

*There you go again, making me feel special.* "You don't have any bloodborne diseases I should know about, do you?"

He held her gaze and said, "None. I'm clean as a whistle."

She pictured herself blowing his *whistle* and her whole body flamed.

"What's that blush for?" he asked.

She glanced up, but his wolfish grin told her he already knew *exactly* what she was thinking, which made her entire body tingle and flame. She tried to focus on cleaning his cuts and *not on* the way he was watching her, but it was like working under a heat lamp. She dripped water over his cuts, patting lightly to get the surface dirt off. Even the sight of blood did nothing to tamp down the lust simmering inside her. Every time she patted his leg, the muscles twitched. He closed his eyes and rested his head back. She couldn't help noticing that something *else* twitched when she touched him, too. She breathed deeply, trying to keep herself from thinking about *that* or peeking at it with every touch.

Pure torture.

When she finished cleaning away as much dirt as she was able, she poured a little alcohol on the tweezers and went to work on the gravel embedded in his cuts, saying, "The good news is that none of the cuts look deep enough for stitches. But this might hurt. I'm going to use tweezers to get out the pieces of gravel."

He gritted his teeth, sucking in sharp breaths and making a grunting noise every time she picked one out.

"Too hard?" she asked.

"No, keep going."

She plucked out another piece, and he gritted out, "*Christ* that was deep."

"I can stop."

"No, you're good. Just keep going. Faster, if you can."

"How's this?" She tried to use a lighter touch but had to dig in a little deeper for the tweezers to take purchase.

"*Holy...*"

"I thought you could handle anything," she joked.

"I didn't expect you to go at me with teeth and nails."

"*What* is going on here?" Rick's voice boomed as he plowed into the office.

"Rick!" Daphne went up on her knees to see over the desk, panicked at the anger in his voice. Rick was scowling, standing beside Brody Brewer, their surfing instructor, who looked amused. "I was just helping Jock," she explained. "He hurt himself."

"*I* want to hurt myself," Brody said with a waggle of his brows.

"That's enough, Brewer." Jock swiveled the chair and pushed to his feet, glowering at Brody.

"Hey, Jock. Daph's my girl." Brody looked at Daphne and said, "One day I'm going to get her out on my board, right, babe?"

Daphne was thoroughly confused by Rick's anger and she had no idea how Jock knew Brody. Brody had been away for the last few weeks. "You two know each other?"

"Yeah. He's from Harborside. Levi and our cousins live there," Jock explained. "Rick, I'm sorry to take Daphne away from her work. I had a run-in with a bike."

"No worries. I'm just happy you have pants on." Rick scrubbed a hand down his face and said, "From out there it looked and sounded like something else was going on."

Jock shook his head, stifling a grin.

It took Daphne a second to realize what Rick meant. "You thought I'd do *that*? *Here*? Anybody could see us through the screen door! That's...that's..." *Exactly what I was thinking about when I was on my knees.* Holy cow, she *had* been reading too much erotic romance.

"I'm sorry, Daphne," Rick said. "But you've got to admit, if you saw Jock's bare shoulders and heard the things he was saying and the noises he was making, you'd wonder, too."

"I would *not* jump to that conclusion," she insisted.

Jock touched her arm and said, "Thanks for your help. I can finish this up at my cottage."

"No you can't," she snapped, her annoyance at Rick thinking she was doing something dirty coming out at the wrong person. "Just sit down and let me finish."

Jock glanced at Rick, and Rick said, "I'd do what she says. She's using her mom voice."

Brody chuckled.

"C'mon, Brody, in my office." Brody followed him into his office. Rick sat on the edge of his desk, arms crossed, talking with Brody, but his eyes were trained on Daphne and Jock.

She crouched to finish cleaning Jock's wounds, hoping she wasn't in trouble and frustrated that Rick would assume something like that about her.

Jock leaned forward and ran his fingers along her jaw. "Guess I'm all yours, Daph."

She swallowed hard. He was dangerously charming. That seductive look in his eyes was surely meant to make her blush and tingle. Which it *did*. She tried to avoid looking at anything but his leg as he gritted out sounds at the poke of the tweezers.

Rick was right—those were the type of sounds she knew she'd imagine coming from Jock late at night in the darkness of her bedroom.

"Just so you know," he said quietly, "those are not the noises I'd make if you and I were—"

Her eyes shot up to his, silencing him and earning a sexy-assin grin. As much as she hated blushing, she loved their banter. Jock made it easier for her, joking and teasing her out of her disgruntled state. No man had ever flirted with her like he did, but it was more than the flirting that had her tied in knots. She had fun with Jock. She could let her guard down and tease him as much as he teased her, even dipping her toes into the sexual teasing pool, like she'd done last night—and she loved it.

When she was finished, she sat back on her heels and said, "Are you heading home to shower?"

Heat sparked in his eyes again. "Why? Do you make house calls?"

"You're impossible. As soon as you walk out that door, I'm going to google remedies for blushing so you can't do that to me anymore."

"That's just cruel and unusual punishment. I love seeing you blush."

He said it so sincerely, she almost felt bad for threatening to stop.

"I only asked because I don't want to put antibiotic ointment and bandages on your cuts if you're just going home to shower."

"I am going to shower," he said. "Thank you for taking care of my cuts. Are we still on for tonight?"

"Oh," she said with surprise, excitement, and nervousness tangling up inside her. "I thought you were kidding about that.

You don't have to make me dinner."

"I want to. How about I come over at seven?"

*You want to! Ohmygoodness, you want to…*Her emotions reeled. *This is a date, right? Wait. Is this a date? Is it wrong to be excited if you haven't had a chance to try to react better to Hadley yet? I can't help it. I'm excited!*

"Daph? Does seven work?"

"*Sorry.* That's when I put Hadley to bed."

He nodded, brows knitting. She wondered if he was going to rescind the offer.

"Seven thirty?" he asked. "Eight? Does that give you enough time to get her tucked in?"

"Sure. Anytime after seven thirty should be fine. What should I get from the store?"

"Absolutely nothing. Do you have any food allergies I should know about?"

"Nope."

"Great. Then we're all set. I look forward to it."

They walked around the desk as Brody and Rick came out of Rick's office, and Rick said, "Daphne, we can book surf lessons for Brody for Tuesday through Friday for the next three weeks."

"Okay." *Remind me when my head isn't spinning.*

"I'm going to head out and see if I can find a biker to run me over," Brody said. "Be back soon, Daphne."

"My ass you will." Jock hooked an arm around Brody's neck, dragging him toward the door. "I'll take your trash out, Rick."

Daphne was glad to hear them joking around as they headed down the steps. She exhaled a breath she hadn't realized she was holding, and when she turned around, Rick was perched against the front of her desk, arms crossed.

"I'm sorry for helping Jock, but I couldn't just let him bleed," she said.

"What are you talking about? I don't mind that you helped Jock."

"Then why do you look like you're about to reprimand me?"

"Do I?" He stood up and pushed his hands into the pockets of his jeans. "Sorry. I'm just concerned as your friend, not your boss. What's going on between you two?"

"What do you mean? We weren't doing anything."

"I don't think you were. But you two looked pretty cozy, and Desiree said Emery and Dean found you two together last night. I like Jock. We all do. But I know how he is with Hadley, and I just don't want to see you get hurt."

"Oh." She wasn't expecting to hear that, or to feel the pang of guilt it stirred. "Thanks for worrying, Rick, but we're just friends and we're getting to know each other better. We talked about his reactions to Hadley, and he apologized. I think there's a lot more to Jock than meets the eye."

"I get that feeling, too. I'm glad he apologized. Just be careful, okay?"

"I always am."

Rick went back to his office, and Daphne took the phones off the answering service, trying to push that pang of guilt away. She would never do anything that could hurt Hadley. Hadley would be asleep when Jock came over. She'd been careful for so long, it was nice to have a chance to let her hair down and be a regular twenty-six-year-old woman hanging out with a man she was attracted to. Was that such a crime?

She sat at her desk, the events flyer staring back at her.

*Events other people get to plan.* She'd spent her entire life being careful, and she was tired of it. Being careful was exhausting, and limiting. Maybe Rick and the guys weren't the only ones who needed a nudge.

Gathering her courage like a cloak, she pushed to her feet and strode into Rick's office. When he looked up from his computer, she said, "Do you have a sec?"

"Sure. What's up?" He waved to the chair across from him.

She sat down and said, "We got another call about hosting a wedding—a small one, only fifty guests. I gave them a few recommendations, but I've been here two years now, and you know I have the experience to handle event planning. I was thinking that maybe we could start with a small event and see how it goes."

Rick sat back, nodding, and a kernel of hope bloomed inside her.

"I have no doubt that you're capable of handling events. We've all seen how great you are at everything you do. I know we said we'd like to eventually host holiday events and such, but with Aaron, and Dean's baby on the way, and Drake's music stores taking off, I'm not sure this is the right time to do it."

She felt deflated, but she refused to let herself sink just yet. "I know how busy life is with a new baby, and I realize you guys don't have much time. What if I handled all of it, start to finish? I'd just need you to approve budgets."

"Daphne, you already have a full-time job."

"I know but…" She wanted to say she'd work extra hours to pull it off, but she didn't want to do that and lose out on time with Hadley. He was right. She couldn't do the job of two people, no matter how much she wanted to. One of the two would get slighted.

"You're right. I wouldn't be able to do it without working a lot more hours, and I can't do that to Hadley." She pushed to her feet and said, "Thanks for taking the time to talk about it."

"I'm sorry, Daphne. Maybe in a year or two we'll be in a better place to reassess and take on more."

"Sure. Or maybe you and Desiree and Emery and Dean will be having more babies."

Rick winked and said, "If I have it my way, we will."

"I hope you do. If I had been in a position to have more, I definitely would have."

She left his office battling her own disappointment against their happiness. They'd worked hard to achieve their dreams, and they were finally in a position to enjoy them.

Maybe it was time for her to start working toward her dreams, too.

# Chapter Six

JOCK CARRIED THE groceries he'd bought up the steps to Daphne's apartment Thursday evening, asking himself the same questions he'd been asking all day. Was he being fair to her? She was so open and giving. Was he being selfish? Would he ever be able to overcome his triggers? He had no idea why Hadley had chosen him as a target of her affection, but every time she clung to his leg, he'd wanted to scoop her into his arms and earn the smiles she gifted him. He wanted to hear her sweet giggles float in the air like brass rings he'd give anything to catch. And when she cried, he wanted to hold her and soothe her tears away, but he couldn't get past the memories those sounds dredged up.

He stepped onto the landing knowing the answers, and they weren't pretty. He wanted so much more than a clandestine friendship with Daphne, and he knew that wasn't fair to her. But how could he walk away from the only woman who had made him *feel* anything since his world had been turned upside down? The only woman who made him lust and laugh and want to be a better man? The situation was torturous, but he wasn't a completely selfish bastard. No matter what he felt for Daphne, until he got his shit together, there was no way he'd put Hadley in another situation that could possibly end with her in tears. Until he figured out how to conquer the beast, he would continue seeing Daphne only when Hadley wasn't around.

He knocked on the door, hoping he didn't appear as nervous as he felt. When she opened the door, their eyes connected with the heat of a torch and somehow also the light of a summer day. He knew in that moment that it would be impossible for him to walk away even if he wanted to.

"Hey, gorgeous." When he'd seen her that afternoon, she'd looked beautiful in a sleeveless paisley top and white capris. Now she wore faded jeans and a white T-shirt that had OH BABY! in pink script across her chest, and she looked even more ravishing.

"Hi." Her eyes swept over his button-down shirt and black jeans, and she looked nervously down at her clothes and said, "I didn't know we were dressing up. I was worried that if I dressed too nice, I'd look like I was making more out of this than I should or that I was trying too hard." Her words flew fast and breathless. "Sorry, but it's not a reflection on how I felt about having dinner with you. Not that I'm thinking anything *big*. I just...I'm rambling. Sorry."

"I like to hear you ramble. You could wear a burlap sack and you'd look like a million bucks." He leaned in and kissed her cheek, inhaling the floral scent of her perfume. "*Mm*. You smell good, too."

She smiled and said, "You're not allowed to make me blush tonight."

"Then I guess I shouldn't give you these." He reached into the bag, withdrawing a bouquet of flowers.

"Oh, *Jock*. They're beautiful. So much for not blushing." She lifted them to her nose and said, "You didn't have to do this."

"Despite the way I freeze around Hadley, I *was* brought up to be a gentleman."

"Well, remind me to thank your parents for that. Come in. Let's put these in water."

She motioned for him to follow her. He stepped inside, noticing Hadley's tiny shoes and sandals lined up beside Daphne's beneath a table in the foyer. On top of the table were two pretty candles and a decorative bowl with a key ring in it.

She led him through the cozy living room, and he imagined Daphne and Hadley cuddled up on the teal couch surrounded by the yellow and beige throw pillows. Above the couch was a large painting of a meadow with a little girl running through it. It looked happy and peaceful, like Daphne. The coffee table was stacked with children's books, and a pale-yellow chair, showing the indentations of an old favorite, was tucked in the corner of the room beneath a light. He could see Daphne reading there in the winter. Cubbies filled with stuffed animals, dolls, and other toys lined the wall beneath the window. There were baskets overflowing with toys by the couch and chair and another by the half wall separating the kitchen from the living room. On top of the half wall were pictures of Hadley and several more decorative candles.

He followed her into the simple and clean kitchen, with white cabinets and a wooden table for four with pretty blue cushions on the chairs. There was a hook on the wall with a set of blue oven mitts hanging from it and candles decorating the windowsill. He noticed that all of the wicks were still pristine. A stack of coloring books littered a child-size plastic table, and several of Hadley's scribble drawings hung from colorful magnets on the refrigerator. Everything in Daphne's apartment was as warm and heartfelt as the aura she gave off.

"Hadley's quite the artist," he said, admiring the drawings.

"I love when she gives me her drawings. She's always so proud of them."

"As well she should be. You must love candles. Are they all just for decoration?"

"They're not supposed to be. My grandmother used to light candles at night when I'd visit. She said nothing soothed the soul like the scent of candles. She passed away a few years ago. I keep telling myself I'll use the candles because they bring such good memories, but I don't want to light them with Hadley around, and after she goes to bed, I never think about it."

"Well, they're very pretty." He set the grocery bag on the counter and said, "Your whole place is nice."

"Thanks. We like it." Daphne moved a chair from the table to beside the counter and climbed onto it.

"*Whoa.*" He put his hand on her back in case she lost her balance and said, "I can get whatever you need."

"It's okay. I've got it." She opened a cabinet and retrieved a vase from the top shelf.

As she climbed down, he said, "You have to be careful climbing up on chairs like that."

"Are you kidding?" As she filled the vase with water, she said, "Single moms have to be nimble and quick. We scale counters, climb trees when balloons get stuck in them, and we'd crawl into sewers if we had to."

He moved the chair back to its place, loving that she wasn't afraid to be herself around him. "You'd crawl into a sewer?"

As she arranged the flowers in the vase, she said, "For Hadley? *Of course.* This one time—"

"*At band camp...*"

They both cracked up.

"I *love* that movie," she exclaimed. "Please tell me you did not bring apple pie for dessert."

"You mean I don't get your *muffins* for dessert?"

"*Ohmygod*," she whispered, turning beet red.

"I'm kidding, Daph. I brought chocolate cream puffs."

"*Mm.* Sounds delicious."

"Then I guessed well. Now, about that band-camp story. Did it involve a flute?"

She swatted his arm. "You're terrible. There is *no* band camp in this story. It's a goat story."

"I'm pretty sure that's illegal," he teased. Her pink-cheeked disapproving look made him want to kiss her again. "I'm sorry, but it's a classic line. I couldn't resist. Go ahead. I promise to behave."

"Last year I took Hadley to a petting zoo, and she brought her favorite stuffed monkey. She always brings stuffies with her. Anyway, I turned my back for three seconds to get goat food out of the dispenser, and she fed her stuffy to a goat! Apparently goats eat anything. I knew the second Hadley got sleepy, she'd want that monkey, so..." She shrugged and said, "I might have taken a mama goat down to save my daughter's stuffy."

"Damn. You can deal with blood without passing out and take down a mama goat? Beneath all that blushing you are one tough cookie."

"Once you've given birth, you see the whole world differently."

He could say the same thing about losing a child, but he wasn't going down that path tonight. He shook off those dark thoughts and focused on Daphne.

"I'd do anything for my baby girl." She peered into the bag

he'd brought and said, "What's going on in *here*? I see wine. Yummy."

He took out the bottle. "Where do you keep wineglasses?"

She wrinkled her nose. "I don't have any. But I do have regular glasses." She grabbed two glasses from a cabinet. "Or I can offer you a wide array of sippy cups."

"Regular glasses it is. I guess that means you don't have a corkscrew?"

"Actually, I do. I got it as a secret Santa gift ages ago." She snagged the corkscrew from a drawer and handed it to him.

While he opened and poured the wine, he said, "I hope you like fettuccini Alfredo and shrimp."

"That sounds heavenly."

He handed her a glass and picked up his own. "Here's to secret Santa and new friends."

They clinked glasses, and as she took a sip, he said, "And to your muffins."

She choked, turning just in time to spray wine into the sink as laughter bubbled out of her mouth.

He passed her a napkin from the holder on the table and put a hand on her back. "Sorry, I couldn't help myself."

She wiped her mouth and her pink cheeks and said, "That happens to you a lot."

"Only around you," he admitted.

"I'm sure I'm nothing like the girls you're used to hanging out with. And I'm definitely not used to this kind of friend-ship."

"I'm not used to it either, so why don't we relax and enjoy our evening." He set down his glass and rubbed his hands together. "Let's get started, blondie. Where do you keep your pans?"

They cooked dinner together, because Daphne insisted that moms were not good at letting someone else do all the work. It was a simple dish that involved boiling fettuccini, simmering ingredients for the sauce, and cooking shrimp, but working side by side with Daphne was anything but simple. She was so frigging cute and funny. He loved her laugh, and she was sexy, and so honest and real, by the time they were ready to eat, Jock was even more drawn to her.

Daphne put place mats at either end of the table. He moved them closer together and said, "I know it's a small table, but that was still too far apart."

After they set out the food, he said, "Just one more thing. Do you have a lighter or matches?"

"Yes. In the biggest drawer behind you."

"Why don't you hit the lights and we'll bring out those happy memories." As he lit the candles, happiness sparked in her eyes. "Who knows, maybe we'll even make a few of our own memories to go with them."

He pulled out a chair for her, and as she sat, she said, "Your parents really did raise a gentleman. Everything smells so good. Thank you for showing me how to make this. It was fun. I feel like I'm at a restaurant."

"*Chez Daph*?" He sat down and said, "We make a good team, and it was the least I could do. After all, you probably saved me from getting a duct tape infection."

She took a bite and closed her eyes for a second in pure satisfaction. "*Mm.* This is delicious. After I cleaned up your leg, I remembered that you probably have a lot of medical experience, since you cared for Harvey."

"I have some, but we've talked about me for two days. I want to hear about you. Have you always lived here?"

She twisted fettuccini around her fork and said, "I grew up here, but I moved away when I got married and came back when I got divorced."

"I take it your ex isn't from here?"

"He was from Wilmington, North Carolina. I was eighteen and working at a resort in Chatham when we met. I worked at the front desk and helped the event planner. He was twenty-two, a management intern. We had a lot of interaction because of our jobs, and a bunch of the staff used to hang out after work. I got to know him over the span of several months, and one night he and I got together."

"Whirlwind relationship?" he asked, taking another bite.

"No. I can't even blame my bad decisions on that. Tim and I dated for a few months while he worked here, and when he went back home, we did the long-distance relationship thing. After a year of going back and forth, he proposed. We got married in the courthouse, and I moved to Wilmington, where I worked at a resort doing event planning, which I *loved*."

"You didn't want a fancy wedding?" he asked.

She shrugged. "I always wanted a pretty wedding, but not too fancy. Something smallish. I had visions of a beautiful white wedding gown, and I know most girls want a spring or summer wedding, but I always dreamed of getting married in the winter. I *love* the winter. Everything feels so crisp, and the holidays and New Year's are so festive. But Tim had to get back to work, and I don't really know why we didn't wait to have a wedding. We just sort of decided, I guess, and ended up at the courthouse." She pushed food around on her plate and said, "Two years later I got pregnant with Hadley, and after she was born, we separated, and I came back home. Then we got divorced."

Her tone was too casual for the pain in her eyes. "Is he still in the picture?"

"No. He didn't want children."

He touched her hand, bringing her eyes to his. He wished he could erase the sadness he saw in them. "I'm sorry you went through that. You didn't know he didn't want children when you got married?"

"No. He said he wanted a family *one day*, and I've always wanted a big family. But when I got pregnant, he started working more hours. I knew things weren't great, but I was busy with my own work at the resort, and I wasn't one of those *cute* pregnant girls, so I assumed he was just keeping himself extra busy so he wouldn't have to...you know," she said softly. "Be close to me."

"*Christ*, Daphne." Jock gritted his teeth, wishing he could track down the prick and tear him apart for hurting her. "He didn't deserve you. You're *gorgeous*, and I'm sure when you were pregnant you were even more beautiful."

"Thank you, but I wasn't. I should have seen the writing on the wall over those nine months, but I guess I didn't want to. He was never interested in doing all the fun things couples do to prepare for having a baby, like setting up the nursery, talking about names, making future plans." Her gaze fell to her plate again, and she said, "It doesn't matter."

"It *matters* a hell of a lot." He covered her hand with his and said, "Look at me." When she did, his heart swelled at the courage looking back at him. "*You* matter, and your feelings matter, every minute of every single day. That's always the case." He didn't think it was possible to feel worse about the way he reacted to Hadley, but knowing that little girl's own father had turned his back on them did the trick. He was more determined than ever to try to find a way to fix it.

"Thank you," she said softly. "I have learned that. I was so young and naive back then. When my mom had my sister, my father bought her a charm bracelet with a charm of a little girl with a pink stone in the belly. Then, when Sean and I were born, he added to it. Sean's was a blue stone. She still wears it. I always loved that bracelet. I had dreams of being given one for my own daughter. I imagined a big, happy family with trips to the park and flying kites on weekends. I dreamed of movie nights where we all cuddled together and having that feeling where it didn't matter how stressful anything in life was, because at the end of the day, I would have this great family to cherish and a husband who would rather be with me than anywhere else." She had a faraway look in her eyes, but she sighed, and that look changed to something *less*. "But those are pie-in-the-sky dreams. Hadley wasn't planned, obviously. I had an IUD and it didn't work. Learned my lesson with that one. But I was happy about the pregnancy, and I believed in marriage. My parents have a great marriage, so I thought once the baby was born and I lost the baby weight, we'd find our way back to each other. Babies are supposed to bring people together, right?"

"You weren't naive, and what you went through had nothing to do with your weight, Daphne. A man who can turn his back on his pregnant wife doesn't deserve to have a wife."

Her expression turned more fierce than sorrowful, and she slipped her hand out from beneath his. "He turned his back on Hadley, and that was worse than turning his back on me. The night she was born, he told me he'd made a mistake and he didn't want a family after all. He hasn't seen her since she was a week old. He didn't even want her to have his name," she said with a biting tone. "That was actually good, because I was so hurt and angry for Hadley, I didn't want her to have his name, either. I gave her my maiden name, and I went back to using it after the divorce."

"You were hurt and angry for *Hadley*, but what about for yourself? You trusted him. You gave up your life here for a new life with him, and he pulled the rug out from under you. I wish I had known you then so I could have helped you through it."

"You're so nice," she said softly.

"Anybody would want to help you."

"My family was there for us when I came home. It wasn't easy, but we made it."

"I'm sorry to say this, but Tim sounds like an ass. Marriage vows are one of the few things in this life that a person should be able to count on to mean something." He took her hand and brushed his thumb over the back of it. "He should have been pampering you and telling you how beautiful you were during your pregnancy, not staying away and making you feel bad about yourself for carrying a baby he helped create."

"That seems like a fairy tale to me."

"It's not a fairy tale. It's *love*, Daph. When you love someone—as a friend or as something more—you can't help but shower them with it."

She glanced at their joined hands and said, "It sounds like you have firsthand experience. Have you ever been in love?"

Guilt wound through him like a serpent seeking prey. He let go of her hand and finished his wine, eating in silence as he pushed the ugliness of his past aside.

"Should I take that as a yes?" she asked carefully.

"No," he said, meeting her gaze. "I've never been in love. I just know it exists." He'd heard it in every one of Harvey's stories about his wife, seen it between his parents, and he'd seen it in Kayla's eyes even if it hadn't been aimed at him.

He wanted to tell Daphne the *rest* of his truth, but she was looking at him so adoringly, free from the shadows of his past. He didn't want to take the chance that the truth would make her see him differently. He wanted to give himself tonight to bask in her light, to enjoy the friendship of this incredible woman who made him laugh, and feel, and want so much more of a life than he'd seen in his future. *Just one night* and then he'd tell her everything.

"I know it exists, too," she said. "Even if it's not in the cards for this package deal."

"You worry a lot about that, don't you? The fact that you're a single mom and how men see you because of that?"

DAPHNE PUSHED THE last of her noodles around on the plate, feeling like she was about to reveal her underbelly, which was silly given what she'd already revealed, but it was true. What happened with Tim was in her past, and she'd gotten out of that bad situation, but Jock had touched on a subject nobody had ever asked her about. Not even her family. She talked superficially with her friends about dating as a single mom, but they'd never even dug into her feelings. That made her want to open up with him.

"Hadley changed everything about me, mostly in a good way. I know that the majority of guys aren't looking for an instant family, and it's not like I'm out there desperately seeking a husband. While I'd like to fall in love and all of that, my focus isn't on that. It's on keeping my head above water and taking care of my little girl. My grandmother once said that single people in their twenties are the *stars* of the show, young families are who those stars aspire to be, and empty nesters are invisible. I think she needed another category for single moms. We're pretty invisible, too. But single dads? They're every girl's dream, because if a man can put a child above all else, then he has an amazing capacity to love. So to answer your question, do I worry about being a single mom? No. I *am* a single mother, and I would never want a life without Hadley in it. I accept and *love* my reality. But I know where I stand in the social atmosphere. Having a child on my hip makes me invisible to most guys."

"A man would have to be blind not to see you." He touched her hand again, his gaze soft and emphatic, like he really wanted her to *hear* whatever he was about to say. "Your *reality* is that you're an amazing woman and mother, and a great friend, and you have a sweetheart of a little girl. You *both* deserve to be loved and to be treated like the special ladies you are."

The way he was looking at her, his touch, and the sweet things he said made her feel like she was floating. She'd never felt so *seen* and appreciated. She wanted to float right out of her chair and into his arms. She knew she shouldn't feel that way given his trouble with Hadley, but heaven help her, because if she could float, there'd be no stopping her. But they were supposed to be *friends*, and this wasn't a date, which meant she was reading everything wrong again.

Embarrassed and flustered, she said, "Are you ready for dessert?" She pushed to her feet and carried her plate to the sink. Her heart was beating too fast to even think about eating. She turned around, and Jock was *right* there, pinning her in place.

"Did I say something wrong?" he asked carefully.

"Wrong? *No.* Of course not. Nothing wrong, all good. I just thought you might be ready for dessert."

She tried to step around him, but he touched her hip and guided her in front of him again. He stepped closer, his fingers pressing into her. She was so nervous she must be hallucinating, because she swore the air between them crackled and popped.

"Talk to me, Daph." His eyes brimmed with desire. He brushed her hair away from her face with his fingertips, an intimate and excruciatingly sexy touch. His lips curved up, and he said, "There are those mesmerizing eyes of yours."

"You can't say things like that. It's confusing. Candles and wine, cooking together, and talking about my *muffins.* Maybe it's because I haven't spent time alone with a man in forever, but when you call me pretty and say I'm special and everything else you've said, I feel things that I shouldn't. I know you just want to be friends, and that's *good.*" The words flew from her lips faster than she could think. "I like you. I want this friend-ship. I want *you.* Oh *geez!* I didn't mean to say that. But I have all these other thoughts, and I mean"—she looked down his body, and what a magnificent body it was!—"they're *not* clean thoughts. They're not *friend* thoughts. They're thoughts I have no business thinking, and I don't know how to—"

He crushed his lips to hers so unexpectedly, she didn't re-ciprocate in those first few electric seconds as she processed the taste of wine and lust in his sensual demand. His arm circled her waist, crushing her to him, not too hard, but definitely possessive and eager. His tongue swept over hers, probing deep and erotic, then easing to a kiss so sweet she wanted to live inside it. Just when her legs turned to jelly, he probed deeper again, and her thoughts spun away. His hand pushed beneath her hair, cradling her head as he angled her mouth beneath his, holding her exactly where he wanted her. He wasn't just kissing her. He was possessive, claiming, and suddenly she was right there with him, giving herself over to their passion. He made greedy noises, like he'd been waiting his whole life for this very moment, and *oh*, what that did to her! He was so big, so hard and delicious, she wanted to savor everything—the taste of his mouth, the feel of his tongue as he took his fill, the slamming of his heart against her, and the press of his hand on her bottom. She ran her hands up his arms and over his shoulders, moaning at the feel of his muscles. When he eased his efforts, she went up on her toes, desperate for more. Their bodies ground together, and she pushed her hands into his thick hair, holding tight. He groaned low in his throat, his hips pressing forward, grinding against her, and she felt herself go damp. She was dizzy with desire, her body pulsing with need. She'd never kissed any man so freely or feverishly. Their kisses went on and on, and when their lips finally parted, she felt him trembling just as she was.

"*God*, Daphne," he whispered. "I've wanted to kiss you since I first saw you last summer."

His confession sent her emotions reeling. She couldn't speak, could barely move for the need coursing through her veins. That was okay, because she didn't want to *talk*. She pulled his mouth back to hers, and he devoured her with slow, drugging kisses.

"Mommy—"

They jerked apart at Hadley's cry. Jock's hazy gaze quickly sharpened, snapping Daphne's mind back to reality. He stepped away as Hadley cried out again.

Breathless, she said, "I have to—"

"Yeah. I'll take off."

"I'll just be a few—"

Hadley's cries escalated.

Jock glanced down the hall, at the dishes, the table, and finally at Daphne, the apprehension in his eyes unmistakable. "She needs you. We'll catch up tomorrow."

As he headed for the door, she went to take care of Hadley, trying to ignore the disappointment filling her up inside. She heard her apartment door close as she lowered herself to the edge of Hadley's bed and caressed her daughter's cheek. "Shh. It's okay, baby. Mama's here."

Hadley whimpered, "*Owly.*"

Daphne found her owl beneath the blanket and Hadley clutched it to her chest, letting out a long, relieved sigh, and closed her eyes. Daphne lay next to her, gently rubbing her back and staring into space. The apprehension on Jock's face flashed before her eyes. How could she have been so stupid to allow herself to get lost in a man who she knew bolted when he saw her daughter? A knot of self-loathing tightened in her chest.

*This* was her life, bedtimes and wakeful nights, sippy cups and stuffies. Her misguided fantasy with Jock had no place in her little girl's world, and that world was all that mattered. If tonight proved anything, it was that she couldn't just be friends with Jock, and anything else would only cause her, and possibly Hadley, pain. She had to put a stop to this madness. No more late-night chats and definitely no more scintillating kisses.

She climbed out of Hadley's bed and made her way back to the kitchen. Flames from the candles danced in the darkness. The unopened bakery box sat on the counter, and dishes cluttered the table. She had a sinking feeling in the pit of her stomach. She knew she was making the right move by ending things tomorrow. So why did it hurt so badly?

# Chapter Seven

JOCK STRODE OUT of the boxing club Friday afternoon just as angry at himself as he'd been when he'd walked in. He'd sparred several rounds with Brock, who had gone at him *hard*. Unfortunately, not hard enough to obliterate the hurt he'd seen in Daphne's eyes when he'd left last night. He hadn't even gotten halfway to his cottage before he'd stopped and debated going right back up to her apartment to apologize and to try— just fucking *try*—to get through Hadley's cries without being thrown back into the nightmare that plagued him. But he'd already hurt Daphne enough. She deserved a man without a head full of ghosts.

He'd spent the rest of the night trying to convince himself to let her go. But their nights together replayed in his head like the best movies, and their kisses…

*Holy hell, those kisses.*

When he'd kissed women in the past, he'd never thought about much, and certainly not about the actual kiss. But kissing Daphne had been different from the very first second their lips had touched. It had been a whole-body experience. He'd been acutely aware of everything about *her*. Her lips were warm and sweet, but he'd felt her hesitate, which had made his protective urges surge. He'd gone from *taking* to coaxing her into the safety of him, easing his efforts, giving her room to retreat, learning what she responded to, and wanting her to trust him as badly as he'd wanted her kisses. But she *hadn't* retreated. She'd given in to her desires, going up on her toes and fisting her hands in his hair. He fucking loved that. His heart had beat faster, he'd held her tighter, and he'd been rewarded with the eagerness of a seductress. He'd gotten swept up in all of her, from the lustful sounds she'd made to the tiny gasp that had followed each one, as if she were embarrassed but couldn't stop herself. When she'd pressed all of her luscious body against him, it had taken a will of steel not to touch her in all the places he wanted to, to show her how beautiful she was by cherishing every glorious curve.

He'd been kicking himself all day for not getting her number. He'd wanted to apologize this morning for the way he'd taken off, but she must have left early with Hadley because she was gone by the time he got outside. He was biding his time until she was free after work. He'd tried to distract himself with writing, but it was like pulling teeth. He'd gone for a run, but five miles later the hurt in her eyes still plagued him. He'd hoped boxing would clear his head, but that was a bust, too.

He'd earned her trust only to break it by leaving, and that gutted him.

He climbed into his SUV, glancing at the time as he drove out of the parking lot. It wasn't quite noon. There was no way he'd make it all day without losing his mind. He made a U-turn and headed for the café on the corner. Maybe Daphne would have a few minutes to talk with him during her lunch break, even if it had to be at her desk.

By the time he left the café, he felt mildly less pissed off. At least he had a plan.

He parked at his cottage and walked up to the office, hoping she could spare a few minutes and mentally rehearsing and tweaking his apology. He heard voices as he climbed the porch steps. When he opened the door, a group of people standing in front of Daphne's desk turned. *Fuck.*

"Excuse me." He stepped around them, aware of everyone watching him, probably thinking he was butting in line. When Daphne came into view, everything else disappeared. The phone was balanced between her ear and shoulder as she typed on the computer. Her eyes shifted his way, but a strained, icy smile lifted her lips. His gut plummeted. He'd give anything to see the smile he was used to. The one that lit up her beautiful face and righted all the wrongs in the world.

He set the lunch bag on the desk and whispered, "Lunch."

Her brows knitted, and she mouthed, *Thanks.*

"We'll talk later," he said, hoping he might get a real smile, but her lips pursed, and she returned her attention to the computer.

He left the office and headed back to his cottage feeling uncomfortable in his own skin. He took a shower, cursing himself for fucking up their night, and then he paced the hardwood floor, wishing he were still pounding the hell out of something or someone. The trouble was, the only person he wanted to beat the shit out of was himself.

He snagged his car keys and headed out. Maybe a drive would clear his mind.

Jock had never been good at doing anything aimlessly, which was part of the reason he was furious at the situation he'd put Daphne in. When he'd worked for Harvey, he'd been a *doer*, a fixer, the man who got shit done for the theater and for his friend. Why was it easier to fix a business and help an old man than to turn those skills inward and fix his fucking self?

Twenty minutes later, he found himself turning down the wooded road that led to what had been his home for a decade. As the stately mansion came into focus, a sense of comfort washed over him, and on its heels came a wave of sadness. He pulled down the empty driveway, glad Tegan was out, and parked in front of the house. Years of memories slammed into him as he stepped out of the vehicle and made his way across the lawn toward the gardens.

He walked past the stone amphitheater and the chairs set up for the production taking place later that afternoon, and memories of Harvey watching the shows as he listened to the children's laughter and comments flooded his mind. Harvey would recall those moments for days. Near the end, Harvey had to watch from his bed inside the mansion, listening through the open windows. His wife, Adele, had loved children, and in their laughter, Harvey had imagined Adele laughing, too. Jock had done all he could to keep Harvey laughing. He walked past the white tent where Harvey had offered a buffet after each performance so the children could run around and play with the new friends they'd met at the show. He was glad that when Tegan had inherited the amphitheater, she'd continued the tradition, although she'd changed the name of the amphitheater from the Cape Children's Amphitheater to the Harvey and Adele Fine Amphitheater, HAFA, both to honor her relatives and because she and Harper were offering adult productions in addition to the children's shows.

He entered the maze of gardens, which overflowed with colorful flowers and untamed greenery, and made his way to the biggest rosebush, where Harvey had spread Adele's ashes and

Jock and Tegan had later spread Harvey's. Harvey had spent a lot of time visiting Adele in the gardens, telling her about the productions and his life. A few months ago, when Jock and Tegan were going through Harvey's things, they'd found a wooden box of love letters that Harvey had written to Adele after she'd died and they'd buried it beside the rosebush and marked the location with several large stones.

Jock stood beside those stones now with a sense of peace in his heart, knowing that Harvey and Adele were finally together again. He missed the hell out of the old man. So much, he could practically hear Harvey's rickety voice now. *What's got you tied in knots, boy? Come on, spit it out.*

Jock sighed heavily, emotions thickening his throat. "Hey, old man. I miss you."

He imagined Harvey grumbling, *Eh, I wasn't so great. Go live your life.*

"I'm trying, you old bastard. For ten years you were my sounding board, my prank partner, my fucking therapist. I was as solid as they come when you were around. Now look at me. I'm talking to rocks. This was all part of your grand prank, wasn't it? I bet when you first saw me in that hospital, you thought to yourself, *I'm going to get this guy good.*"

He imagined Harvey laughing.

"Yeah, you laugh, old man. You're probably up there with Adele, shaking your head at all my screwups. I've got a lot of them, so you should be pretty entertained." He paced by the rocks, his thoughts coming out as easily as if his buddy were still alive. "You once told me that the most important thing I can do for a woman is listen to the things she says and *hear* the things she doesn't. You said to see the woman she wants me to see but *know* the woman she's afraid to set free. Well, guess what, Harv?

You were *wrong*. That advice got me into deep shit."

His hands fisted by his sides as he wore a path in the dirt. "Yeah, I know. I got *myself* into deep shit. I'm not blaming you. I should have kept my distance, but that's like asking me not to breathe. Every time I think of Daphne, I get *happy*, and I want…I don't know what. I want to be around her. And yeah, she gets me hot, which is fucking *fantastic*. How long has it been since I felt that?" He scoffed. "Remember how often you'd try to kick my ass out of the house to get some action?" He huffed out a laugh. "I don't know what to do, Harv. Her little girl looks at me like I've hung the moon, and you and I both know that isn't right. I couldn't save my boy, and when Hadley cries, I hear him. I see his little face…"

Tears burned his eyes. "How can I get past that?" He dropped to his knees by the rocks with a crushing feeling in his chest. "I've spent a year trying to figure my shit out, and I ended up right back here where I started. But I *want* what Daphne makes me feel, and I want to give that back to her and her daughter ten times over. I wish you'd met her. She is as strong as the sea, as light as the air, and as joyful as the laugher you craved. When I look at her, so open and hopeful, I want to tell her *everything*. But mine is such an ugly story, and she's got a beautiful life and an adorable little girl. I should leave, *right?* Take my baggage as far away as I can get?" He stared down at the rocks, gritting his teeth, and said, "Give me a sign, Harv. Give me a fucking clue, because I don't want to leave. I want to conquer the darkness inside me and climb out of it forever. I want to show Daphne she's worth so much more than what her asshole ex gave her, but when her daughter cries…I can't even stick around long enough to *try*. What the fuck is that? That's not the guy I used to be. That's not the man I *want* to be."

He pushed to his feet, pacing again, his heart slamming against his ribs. "I need to get this elephant off my chest so I can *breathe* again. I don't want to be the guy Daphne's afraid to have around her daughter. Hadley's goddamn father turned his back on her. What kind of man am I if I can't be better than that? I want a life, Harv. And maybe that life can't be with Daphne. Maybe I'm too messed up to be the man she needs. But how can I know unless I face my shit head-on and try?" He glared at the rocks and said, "You shouldn't have left me a typewriter. You should have left me a how-to-get-over-my-shit manual."

Harvey's face appeared in his mind, mapped with wrinkles, serious gray eyes boring into him, as he said, *I did.*

A shiver ran through Jock.

"Jock?" Tegan's voice was laden with concern.

He spun around, meeting Jett's and Tegan's worried eyes, but his mind was still on Harvey. His voice had sounded real. Was he losing his mind?

"Holy shit, man. Are you okay?" Jett asked. "You look like you've seen a ghost."

He tried to process Jett's question, but he was too busy mentally traipsing through the things Harvey had given him over the years, the stories he'd told, scrambling to make sense of what he'd just experienced. But Harvey had given him so much. How could he ever figure this out? *The storage unit.*

Tegan touched his arm. "Do you want to come inside for a minute? Are you feeling okay?"

"I don't know," he said, striding past them. "But I'm about to find out."

TWO HOURS LATER Jock stood in the middle of the storage unit scratching his jaw, surrounded by shelves and open boxes filled with books, heirlooms, costumes they'd dressed up in for Halloween, trinkets, and a host of other things. But among those good memories he found nothing that resembled a manual. *Damn it, old man. Even from the grave you're pranking me. You got me good, didn't you?*

He began sealing and restacking boxes and noticed an unopened crate in the corner beneath an old suitcase. He cleared a path, moved the suitcase, and worked the crate open. He was struck numb at the sight of the rosewood and leather trunk Harvey had given him the first Christmas after he'd moved into the mansion. His pain had been so raw back then, he hadn't wanted to celebrate. He'd wanted to climb into a hole and disappear. But Harvey had insisted, and for Harvey, Jock had played along. To an outsider, that night would have looked like a postcard-perfect celebration. Christmas lights had shimmered on a tree by the window, and a roaring fire crackled in the fireplace. Jock had given Harvey a watch because the old man had constantly asked him what time it was. Harvey had never once worn the damn thing, insisting the band irritated his skin. Jock hadn't learned the truth about why he hadn't worn the watch until years later, when Harvey had told him that he'd needed to hang on to every connection he could to pull Jock out of his own head and the dark place where he'd retreated after the accident.

Jock lifted the trunk out of the crate and set it on another box. He didn't remember it being that heavy, though he'd never even unlocked it. He'd put it in the back of his closet and hadn't given it another thought until he'd moved his things into storage. Even then, it had only been a passing thought while coordinating his move.

He ran his fingers over the leather and brass corners and the gold plaque on the top inscribed with JOCK and beneath that, MAN OF STEELE. Jock had told Harvey that he felt more like kryptonite than Superman and that he'd spelled *steel* wrong. Harvey had waved his hand dismissively and told him he was more deserving of the title than some guy in a jumpsuit who could be taken down by a mineral.

Jock shifted the trunk so he could see the back of it and found the key still taped there. He unlocked it and shoved the key in his pocket as he lifted the top. His gaze moved over a stack of books, the top one being his own, *It Lies*.

"Are you shitting me?" He'd actually thought there might be something helpful in there. He took out the book and opened the front cover. Inside was a handwritten note from Harvey.

*A great man wrote this book. Never forget what you're capable of. Yours truly, Harvey "the Great" Fine*

Jock's chest constricted as another memory rolled in, this one from the night he'd met Harvey. He'd been standing in front of the nursery in the hospital after the accident when a private nurse had pushed Harvey's wheelchair up to the observation window. He'd had oxygen tubes in his nose and IVs snaking from his arms. Harvey hadn't said anything for a few minutes. Then he'd motioned for the nurse to come closer, and he'd whispered something to her. The nurse had looked at Jock and said, *I'd like to introduce you to Harvey "the Great" Fine, man of laughter, lover of Adele Fine…and one hell of a pain in the ass.* Based on Harvey's grumbles, she'd ad-libbed that last part.

Struggling against the emotions swamping him, Jock set the book down and peered at a stack of cheap spiral notebooks in the trunk, each labeled STUFF. Harvey had despised the word *stuff*. He'd found it boring and meaningless and had called it a *lazy* word. Jock opened one notebook and found every page filled with Harvey's writing. The script was dark and angry. He flipped through a few of the other notebooks, each filled from the very first line to the last. In the top right corner of each notebook was a number, labeling them one through eight.

Jock began reading notebook number one.

*I have so much hate inside me, I feel like my father. I refuse to become that monster. I have been battling grief like a winter storm, battening down my hatches, hoping to survive it. But it seeps through without warning, drenching me to the bone, drowning me in my self-imposed dungeon.*

He leaned back against the wall, a sheen of sweat on his brow. He could have written those words himself. He hated imagining Harvey going through that pain. They'd met decades after Harvey had lost Adele, after he'd healed and found a way to move on. When Harvey spoke of her, the pain Jock had just read hadn't been nearly as raw.

He flipped through the pages, catching underlined passages like *I'm constantly fighting the urge to fall into the darkness, to let go in hopes of finding you on the other side. I must remember to treasure the beauty of what we had, to hold on to your spirit and the time we were gifted.*

Jock sank down to the floor in disbelief and continued reading what he now understood to be Harvey's how-to-get-over-his-shit manual.

# Chapter Eight

JOCK STARTLED AT the vibration of his phone. He blinked several times, trying to clear his vision and his head. He'd been so entrenched in Harvey's journey out of grief that he'd forgotten he was sitting in the storage unit. The four notebooks he'd read lay on the concrete floor beside him. He pulled out his phone, shocked to see it was after seven, and read Tegan's message.

*Are you okay? Where are you?*

That was a loaded question. Reading about Harvey's devastation, the ways in which he'd grappled with many of the same feelings Jock had been struggling with, made him feel a lot of things, none of which were *okay*. But learning about the steps he'd taken—a litany of trial and error—to escape the prison of grief gave him hope. Every step forward Harvey had taken had given him a glimpse of what could be, and his backsliding had shown Jock what not to do. Harvey's messages came through loud and clear. Jock needed to purge the ugliness before it consumed so much of the good in him he might never get it back. He had to accept his past and his losses for what they were, not allow them to appear like a smokescreen between him and his present, sucking him in at will. He needed to dig deep and find the beauty of the memories, regardless of how brief they were, and treasure them as gifts instead of seeing them only as what had been stolen away from him.

He thumbed out a response to Tegan. *I'm good. Getting some stuff from storage.* He glanced at the notebooks, finally realizing why Harvey had labeled them with a word he despised. That word probably matched how he'd felt about the monster he'd left behind on every page.

Jock pushed to his feet and put the notebooks in the trunk. He carried the trunk out of the storage unit, and as he set it down to lock the unit, his phone vibrated with another text from Tegan.

*Are you coming to the bonfire?*

He hadn't planned on going, hoping to save Daphne from having to deal with his reaction to Hadley clinging to him and the tears that would likely follow. But now the path he needed to take was clear. If he had a chance in hell with Daphne, he had to share his past with her. The confession might bring him to his knees, but wasn't that better than the shitstorm of tears he'd caused Hadley?

IT WAS NEARLY eight by the time Jock stopped at the convenience store to buy sand toys for Hadley and got back to his cottage. He swapped his sneakers for flip-flops, threw on a sweatshirt, grabbed the netted bag full of sand toys, and headed out the back door. The toys were a purely selfish move. He was hoping to distract Hadley long enough for him to talk with Daphne.

He kicked off his flip-flops at the top of the dunes and headed down the path, greeted by the sounds of the bay and the dune grasses swishing in the wind. Knowing that Harvey had successfully beaten his demons made Jock even more determined to conquer his own. But he wasn't fooling himself into thinking Daphne would be forgiving. Especially after last night and her semi-icy reaction when he'd dropped off lunch today. He was as prepared as he could be for her to tell him to fuck off. But at least she'd do it knowing the truth about his past.

The flames from the bonfire came into focus, and his friends' voices carried in the air. Adrenaline coursed through his veins as he strode down the beach, squinting into the darkness, searching for the tiny leg-hugging human who was sure to barrel into him. He was as nervous as a seal in a sea of sharks, unsure if he'd be able to manage spitting out the truth, much less deal with Hadley's cries if the toys didn't do the job. He recalled the words Harvey had written about his early days of talking about losing Adele, when he'd drawn upon his acting career and had seen himself playing a role, distancing himself just enough to ease into the person he'd eventually become. Jock wasn't an actor, as he'd proven every time Hadley had clung to him. He was a writer. Or at least he had been.

As he neared the bonfire, an idea formed. He began narrating his story in his head, thinking in terms of how a character might handle the situation. That modicum of distance eased the tension in his chest just enough for him to breathe a little easier.

"Jock!" Tegan ran down the beach toward him. Her blond hair lifted off her shoulders as she threw her arms around him. "I'm glad you made it. I was worried about you."

"Thanks, Teg. I'm okay." He waved to the others, but Daphne and Hadley were nowhere in sight. "Where's Daphne?"

"She didn't come."

*Shit.* He hoped he hadn't made her too upset to join the others.

Tegan glanced at the toys in his hand and said, "Toys?"

"For Hadley."

"Emery was just telling me she thought there was something going on between you and Daphne." She lowered her voice and said, "Has something changed with you and Hadley? Are things better?"

"No, but I'm hoping they can get there. I'm going to head back up."

"Are you sure you don't want to stick around for a little while?"

"I'm sure. I've got to take care of something."

"Okay. Jett and I are around all weekend if you need an ear or want to hang out."

"Thanks, I appreciate that. Sorry for running off earlier." He gave her a hug and headed back the way he'd come.

He tossed the toys on his patio and went directly to Daphne's apartment, hoping to find her outside. His pulse kicked up as he walked around the office to the chairs where they'd been meeting, but she wasn't there. He tucked away his disappointment and climbed the porch steps to the office, hoping the door was unlocked. He nearly did a fist pump when the door opened. He took the interior steps two at a time, his hopes rising as he reached the landing and knocked.

Daphne answered the door, looking beautiful in a tank top and jeans, but her semi-smile matched her troubled eyes.

"Hi," he said quickly. "I'm sorry to just show up, but I don't have your number, and I went to the bonfire looking for you, but...I wanted to say I'm sorry about the way I took off last night."

She lowered her eyes, her lips pursing.

"Daphne, I—" Over her shoulder he saw a guy carrying Hadley. Her little arms were wrapped around his neck, and she was giggling. Jock's gut seized. "Sorry. I didn't know you had company. I'll catch up with you some other time." He descended the steps, silently cursing himself, his past, and all his other shit that stood between him and Daphne.

DAPHNE CLOSED THE door, her chest aching. When Jock had brought her lunch this afternoon, she'd been so happy to see him, but that motherly voice in her head had quickly reminded her that there could be no more kisses, no more late-night Scrabble games or sharing of secrets. Not when he had such a strong reaction to her daughter. She touched her forehead to the door, clutching the knob, waiting for the hurt to subside.

"Hey, Dee, you okay?"

"Mama?" Hadley said with her mouth full.

Daphne put on her best happy-mommy face and said, "I'm fine," as she stepped away from the door. Hadley had chocolate on her lips, and she was elbow-deep in a giant bag of M&M's that Sean was holding. "*Sean*. Are you *kidding* me?"

Hadley shoved the candy into her mouth as fast as she could. She looked tiny in Sean's beefy arms. Sometimes it baffled Daphne that she and Sean were twins. He was six two and so fit he could bounce quarters off his abs. He wore his blond hair military-short, and he had a flirty smile that probably won him all sorts of favors from women that Daphne did *not* want to think about. But from the moment she'd left Tim and moved back to the Cape, Sean had stepped up for both her and Hadley, which made her love him even more.

At the moment, Daphne didn't feel very loving.

"It's an hour past her bedtime, and now she'll be all sugared up. She'll never go to sleep." She reached for Hadley, but Hadley clung to Sean, scowling at Daphne.

"It's just a little candy," Sean said. "Besides, it's a beautiful night. Take her outside and let her run it off." He lifted the bag for Hadley to take more candy, but Daphne snagged it out of his hands.

"Twin or not, I'm going to k-i-l-l you." Daphne glowered at him.

"*Mowah!*" Hadley reached for the bag.

"No more, sweet pea," Daphne said.

Sean lowered his voice and whispered to Hadley, "I'll bring more next time," earning more grins from his biggest fan. He could show up empty-handed and Hadley would still have a bucketful of smiles for him.

Hadley wriggled down from Sean's arms and darted into the kitchen, yelling, "Owly!"

"He's on the table," Daphne called after her.

"Who was that guy?" Sean asked.

"Nobody," she said, not wanting to face an inquisition.

"He wasn't looking at you like he was nobody." Sean draped an arm over her shoulder and said, "Do I have to nose around with Rick and the guys to find out for myself who he is?"

"*No.* He's just someone staying at the cottages who I've been hanging out with."

"You don't hang out with the guests, Dee."

Sometimes she hated that he knew her so well. "He's a friend. I met him through Tegan. He was here last year, and he goes out with all of us sometimes."

"And…?"

"And nothing," she said, flopping down on the couch.

He sat beside her. "But you like him?"

She shrugged. "It doesn't matter."

"Sure it does. You haven't liked a guy since Tim."

Hadley toddled down the hall toward her bedroom and yelled, "Getting Bird!"

"Dee, what are you not telling me? Did he hurt you? Because I'll fuck him up right now."

She rolled her eyes. "He's not like that. We've been hanging out, getting to know each other better. We had dinner last night, and he brought food, wine, *flowers*, dessert. We cooked dinner together and I had the best time, but it's not going to work between us. Hadley loves him, but he has trouble being around kids. I knew that going into it, but dumb old me…" *Got attached to him.*

"You're the smart one. I'm the dumb fireman."

"Hardly." Sean wasn't dumb. He was dedicated, loyal, and yeah, he had a nose for trouble, but not because he was stupid. He *liked* trouble.

"Why did you have dinner with him if you knew he had trouble being around Had?"

"Because I *like* him, okay? He's a good guy. Maybe even a great guy, except for the whole kid thing. We have fun together. But I know what you're thinking, and he's *not* like Tim. Tim *lied* about wanting kids. Once Jock and I started spending time together, he was up front with me about having trouble being around young children. He also said he wanted to try to get past it. But I realized last night that I was just being stupid. I can't see a guy who isn't able to be around my daughter. You know what? I guess I am the smart one after all, because I know what I have to do."

Hadley came into the living room wearing sweatpants and red rain boots, dragging her sweatshirt in one hand and holding her owl and bird in the other.

"What're you doing, Had?" Daphne asked with a sigh.

"Go for walk." She handed her sweatshirt to Sean and said, "Unca help me?"

Daphne wasn't in the mood for a walk, but before she could say anything, Sean said, "Always," and helped Hadley put on her sweatshirt.

"I guess we're going for a walk. You can take one toy, Had. *One.*" Giving in was easier than arguing. She was in a sour mood, but maybe the fresh air would do her good. She had a feeling even magic couldn't turn her mood around. How could it when she knew she had to end things with the only man she'd wanted to spend time with in the last three years?

She lowered her voice and said, "Just wait until you have children, Sean. I'm going to hype them up all night long, then leave."

"*Me*, have kids?" He laughed.

Hadley put her bird on the coffee table and said, "Owly."

Daphne grabbed her sweatshirt and keys as Sean lifted Hadley into his arms and they headed downstairs. As Daphne locked the office door, Sean's phone alarm sounded.

"I've got to head over to the station for my shift," he said.

"That was your plan? Suggest a walk and ditch us?"

"Nah. I totally forgot about my shift. Are you okay by yourself?"

He'd been like that his whole life, forgetful, thinking about too many things at once, except when it came to fighting fires.

"I've been by myself for nearly three years. I'm fine."

Sean tapped Hadley's belly and said, "You be good for Mommy, okay?"

Hadley nodded.

"I love you, *Hadley Padley*." He kissed Hadley's cheek, and as he set her down on the grass, she said, "Love you, Unca Unca."

Daphne reached for Hadley's hand and said, "Thanks for coming over tonight. It was good to see you."

Sean flashed an arrogant grin. "I had to check on my *baby* sister." He was less than a minute older than her.

As he climbed into his truck, Daphne said, "Just remember, you'll get wrinkles before I do."

Hadley tugged Daphne's hand toward the beach. "*Walk!*"

"Okay, let's go. But we're going on a short walk, okay, pumpkin?" As they walked along the grass toward the dunes, Daphne thought about Jock. She'd been so focused on getting him to leave before Hadley had seen him at the door, she hadn't fully processed what he'd said. He'd gone to the bonfire looking for her? He'd known Hadley would be there. She'd mentioned it the other night in front of him.

Hadley pointed to Jock's cottage and said, "Mine and Dock's house."

Daphne's nerves flared. She and Hadley had lived in that cottage when a storm had caused a leak in the roof of their apartment. They'd loved it so much, Hadley had called it hers. When Jock had moved in, her daughter had simply added him as if the cottage had always been meant for the two of them.

"Keep going, Had. We're taking the Lefty Loosey trail."

The trail to the right of Jock's cottage led to where her friends would be having the bonfire, and Daphne wasn't in the mood to hang out with them. She was nervous and unhappy about what she had to tell Jock, and now it looked like she'd be this way for another night.

"Lefty Loosey!" Hadley said as they walked past Jock's cottage.

"Daphne?" Jock stepped off the back patio.

Hadley spun around.

*Oh, no, no, no!*

"Dock!" Hadley charged toward him.

His jaw clenched, a stark contrast to the glee on her daughter's face. Daphne's heart ached for both of them as Hadley plastered herself against his leg. Jock's eyes found Daphne's. The mix of torture and hope in them wrecked her.

He put his hand gently on the top of Hadley's head, as if he were testing his own reaction, and said, "Hi, Had."

*Holy fudge.* Daphne didn't know what alternate universe they'd fallen into, but her heart melted at his efforts. She didn't want to push their luck, so she said, "Had, come take Mommy's hand," and hoped Hadley wouldn't pitch a fit.

Hadley looked up at Jock, her rare and perfect smile curving her little lips. She held up her owl like a prize and said, "Owly!"

Jock's lips twitched, though the tension wafting off him was palpable as he said, "I see that. Maybe you should hold Mommy's hand."

Hadley skipped across the grass to Daphne and took her hand, leaving Daphne dumbfounded.

Jock's chest rose with a deep inhalation, relief rising in his eyes as he met Daphne's gaze and said, "I wish you had told me you were seeing someone."

"Seeing someo…? I'm not…" *Ugh!* Her heart was racing and her nerves were on fire, but she had to get it out, even with Hadley by her side. She lowered her voice and said, "It doesn't matter if I am or if I'm not, because whatever this is between us can't be. I really like you, Jock, but I've been with a man who didn't want children, and I can't do that again. I can't sneak around and pretend to have a personal life that is *mine,* when my life belongs to her. She comes *first* and she always will."

"I know that, and it's good. That's how it should be," he said quickly. "I don't want to be that guy, Daph. I just want a chance to explain."

Hadley tugged on her hand. "*Lefty Loosey*, Mommy. *Walk!*"

"Please just hear me out." Jock's eyes implored her. "That's all I'm asking. If you don't want to see me afterward, I'll not only leave you alone, but I'll get another place to stay away from Bayside."

"*Mommy!*" Hadley yanked her hand. "Dock walk? *Dock?*"

Hadley's patience was fraying fast. The last thing Daphne needed was a meltdown when she was holding on to her own sanity by a thin thread. She looked at Jock and said, "Can you handle walking with both of us?"

The relief in his eyes was unmistakable. "I'd like to try."

# Chapter Nine

JOCK PICKED UP the netted bag of beach toys, thankful and nervous at once. He had no idea how this would go, but at least Daphne was giving him a chance. "Should I grab a blanket in case she gets cold? A towel?"

"Sure, I guess. But she doesn't need more toys," Daphne said, watching Hadley play with her owl at the edge of the patio.

"I'm not trying to buy your affection through Hadley. I assumed I'd find you down by the bonfire and thought she might play with them long enough for us to talk."

Her gaze softened. "For a guy who has a hard time around small children, you can be very thoughtful toward them when you want to."

"I'm *uncomfortable* around small children. I don't hate them. I actually love kids. I always have. I just…Let me grab a blanket and towel and then I'll explain."

A few minutes later, they left their flip-flops and Hadley's boots at the head of the path and made their way down to the beach. Daphne nudged Hadley in the opposite direction of the bonfire. Jock was thankful they wouldn't have an audience. They followed Hadley as she toddled along the shore, stopping

141

to pick up shells and inspect rocks and holes in the sand. Jock tried to figure out how to start the conversation. He had a lot to say, and he knew he'd have only one chance to do it, so he led with "Thank you for letting me come on your walk."

"You touched Hadley's head, and you encouraged her to come to me." Daphne glanced at him and said, "I know that must have been difficult for you, so I figured I should hear you out. But I meant what I said, Jock. I don't want to exclude her from any part of my life."

"I understand, and I don't want you to, either. I thought I had most of this worked out in my head, but now I'm not even sure where to start."

"How about starting at the beginning, wherever that is? Just keep in mind that it's late and Hadley might not last long."

"The beginning is hard to define," he said honestly, and then he dove in with both feet. "You know that I'd written a screenplay that I turned into my novel while I was in college. I was going to school in New York City, and a few months before graduation, Archer called and asked me to reach out to his best friend, Kayla, who had moved to the city for a job in the fashion industry. She grew up with us on the island, and he wanted me to make sure she didn't run into any trouble since the city is so different from the island. But I was busy with school and friends and never got around to it. A few weeks later, I was out at a club and I saw her. You'd think because Archer and I are twins, Kayla and I would have been close friends, too, but it wasn't like that. She was always Archer's friend, and that's pretty much how I always saw her. Anyway, we had a few drinks and we were having a great time, and we hooked up. Neither of us was looking for a relationship. We were just having fun."

"Did Archer know?"

"Yes. I told him. I was so cocky back then, I probably bragged, you know, one-upping him since I knew they had never hooked up. Everything came easy to me then—school, sports, women. Archer and I were pretty competitive, and maybe that was part of why I did it. I don't know. But I liked Kayla, and Archer was cool about it. He told me he'd kill me if I screwed her over, which was fair. But she and I were doing the casual thing, you know? Hanging out, hooking up, not even talking about commitment. We were having too much fun." He paused for a moment and said, "Then we found out she was pregnant, and that was a shock for both of us. We weren't prepared, and we weren't in love, but we were good together as friends and we decided to try to make it work."

"Make it work as a couple?" Daphne asked.

"Yes. We told our families, and she moved in."

"So, you are—or were—married?"

"No. What I said to you over dinner is truly how I feel. Marriage vows are one of the few sacred things in life that should mean something. It probably sounds weird, but we had our own lives, and yes, we were trying to *be* a couple and we had every intention of raising our baby together, but it's not the 1950s. We didn't feel pressure to rush into marriage just to appease others. We knew we needed to talk to our families about it, but the pregnancy was a *big* bomb to drop, so we decided not to tell them we weren't in love. We told them we wanted to be sure we were right for each other before we got married. I have since told my parents the truth, but the rest of our family members don't know."

"So what happened? Where is she? Where's your son or daughter?"

Hadley plopped down in the sand, and they stopped walking. Emotions clogged Jock's throat. He needed a minute to try to clear them away and said, "Should we give her the sand toys?"

"Sure."

While Daphne took the plastic toys to Hadley, Jock spread out the towel for them to sit on, and used that moment to regain control, telling himself to get it all out as fast as he could.

Daphne brushed the sand from her knees and joined him.

"Do you want to sit down?" he asked.

They sat down, and she said, "Where were we? Oh yeah, you weren't married, but you and Kayla were going to have a baby."

"Yeah. Things were good. I got my book deal and I was working with a publicist to prepare for the launch in the fall. Kayla was working and having fun in the city with her friends. As the months wore on, we found out we were having a boy and set up a nursery for him. I had wondered if we'd fall in love, you know? Like you said, a baby can bring a couple closer together. We tried to force those feelings, but we realized they weren't going to develop."

"That must have been hard."

"I wouldn't say hard, because neither of us was pining for the other. But it was sad. We wanted to raise our child together, but as time passed, we realized that would mean we would never experience being in love. I was okay with that for me, but not for her. I knew things had to change. She spent more time talking to Archer than to me, and I tried to talk with her about it a number of times, but she didn't want to. Then my book hit the *New York Times* bestseller list, and she was really distracted all day. I thought maybe she was finally ready to talk about it, and I tried to bring it up before we went out to celebrate with friends that night, but she said she didn't want to put a damper on my big night. She was like that, always looking out for everyone else. Anyway, we went out and I had a few drinks. *Three* drinks. Not enough to miss that she spent the whole night texting with Archer, sending him pictures under the guise that she didn't want him to miss out on the celebration. But that night I realized that she always shared everything with Archer first. It had always been him and then me."

"Oh, Jock. That had to hurt."

"It was a blow to my ego, but not my heart. I know this is going to sound untrue, but it's not. I had a gut feeling that she was in love with him, and I wanted her to be happy. And Archer's my twin, my blood. I wouldn't have held him back. Anyway, after our friends left the restaurant, she and I talked. She admitted she was in love with Archer. She thought she always had been, but that she'd get over it. She had no idea if he felt the same way, and I didn't either. It was weird, because Archer and I were always competitive, but that night I didn't feel that way. I hoped to hell Archer loved her, because she deserved to be loved."

"But still. It had to hurt to hear that."

"It did, but like I said, we weren't in love, so it was a different kind of hurt. I don't know how to explain it. I loved her deeply as a friend, and as the mother of my child, but I wasn't in love with her. That's why when you told me about Tim turning his back on you and Hadley, I couldn't even…" He shook his head, anger bubbling up inside him again. "It's unfathomable to me. When Kayla was pregnant, as her belly grew, I thought she was more beautiful than ever. I would run out at midnight to get things she craved. I rubbed her back, her feet. I would have done anything for her. Anyway, by then she was thirty-four weeks pregnant, and we agreed to go home that weekend so she could tell Archer, and once we knew where he stood, we were going to let our families know the situation."

"You were willing to give up your baby for your brother?"

"*No*," he said emphatically. "I would still be in the baby's life, but I wouldn't stand in their way if they were in love."

"Mama!" Hadley toddled over with a bucket and crouched in front of them. "Shells for my Dock."

She stuck her hand in the bucket and thrust her fist toward Jock. He held out his hand, and she opened hers. Three tiny shells fell onto his palm.

His chest tightened. "Thank you, Hadley."

"Mommy shells." She grabbed another handful from the bucket and gave them to Daphne.

"Thank you, baby. Are you getting tired?"

Hadley shook her head vehemently. "I'm playing!" She ran back to her toys.

"That wasn't so hard, was it?" Daphne said.

"Daph, it's not...Let me finish." He curled his fingers around the shells, the jagged edges digging into his palm. "Kayla never got a chance to find out how Archer felt, and neither did I. Since I'd had a few drinks, she drove home from the restaurant. It was raining and cold, and she was so happy about our decision, she was talking a mile a minute over the sound of the heater. We went through an intersection and she glanced at me with this big smile. I registered the headlights glowing over her shoulder from a truck that had run a red light a split second before impact." Tears welled in his eyes, but he forced the words to come. "When I came to, there was so much blood. There were lights, sirens. I reached for her hand. It's all pretty fuzzy. I was going in and out of consciousness, and she kept saying,

'Tell him I love him.' The next thing I remember was waking up in the hospital. They told me Kayla was gone and our son wasn't going to make it." He gulped a lungful of air, looking away from Daphne as the rest spilled out. "I held our son, Liam. Kayla had picked out his name. He was so tiny, his cries were so weak. Other babies' stronger cries echoed in my head, and I remember trying to block them out, thinking our baby was crying for Kayla, and I couldn't...I *couldn't*...And then he stopped breathing. He was gone."

He swiped at his tears, and he realized Daphne was crying, too, which broke his heart all over again. "I'm sorry," he said, drawing her into his arms. She held him as tightly as he held her. "I'm sorry. I'm so sorry." He couldn't stop saying it. He'd kept it all in for so many years, he didn't know who he was apologizing to—Daphne, Kayla, Liam, Archer...*everyone*.

"Dock *cwying*?"

Jock felt Hadley's hand on his arm, and he released Daphne, wiping his eyes.

Hadley stepped closer and sat on her heels, her big blue eyes moving between Daphne and Jock. "Mommy *cwying*?"

"Mommy's okay, honey," she said.

"No *cwy*, Dock." Hadley leaned forward and pressed her tiny lips to Jock's cheek in the sweetest kiss he'd ever received, drawing more tears from Daphne's eyes and filling him with...he had no idea what. It felt good and sad at once.

He choked out, "'Kay," and cleared his throat.

Hadley crawled into Daphne's lap, resting her head against her chest. Daphne rocked her and said, "I'm sorry, Jock. I don't even know what to say."

They sat in silence for a while, the bay breeze sweeping over them. When Hadley's eyes fluttered closed, Jock slipped the shells she had given him in his pocket and draped the blanket around her.

"Thank you," Daphne said softly. "I'm so sorry for everything that you've gone through."

"Thanks. I haven't told anyone about holding Liam except Harvey, my parents, and Kayla's parents. But I wanted you to know."

"I appreciate you trusting me enough to share that." She kissed Hadley's head and said, "I can't even imagine how you got through it."

"If not for Harvey, I'm not sure I would have. After Liam died, I was in a fog. Most of that night has blurred together. Our families came to the hospital, and everyone was a mess. When Archer heard about Kayla, he came at me fists flying. My father stepped between us, and Archer nearly broke his jaw. I was sitting in the hospital bed, and if my father hadn't stepped in, I would have gladly let Archer kill me, because *I* should have been driving that night. It should have been me who died, not them."

Tears welled in Daphne's eyes again. "I understand why you're saying that, but please don't. It's too hard to hear."

"I'm sorry, but it's true. I know I can't change what happened no matter how much I wish I could. And trust me, I would give anything to take it all back. If we had just stayed ten minutes longer at the restaurant, or if we had left with our friends and talked after we got home. I know those thoughts won't bring them back, and I want to move forward. But there's more that you need to know. That night in the hospital Archer told me that as far as he was concerned, I was dead to him, and then he took off."

"Oh my God." Tears slid down her cheeks.

"I don't blame him. She was his best friend, and she was gone because of me."

"So he *was* in love with her?"

"I don't know. We've never talked about it. He took off, and I had broken ribs and a concussion and had to stay in the hospital. I was in shock. I couldn't believe Kayla and Liam were gone, and then Archer...Later that night, after my family left, nothing felt real. I couldn't close my eyes without being barraged with flashbacks. I was so numb, I didn't even feel my injuries. So I went to the nursery. Liam had died in the PICU, but I wasn't thinking straight, or maybe I just needed to see for myself that he wasn't in the nursery like all the other babies. I don't know how long I was there, maybe a couple of hours, but that's where I met Harvey. He was recovering from a lung infection—he'd been in New York visiting friends when he'd come down with it. He was in a wheelchair, and a private nurse was with him. He introduced himself and tried to strike up a conversation. I don't know why he bothered with me, but every time I walked away, they followed. I couldn't get rid of him. I don't know if he could tell I'd lost Kayla and Liam—"

"And Archer," Daphne said softly.

Jock nodded, the ghosts of his past perched on his shoulders like birds of prey, talons digging into him. "Harvey told me about his wife, Adele, who had lost both of her legs in an accident on their seventh date. She'd wanted to give up, and he said she tried to push him away, doing and saying all sorts of things, but he was in love with her, and he refused to let her give up." Jock met Daphne's empathetic gaze and said, "*That's* what love is, Daph. It's not a choice, or something you can control. It's its own entity, an unstoppable driving force. Harvey stuck with Adele through her recovery and therapy, using laughter to break down her walls, and then they got married. But he lost her to cancer just eight years later."

"That's so sad."

"I know. Their love story is a tragic one. I met Harvey decades after he'd lost Adele, and his love for her permeated everything he said and did until the day he died. That kind of love? That's what marriage vows are for. The night I met him, I didn't want to hear about what he'd lost, but like I said, when I walked away, he followed me. I didn't know this then, but he didn't make me listen to the worst of it. He talked all night, and I can't even tell you what he said. But I felt safe around him. I felt *understood*. I woke up in the chair in his hospital room. I can't explain any of it—our connection, the way I felt around him, how I knew I belonged in his house. But that morning he said I seemed to want to fall into a well and never climb out. I told him I did, and he said he had a well and I was welcome to it."

"That's kind of sweet *and* awful."

Jock laughed softly. "It was, but the old bastard knew what to say. I went home to the island, and we had the funerals. The whole town was mourning Kayla and Liam. The rest of my family tried to get me to stay on the island, but that was Archer's home. He'd never wanted to do anything but work with my father on our family's vineyard and in the winery. He never went away to school. He stayed and built his life there. When I'd left for college, I had no plans of ever going back for good. And then, at the funerals, I was so consumed with guilt and sadness, all I wanted to do was find that well Harvey had talked about and dive in headfirst. So I canceled the book tour, signings, everything. I broke my lease and went to see Harvey. Not long after that, Kayla's family moved away from the island, too."

"Probably because of all those memories. It must have been awful for them. What happened with Harvey? He just took you in?"

"Yes. But don't be fooled by the way he did it. He was a shrewd businessman. I found out later that he knew everything about me when I showed up that day. He'd done his due diligence, but he stayed true to his word. He took me in and let me drown in my grief. But not for long. Within a couple of weeks, he was asking me to help him with things. At first it was his business, then driving him places, helping with household issues. Then he fired his nurse and nudged me into taking care of him. I later found out that he'd fired every caretaker who had worked for him within a few months of hiring them. He said they treated him like a dying old man, and he had a lot of life left to live. I kept waiting for him to send me packing because we bickered a lot, but I think he saw himself in me, and he liked our bickering. That bickering fueled a fire in me, made me fight back. I didn't realize it until months later, but he'd known exactly what he was doing and how to get to me. He kept pushing me to do more. He forced me to dress up every day in slacks and a button-down shirt, to handle more important business transactions, manage the household, his staff, and of course take him to meetings and accompany him to every children's show."

"Were the children's shows difficult for you?"

"Everything that first year was difficult, but I know what you're asking. I was there for Harvey, not for the kids. None of the children were looking up to me, hanging on me, or anything like that. I had built pretty substantial walls around myself. I don't think I was very approachable until years later.

And even then, the kids weren't ever looking to me for anything, so I wasn't affected by them."

He gazed out at the water and said, "Harvey brought me back to life and into a world that was different from anything I had ever imagined for myself. I grew to love him like I love my own father. I brought a nurse in to help me learn everything I could about the realities of living with a man in his condition and the care he'd need. He gave me purpose, a reason to get up every day and move forward. I don't know how he knew that I needed him, but I'm grateful every day of my life, and I never saw him coming." He met Daphne's warm gaze and said, "The same way I never saw you coming."

She looked away a little nervously and pressed a kiss to Hadley's head.

"From the moment Harvey stopped letting me drown in grief, everything I did was for him. I thought after all these years, I had healed and moved on. But it turned out that my life had been so consumed by caring for him, there wasn't space in my head for anything else. Because of what had happened with Archer, I used my relationship with Harvey as an excuse not to go home for more than a few hours a couple of times a year. Now the ghosts of my past are rattling the chains on the dungeon where I buried them. They want to come roaring out every time Hadley wants me to hold her. I hate my reaction when she looks up at me with her big blue eyes, and I don't like being scared to hold Rick's baby, afraid I'll have a bad reaction to him, either. It's like I'm a prisoner in my own head. And man, I hated keeping my distance from my niece until she was old enough that she no longer triggered those memories."

"When did that stop with her?"

"A few years ago. She's almost eight, so maybe when she was

four? I'm not sure. But Daphne, you need to understand that I'm not triggered by just being around children. What triggers me is when Hadley, or any other little kid, looks to me for *care*. When she clings to me and wants me to pick her up. I couldn't save Liam, and I know that Hadley isn't Liam and that Rick's baby isn't Liam, but at those times, it all comes rushing back, and I remember my son lying helpless in my arms, the sound of his weak cries, and then...nothing."

"I understand completely, and I'm so sorry."

"I want to get past that, Daph. I don't want to freeze up when Hadley hangs on to me and looks at me like..."

"Like she adores you?"

He nodded. "Yeah, I guess. I'm sorry I'm so broken."

"You suffered a devastating loss. After what you've been through, I don't think you're *broken*. Everyone has emotional battles. When I got divorced, I couldn't think about my ex without bawling for a long time. And it felt like forever before I could see any man and think in good terms instead of bad. Rick and the guys helped with that. They're so good with their significant others, and with me, really. They restored my faith in the male species." She smiled and said, "I think broken is the wrong word for you, Jock. Maybe wounded is better. You just have a different emotional battle than some of us do."

"That's a very kind way to put it." The knots in his chest began unfurling. "Right before Harvey died, I thanked him for saving me, and he told me that *I* had saved *him*. He had emphysema, and he said he knew when we met that he was facing life in a wheelchair and had wanted to crawl into that well he'd told me about and never come out. But then he met me, and he saw that I needed it more than he did. He told me that after he was gone, he wanted me to get the hell away from that place and live my life." He looked at Daphne holding her sleeping daughter and said, "I want to get past this, Daphne. I want a full life, free from triggers. I want to be that guy I used to be, only smarter. You need to know that I never have more than one drink when I go out, and I'll never put anyone in that position again."

"I've noticed that you don't drink much when we're out with everyone."

"Having Kayla drive was the biggest mistake of my life. I can't fix that, but I do want to make things right with Archer and spend time with you and Hadley to see if we're as special together as it feels like we are. But I'm not sure how to do it, or if it's even fair to you and Hadley after what you've been through with your ex. I would totally understand if my past scares you, or if it's just too much for either of you to deal with, because the truth is, I have every intention of doing what I can to fix it, but I'm not even sure where to start."

AFTER EVERYTHING JOCK had said, after shedding tears and baring his soul, he was comparing himself to her ex? Daphne couldn't believe it. She thought he'd walk away when she'd said she couldn't be with him, and instead he was fighting for a chance to be with them. Her heart broke for all that he'd lost, and her faith in him grew for his openness and honesty.

"You're nothing like Tim. You and I have known each other a year, but we've only just started getting close, and you told me things you said you haven't shared with anyone but family. That's totally different from him."

"Good." He sighed with relief.

"And you've already started making changes. Look how you handled Hadley tonight."

"I knew I had to do something, or I'd never get this chance to tell you what I've been through. Just knowing you're aware of my triggers takes the edge off. I feel a hundred pounds lighter, and that gives me hope that I can change my reactions to her. It felt good to see her smile instead of making her cry, and that's what I *want*, Daph. To see both of you smile. I don't want to freeze every time she hangs on me. You make me feel things I *never* have. I see you and my pulse kicks up. You smile, and it lights up everything around you, including me. I have pined for you for a long time."

"*Pined* for me? No one has ever pined for me."

"I don't believe that for a minute." He shook his head. "You're the *clue misser*, remember? And that makes me the luckiest of them all, and I want to explore what we are with you. But what I want is the least of my worries. What do *you* want? If you're not comfortable trying to work through this with me, or if you don't trust me on any level, then, as I said, I'll take off."

"If I didn't trust you, I wouldn't be here right now." He'd revealed so much, she wanted him to know how she felt, too. She mustered her courage and said, "My daughter has a thing for you, and I think you know she's not the only one. I'd like to try to help you through this and see what this is between us, but I have to be careful. I don't want Hadley to get hurt."

"Neither do I."

"I've obviously never gone through anything like the death of a child, or your losing Kayla and your relationship with Archer. But when Tim and I separated, I had to figure out who I was as a new single mother. And I know it's not at all the same, but I lost a husband who I trusted to be there through thick and thin. I grieved the loss of my marriage and the loss of who I was and what I believed in, and I grieved for Hadley not knowing her father. I'll probably always have moments when I get angry about how easily he walked away from us. And I'd think that you'll probably always have moments where you think of Liam and Kayla, too. That's just how life is. I'm not an expert on grief, but for me, when I got divorced and moved back home, when I was trying to find my way as a single mom, even with my family's help, and I was grieving everything at once, I felt like I was adrift at sea. I could go weeks drifting along, making it from one day to the next, and then someone would say something, or I'd see a young family or a couple that reminded me of me and Tim, or I'd look at Hadley, and sadness or anger would suddenly crash over me like a tidal wave. I think that's the nature of grief. It sneaks up on you and drags you under, and sometimes you have to fight with everything you have to come back up to the surface. Or in my case, you have to cry your eyes out late at night when nobody will know."

"Aw, Daph. I hate that." He reached over and touched her hand. "I'm sorry."

"It's okay. It made me stronger. Once I figured out what was causing those reactions, I took steps to learn how to take the power away from them so they didn't impact me so strongly. I have some ideas that might help if you really want to try to deal with your triggers, but I'm not sure if they'll work."

"I'll try anything. I'd stand on my head and spit wooden nickels if it would help me figure this out."

"I'm not sure that would help," she teased to lighten the mood. "But I have a few thoughts. Now that I know what causes your anxiety, I can intervene in a gentler way and try to dissuade Hadley from clinging to you from the get-go. I can teach her how to be more like she was tonight."

He shook his head. "I don't want to do anything that will make her feel like she's not wanted or she's doing something wrong, because she's not."

"Neither do I. I just meant that tonight she seemed happy that you touched her head and walked with us, and I can try to build on that. I think she clings to you because she's afraid you're going to run away."

"Smart girl." He stroked Hadley's back, and Daphne's heart squeezed at his effort. "I appreciate that you're willing to try to work with Hadley, but instead of trying to alter her behavior, let's try to change mine. This is my issue, not hers."

"Okay, well, I do have one idea. When Hadley was a baby, I used the Ferber method to get her to sleep through the night. I basically taught her to self-soothe by letting her cry for a little longer in between the times I'd go in and comfort her."

"Levi did that with Joey. He said it was hell."

"Oh, it *is*. It was excruciating listening to her cry. But I think the idea of easing into something you're not comfortable with could work for you."

"Small doses of leg clinging?" he asked with a smile.

She liked his smile even more now that she knew his past. It was less mysterious and more vulnerable, which endeared him to her.

"Something like that," she said. "You got through tonight by just putting your hand on her head and accepting her shells. That's what she wants, to connect with you on some level. I'm just suggesting more of the same, little alterations in your reactions. Taking a few seconds to breathe deeply and think about not walking away, but how to work around what she wants by doing something you *can* handle. If you think it's doable."

"I *cried* in front of you tonight," he said. "I don't know what kind of spell you cast on me, but I think it's safe to say there's nothing I won't try to do for you and Hadley."

He couldn't possibly know how much his words meant to her. She wasn't sure how to react to such a declaration, so she went for humor to lighten the mood. "I slipped a witch's brew into your dinner last night."

"That's not all you slipped into me. I'm pretty sure you had Viagra on your tongue when we were kissing."

She felt her cheeks flame. "You're not allowed to make me blush tonight, remember?"

"I've never been good at sticking to the rules." He brushed his fingers over her hand, sending tingles skittering through her.

She rubbed Hadley's back, futilely trying to stifle a grin. She wanted to talk longer, to get knee-deep in sexy banter, to feel the butterflies he stirred all night long. But it was getting late, and she needed time to think about everything he'd shared, so she said, "I should probably get Hadley to bed."

"Right, of course. Thank you for giving me the chance to talk with you tonight." He helped her to her feet and began gathering their things.

As they walked up the beach, he kept one hand on her lower back. She liked that he wasn't keeping his distance or acting awkward. Hadley was sleeping, but still it meant he was making an effort.

When they turned up the path, he said, "So, how do we do this?"

"Good question. *Baby steps*, I think." She knew all about baby steps. She'd taken enough of them during her separation and divorce to appreciate how much effort they took. But something else was nagging at her. "Jock, you lost a child. Are you sure you want to do this? There are plenty of women out there without children who I'm sure would give their eyeteeth to go out with you."

"Seriously? After everything I just said, you think I want to find someone else?"

"I'm just being cautious, making sure you know all your options."

"Daphne, I've had years of options, and not one of them has turned me inside out the way you do. Not one. Do you know that when I went traveling after Harvey died, I tried to forget you? But I could no sooner forget you than I could have walked away from Hadley tonight. I want to do this more than you could ever know. I told you I want a full life, and I meant it. I want a family of my own one day—three, four kids. I want to hold my friends' babies and children and be *fun* Uncle Jock, the guy who will get down on the floor and play with them, or toss a football, or have a freaking tea party. I would not be walking beside you if I didn't want all of those things."

Her heart beat faster. "Okay. I just wanted to make sure. Then you need to know that you can talk to me about Kayla, Liam, or Archer anytime. They're all a part of you, and I don't want you to feel like this was a one-time conversation."

"I appreciate that." He pulled her a little closer as they walked up the dune. "Now, how about we talk about those baby steps?"

"I was thinking, we're going down to the beach tomorrow. If you want to try to spend some time around Hadley, you're welcome to join us, or even just come by and say hi. Ease into it, like you did tonight. Or not. No pressure. Whatever you want."

"You make me *want* a lot of things, Daphne."

"*Stop*," she said, bumping against his side.

"I wasn't trying to make you blush. That was just an added benefit."

Boy, she really liked him. When they reached the top of the path, he moved her flip-flops so she could slip her feet into them, and he carried Hadley's boots. Like the apology gifts, and the beach toys, those small, thoughtful things were the ones that proved what Tegan had said about him. Beneath the pain and the triggers was a man worth being patient for.

He dropped the towel on his patio and as they headed for the office, he said, "Will you be wearing a bikini to the beach?"

"*No*. Will you be wearing a Speedo?"

"If you'll wear a bikini, I'll wear a thong."

She laughed. "There will be no *thongs* around my little girl, thank you very much."

As they climbed the porch steps, he said, "Please tell me the door is locked."

"It is." She shifted Hadley and pulled the keys out of her pocket.

He took them from her and unlocked the door. As he followed her through the office and up the interior steps with that protective hand still warming her back again, he said, "Why won't you wear a bikini?"

"Because I'm not Kendall Jenner."

"Thank God for small favors. You've got a better body than she ever will."

"Not according to my ex," she said as Jock opened her apartment door.

He set the beach toys in the foyer, remaining on the landing with her. She hoped they could sneak a good-night kiss without waking Hadley.

"We've already established that your ex is an idiot." He put a hand on her hip, squeezing just enough to send even more awareness gusting through her, and said, "If you wear a bikini, I'll come to the beach tomorrow."

"Jock, trust me, that's not something you want to see."

He gazed into her eyes with a hunger that made her breath catch. "Babe, believe me when I say you are gorgeous, and I would very much like to see more of you."

"I don't even own a bikini," she confessed.

"That's a damn shame and something we definitely need to rectify. But you in a bathing suit is enough to get me to go anywhere." He ran his hand down Hadley's back and said, "That and trying to make things right for this little one, of course."

The sincerity in his voice was *everything*. Neither one said a word as they gazed at each other, the air between them pulsing with heat. Daphne was getting more nervous by the second, and Jock looked like he was, too. His brows knitted, and he took her hand and placed her keys in it, but he didn't let it go.

"I want to kiss you good night. Is that inappropriate if you're holding your daughter and she's sleeping?"

"Just don't wake her," she said breathlessly, leaning forward to meet him in a long, slow kiss that turned her tingles to full-on fireworks.

When their lips parted, he stayed close, brushing his lips over hers, light as a feather, and said, "See you tomorrow." He took a step away and stopped. "You have to lock the office door. You need a better system."

"Shoot. I'll get it after I put her down. You can go."

"No. I'll wait here while you put her to bed. Is this the only door to your apartment? I saw stairs out back."

"Those lead to my bedroom balcony," she said quietly. "There's an entry door there, too, but the steps are so steep for Hadley. Although I could use it when she's sleeping, I guess. Oh well. Let me put her down. I'll be right back." She hurried inside and put Hadley to bed. Her body was still humming as they made their way down the steps. All she could think about was another kiss.

When they reached the office door, he drew her into his arms and said, "Put me out of my misery and tell me who that guy was in your apartment earlier tonight."

It felt like it had been *days* since he'd shown up at her door. She loved the flare of jealousy in his eyes. He'd kept it under wraps well. "That was my brother, Sean."

"Thank Christ. I know we're not an item, and I have a long way to go before we can be, but for the first time in my life I was jealous, and I didn't like the way it felt."

She giggled, and then he lowered his lips to hers, turning her giggles into white-hot desire.

"Maybe you don't need a better system after all. Saying good night to you twice has its benefits." He touched his lips to hers in a tender kiss and said, "I'd better go before I get us both in trouble."

As she locked the door behind him, she knew it was too late. They were already in trouble.

# Chapter Ten

THE SOUNDS OF children playing hung in the air. The salty bay breeze brought summery scents of sunscreen and happiness. Sandpipers danced along the water's edge, and herring gulls slowly floated down to scavenge near the rocks. Hadley was playing with a castle they'd built in the sand. She pushed to her feet in her favorite pink bathing suit with a glittery fish on her belly and CUTEST CATCH written in yellow above it.

"Dock!" Hadley hollered, and took off running down the beach.

Daphne went after her, spotting Jock heading their way. Her daughter definitely had a built-in Jock Steele homing device. Daphne lifted Hadley into her arms and twirled her around, turning her aversion tactic into a game as she whispered, "Shh, let's surprise him."

Hadley nodded, mimicking in her whisper, "*Supwise.*"

Daphne had been a nervous wreck all morning, anxious to see if Jock would show up and about finally wearing the new black bathing suit Tegan and Chloe had convinced her to buy several weeks ago. It was racier than what she was used to, but her friends had said the high-cut bottom flattered her full hips and set off the dip of her waist, and the lace-up bodice showed just enough skin to draw the eye. That laced-up area started at her *belly button*. She had shorts on, but she still felt overly exposed, and despite what Jock had said, she worried that in the flesh, he might not find her size fourteen/sixteen, dimply, stretch-marked body *beautiful*.

He was heading their way wearing only black bathing trunks. A towel was draped casually over one shoulder and a backpack hung from his hand. Daphne's breath caught, as it had last night. He was beautiful, which might be a funny way to describe such a big, manly guy, but it fit him perfectly. He was the perfect mix of rugged and refined, and as he strode toward Daphne, he drew the eyes of nearly every woman on the beach. But his eyes were locked on *her*, and that made her feel good all over.

A sexy smile lifted his lips. His gaze shifted to Hadley, and Daphne saw the slightest twitch in his jaw, making his smile a little rigid.

"*Supwise!*" Hadley threw her arms up, startling Daphne, but she was quick to react.

"Yay! Surprise, Jock. We're at the beach, too," Daphne said, hoping Jock would catch on and not think she'd lost her mind.

"Today is my lucky day. I get to spend time with the most adorable girl on the beach and her gorgeous mama." He leaned in and kissed Daphne's cheek, whispering, "Thank you for intercepting her, but I *am* prepared to try."

Daphne's heart fluttered at the determination in his voice.

He tickled Hadley's belly—*Tickled. Hadley's. Belly!*— earning joyous giggles, and said, "*Cutest catch* is right."

"Down!" Hadley wriggled out of Daphne's arms and grabbed Jock's fingers, pulling him toward their blanket. "See my castle?"

Daphne's first instinct was to try to save him from that connection, but he wanted to try, so she bit her tongue, hoping for the best.

"You coming?" he asked as he shouldered his backpack, allowing Hadley to lead him by the fingers down the beach.

*I guess we're really doing this.*

She caught up to them and watched with awe as Jock stood with his hands on his hips, listening to Hadley jabber about her castle being *pointy* and having rooms for her bird and her owl, which were not allowed on the beach because it was too sandy. Daphne noticed that Jock kept a little distance between them, his legs planted firmly in the sand. Hadley toddled over to him and he crossed his arms, his muscles flexing. He was making a valiant effort. If Daphne hadn't been looking for hints of discomfort, she probably wouldn't have noticed those things.

"You make a castle?" Hadley looked hopefully up at him.

"Sure," he said evenly.

Her fearless daughter picked up a bucket and ran toward the water. Daphne ran after her, but Jock was two steps ahead. He circled in front of Hadley and crouched in about eight inches of water, putting his hands up in front of him, fingers splayed, and said, "That's far enough."

Daphne didn't know if she should laugh or swoon. He might as well have said, *I'm not going to touch you, but I'm not going to let you drown, either.* He looked vulnerable *and* protective of her little girl. That protective instinct told her more than words ever could.

Hadley crouched in front of Jock, filling her bucket with water. Jock's unsure gaze moved to Daphne. His brows rose and a small shrug lifted his shoulders, and she knew she'd made the right decision by inviting him to join them.

They built sandcastles, and Hadley decorated them with shells. When Jock's cell phone rang in his backpack, he paced a few feet from them as he took the call. Hadley watched him like a hawk, serious faced, as if she were making sure he wasn't going to leave. Jock looked as serious as she did. His eyes were trained on the sand as he wore a path in it. When he ended the call, he sat on the edge of the blanket, staring out at the water.

Daphne sat next to him and said, "Is everything okay?"

"Yeah. That was my sister, Jules. My grandmother's birthday is coming up, and she's been badgering me to go to her party."

"And you don't want to?"

He glanced at Hadley, pushing a plastic boat in the sand and making motor noises, and his lips curved up. He put his hand over Daphne's and said, "Things with me and Archer aren't good."

"Well, maybe you should make an effort there, too," she said carefully.

"Maybe one day I will." He ran his hand up her arm and said, "Why don't you take those shorts off?"

Tim had always encouraged her to wear shorts over her bathing suit, but she didn't want to tell Jock that. "I'm okay."

"*Okay* is not happy or comfortable. You're gorgeous, Daph." He glanced at Hadley, who was still preoccupied, and then he kissed Daphne's shoulder and continued pressing tantalizing kisses along her neck, sending shivers of heat through her, and whispered, "Let me see more of you."

Her nipples pebbled, and she felt a tug low in her belly. He must have noticed, because his eyes turned dark as night, and he said, "Come on, babe. Take a baby step for me."

How could she say no given his efforts with Hadley? She

stood up and shimmied out of her shorts. She was rewarded with the most lascivious look she'd ever seen.

"Hot, Mama?" Hadley asked.

"She sure *is*," Jock said with a smirk.

Now she was blushing *all* over. She grabbed the sunscreen to distract herself, and as she put it on, she said, "*Happy?*"

"Very," he said, his gaze moving languidly from her face all the way down to her toes, making her body sizzle and burn.

She thought the *sun* was hot, but *one* of his spine-tingling leers was hotter than a thousand suns. How was she going to make it however long he stayed?

The morning passed with sandcastles and gathering shells, with laughter and a few tears from Hadley that caused Jock to bristle. But he handled it well, shifting to the edge of the blanket, or getting up and walking off his discomfort. Daphne was surprised that Hadley didn't cling to him. It was as if her little girl knew she needed to give him some breathing room.

They ate the lunch that Daphne had packed, and she was glad she'd thought to bring extras for him. Jock tossed a wink here, a caress of her cheek there, and a tease to make Hadley giggle just about every chance he got. He stole kisses and cast so many of those steamy looks her way, Daphne would probably go home ten pounds lighter just from sweating. She tried not to make too much out of his efforts with Hadley, but it was impossible not to fall a little harder for him.

"What's in your backpack?" Daphne asked as she zipped her cooler closed.

"A notebook, a novel, my phone, water, sunscreen. The usual. I'd love to get your number, by the way. I keep forgetting to ask you for it."

He took out his phone and she programmed in her number.

As he put it away, she said, "I checked your book out of the library this morning."

"Really?"

"Mm-hm. Hadley's staying at my mom's tonight, and I have a date with *It Lies*. I'm nervous about reading it, though. It might give me nightmares."

"You have a free night, and you're spending it reading?"

"Sure, why not?"

"Because you could spend it with me."

Her pulse skyrocketed.

"You're used to reading romance. You can't just jump into horror. You need to *ease* into it, with a little help from a friend." He put his hand on hers and said, "You need to go slow, enjoy the thrill of anticipation, the heightened sensations, the fear and excitement as your pulse quickens and your skin grows hot, so you're ready for the rush of adrenaline when it pumps through you."

"*Yes please*," she said in one long breath.

A slow smile crept across his face.

She realized how she'd sounded and quickly said, "I mean, that sounds like the right approach."

"I liked your other response better," he said, making her blush feverishly *again*. "How about I take you to dinner, and then we can go back to my cottage, and I'll show you my collection of horror movies."

"I'd rather see your romance collection" slipped out under her breath before she could stop it.

"Even *better*."

*Ohmygosh!* "I didn't mean to say that."

"Mean what, Mommy?" Hadley asked from a few feet away, where she was playing in the sand.

"Nothing. Let's go down to the water for one last swim." *Mommy needs to cool off.*

As she stood up, Jock held her hand and said, "Pick you up at seven?"

"Okay," she said, and hurried down to the water with Hadley. *See your romance collection? Ugh.* She was so bad at this. Jock was watching her and Hadley, as he'd been doing all day, looking out for them. Chloe's voice traipsed through her mind. *I haven't seen him look at anyone else the way he looks at you… That man knows true goodness when he sees it.*

There were plenty of pretty women lying in the sun, frolicking in the water, and walking along the shore. He could have his pick of any of them, but he'd *chosen* her, and he hadn't walked away last night when she'd said Hadley had to come first. He'd also been with them all day. Did he even know what baby steps meant?

Daphne knew true goodness when she saw it, too, and he was pushing to his feet and heading straight for her.

"Dock, look!" Hadley jumped into the ripples of a broken wave, splashing sand and water everywhere.

"Watch *this*, Had." He picked up Daphne like she was light as a feather, making her squeal, and strode into deeper water. "Mommy needs to cool off."

"Don't do it! Please don't do it!" Daphne pleaded.

"Mommy!" Hadley ran toward them.

Jock spun around, rushing back toward Hadley. "You're so lucky," he said as he set Daphne on her feet and Hadley barreled into his legs.

"Me! *Cawwy me!*" Her grabby hands shot up. "Up! *Up!*"

Jock's jaw clenched, and he said, "How about I hold your hand?"

169

"Up! *Please!* Up!" Hadley begged.

Daphne reached for her, but Jock touched Daphne's arm, stopping her.

He crouched, meeting Hadley eye to eye, and said, "Sometimes all I can do is hold hands."

"Why?" Hadley asked.

"It's just hard for me to pick people up sometimes," he said. "But maybe one day it won't be so hard."

Hadley took his hand and reached for Daphne's as a wave rolled in. Jock's eyes connected with Daphne's as they lifted Hadley above the rolling wave and she squealed. When they lowered her toes to the water, she cheered, "Again!" As their laughter joined her daughter's, Daphne didn't even try to tamp down the joy filling up her hopeful heart.

# Chapter Eleven

"*DAMN…*" JOCK STOOD in Daphne's doorway, spellbound and speechless, Saturday night. Every time he saw her, he thought she couldn't possibly get more beautiful. Then she proved him wrong.

*Every. Damn. Time.*

She was beyond stunning in a rust blouse with white polka dots, tied casually just below the waist of her gauzy black skirt, which drifted above her knees. Her skin held the glow of a fresh tan, her hair cascaded over her shoulders, begging for his fingers to thread through it, and she'd done something with her makeup that made her blue eyes even more alluring.

She looked down at her outfit and said, "Oh, *stop*."

He swept his arm around her and crushed his mouth to hers, taking her in a long, slow kiss. He'd been waiting all day to do it. Holding back as she pranced around in that sexy black bathing suit had been torture. Did she know how incredible she was? How amazing of a mother? How all of her stolen glances had sent his heart into a tizzy when she'd look at him like he was the best dessert on the planet? And these kisses. *Holy hell.* His body burned with desire. He wanted to ravage her warm, willing mouth and put *his* on every inch of her. She was right there with him, clutching at his back, making those sinful noises that made his body throb and ache. He felt so close to her after they'd spent the day together. He didn't even know how that was possible after only a few short hours, but his burgeoning emotions had seeped into every part of him. He kissed her longer, deeper, more passionately than he'd ever kissed a woman, and he didn't want to stop. But he knew he had to, and he forced himself to break their connection. Her cheeks were flushed, her lips dark pink from the force of their kisses.

"I'm sorry," he panted out. "I had to get that out of the way if I'm going to sit across from you at dinner and keep my hands to myself." He tightened his hold on her, craving another kiss, and said, "I learned something today."

"Was it how to greet a woman, because…*wow*."

He grinned. "I learned that going to the beach with you is as dangerous as everything else." He brushed his lips over hers, tasting her desire, and said, "I had to keep my hands off you all day as you ran around in that sexy suit, your carefree laughter shining brighter than the sun."

She made a whimpering, needy sound that drew his lips to hers in another intoxicating kiss. He splayed his hand over her ass, pressing her to him so she could *feel* what she did to him, earning a long, sensual moan. He wanted to say *fuck dinner*, carry her into the bedroom, and make love to her until they were both too spent to move. But what he felt for her was too big, and she was too important, to allow her to think he only wanted sex.

He drew back, both of them breathless, and said, "You know I want to take you into the bedroom and make you mine, right? But you're too special, Daph. I'm not going to cheat either of us out of a real date."

She blinked, looking a little hazy. Her tongue swept over her lower lip, leaving it slick and enticing.

A hungry sound left his lungs. "We've got to go *now* or we never will," he practically growled.

Daphne was quiet for the first few minutes of the drive to the restaurant, nervously fidgeting with the edge of the seat. Jock reached across the console and held her hand, loving the mix of innocence and hunger in her eyes.

"I had a good time today." He pressed a kiss to the back of her hand.

"We did, too," she said a little breathily.

Seeing Hadley running toward him on the beach had been nerve-racking when he'd first arrived, but he'd made the decision to do everything within his power to conquer his anxiety, and in the end, it hadn't been as difficult for him to jump over some of the hurdles and navigate his fears as he'd thought it might be. He had a long way to go, and he knew it wouldn't be easy, but Daphne and Hadley were worth whatever pain he had to endure.

"When I dropped Hadley off with my parents, she couldn't stop talking about her friend *Dock*," she said more confidently. "I had to rush out of there before they started asking questions."

As he turned toward the restaurant, he said, "So I'm going to be your dirty little secret?"

She gave him one of her sweet smiles and head shakes that said she knew he was kidding. "You could never be a *little* anything."

"Good thing you've accepted the dirty part." Oh, man, her blush was going to do him in.

A little while later, they were sitting at a table on the second-floor balcony of the Bookstore Restaurant overlooking

Wellfleet Harbor, the heat between them crackling like live wires. They made small talk as they shared stuffed-mushroom-cap appetizers and scallop and lobster dinners, exchanging steamy glances and furtive touches. It was all he could do to keep from hauling her into his lap and devouring her.

Daphne teased him about looking like a catcher at a baseball game when Hadley had run down to the water, though the appreciation in her eyes was unmistakable. He made her blush, raving about how lucky he was to be seen with the sexiest woman on the beach. They talked about music and found they liked some of the same groups, and as they waited for dessert to be served, they talked about growing up as twins.

"My parents never dressed us alike or any of that. They always encouraged us to have our own identities," Jock explained. "We're pretty different anyway. I was a really positive kid, and Archer always had a chip on his shoulder."

"Even before the accident?"

"Yes, but before the accident his attitude wasn't usually aimed at me. We were competitive, but we were also best friends. You know how it is with a twin. You said you and Sean are close."

"We are. But we're also close with our sister, Renee. Sean and I didn't have to worry about having separate identities, since he's a guy and I'm a girl, but he did get to take liberties that Renee and I weren't allowed to take."

She sipped her wine, their eyes connecting over the glass, and as her cheeks burned pink, he realized why he loved seeing her blush. Most women he knew were overtly flirtatious, like they did it all the time. He loved knowing that he was as special to Daphne as she was to him.

"Ah, the old double standard. My sisters hated that," he said as the waiter brought their chocolate-dipped fruit for dessert.

Daphne picked up a chocolate-covered strawberry and bit into it. She closed her eyes and said, "Mm."

She had no idea how her moans and that look of sheer pleasure on her gorgeous face sparked images of her lying naked and blissed out beneath him. He ate a piece of fruit, too, because if he didn't keep his mouth busy, he was going to take the kiss he was dying for.

"Now that I have Hadley, I understand why my father had a double standard. But he was really strict about it." She licked chocolate from the corner of her mouth and said, "He wouldn't even let us date until we were seventeen. Of course, my sister found ways around it. She was always rebellious. I swear she had boys chasing after her from the second she turned thirteen."

"And you?" he asked, trying to picture bashful and beautiful Daphne in high school.

"I wasn't a rule breaker. But I also didn't have a line of boys after me like she did." She picked up a slice of chocolate-covered pineapple and bit into it, sharing another eyes-closed appreciative moan.

If she kept this up, he'd never make it through dessert.

"I can't believe that. I think you must have been as clueless to cues from boys then as you are now from men."

She pointed the remaining piece of pineapple at him and said, "I think you're on a sugar high."

He wrapped his hand around her wrist, and their eyes locked. Her jaw dropped as he drew the pineapple into his mouth and then kissed her fingertips, desire glittering in her eyes. Every touch of his lips brought a sexy little gasp. He'd never met a woman who was as genuinely sweet and unknowingly seductive as her, and he wanted her to know it. "Then I've been on a sugar high since we met last year."

She grabbed her wineglass, finishing the wine in one gulp, and said, "You should see a doctor about that."

"I'm not looking for a remedy." He paused, letting his words sink in, and went for a less intimate comment before they combusted. "But if you're right about not missing the cues, then your brother was keeping boys away from you."

"You're crazy." She laughed.

"Is he protective of you now?"

"Yes, but—"

"Then I'm sure he was always protective of you. I did the same thing when guys flocked to Sutton, and I would have done the same for Leni and Jules if I were around, but they're much younger than me. Levi usually cracked that whip."

"And who cracked the whip for *you*? What were you like in high school? Did you charm the pants off every girl on the island?"

He brushed his thumb over the back of her hand and said, "I only made it through the fifteen- to twenty-five-year-olds." Damn, he loved the shock rising in her eyes.

"You dated *twenty-five*-year-olds when you were in high school? You are *so* out of my league."

He laughed. "I was kidding, and there are no leagues, Daph. If there were, you'd be out of mine. I wasn't like that in high school. I know the guys at Bayside say gossip travels fast around here, but they've never lived on Silver Island, where it travels faster than the speed of light. I swear if I even thought about kissing a girl, everyone knew it. My parents' closest friends are the Remingtons and the Silvers. They have big families like we do, and all the kids pretty much ran in *packs*. We all had our secrets, but our parents had eyes everywhere. My family owns

Top of the Island Vineyard, the Silvers own the Silver House, where Gavin and Harper got married, and the Remingtons run Rock Harbor Marina. We were always traipsing around those places."

"That sounds like so much fun. I know a guy named Rowan Remington. He has a little girl named Joni. Do you think he's related to your friends?"

"Rowan and I grew up together."

"Really? Small world." Daphne ate a slice of chocolate-covered apple and said, "Did you like growing up there?"

"Oh man, did I *ever*. It was like our own world, with virtually no crime, so we could pretty much run wild. There was always someone to prank and something going on. I played every sport and had a great group of friends. We all watched out for each other. Like you do at Bayside with Desiree and the girls. And our parents were tough about grades and being respectful, but they also valued our childhood."

"What do you mean?"

"They supported our craziness. We didn't get in trouble for pranking, unless we stepped over a line—like when Archer and I threw together homemade flight suits and went in search of a roof to jump off, my dad took us skydiving. We had to go with instructors, but they could have just punished us and been done with it. It taught us to appreciate doing things the *right* way. They were supportive in lots of ways. We used to love playing in the vineyard at night, popping out of the dark to scare each other. I think most vineyard owners wouldn't want their kids running around the vines, but we were taught where we could go and where we couldn't, and we listened, because we *wanted* to be there. By the time we were teenagers, half the kids on the island were running around there with us. Instead of getting upset, my parents made a Halloween event out of it and set up ground rules for the kids. That's how they created the Field of Screams. They rope off part of the vines for a haunted walk, they make cider and cookies, do bobbing for apples. It's a community thing now, but it all stemmed from our love of scaring people. The whole family dresses up, and my siblings and I used to hide in the dark and jump out to scare people. They still do it, but I obviously haven't since the accident."

"Your parents sound incredible."

"Yeah. I'm lucky."

"But if you loved it so much, why wouldn't you want to live there? You said when you left for college you had no intention of ever moving back."

He shrugged and ate another piece of fruit. "My plan was to become a screenwriter and make great movies. I assumed New York or LA were the places to be. Then my film professor put me on a path to novel writing and it felt like I'd found my niche. I never really thought about *where* I would write until after graduation, and then Kayla had her job in the city, and it made sense to stay there. And after the accident, home was off the table completely."

"That's a shame, given how much you love it."

"Yeah, but I'm glad I ended up here. Otherwise I never would have met you. How about you? Do you see yourself staying at Bayside?"

"I don't know. I've been asking myself that a lot lately. I love the people, but I miss event planning, and I can't do that at Bayside anytime in the foreseeable future."

"What do you miss about it?"

"Everything," she said wistfully. "I miss working with brides and families, putting all the pieces of their events together, seeing all my hard work come to fruition. It's exciting. When we went to Gavin and Harper's wedding, it brought back so many memories of the work I did with the resort in North Carolina, so it made me think about it more seriously. And I love living at Bayside, but now that Hadley's getting older, I worry about her not having friends her age around to play with."

"If you miss it that much, why not look for a job in that field?"

"Because the guys have been great to me, and I love our friends there, although the girls aren't around very often anymore. And while I worry about Hadley not having friends where we live, she starts preschool Monday with all the kids she's been in daycare with. Moving to a new home and possibly a new school could throw her for a loop. What if it doesn't work out at a new job? What if we move someplace that looks great, but we don't find the right friends for either of us? Then I'm back to square one, and Hadley's the one who suffers."

"What if it *did* work out?"

"I get it—glass half-full and all of that. It's such a double-edged sword. I just don't want to make the wrong move for Hadley."

"You're a very devoted mother. Hadley's lucky to have you. It's got to be nice to have your family close by, too, for both of you."

"It is, although no matter where I live, we'll always be close. I didn't feel like we were too far apart when we lived in North Carolina. We visited my family, and they'd come see us. It's scary looking for a new job as a mom. It's different than just looking for myself. When I interviewed at Bayside, I knew *instantly* that I wanted to work there. It was the right opportunity at the right time in mine and Hadley's lives. So unless the perfect job comes along, one where I know without a shadow of a doubt that moving Hadley and giving up our security is the right thing to do, event planning is just a pipe dream."

"Well, I for one would love to see your pipe dream come true."

Her lashes fluttered as she lowered her gaze. "Thank you."

He took her hand in his and said, "Everything you say and do makes me admire you even more, from the way you are with Hadley, to your hopes and careful thought processes." Her eyes flicked up to his. "To the way you're looking at me right now and the pink spreading across your cheeks. You make me want so many things, Daph. Not just for me, but for you and Hadley. How about letting one of my dreams come true and allowing me to kiss you so everyone in here knows you're mine?"

That sexy smile he loved appeared, and her eyes shifted nervously around them.

Leaning closer, he said, "You've got about seven seconds to tell me no."

"I don't even need *one*."

She pressed her lips to his, surprising him. He felt her smiling, just as he was, and he slid his hand to the base of her neck, taking the kiss deeper. Her cheeks were soft, and her lips were warm. She kissed him eagerly, and when she put her hand on his leg, he put his hand over it to keep from touching her in ways he shouldn't in public. As badly as he wanted to earn one of her sexy moans, he didn't want to embarrass her, so he savored the last few seconds of their kiss and eased his efforts to a series of tender kisses before finally putting space between them. Her face was flushed. Her eyes hazy with lust. He pressed his lips to hers again and said, "What do you say we get out of here?"

"I'd like that."

He flagged down the waiter and paid for dinner. Then they left the restaurant hand in hand, stealing kisses as they hurried across the street to the parking lot, laughing like teenagers. He'd woken up that morning vowing he would *not* let her down with Hadley, or in any other way. She not only trusted him with her daughter, but also with her heart. He knew that must be hard for her after all she'd been through. His own heart beat with an unfamiliar passion and renewed strength, even more powerful than the thunder he'd lost long ago.

He drew Daphne into his arms, feeling more confident, sharper, *happier* than ever, and gazed into her eyes. "What are you doing to me, beautiful girl?"

He lowered his lips to hers, taking her in a long, sensual kiss that had her melting into him, making one of those pleasure-filled sounds that sent heat straight to his groin. He told himself to slow down, to be careful with her, to give her room to make her own decisions without the pressure of his desires. It was not an easy task, but he reluctantly drew back.

Her eyes caught his, and so many emotions passed between them, he could barely find his voice. "My cottage? Or…?"

"Your cottage sounds good."

Daphne was quiet on the drive back to Bayside. Jock reached across the seat for her hand. "I'm sorry if I went too fast, Daph. I don't have any expectations tonight. I just want to be with you."

"You didn't." She sat up a little straighter, holding his hand tighter, and said, "If I didn't want to kiss you, I wouldn't have. I'm just nervous, that's all."

"Because you're still not sure if I can handle Hadley?" Today made him believe he could get perspective on his past and learn to deal with his triggers, but it was only the beginning and it would be understandable if she were concerned.

"No, you did so well with Hadley today, you surprised me. You knew just how to handle her, and you were honest with her about it being hard for you to pick her up. That was...that meant more to me than you can imagine. So many people treat children like they don't understand the real world. Sometimes I think she understands it better than we do. I know it would have been easier for you to walk away."

"Actually, it would have been harder to walk away. She trusts me, or she wouldn't keep approaching me, and *you* trust me. I want to be worthy of that trust. I surprised myself, too, but I realized last night that I've never actually *tried* to face my triggers. Once I made the decision to confront them for you and Hadley, and for myself, it was easier than running away from them. I felt like such a failure all those times I'd walked away, but I was afraid of what the memories would do to me if I picked up Hadley and she cried. Sharing my past with you last night was cathartic. You make me want to be a better man, Daph, and with you I feel safe enough to admit the things I need to work on. I have more work to do, of course. There were times on the beach when Hadley cried that I had to remind myself that I wasn't in that hospital again, that she wasn't going to stop breathing."

"You handled everything well. It's okay to take a breather, and now that I understand it, I'm not offended by it."

"Thank you. That's why I didn't hold her when she asked me to down by the water. I don't know if it will trigger the memories or not, and I don't want to risk it."

"After what I saw today, I have faith that you'll eventually be able to hold her if you want to," she said sweetly. "But I don't think you know what *easing* into something means. Today you didn't *Ferberize* yourself. You jumped in with two feet."

"I've never been good at easing into things. I'm an all or nothing guy." As he turned in to the resort, he said, "But I want to do right by you and Hadley, and if you need us to go slow, we will."

She lowered her eyes and said, "It's just been a long time, and I'm not used to…you know."

He parked in front of his cottage and squeezed her hand. "That makes two of us." He climbed out and went around to her side, taking her hand as he helped her out of the vehicle. As they walked up to the front door, he said, "How often do your parents keep Hadley overnight?"

"Every few weeks. They'd keep her every night if I let them. They love spoiling her, and she can't get enough of Nana and Pop Pop."

"Nana and Pop Pop. That's cute. What do you usually do on those nights?"

"Have dinner with the girls, read, or go out with our friends, but you're usually there, and we don't do that often now that everyone is coupled off."

He opened the door and said, "After you."

He followed her in, and though she ran the resort and had probably been in the cottage dozens of times, he tried to see it from her eyes. The bookshelves now held *his* books, pictures of Harvey, and a few decorative things he'd picked up in his travels. He didn't display pictures of his family because it made him too sad. His laptop and notebooks sat on the table, and the wooden trunk with Harvey's handwritten manual in it was still on the floor by the patio doors. It wasn't *home*, but he didn't even know what a home would feel like anymore, and at least it didn't feel as much like a rental.

"How do you like staying here?" Daphne asked.

"I like it. I lived in the mansion with Harvey for the first two years, but once he believed I wasn't going to *off* myself, I moved into the caretaker's cottage at the rear of the property. The one where Tegan and Jett live now. This cottage is smaller, but it reminds me of that one. I like the open floor plan, and you can't beat the view."

She walked over to the patio doors and gazed out at the moonlight shimmering off the bay. "Hadley and I stayed in this cottage in the spring when a storm came through and the roof in our apartment leaked. She calls it *our* house. Well, now she calls it 'Mine and Dock's house.'" She laughed softly. "One day I want to have a home like this for Hadley, with a backyard where she can play, near friends her age that she can grow up with, get into trouble with—not too much trouble."

His mind skipped ahead, to thoughts of the future, of being there with them, watching Hadley play, picking her up and swinging her around as Daphne had done on the beach. He tried to rein those thoughts in as he put his arms around Daphne from behind, but when they were together, despite the struggles he still had to move past, nothing had ever felt so right.

He kissed her neck and said, "You mean, we've already slept in the same bed?"

She turned in his arms, *want* simmering in her eyes. "If we did, it doesn't speak very highly of your bedroom expertise, because I don't remember it being that thrilling."

He laughed. "Is that a challenge?" That earned an adorable

blush. He teased his lips over hers and said, "I promise you, Daphne, when you're ready and you and I get together, the earth *will* move."

DAPHNE COULD STARE into Jock's honest eyes for days. He made her feel feminine and beautiful, and she trusted him implicitly. But this moment could change everything. She could finally get her hands on the man she fantasized about when she used her battery-operated boyfriend. Her pulse quickened at the thought. She wanted him so badly she could taste his salty skin. But was she ready to open herself up in a way that she could never take back? To bare not only her heart but her mom bod? Loving her own body was one thing, but baring herself to a man was a whole different ball game. She could hardly breathe for the butterflies in her stomach. Seconds ticked by like minutes. She needed to make a decision. Trust her instincts and let go of her fears, or redirect all her pent-up desires and go for the movie? He held her a little tighter, his eyes boring into her with dirty promises she wanted him to fulfill.

She was so nervous, she didn't know what to say. But it turned out, her heart did, because when she opened her mouth, "I've never felt the earth move" came out.

"Oh, my sweet Daphne. You are going to test my every limit, aren't you?"

His lips touched hers in a series of tantalizingly tender kisses, each one leaving her aching for more. "Your lips are magnificent," he whispered, and traced her lower lip with his tongue. "Delicious."

The words he used to describe her excited her as much as his touch did. Lust billowed inside her as he teased and tasted her lips. Every slick of his tongue, every erotic *nip* caused a needy gasp. He brushed his scruff along her cheek, pressing a kiss beside her ear, speaking huskily. "There are so many things I want to do with you. *To* you." He slid one hand along her cheek and threaded his fingers into her hair, holding tight, his other hand pressing on her lower back, keeping their bodies flush. His arousal pressed hot and hard against her belly. His lips hovered over hers, his tongue gliding along her lips excruciatingly slowly. The anticipation was agonizing and luxurious at once.

"I want to show you how exquisite you are. I want to *treasure* you, *taste* all of you."

She inhaled shakily, her fingers digging into his sides as his mouth covered hers in a penetrating kiss that bound together with his dirty talk, making her damp. She'd read all kinds of books with dirty-talking heroes, but she'd never heard a man say such things in real life. They felt wicked coming from Jock. She never realized how much she liked *wicked*. His fingers tightened in her hair as he intensified the kiss, and just when a moan left her lips, he eased his efforts as he had the other night, making her *crave* more.

"I want *your* beautiful mouth on *me*," he said gruffly, sending her entire body into a frenzy of fiery pinpricks.

His mouth claimed hers again, warm and insistent. She opened wider for him, wanting *everything* he had to give. His tongue probed deep and sensual, as if to show her *how* he wanted her mouth on him. Her body screamed *Yes!* but her nerves had her shaking like a leaf in a storm.

He drew back, his eyes dark and possessive, and said, "Don't get scared, sweetheart. Not tonight. *Someday*, when and if you want to, my body is yours to explore and enjoy."

*Oh. My. God.*

How would she make it through a *minute* without thinking about *that*?

He led her to the couch, which was a good thing, because she was dizzy with desire and her legs weren't going to hold her up much longer. They sat down and he put his arm around her, playing with the back of her hair, their faces a whisper apart. When he looked at her like that, so different than she'd ever been looked at before—full of emotions, with as much admiration as hunger—she felt like he truly saw her, *all* of her: the responsible mom, the caring friend, and the sensual *woman*.

"I could kiss you all night long." He kissed her lips, her jaw, and the curve of her neck, sending heat blazing through her core. He put his hand on her thigh, and his brows knitted. "You're shaking. Do you want to stop?"

"No," she said barely above a whisper.

He squeezed her thigh and said, "Don't be nervous. I'll never ask you to do anything you don't want to. I just want to make you feel good."

*God.* Did men like him really exist? He was generous in every sense of the word.

His lips descended slowly, *intimately*, upon hers, as if he were savoring every blessed second. Lust spread through her entire being, burning between her legs like hot coals. His tongue swept greedily over hers, stealing her brain cells one lick at a time. She didn't fight it. She didn't want to think; she only wanted to *feel*. His passion was a drug, taking her higher. She wanted to revel in the rush of desire consuming her, the feel of his hands exploring her torso, the scratch of his rough scruff on her cheeks as he devoured her. *Oh*, how she loved that! Her sense of time and space blurred, fading until there was only the two of them and the raging emotions binding them together. He kissed her slower, more intensely, so thoroughly she couldn't stop the moans coming as he lowered her to her back.

He perched above her, his hard length pressing against her center. "*Daphne*" came out rough and pleading as he shifted, bearing his weight on one arm.

"Touch me." She pulled his mouth to hers, arching beneath him, wanting his touch as much as he wanted her kisses. His hand covered her breast, groping greedily, then caressing as if she were precious. His thumb brushed over her nipple, bringing it to a taut, aching point. It had been so long since she'd been touched, she tore her mouth away, panting out, "*Yes...*"

He trailed openmouthed kisses down her neck, slowing to take a tantalizing suck here, an erotic nip there. She felt like a bundle of raw nerves as he touched the buttons on her blouse, his adoring eyes silently seeking her approval. Her heart stuttered. She nodded, sure she was blushing from head to toe, which she knew he'd love. Just the thought of him loving that part of her made her want him even more. He pressed his warm lips to her breastbone and dusted kisses along her chest as he unbuttoned her blouse. He didn't rush, didn't try to hide his greedy, appreciative looks as he unclasped her bra and bared her breasts. She'd never had perky breasts, and nursing Hadley had definitely taken a toll. Her belly was anything but fit and hadn't seen sun since the seventh grade, but when Jock's eyes met hers, sheer, unadulterated *awe* stared back at her.

"You are absolutely breathtaking." He ran his fingers lightly over her breasts, leaving goose bumps in their wake. "More beautiful than a Renoir."

She knew Renoir was a famous artist, but she had no idea what he painted. It didn't matter, because Jock's tone made it clear that a Renoir didn't hold a candle to *her*, and *that* overwhelmed her. She was bewildered by his appreciation, consumed by feelings bigger than happiness, more powerful than exhilaration. Similar to the day Hadley had come into the world, only totally different. She scrambled for the right words, but there were none special enough to describe all the things he made her feel. He lowered his mouth to her breast, loving her so perfectly, she had a hard time holding on to her thoughts. He whispered, "So sweet." *Kiss, suck.* "I've wanted you for so long..." rendering her unable to think at all. Every suck brought a tug between her legs, every caress, a rock of her hips, until she was writhing in pleasure, hanging on to reality by a thread. A stream of indiscernible noises fell from her lips.

"That's it, baby," he coaxed, his voice thick with desire.

With his mouth on her breast, his hand moved to her thigh, and she opened her legs, giving him the approval she knew he'd seek. He shifted higher, gazing into her eyes as his fingers traced the skin along the edge of her panties, so close to her sex she was going to lose her mind. He didn't say a word, and from the fire in his eyes, the tension in his jaw, she wondered if he wasn't able to. He lowered his mouth to hers, rough and demanding as his fingers pushed into her panties, sliding over her wetness. *Yes...*She rocked her hips, her whole body bowing up as he teased her into a moaning mess of desire. He kissed her like he was making love to her mouth. His thick fingers entered her slowly, stroking over the magical spot that made her whimper like the needy girl she was. His thumb zeroed in on her most sensitive nerves, sending electric currents racing through her.

"Let go for me," he said against her lips before reclaiming

them with a passion unmatched by anything she'd ever felt.

She was lost in a sea of sensations she'd never known existed. He was some kind of make-out god, *giving* and *taking* in a mind-numbing rhythm, taking her up, up, *up*, until every breath felt like her last. She clawed at his arms, moaning, aching, her body pulsing with need, and then he finally, blissfully catapulted her into a wild, sensual ecstasy. He swallowed her cries of pleasure as she surrendered to a climax that hit like a tidal wave, engulfing her, dragging her under, then tossing her up toward the stars. Her toes curled, her hips bucked uncontrollably, and the sounds she made were unrecognizable to her. It should have been terrifying to be so vulnerable, mortifying to completely lose control, but as she finally started to come down from the peak, he cradled her in his strong arms, her head clearing with each tender kiss, and all she felt was blissful and safe. His eyes found hers, and those pools of darkness held so many emotions, for the first time in her life, she felt truly, deeply *adored*.

He touched his smiling lips to hers and whispered, "Welcome back, beautiful." He kissed her again, sweet and tender. "You are truly magnificent."

As reality sank in, embarrassment was not far behind. He was fully dressed, and she was lying there bare breasted, her skirt bunched around her waist, one arm hanging languidly off the couch, in a miraculous state of heavenly bliss. Several thoughts hit at once—*Holy cow, that was amazing. He looks as blissed out as I am. Oh my God, he's waiting for me to reciprocate. I suck at this.*

"Hi," she whispered, and reached for the button on his jeans. "I should…I'll…"

He intercepted her hand, laced his fingers with hers, and

kissed her knuckles.

"No, sweetheart. I just want to be close to you." He placed her hand on his hip and smoothed her skirt down her leg. Then he kissed her breast and somehow managed to refasten her bra with ease, while she always felt like she was wrangling baby elephants into hammocks.

"But...?" Tim had never touched her without wanting something in return. *Oh no.* She'd been totally out of it when she came. What if she'd acted in a way that turned him off and made him *not* want her to touch him? What if he just wanted her to leave? Her head spun with worry. She chanced a glance at him, and her insides turned to mush at the way he was looking at her, like she was all he ever wanted, easing her worries and her embarrassment.

"No *buts*, beautiful." He righted her shirt, covering her bra, and said, "There's no need to rush."

"If this is you not rushing, I'm not sure I can handle you at regular speed," she said as they sat up and she buttoned her shirt.

"I've been dying to touch you." He kissed her softly. "And making you come?" He flashed a sexy grin. "I've found my new favorite activity."

"*Ohmygod.*" She covered her face. "You're going to make me live in a constant state of embarrassment."

He laughed and moved her hands. "Get used to it. I like you, Daph, a whole hell of a lot more than I've ever liked anyone, and I'm not ready for tonight to end. Can you stay for a while? I promised to ease you into horror. We can watch a movie, and then I'll walk you home."

She definitely wasn't ready for the night to end, either. "I'd love to. But I think I need some wine if I'm watching horror.

Do you mind if I use your bathroom?"

"Go ahead. I'll get the wine."

She hurried into the bathroom. Her hair was tangled from his hands, her lips were a little swollen and pink from their kisses—*oh, those kisses!*—and her skin was flushed. If he could do that to her with one hand and his incredible mouth, she had no doubt that he could make the earth move with the rest of his body. After using the bathroom, she washed her hands and finger-combed her hair, lingering in the bathroom, waiting for her pulse to calm. But every time she thought about going out there, her body threw another party.

She finally gave up and went to join Jock.

He was sitting on the couch and stood as she entered the room, reaching for her hand. "You okay?"

*My body won't stop singing your praises.* "Mm-hm."

"You're nervous again." He put his arms around her, and his all-seeing eyes smiled down at her. "I'm nervous, too. I told you it's been a long time since I've been with a woman. It's actually been an embarrassingly long time. More than a year. I want you to know that I don't take intimacy lightly. What we did—hell, Daph, when we *kiss*—it's all special to me."

Now that she knew him better, his confession didn't surprise her, but it did make her feel a little less nervous. "I know. I feel that when you touch me."

He exhaled loudly, as if he'd been holding that in for a while, and said, "Okay, then. Ready for a little horror?"

"No, but I'm willing to try."

He turned off the lights and said, "I'll keep you safe."

He toed off his shoes and she took off her heels, and they settled into the couch. Daphne sipped her wine as he queued up *Scream*.

"I love Drew Barrymore." She set her glass on the table. When the movie started, it had an eerie feel to it. Daphne tucked her feet up on the couch beside her, snuggling closer to Jock.

He kissed her cheek, hugging her against his side. In the movie, Drew answered the phone, talking to the stranger on the other end.

"Well, that's stupid," Daphne said. "Why would you tell someone you don't know that you're making popcorn? Do people believe this? That's not scary. You don't tell a stranger you're going to watch a movi—" She gasped when the man on the phone said he was watching Drew. Daphne sat up waving her hands and said, "*Nope.* I can't watch it. I'm sorry, but it's just me and Had in the apartment. I'll have nightmares."

He turned off the movie and threw his arms around her, hugging her as he laughed. "Do you have any idea how crazy about you I am?"

"Oh yeah, right. You've got yourself a real winner," she said sarcastically. "I can't even watch five minutes of the movies you like."

"I don't care. And I have a backup plan. Get cozy, buttercup." He navigated around the Netflix site and started the movie *Love Actually.*

She melted against him. "Are you sure you haven't done this in a while? Because that's one of the all-time best romance movies around."

"Positive. But I do know how to research good date movies."

"You did research for our date?" *There's your brownie points.*

"I scored a date with the only woman I have thought about for the last year. I wasn't about to mess it up."

"Jock Steele, you are surprising me at every turn. I better snatch you up before all the single girls in town find out about you."

"Baby, you're the only single girl I want." He pressed his lips to hers and said, "Now watch the movie, or I'll snatch you up and carry you off to my bed."

She was dangerously close to saying *Yes, please...*

# Chapter Twelve

THE NEXT MORNING Jock carried a box of pastries up the back steps to Daphne's bedroom balcony, as anxious as a teenager seeing his first crush—magnified by about a *zillion*.

He'd loved cuddling with Daphne on the couch watching a movie, holding hands, stealing kisses, and hearing her dreams of event planning and owning a little cottage for her and Hadley. And finally touching her? Experiencing her in the throes of passion? Holy hell, he couldn't *stop* thinking about how incredible that was. He'd been *this close* to asking her to stay last night, but he hadn't wanted to rush her. When he'd walked her home, they'd kissed for so long, he knew she wanted him as much as he wanted her. But just as she was trusting him to find his way with Hadley, he was trusting her to find her way with them. He promised himself he'd take their relationship on *her* timeline, even if it meant cold showers three times a day. If this morning was any indication, three might not be enough.

When he was younger, he hadn't understood the way his parents had talked about love like it was something that just *was*. As if it were a tangible being with a mind and will of its own and its victims had no say in surrendering to it. He believed it existed because he'd seen it in his parents, and

Harvey's love for Adele validated the force of love even more. Jock had felt lust, and he'd felt need, but what he felt with Daphne was different. This was lust, need, *greed*, and something much deeper, accompanied by protective urges so strong, they were driving him to face his demons head-on. When those feelings bound together, they were all consuming. Was that *love?* He had nothing upon which to gauge his feelings, except that *something* had motivated him to drive to the bakery at six thirty in the morning and get the blueberry-cream-cheese breakfast pastries Daphne said were her favorites. Waiting until a reasonable hour to knock on her door had also been *hell*. Six fifty was close enough to seven o'clock.

Or at least he hoped it was as he knocked.

He heard fast footsteps and imagined Daphne running to answer the door, missing him as much as he missed her. The door swung open. Daphne was breathing hard. Her hair was tousled, her skin flushed, cheeks stained pink, and the short, sexy robe she wore was on inside out and cockeyed, exposing half of one breast. Over her shoulder he saw her unmade bed, the blankets bunched at the foot of it. If he didn't know better, he'd think he'd caught her having sex.

"Jock?" she said breathlessly. "Hi. I was just...doing *yoga*."

"*Naked* yoga?"

She crossed her arms over her middle, her blush deepening. "*Mm-hm.* It's all the rage."

*Yoga my ass.* He heard something—a buzzing or a knocking. "What's that noise? Did you leave something on?"

Her brows knitted. Then her eyes opened wide, and she gasped. She whipped her head to the side, looking over her shoulder, and made a tortured sound as she ran around the bed. She reached into the nightstand drawer, fiddling with something and whispering harshly to herself. The noise stopped. As she sank down to the edge of the bed making more embarrassed sounds, understanding dawned on him, igniting the inferno that had been simmering inside him all night. He closed the door and went to her.

She covered her face with her hands, turning away as she said, "That did *not* just happen."

She was so damn sexy, he was going to lose his mind. He set the bakery box on the nightstand and knelt before her, resting his hands on her thighs. "Baby—"

She spread her fingers, peeking out from between them, and said, "*Don't.*"

"*Don't* think you're the hottest woman I've ever known? Sorry, I can't help that." He lowered her hands, his heart aching for her. "I spent the night wishing I had asked you to stay with me. This morning I went for a run at five o'clock, took a cold shower after that, and still had a raging hard-on because I wanted to make love to you so badly. I had to take things into my own hands just to make it through the morning, and look what seeing you in that robe, and knowing what you were doing, has done to me."

Her gaze moved to his erection straining against his sweats. His going commando left nothing to her imagination. Her eyes sparked with so much heat, he had to grit his teeth to keep a growl from coming out.

She swallowed hard and said, "I thought about you all night, too, and then I had this dream, and I woke up all hot and bothered."

"I'm right here if you want me."

"*If* I want you?" She snort-laughed. "I want you more than I've ever wanted *anything*, but you've probably been with dozens of women, and I've been with only two men. *Two.* And I haven't been with anyone since before Hadley was born. That's a *long* time. I've forgotten everything about sex, and I never knew that much about it to begin with." She was talking so fast, he couldn't get a word in. "Nobody and *nothing* has ever made me feel like you do. So, *do* I want you? You're damn right I do. But I'll just mess it up. I think I need about five years of practice firs—"

Her words were smothered by the firm press of his lips. He wrapped her in his arms, kissing her slow and deep, trying to ease her panic. She went soft in his arms, and he kissed her longer without any endgame. He just fucking loved kissing her.

She came away flushed and breathless all over again. He held her beautiful gaze as he ran his fingers up her thighs and said, "Let me make love to you the way you deserve to be loved."

A needy whimper left her lips.

He wasn't taking any chances of misreading her, and said, "I can leave, or I can stay. Tell me what you want."

"*You,*" she said with confidence and a hint of vulnerability. "I want you, Jock."

His heart thundered at her confession. He took her hand and rose to his feet, bringing her up with him. "Hearing you say that and seeing you in this sexy robe…" He untied the robe, and it fell open, catching on her breasts. "It's almost too much to bear."

She looked nervously around the room. "It's too light in here."

"Perfect for me to admire your gorgeous body." He put his fingers beneath the shoulders of her robe and gently lifted it off. The silk slipped off, puddling at her feet. He looked his fill, heat thrumming through him. She crossed her arms around her middle, and he guided her hands to his hips. "I want to see all of you. I want to *feel* all of you."

He stepped out of his flip-flops and tugged his shirt off, tossing it to the floor. Her eyes locked on his chest, and when he pushed his sweats down and stepped out of them, those sweet baby blues followed. Having her eyes on him made his cock twitch eagerly. He drew her into his arms, savoring the first touch of their bare bodies. She inhaled sharply, and he gritted out a curse at the sheer pleasure of feeling her. He should bow down and pay homage to her silky skin, the way her soft curves molded to his hard frame. He would, in time. But her heart was pounding frantically, and though he loved her rosy cheeks, he needed to waylay her embarrassment and show her just how perfect they were together.

"Feel that, sweetheart?"

She made a breathy sound of affirmation.

"That's your beautiful body making me feel good all over." He cradled her cheek in his hand, lifting her face so he could gaze into her eyes, and said, "I'm not going to hurry, and you're *not* going to hide."

He forced himself to go slow, even though he was dying to bury himself deep inside her, for them to get as close as two people could be. As he ran his hand down her side, over the swell of her hip, her innocent and nervous doe eyes held his rapt attention. "I've got you, sweetheart, and I'm going to make you feel even better than last night."

His mouth covered hers firmly, authoritatively, devouring her sweetness. He reveled in the feel of her sexy curves pressing into him, her fingers digging at his flesh, sending heat coursing through his veins. His hands wandered over her supple skin, memorizing the dip at her waist, the curve of her lower back, and enjoying the feel of her gorgeous ass filling his hands. He moaned into their kisses, but just touching her wasn't enough. He wanted to cherish her so thoroughly, she'd never feel the need to cover up again. He drew back, trapping her lower lip between his teeth and giving it a gentle tug. Her eyes opened, full of *want*. He trailed kisses down her cheek and across her shoulder as he moved behind her.

"Jock," she whispered nervously.

"I'll never hurt you, sweetheart. I want to admire all of you." He gathered her hair over one shoulder, kissing the curve of her neck, his arms circling her waist. "I want to touch all of you." He sealed his mouth over her neck, sucking as his hands played over the soft, supple curves of her thighs and hips, loving the feel of her. "You're perfect, baby." He ran his hands up her belly, kissing and whispering, rubbing his hard length against her lower back. "Feel what your beautiful body does to me." He caressed her breasts, rolling her nipples between his fingers and thumbs.

"Oh God," she whispered.

"Like that, baby?" he asked between kisses. She moaned in response. He kept one hand on her breast, moving the other between her legs to her slick heat, and groaned, his hips thrusting in response to the feel of her arousal. "So ready for us."

"You can thank *BOB* for that," she said in a shaky whisper.

He stilled. "Who the hell is Bob?"

"My battery-operated boyfriend," she whispered sharply, as if he should *know* the answer.

He chuckled and nipped at the back of her neck. "Guess what, buttercup? BOB is out of a job. You've got me now." He sucked her earlobe into his mouth, earning a needy moan. "BOB can't appreciate your beauty the way I do." He kissed his way down her back, loving every dimple, every lush curve. "I love these *muffins*," he said, taking a small bite of her ass, earning a surprised squeak. He kissed every inch of each soft globe, touching *all* of her as he moved around her, loving her hips and waist. When he stepped in front of her, he kissed her softly and said, "If my girl likes toys, I'm happy to oblige."

Her eyes widened.

"There's nothing I won't do for you, gorgeous." He loved his way down her body, kissing, sucking, tasting her breasts, her rib cage, and the swell of her belly, earning tiny gasps of pleasure. He traced her stretch marks with feathery kisses, his heart swelling for the beautiful mother in his arms. He trailed kisses over her hips and slowly dragged his tongue along her inner thighs. The scent of her arousal made his cock throb. He slicked his tongue along her wetness, her essence spreading through his mouth like the sweetest honey. She grabbed his shoulders, and he grabbed her ass, nudging her legs open wider with his knees. He licked and sucked as she writhed and moaned. He fucked her with his tongue and teased over her most sensitive bundles of nerves. She went up on her toes, whimpering, digging her nails into his flesh as he teased and tasted his girl. His cock wept for her.

When she fisted her hands in his hair, he ground out, "Come for me."

He stayed there on his knees, loving her with his hands and mouth. She was shaking, moaning, pulling his hair so hard he was sure she'd pull it out—and he didn't care. Loving Daphne was the best thing he'd ever experienced. He pushed his fingers into her tight heat, seeking the spot that would make her shatter for him, and used his mouth on her other magical detonator.

"Oh God...*Jock*..." She panted. "*Don't stop.*"

He quickened his efforts, and her hips shot forward. He held her right where she needed him most, relentless in his pursuit of her pleasure.

His name flew from her lips like a prayer. "*Jock!* Oh, oh, *ooooooh—*"

He stayed with her, devouring her sex as it pulsed and quivered, and she panted out sinful sounds he knew he'd hear in his dreams. When the last shudder rolled through her, he pushed to his feet and crushed his mouth to hers. She didn't pull away at the taste of her arousal. She feasted on his mouth as he feasted on hers, and *fuck*, that nearly sent him over the edge. Then her delicate hand slipped from his body and she cupped his balls, stealing the breath from his lungs. She fisted his shaft, stroking him tight and perfect, shocking his brain into gear.

"*Fuck.*" He grabbed her wrist.

"Did I do it wrong?"

The innocence and worry in her eyes cut straight to his heart. "No. You're incredible, but I want to make love to you." And then he realized his mistake, and it was a big one. "Shit, *Daph*. I don't have a condom. I didn't think we'd end up here."

"I'm on birth control, and you said you were clean as a whistle." She squeezed his cock, and he ground out a curse. "Is *this* whistle clean?"

"*Yes*," he said with a laugh. "I wouldn't be naked with you if I wasn't."

"Then..." She raised her brows in the sweetest, sexiest invitation he'd ever received.

"You're too fucking adorable for words." He crushed his mouth to hers, needing so much more of her. He'd promised her slow, but he couldn't hold back any longer. They kissed as they stumbled to the bed, and he laid her on her back, taking a long, lustful look as he came down over her. "You're gorgeous, Daph. Know that, sweetheart, because it is true."

"You make me feel beautiful."

"Then I need to try harder, because you are utterly *divine*."

He lowered his mouth to hers, and as their bodies came together, waves of soul-drenching pleasure crashed over him. His emotions whirled and skidded, rendering him speechless. He crushed his lips to hers, and their bodies took over, urgently pumping and grinding, groping and clawing. Their kisses were deep and agonizing, both desperate for more. Their skin grew slick, the sounds of their lovemaking filling the room. Jock pushed one hand beneath her, cupping her ass as he took her deeper. She moaned into his mouth, and the vibration set his heart on fire. He reared up, needing to see her face. Her eyes opened, and he slowed his thrusts, savoring the feel of her tight heat, her hands holding him like she never wanted to let go.

"I've waited so long," he whispered. "You're so..." He searched for the right words, but she was looking at him like he was the only man she'd ever wanted, and he clung to that, wanting to be that man, because that was exactly how he felt about her. "You're *everything*, Daph. *Everything*." Their mouths came together, and they found a new rhythm, slower, more intense. But *slow* didn't last as their passion mounted, rising between them like the hottest fire. Tremors started in her thighs, her nails dug into his arms as her hips rose off the bed, and her head fell back.

"*Jock*—" flew from her lungs as her orgasm crashed over her.

Her hips bucked, and her body clenched so tight, heat skated down his spine, hurtling him into his own explosive release.

He buried his face in her neck, gritting out her name as they rode the waves of ecstasy. Their climaxes went on and on, until they lay tangled in each other's arms, too spent to move. He kissed her softly, their hearts beating as one as he ran his fingers through her hair, down her back, along the curve of her spine.

She drifted in and out of sleep in his arms, beyond beautiful, with the sunlight illuminating her voluptuous body. A long while later, her eyes fluttered open and her lips curved up. "I just want to stay in your arms all day."

"I would like nothing more." He kissed her softly, but it wasn't enough for either of them, and they deepened the kiss. Their hands moved greedily over each other's bodies, Daphne's soft fingers pressing into his skin. Her touch was like a gift he couldn't get enough of. He felt like he was floating down an endless river on the most luxurious ride, and he never wanted to get off. But he had a feeling today wasn't totally theirs. "When do you have to get Hadley?" he whispered against her lips.

Her smile grew, and she ran her fingers lightly along his back, making him even harder. "I love that you worry about her."

"She's part of you. Of course I do."

"I have to get her in a few hours." She cuddled closer, pressing against his erection. Her trusting eyes met his, and she whispered, "After we do that again."

"Aw, baby." He moved over her, feeling *free* and *whole* for the first time in years, and when she whispered, "Love me, Jock," he had a feeling he was already well on his way.

# Chapter Thirteen

DAPHNE WAS STILL floating on air from her morning with Jock when she headed up her parents' driveway late Sunday morning to pick up Hadley, thumbing out a text to Chloe. *SOS. Need girl talk.* She added an eggplant and a peach emoji and sent it off. She knew Chloe was on her weekly motorcycle ride with Justin and other Dark Knights, but she was dying to talk to her. She hadn't been able to stop smiling since Jock had knelt in front of her in what she considered to be the most embarrassing moment of her entire life. She still couldn't believe that had happened, much less how he'd made it seem *natural* to be caught using a vibrator.

How had he known just what to say and do to make her not only feel at ease, but also beautiful and sexy? She wanted to bottle up the things he did and said, the way he touched her, *looked* at her, and revisit them later to make sure she hadn't dreamed them up. After they'd made love a second time, they'd lain in bed for the longest time, nibbling on the treats he'd brought and talking about silly things, like their favorite seasons—they both loved fall and winter because of the colors and cooler weather—and their favorite colors—hers was rust, because it was unique and pretty, and his was blue, because it had always been blue. She'd thought it funny that he hadn't had a reason. He'd asked about her plans for the day, and she said she was hoping to play with Hadley, answer forum questions for the book club, and get some laundry done. Although she was in no rush to wash her sheets. She loved having his scent on them. He'd said he was feeling inspired and hoped to write. Daphne tried to coax him into taking a shot at writing romance, since he was so good at living it, but he'd refused. They'd had a few laughs making up romantic story lines that he injected with death and gore just to get a rise out of her. He suggested they take Hadley out for ice cream that evening. She was thrilled that he was taking steps toward making things better with Hadley.

"Mom?" she said as she walked through the kitchen of her childhood home, a modest four-bedroom Cape Cod with a glass breakfast room that Daphne had always loved. The rooms were rather small, and the furniture had been the same for as long as she could remember, but that consistency brought comfort.

"In the playroom!" her mother called out.

Daphne went through the living room and down the hall to the playroom, which they'd called the *rec room* when Daphne had been young. Back then it had been her and her siblings' hangout, boasting a large flat-screen television, a computer desk, and two comfy couches. Now those couches were pushed against the wall and there were shelves and buckets filled with Hadley's toys. The room was always in a state of chaos, littered with dolls, coloring books, plastic vehicles, and dozens of stuffed animals.

It was a bright, sunny room, and in the middle of the floor Renee and their mother were having a tea party with Hadley and several of her stuffies.

"Mommy!" Hadley jumped to her feet and ran to her.

Daphne scooped her into a hug. "Hi, baby girl. Are you having fun?"

Hadley nodded. "Auntie Nay is here!"

"I see that." Daphne glanced at her sister, who was looking at her curiously.

Renee was tall and lean with high cheekbones and a perky nose, like their mother. She was into every fitness trend there was, from Pilates and kickboxing to hot yoga and mountain climbing. When Daphne had been a chubby thirteen-year-old wearing a D-cup bra, she'd been jealous of her gorgeous and popular fifteen-year-old sister. But then she'd overheard Renee crying one afternoon with a girlfriend about how she was too skinny and complaining that her younger sister had a better body than she did. Hearing that had affected Daphne so strongly, she'd gotten up the courage to talk with Renee about it later that night. Renee had told her that *every* girl hated their body, and that she'd give anything to find a way to love hers. That conversation had been the catalyst for Daphne to stop comparing herself to everyone else and to embrace her fuller body. She faltered from time to time, wishing she had fewer dimples or less cellulite, but more often than not, she was glad she could be comfortable in her own skin.

Until she was naked with a man.

At least that had been the case before Jock. Embarrassingly, she couldn't wait to get naked with him *again*. She tried to push those thoughts away as she set Hadley down and said, "Where's Dad?"

"He and Sean had a meeting at the firehouse about the carnival," her mother explained. The carnival was still several weeks away. Every year the firehouse ran a dunk tank, and it was always mobbed with single women.

"Sorry I missed him," Daphne said. "Renee, I didn't know you were going to be here."

"I got that new line of clothes in for the boutique that I told you about. I picked out a few things for Mom. I knew you'd want to pick out your own next time you come by." Renee pushed to her feet in her spandex capris and tight white tank top. She flipped her long chestnut hair—which she swore was dirty blond—over her shoulder, keeping her scrutinizing gaze locked on Daphne. "I'm glad I made it, because Hadley told us *all* about her new friend *Doc*. She seems to really like him."

"I love my Dock," Hadley said matter-of-factly as she plopped down on her bottom to play with her stuffed owl.

Daphne felt her cheeks burning and quickly looked away from Renee, who had somehow known with a single glance about Daphne's first kiss, the first time she'd been felt up, *and* the first time she'd had sex.

"Is he a doctor?" their mother asked as she got up to hug Daphne. Their mother was always on the move, but she never appeared harried. With delicate features and glossy light-brown hair cut just above her shoulders with a few wispy bangs, she looked like she belonged in a Hallmark movie. "Honey, are you using a new moisturizer? You are positively glowing. You have to tell me what you're using, because my skin has been terribly dry this summer."

Behind their mother, Renee stifled a laugh, pointed to Daphne, and did several hip thrusts.

Daphne turned away to hide her embarrassment and said, "*No*, Mom. I'm not using a new moisturizer."

"Really?" Their mother turned Daphne's face toward her, inspecting it more closely. "Maybe it's that tan you've picked up."

"You *are* glowing, Dee. Is Doc *your* new friend, too?" Renee waggled her brows. "Had said he gave her Owly and that he *cried.* Was that a cry of pleasure, maybe?"

*Ohmygod!* Daphne was going to tape Hadley's mouth shut and slaughter Renee. "He's a friend of both of ours," she said, ignoring her sister's crying comment and nervously putting away toys. "He's staying at Bayside, and yes, he gave her Owly, but he's not a doctor."

"Then why do they call him Doc?" their mother asked.

Renee smirked. "Maybe he likes to *play* doctor."

Daphne glowered at her.

"*Renee,*" their mother chided. Her eyes moved between the two sisters. "What is going on with you two?" She gasped, and suddenly her face brightened. "*Daphne?* Do you have a new beau?"

"Um…" Daphne suddenly felt like she was going to burst at the seams, but she didn't know how to answer. She made a strangled noise in her throat and said, "Maybe? Kind of? I think so, but I don't really know for sure."

"Oh, baby girl!" Their mother hugged her so tight Daphne couldn't breathe. "I want to hear everything!"

"Maybe not *everything,*" Renee said under her breath.

Daphne shot her a pleading look.

Renee took her hand and led her to the couch. "Okay, darling Daphne, talk to me."

Flanked by her mother and sister, Daphne said, "First of all, his name is Jack Steele. Jock is just a nickname given to him by the man he took care of for several years, and Had can't say *J*s, so she calls him *Dock.* He's a writer, but he stopped writing about ten years ago…" With an ache in her heart, she told them everything—from the first moment she and Jock had met and his reactions to Hadley, to the losses he'd suffered, his years with Harvey, and his struggles with writing and finding himself again—because it was the only way for them to truly understand who he was and the extent he was willing to go to for her and Hadley. "I can't explain *why*, given the way he first reacted to Hadley, but he's the only man who has lingered in my thoughts since Tim. And it seems the same for him, since we met last year." She told them about their evenings together—leaving out the dirty details—and his apology gifts, the flowers, dinners, and how he was trying to figure out how to deal with his triggers.

"Oh, honey," their mother said. "Jock sounds like a very special man who has been through more than anyone should ever have to. If he's willing to try to figure out how to move forward after everything he's been through, he must realize how wonderful you and Hadley are. He sounds like a very smart man."

"Thanks, Mom. He is."

"How do you feel when you're with him?" their mother asked.

"He makes me *feel* like…" She looked up at the ceiling, knowing her blush and ridiculous grin were giving everything away. The truth flew out like confetti and glitter. "Like a desirable *woman*. Not just like a mom, although he likes the mom part of me, too."

"I bet he likes the part of you that your baby came out of," Renee whispered for Daphne's ears only.

Daphne shot her a warning look.

"I'm sorry, but you know I'm not great with touchy-feely conversations." Renee's expression turned apologetic, and she said, "It's no wonder you two feel a connection. You're the most caring person I know, and it sounds as though he's very much like you. I'm happy for you."

"He is caring, and careful." She wanted to tell them that he tested her boundaries carefully, too, but that was too private to divulge. "I've never been with a man like him. He looks at me like Dad looks at you, Mom, and it feels so different from the way it was with Tim. Jock notices things about me, things I try to hide from everyone. It's a little scary to be with someone who sees me so clearly, but it's a good scary. And with all the stuff he's dealing with, he still thinks of *me* and Hadley, of *our* needs, *our* happiness. He's thoughtful and protective toward her, even with his limitations. He worries about making sure she doesn't feel like his reactions are her fault." She looked at Hadley playing with her owl and remembered how honest he'd been with her and how he'd sprang into action when she'd toddled toward the water. "I know not to make too much out of it yet, but I like him a lot."

"I'm so happy for you, honey," their mother said.

"I'm really happy for you, too," Renee said. "I've got my eye on a new guy at my gym."

"Really? What's he like?" Daphne asked.

"I don't know. I've only seen him a time or two, and we haven't talked yet. But who knows. Maybe we'll both get lucky."

"It's like I keep telling you girls," their mother said. "Relationships are like golf. If you don't get a hole in one the first time, don't give up. Sometimes you have to try lots of different clubs and angles and stances, use a lighter touch, or a tighter one, and keep at it until you get it in the hole. And then practice, practice, *practice*. Trust me, when you grab hold of the perfect club, you'll *know* it."

Daphne stifled a laugh, but Renee laughed so hard she choked.

"*Mom!*" Renee said between coughs. "You should *never* talk about holes again."

"Oh dear. That didn't sound right, did it?" Their mother covered her mouth, eyes wide, cheeks pinking up as quickly as Daphne's did.

"It's okay, Mom," Daphne said, tingly with thoughts of playing *golf* with Jock. "I get it."

"Apparently you're getting it good, based on that *glow*," Renee teased, making them all laugh.

As their mother wrapped an arm around each of them, Hadley toddled over and climbed onto Daphne's lap, bringing her reality front and center. This thing between her and Jock was much more dangerous than a game of golf. There weren't just two hearts at stake. There were *three*, and they'd all been hurt before, even if the littlest of them didn't realize it.

JOCK WALKED ALONG Wellfleet Pier with Daphne and Hadley, each of them eating an ice-cream cone, and felt like he was on top of the world. After enjoying the most glorious morning with Daphne, followed by his first day of productive writing in forever, he felt like a new man. He'd been astonished when he'd sat down at his laptop and the words had finally come. He had written only two chapters, but they were *good* chapters, even if he didn't quite understand the story they were beginning to form. That was the funny thing about writing. One idea could spark ten more, and the direction of the story could change with each one, until finally the perfect one clicked. But Jock had been elated to have written at all, and he knew that when the words flowed, it was best to let them continue and make sense of them later.

The pier was crowded with families enjoying the unusually warm evening. Teens rode skateboards, and couples meandered along the wharf going to and from Mac's Seafood, the Pearl restaurant, the Frying Pan Gallery, and other local shops. Daphne held Hadley's hand as they walked in the opposite direction of the crowds, toward the stage at the far end of the wharf. The setting sun cast a romantic glow over the bay, making their time together feel even more special. Surrounded by boats, the scent of the sea, and the familiar clank of metal against tall masts, Jock was reminded of home. It had been a long time since he'd let his mind wander in that direction without ghosts pushing it away. But Daphne's comment about making an effort with Archer had struck a chord, and he wondered if she was right. He'd also gotten a call from Levi and Joey earlier, and another from Sutton, both of which he was sure were made at Jules's prompting. Jules was still trying her best to wrangle him into going to their grandmother's birthday party. Talking to Joey had *almost* done the trick. That little girl had him wrapped around her finger, just as Hadley was starting to.

"You look deep in thought." Daphne bent to wipe ice cream from Hadley's cheek and said, "Are you thinking about what you wrote today?"

"I'm trying not to think too hard about what I've written. I don't want to jinx it."

"Good idea. I'm so happy you were able to write."

"Me too. I was actually thinking about home just now." He

leaned against the side of the stage, looking out at the boats as he ate his ice cream. "I spent a lot of time at the marina when I was young. Being here brings back memories."

"You mentioned that at dinner the other night. Are they good memories?" Daphne asked.

"Yeah. I had a great childhood. How could I not with so many brothers and sisters? It was filled with adventures and driving our parents nuts."

Hadley put her back against the stage beside him, mimicking his stance as she licked her cone. Her pink hoodie had drops of strawberry ice cream down her belly, and Owly was stuffed in the pocket. Jock placed his hand on her head, giving her a little pat. He didn't get the twinge of discomfort that he had yesterday.

She tilted her face up and said, "*Twade* ice *cweams?*"

Daphne laughed. "Sorry, Jock. We do that sometimes. Honey, I don't think Jock wants your half-eaten ice cream. Why don't you trade with Mommy?"

"I want *gween* ice *cweam*," she said with the most adorable pouty face.

It struck Jock that the sudden jolt of apprehension he usually felt at the sight of a pout didn't come; instead he felt the urge to do what he could to make her happy.

"It's okay. I like half-eaten strawberry ice cream," he said, and exchanged cones with Hadley. He'd never seen such an enormous smile on a tiny human being, and it tugged at all his heartstrings.

"Thank you." Hadley clung to the double-scoop cone with both hands, eyes dancing with delight as she held it up and said, "Look, Mommy!"

Mommy was looking all right. She was looking at Jock like

he'd hung the moon. And damn, he loved that. He blew her a kiss and finished the child-size cone in three bites.

As soon as his hands were empty, Hadley's arms darted up, nearly dropping the ice cream off the cone, and she said, "*Up!*"

Daphne was quick to snag the cone, looking hesitantly at Jock. She was ready to save him, but after last night and that morning, it was time he started saving himself.

He wanted to hold Hadley, to kiss her sticky cheeks and be the guy who could carry her on his shoulders. He had every confidence that he would get there, but they were having too nice of a night to risk it, so he said, "How about if we sit together?" He lifted her up and set her on the edge of the stage. He hoisted himself up beside Hadley, and put his arm around her to keep her from falling.

"That's fun," Daphne encouraged, giving Hadley back her cone, flashing an adoring smile at Jock, which made him feel like a king.

Hadley took a bite of her ice cream and beamed at him. She put her hand on his knee and said, "My Dock," and kept it there as she ate her ice cream.

Daphne was watching them with a dreamy expression. He winked and hugged Hadley to his side. He was literally holding Daphne's heart in his hand, having no idea how he had ever kept his distance from either of them.

"Maybe you can share Jock with Mommy," Daphne said, her dreaminess turning seductive as she licked around her ice cream with an enticing tease in her eyes.

Oh *yes*, his sweet, innocent Daphne had a wild side, and he couldn't wait to explore it further. She'd awoken the sleeping giant, the man who had known *only* how to pursue and conquer. Now he didn't want to imagine a day without her and

Hadley in his life. He knew in order to deserve them, he had to conquer *all* of the ghosts, not just get ahead of the triggers that losing Liam and Kayla had left behind, but also finally resurrecting his relationship with Archer. The trouble was, as much as he wanted to fix things with Archer, he wasn't quite sure how yet.

After they finished their ice cream, they headed back to the resort. Hadley chattered on about her yummy ice cream and how next time she wanted to get *gween* like Dock.

Jock hung out in their living room while Daphne bathed Hadley and got her ready for bed. He liked being there, listening to their nightly routine. Hadley had a lot to say and Daphne gave her daughter her full attention, answering every question without rushing. She laughed a lot, reminding Jock of his own mother. His mother had never just been in the same room with them; she'd been mentally present, paying attention to everything they said even when they didn't think she was. Jock remembered times when he and Archer would argue quietly and call each other names and their mother would give them one of those looks that only a mother could give, instantly silencing her rowdy boys. His mother also knew when he needed space. Like he had for the last decade. But suddenly the two-hour phone calls they had every few weeks didn't feel like enough.

The chains on his dungeon were rattling again, only this time it wasn't the ghosts trying to come out. It was Jock trying to figure out a way to get back to all the people he'd shut out, back to the life he'd left behind. Sure, he had a couple of short visits with his family each year. But after spending time with Daphne and Hadley, he was feeling the distance. And if *he* was feeling it now that his head was clearing, how strongly had his family been feeling it this whole time? They didn't know about

Archer's scathing declaration standing between Jock and the island. They saw only a son or a brother who had taken himself away from their family.

Hadley toddled out of the hallway in a pair of yellow pajamas and jumped into his lap. His chest tightened and his throat clogged as she threw her arms around his neck and planted a tiny wet kiss on his cheek.

"'Night, Dock. Love you."

She wriggled off his lap before he could react, darting toward her mother. Daphne's mouth hung open as Jock touched that little wet spot on his cheek and said, "'Night, Had. Sweet dreams."

Daphne's eyes glistened.

"'Night!" Hadley yelled, and ran toward the hallway. "Story, Mama!"

As Daphne carried Hadley down the hall, Jock sank back against the couch cushion, steeped in new emotions. His pulse raced, but it was a good feeling, the kind he wanted to run *to*, not away from.

AS DAPHNE READ to Hadley, she knew she'd never forget the sight of her little girl launching herself at big, broad Jock and giving him a good-night kiss as if it were the most natural thing in the world. In just a few seconds, Jock had gone from sheet-white to exuding the warm emotions people couldn't help but emit when they were around a child they cared about. She'd thought nothing could compare to Jock swapping his ice-cream cone for Hadley's slobbered-on cone, but witnessing his transformation and the adoration in his eyes had made her heart soar.

Daphne finished reading and closed the book. As she set it on the nightstand, she noticed Jock leaning against the doorframe watching them with that same warm expression and wondered how long he'd been there.

"I'll just be a second," she whispered. "I usually sing to her."

"No rush. Do you mind if I stay?"

"Stay, Dock," Hadley said sleepily, reaching her little hand out to him.

Goose bumps chased over Daphne's flesh as he came into the room and sat on the floor beside the bed, leaning his back against the nightstand.

He took Hadley's hand and pressed a kiss to the back of it. "Close your eyes, princess."

*Princess.*

Daphne had no idea how she wasn't melting into a puddle of goo and soaking into the mattress. The smile on Hadley's face as she nestled deeper beneath her blankets got her all choked up. With her heart in her throat, she whisper-sang to Hadley. It didn't take long for Hadley to nod off. Jock carefully placed her hand on the bed, his eyes meeting Daphne's as she sang. She felt as though she and Hadley were cocooned by him, and he wasn't even touching her. But in the next breath, he sat up taller, his expression turning serious. He pulled his phone from his pocket and began thumbing something out. She wondered what had changed. Was he having second thoughts about what he felt for them? Was it all too much? Did he need an escape?

Her nerves twisted into knots.

He was still typing when she finished singing, and he didn't look up as she climbed from the bed. She touched his shoulder, startling him. He glanced at Hadley, and a distracted smile lifted his lips as he took Daphne's hand and rose to his feet.

"She's really something." He was still clutching his phone as they went into the living room. "You're amazing with her."

"Thanks, but is everything okay? I'm sorry she got away from me and ran to you like that," she said.

"Sorry?" He looked confused.

"You're typing furiously, like something is wrong."

"Are you kidding? When she ran to me, that was the second greatest moment of my life." He pocketed his phone and put his arms around her. "Daph, you two are changing my world. You've opened some kind of vortex inside me. I'm typing because when I was sitting there, I got an idea for my book. It changes everything I've already written, but I think it's good. Maybe even *fantastic*. I just don't want to forget any of it."

Relief and excitement swept through her. "Then what are you doing standing here? Go write while it's still fresh."

"Really?" he asked, brows knitted. "I don't want you to feel slighted."

"Jock, this is what you have been trying to do for a *year*. How can I feel slighted after the morning we spent together and how you were with Hadley tonight? I'm not going anywhere. But those words in your head? I don't know much about writing, but I'd imagine it's like when I used to plan events. When inspiration hit, I'd get into a *zone*, pull a million things together, and sometimes I *still* couldn't work fast enough to capture every idea before it flitted away." She pressed her lips to his, elated for him, and for *them*. "Go write for an hour, or *five*. Write all night if the inspiration lasts. Whatever it takes, soak up the ideas and turn them into something magical."

"God, I—" He closed his mouth, the muscles in his jaw bunching, but the depth of emotion in his eyes was as inescapable as a warm summer breeze. He crushed his lips to hers and said, "I am so lucky to have you."

He kissed her again, so sensually she couldn't resist putting her hands beneath the back of his shirt just so she could feel more of him.

He made a hungry noise, his muscles flexing against her palms, and said, "The hell with writing. I don't want to leave you."

Her heart leapt, but her mind reined it in. "You have to." She gathered her courage and said, "Besides, you know where those steps to my bedroom door are if you feel like celebrating after you're done writing."

Flames flashed in his eyes, but in the next second worry pushed to the forefront. "What about Hadley?"

There it was again, the very special *extra mile*. "We'll just have to be quiet."

"Hm…" He arched a brow. "Another challenge."

# Chapter Fourteen

HADLEY DARTED INTO the kitchen Thursday morning as Daphne went to the window, hoping they hadn't missed Jock leaving for his run. She and Hadley had been ready a few minutes *early* every day this week, which was a refreshing change. That was a nice side effect of Daphne and Jock's relationship. Their coupledom was doing great things for him, too. The writing bug had hit Jock hard. Sunday night he'd written until nearly two in the morning. Then he'd come to Daphne's bedroom door to celebrate, and *oh*, what a glorious celebration it was! He'd been writing up a storm ever since, though he wouldn't let her read anything he'd written yet. He had come over after dinner Monday and Tuesday night and had helped put Hadley to bed. Last night they'd taken Hadley down to the beach after dinner. Hadley had loved it, and so had Daphne. It was wonderful being a real couple, holding hands and enjoying themselves. Once they were sure Hadley was asleep each night, they'd fallen into each other's arms. Every time they were together was better than the last. Not just because the sex was incredible, but because it brought them even closer together. They'd lie there talking, holding each other, sharing stories and secrets. Daphne should be exhausted, but she felt more alive than ever. Sexier and bolder, too. He made her want to explore her sexuality with him, and he made it easy by making her feel safe and not only desirable, but *cherished*. She wondered how she could have ever felt loved by Tim, when Jock was so much more caring and attentive, interested in every facet of her life and her feelings.

She spotted Rick out the window, heading for Jock's cottage, and called out to Hadley, "Come on, Had!"

Hadley toddled out of the kitchen holding an apple. "Bweakfast for Dock."

Daphne didn't have the heart to tell her that he wouldn't be able to eat it while he was running. She worried a little bit about letting Hadley get too attached to him in case things didn't work out between them. But Hadley had been smiling more these days, and not just for him. Her transition from daycare to preschool had been seamless, which Daphne had hoped would be the case. Maybe it was the start of preschool, or just a coincidence that she and Jock were getting along so well. But Daphne had noticed that she and Hadley were bringing new light to Jock's eyes, too. It turned out that Jock did know a few things about baby steps. He hadn't taken the plunge and picked up Hadley yet, but every day he and Hadley got a little closer.

"Grab Owly and let's go see the girls for breakfast."

"*After* Dock's *bweakfast*," Hadley said emphatically as she snagged Owly from the coffee table.

"Of course." Daphne shouldered Hadley's backpack and her own bag, and they headed out the front door.

"*Huwwy*, Mommy!" Hadley said as Daphne locked the door.

"Yes, ma'am," Daphne teased. "Let's go."

Hadley slid down the steps on her bottom, making her

usual singsong "Ah*haah*ha" noise as she went. The minute the front door was open, Hadley hurried down the steps and ran toward Jock, Rick, Jett, and Dean, who were talking by Jock's cottage. "*Dock!*"

Daphne put their things in her car and followed her daughter toward the man who was rocking her world—in and out of the bedroom. Jock crouched in the grass with a genuine smile as Hadley plowed into him, giving him a big hug, and presented him with the apple. Daphne filled with admiration, and something so much bigger she didn't even try to name it.

Jett looked at Daphne with a quizzical expression and said, "This is new."

Rick appeared as confused as Jett, but Dean was smirking. Daphne wondered about that smirk. She'd told Chloe about her and Jock's relationship, but she'd made her swear not to spill the beans until she and Jock were ready to tell everyone themselves. But they had been so swept up in each other, they hadn't even talked about telling their friends yet. And now she swore the sun was shining on them like a spotlight.

A bead of sweat dotted her brow as Jock rose to his feet, putting a protective hand on Hadley's shoulder. He met Jett's gaze and said, "Yeah, we've been working on it."

"Anything *else* you're working on?" Rick asked, eyeing Jock.

Dean sidled up to Rick and said, "That's none of our business."

The look that passed between Jock and Dean made Daphne wonder if he'd already told Dean about them. But Jock looked at her with that approval-seeking gaze she already knew by heart. She nodded, touched that he'd given her the chance to wait.

"Actually, the answer to that is yes," Jock said. "We are."

Jett and Rick looked at her, and she felt her cheeks burning. Would she *ever* stop blushing, or was she destined to blush forever like her mother?

"Well, *damn.*" Jett slapped Jock on the back. "Great—"

"No hit Dock!" Hadley snapped, scowling at Jett, making everyone laugh.

Jett held his hands up and said, "Sorry, Had. It was a *nice* touch. I like Jock."

Hadley wrapped her arms around Jock's leg and said, "*My* Dock."

A flutter of worry rose in Daphne's chest at Hadley's clinging to Jock's leg, but Jock looked at her with something akin to *pride* in his eyes, washing those worries away. She was amazed at how far he'd come.

"Looks like Uncle Jetty has been replaced," Rick teased.

As the guys teased each other, Jock leaned in and kissed Daphne. "Hey, beautiful. I guess we're out of the closet. Want to have lunch today?"

She nodded. "I'd like that."

"I'll bring sandwiches around noon," he offered.

"I'm hungwy, Mommy." Hadley tugged on Daphne's hand as she called out, "Bye, Dock!"

They headed over to Summer House, where Emery, Desiree, Chloe, Tegan, and Harper were deep in conversation over waffles and berries. Cosmos darted out from under the table as Hadley made a beeline for Aaron's bassinet.

"*Awwon* sleeping, *Desway?*" Hadley whispered as Cosmos sniffed her legs.

"Yes. He's very tired today," Desiree answered. "He was up a lot last night."

"I *kiss'm* soft?" Hadley asked.

"Maybe you should wait until he's awake," Daphne suggested. "Do you want to eat, or play with Cosmos first?"

"Play!" Hadley ran across the yard with Cosmos on her heels.

Harper nudged her red sunglasses to the bridge of her nose and said, "I want to have five little girls just like her." She stood up to hug Daphne, looking cute in a pair of cutoffs and a brightly colored batik top. A thin braid hung down the left side of her long blond hair. "You look radiant, Daph. I don't know what you're doing differently, but keep it up."

"Thanks." *I'm on the hot-sex-every-night regimen.* Daphne sat down and all eyes locked on her. She glared at Chloe and said, "You promised you wouldn't tell."

"Don't look at me," Chloe said. "I'm not the one who just kissed Jock out in the open."

"You guys *saw* that?" Daphne asked.

They all nodded, talking over each other with approving grins.

"Looks like I've missed too many breakfasts," Harper said. "When did you and Jock become an item? How come nobody told me?"

"We didn't know," Tegan said. "But it explains why he's suddenly found his muse."

"How long have you two been doing the dirty?" Emery asked, making Daphne's cheeks burn. "Dean saw Jock climbing the back steps to your bedroom last night at around eleven. I *knew* something was going on."

"Dean *saw* him?" Daphne asked. "His smirk makes much more sense now."

Emery laughed. "Don't worry. He's happy for you guys. He said you've been all moony-eyed around the office since we caught you two playing Scrabble, which I still think was a cover-up for a hot-and-heavy make-out sesh."

"It was *not*," Daphne said with a giggle.

"It's been killing me holding it in," Chloe said exasperatedly.

"You knew about them?" Desiree asked.

Chloe popped a blueberry into her mouth and said, "Daph sent me an SOS text on Sunday with an eggplant and a *peach* emoji."

Emery and Tegan gasped.

"No!" Tegan covered her mouth. "I had no idea Jock was so dirty."

"Thanks, Chloe," Daphne said sarcastically. "I didn't know a peach meant *butt*." She lowered her voice and said, "I thought it was like, a *lady peach*."

Everyone cracked up, except Daphne and Desiree.

"You should have seen me when I got the text," Chloe said, trying to catch her breath between laughs. "I was like, *What? You let him do that to you already? You are a dirty girl.*"

Daphne covered her face.

"I'm *so* confused," Desiree said. "A peach means a *butt*? I don't unders…" Her eyes widened, and then she gasped, her cheeks pinking up. "*Oh my goodness.* Oh no! You guys, I texted Violet the other day and said that Rick ate my peach pie, and I used the emoji for peach! No wonder she responded with the shocked emoji and flames."

They all laughed hysterically.

"That's worse than me," Daphne said as she put food on her and Hadley's plates.

"But Daphne *did* send Chloe the eggplant, and we all know what that means," Harper said. "Our sweet Daphne is getting a little mattress action."

"*Stop*," Daphne whispered. But she couldn't help adding, "There's nothing *little* about the action I'm getting," earning more uproarious laughter.

"I want to know *everything*," Tegan said. "I told you he was worth being patient."

Daphne kept an eye on Hadley playing in the grass with Cosmos across the yard while she filled her friends in about all things Jock related. Much to her friends' disappointment, she didn't spill the dirty details of their incredibly hot love life, but she did tell them about their outings and the romantic things he'd said and done. "I've never been happier. I know it's been years since I've even kissed a man. But kissing Jock is heavenly. It's even better than the erotic, sensual kisses in our romance novels. I could kiss him for *days*."

"There's nothing quite as nice as a man who knows how to use his mouth," Emery said with a wink.

"I know it's fast, and he still has a way to go with Hadley, but it just feels so *right*."

Chloe scoffed. "*Fast?* You and Jock started making eyes at each other a year ago, and I bet if he didn't have issues with kids, you two would have gotten together then."

"Agreed," Tegan said.

Daphne thought back to Gavin's birthday party, and she knew in her heart they were right. She was beginning to think they were written in the stars.

"Remember at my wedding how he kept looking at Daphne?" Harper said. "I thought for sure he was going to ask you to dance."

"I don't know about that, but I know I was looking at *him* that night. He's always hot, but in that suit? *Whew...*" Daphne fanned her face. "That man makes me tingle all over. Not only that, but he's been helping me put Hadley to bed, which is huge in and of itself, given his trouble with kids." She lowered her voice and said, "But I never knew that could be an aphrodisiac. Seeing his feelings for my daughter grow makes me fall even harder for him. I even went out and bought sexy lingerie yesterday before I picked up Hadley."

"Damn, girl," Chloe said. "You didn't tell me about the lingerie."

"It was a last-minute decision. I feel so much more for him than I ever did for Tim. What does that say about me? Something bad?"

"It says you have good taste," Emery said.

"You were a teenager when you met Tim, right? You were too young to know the difference between infatuation and something deeper," Desiree said reassuringly. "And now you're a mother, and we both know that motherhood changes everything."

"I definitely view things differently now," Daphne agreed.

"Let's not forget that Tim was an ass," Chloe chimed in. "He was also in his early twenties. He wasn't a *man*, like Jock."

"And Jock hasn't lived an easy life," Tegan pointed out. "There's no comparison even to most guys his own age."

"I guess that's true," Daphne said. "There's so much to think about, and when we're together, I really don't want to think at all. But we're trying to do right by Hadley, so while we're *together* every night, Jock leaves before she gets up in the morning. But I hate that. Last night we set an alarm for four a.m. so we could sleep in each other's arms for part of the night. It was wonderful to be able to fall asleep after...you know...and not feel rushed. I'm not saying I *would* have him stay until morning because it's too soon for Hadley, but I want him to *so* badly. I haven't been in a relationship for so long, I'm not sure what's normal and what's not. Is it weird that I wish he could stay over even though I know he can't?"

The girls exchanged knowing glances and said "No" in unison.

"That's just *one* of the ways I knew Dean was the man for me. I wanted to be with him all the time," Emery said.

"Same with me and Justin," Chloe said.

Tegan waved her hand. "Me and Jett, too."

"You know it was like that for me and Gavin," Harper chimed in. "Heck, I still miss most of our breakfasts because we don't want to get out of bed."

"It was like that for me and Rick, too," Desiree said. "But as a mom, I understand your worry, Daphne."

Daphne pushed to her feet to intercept Hadley on her way to the table and said, "I'm pretty sure he feels the same." She thought about how it had taken them nearly twenty minutes to finally say goodbye in the wee hours of the morning and how Jock had gazed into her eyes and said, *How can I miss you when I haven't even left yet?* She scooped her giggling daughter into her arms and said, "Actually, I *know* he feels the same, but as I said, I've got a chickadee to think about."

"*I'm* chickadee," Hadley said.

"Yes, you are." *And I wouldn't want it any other way.*

AFTER HIS RUN, Jock spent the morning being led down a literary path he was still trying to understand. The story he'd started writing over the weekend had been about a serial killer stalking women in a small Southern town. The villain tortured his victims for weeks in the cellar of an old mansion, keeping the women caged, in various states of despair. But over the next few days, as Jock had honed in on crafting his characters' personalities and backstories, he started feeling protective of the heroine. Every time he tried to give the villain an opening, he found himself devising ways in which the heroine avoided capture, which made the story's progression next to impossible. But the words kept flowing, and though they weren't leading in the direction he'd anticipated, he was building an impressive world with complex characters facing real-life problems, and he was loving it. Something inside him had definitely changed. He found himself giving more depth and story to the detective who was tracking the villain rather than the villain himself. Making the detective keener, giving him more resources and unexpected emotions. He'd tried to force the darkness onto the page, but it was like swimming against a riptide.

At first he'd thought he was just so into Daphne, she'd infiltrated his every thought. But while that was true, those feelings weren't *hindering* his writing. She'd coaxed the writer in him out from the darkness by making him feel again, and those feelings were making his writing *stronger*, his story deeper and more meaningful. She and Hadley brought beauty into his life, and after living through enough horror and pain for three lifetimes, he didn't want to inflict torture on anyone, not even on fictional characters. He didn't even want to *think* dark thoughts. Not when he had someone so full of sunshine and positivity to share his life with.

He pulled into the resort with lunch, excited to see Daphne, and was shocked to see his sister's bright-yellow Jeep with the

Happy End gift shop sign on the door parked out front. He'd given Jules a hard time about naming her shop Happy End because he didn't like the jokes it spurred from guys. But while Jules was the most effervescent woman he knew, she was also one of the most stubborn, and she had insisted it made perfect sense since her shop was located at the end of Main Street.

He grabbed the lunch bag and headed up to the office wondering what she was doing there. He heard Jules talking as he climbed the steps to the porch.

"I understand that you *normally* don't give out the cottage numbers of guests, but I'm his *sister*. Can't you make an exception just this once?"

"I wish I could," Daphne said sweetly. "But you'd be surprised how many people have used the *sister* or *brother* line. Can't you just call him? Let him know you're here?"

"If you knew my brother, you wouldn't ask that. He's as reclusive as they come, and he'd just claim to be busy. Although..." Her tone lightened and she said, "He is handsome and single. I bet you could bring him out of his shell—"

Jock pulled open the screen door before Jules could pimp him out, and both women looked over. Daphne appeared amused, smiling brightly, and Jules looked like she'd just walked off a college campus, in shorts and an embroidered tank top. Her hair hung in loose golden-brown waves down her back, with the top layer in a ponytail in the middle of her head. That *water fountain* had been her signature look since she was a little girl, and it made her look about nineteen instead of twenty-five.

"Jack!" Jules launched her petite, energetic self into his arms.

"Hi, Jules." He winked to Daphne as he embraced his sister. "What are you doing here?"

"I had to pick up a few things from a local artist for my

shop, and I thought I'd stop by to see your new digs and take you to lunch." Jules waved at Daphne and said, "But this charming woman, *who just might be single*, runs a tight ship." She whispered the part about being single.

"Her name is *Daphne*," he said, not buying her reason for the visit.

"Well, Daphne wouldn't give me your cottage number."

"I'm sorry," Daphne said. "It's company policy. Jock and I are friends. I wouldn't try to keep you from seeing him."

Jules's eyes sparked with curiosity. "How good of a friend *are* you? Because I could really use some help convincing him to come to our grandmother's birthday party the weekend after next."

"*Jules*," Jock warned. "I knew there was a reason for your visit."

Jules threw her hands up. "Of *course* there's a reason. If you weren't so stubborn, I *could* be here for a fun visit. But it takes an act of God to get you home, and Grandma might not have many birthdays left." She sniffled, and tears sprang to her eyes, as if he would buy that she might cry. "Do you have any idea how hard it is for the rest of us to not see you? I *miss* you, Jackie."

Daphne's expression softened, and she gave him a pleading look.

"Don't buy into her performance, Daph." He put the lunch bag on Daphne's desk and said, "Jules was named Best Actress in high school."

Jules bounced on her toes. "I *was*! That was pretty believable, wasn't it, Daphne?"

"I thought so," Daphne agreed. "I thought your tears were real."

Jock shook his head. "We've taken up enough of Daphne's time."

"Wait. Daphne, are you single?" Jules grabbed Jock's arm and said, "Because beneath his stubbornness, my brother is an amazing guy, and he's *very* single."

"I'm not single, Jules." Jock pulled his arm free and reached for Daphne's hand, earning a blush.

"You two are a couple? *Yay!*" Jules clapped her hands. "No wonder you didn't take my call that night. You can bring her to the party! You'd love it, Daphne. We all pitch in to help set up at the winery, and then we play touch football, a Steele-family tradition. Everyone goes all out and dresses up for the party, and all of our closest friends, and my grandmother's *Bra Brigade*, come for a fancy dinner and dancing."

"That sounds amazing, but what's a Bra Brigade?" Daphne asked.

"You wouldn't believe it if I told you. Let's just say my grandmother and her friends have wilder sides than I do," Jules said with a giggle. "I hope you'll come. It's an all-day affair…"

As his sister went on about the afternoon and the party, Jock whispered in Daphne's ear, "I brought your favorite sandwich from the Sundial Café."

"Were you two supposed to have lunch together?" Jules asked. He'd forgotten she had supersonic hearing. "I'm sorry. I didn't mean to mess up your date."

"It's fine," Daphne said. "You two should go have lunch and visit. I have loads of work to do for my book club anyway."

"You're in a book club? How fun. I'd love to hear about it." Then Jules whispered, "At the party!"

"Daph, do you mind if I get her out of here and make up for our missed lunch tonight?"

"Of course not," Daphne said.

"You guys are so cute together." Jules hurried over to Daphne and said, "I'm a hugger." She threw her arms around Daphne.

Jock kissed Daphne, and then he took Jules by the arm and said, "Let's go, nosy."

"It was nice to meet you," Daphne said as Jock dragged Jules toward the door.

Jules looked over her shoulder and said, "Please work on him! You'd love our family, and I want to hear about your book club!"

Jock walked her down the steps to his SUV, and as he opened the passenger door, he said, "You can't seriously think it would be a selling point to bring her around me and Archer, do you?"

"I *like* her. Why didn't you tell me you had a girlfriend?"

"Do you really have to ask?" He went around to the driver's side, and as they settled into their seats, he said, "And don't go blabbing about me and Daphne to anyone back home, okay? I'm just starting to write again, and the last thing I need is to get a hundred phone calls about my private life."

"You're *writing*?" she asked as he drove out of the parking lot. "Look at you, getting your groove on in the bedroom *and* at the computer."

He looked at her out of the corner of his eye and said, "Nice talk coming from my baby sister."

"I'm happy for you, Jack. I worry about you closing yourself off for all those years and then traveling to who knows where. You could have come home, you know."

"I did come home, and for the record, I called you several times when I was traveling." He tried to always keep in touch with her. She'd beaten cancer, but cancer was a fickle beast, and he would always worry about it coming back.

He drove down the main drag in Wellfleet, heading for the Flying Fish café, Jules's favorite pizza and sandwich restaurant. It was tucked away on a side street, where they could sit outside and talk without having to deal with crowds.

"Stopping by Mom and Dad's for twenty minutes after a wedding is hardly considered coming home," she said. "I want to hear all about Daphne. She's beautiful, and when you kissed her, she *blushed*. I haven't seen a girl blush since high school. She must be really sweet."

He parked and said, "She is, and she doesn't need the nightmare of me and Archer thrust upon her, okay?"

Jules rolled her eyes as they climbed out. "Does she know about it?"

"Yes," he said as they headed up to the deck. He ordered two iced teas from the window. They grabbed menus and their drinks and sat at a table beneath the umbrella of a large tree.

"She does? About the accident and everything?"

He nodded and stared at the menu.

"You really like her, don't you?" Jules asked.

"Yes, very much."

Jules put down her menu and drummed her fingers on the table. "Then tell me about her."

"Jules, can we drop it? I don't need to become the talk of the island."

"I'm not a blabbermouth." She sat back and crossed her arms, eyes narrowing.

He cocked a grin. "I seem to remember a number of times when you got me and Archer in trouble."

"I was a little kid," she countered.

He set his menu down and said, "I got a call from Levi and Joey, and one from Sutton last weekend. Any of that ring a bell?"

"That was *different*. I can't do all the heavy lifting in the family." She stirred her iced tea with her straw and said, "Come on, Jackie, *please*? I promise not to tell anyone." She drew an *X* over her heart.

Resisting Jules over the phone was one thing, but he'd never been able to deny her anything when they were face-to-face because he would forever see her as his baby sister lying in a hospital bed. "Fine. Let me place our order first," he relented. "P and P?" Pepperoni and pineapple pizza had always been her favorite.

Her face lit up. "You know it."

He ordered their pizza, giving himself a few minutes to think about how much to divulge about his and Daphne's relationship. Just thinking about Daphne made him want to tell Jules everything about her, but he knew that once she heard about Hadley, she'd have dozens of questions, and he didn't want to deal with that. He decided not to mention Hadley. His decision came with a hefty dose of guilt, but for now he'd rather err on the side of sanity.

"How long have you been seeing her?" Jules asked as he sat down.

"We met last year at a party. It feels like we've been seeing each other for months, but it's pretty recent." He sipped his drink, thinking about how much had changed since they'd started seeing each other.

Jules tapped her fingernails on the table. "She really does have you twisted up, doesn't she?"

"You could say that, but it'd probably be more accurate to

say she's *untwisting* me. She took me by surprise. I haven't ever been drawn to anyone like I am to her."

"So, my brother the hookup artist is taming his wild ways?"

Jock shook his head. "You know me better than that."

"No one really knows you anymore, Jack. I remember you as a cocky guy who all the girls loved when you lived at home, but I don't know if you're a hookup artist or what now. I only know what you tell me, which I could recite in my sleep—*you're fine, you're trying to write, you're not coming home*. So please tell me who you are, because I want to know."

Emotions stacked up inside him at the plea in her voice. Had he really been *that* closed off? "I'm not an asshole, Jules. I used to be cocky—you're right about that. But I was never a hookup artist, and after losing Kayla and Liam, women were the last thing on my mind. But shortly after Harvey died, I met Daphne, and for more than a year, I couldn't get her off my mind."

"Then why did you leave the Cape and travel? Why not stay and ask her out?"

"Because I was messed up. I'm still messed up, Jules. This crap between me and Archer isn't right, and I'm dealing with a hell of a lot of other stuff, too. I left to travel in an effort to clear my head. I thought I could figure out how to fix things with Archer, and forget Daphne, because I didn't think she needed a guy like me in her life. But there was no forgetting her. She's one of the reasons I'm here."

"Well, first of all, you're a great guy, Jack. You have the biggest heart of anyone I've ever met. You're creative, and you're funny, and you're *kind*, which is hard to find in guys these days. But I thought you came back to the Cape to help Tegan."

"I did. But Tegan doesn't need my help anymore. I stayed, and I'm renting at Bayside, because Daphne is there. I've never met anyone like her. She's obviously gorgeous, but she's also sweet, strong, and smart. She makes me laugh, and she makes me feel things I haven't felt in a long time. She's incredibly insightful, and she's interested in who I am as a person. I've never been with a woman who was interested in me in that way. I was so young when I was with Kayla, everything was different. We lived together, but we were in a whole different place in our lives. We were out having fun, living the high of my good fortune." Though Jock had never admitted that he wasn't in love with Kayla to any of his siblings, now he wanted Jules to know the truth, if only to show her the difference in how he felt about Daphne. "You were so young when Kayla and I were together, I'm sure you never thought about my feelings for her. This might come as a shock—you might not want to hear it, and I'm pretty sure you won't understand it—but I wasn't in love with Kayla. I never felt for her what I already feel for Daphne."

She studied his face for a moment, her brow furrowed. "I didn't know that, but why wouldn't I understand it?"

"Because she was pregnant, and we lived together."

"A baby doesn't equate to love, Jack. But you always did the right thing, so it doesn't surprise me that you stayed with her. Does Archer know? Is that why he's still so angry with you?"

"No. I never told him. He's angry because she's gone, and she was his best friend."

"Was she in love with you?" Jules asked.

"No. But you need to keep all this to yourself."

"You already told me that."

He raised his brows.

"Okay. I get it. But I'd never say anything about this. Getting you to come home is one thing, but what you went through with Kayla is totally different. I know how private that is. Thank you for trusting me."

"Things were different with me and Kayla. We were friends who were going to have a baby together and try to make it work. I wanted to love her, for the baby's sake, but I never really knew what was missing. I'm starting to understand it now. I've only been with Daphne a little while, and I care about everything she does, what she's been through, what she dreams of. When she told me about her past and how she'd been hurt, I hurt *for* her. Kayla and I never had that kind of relationship. We didn't talk about anything of substance, not my writing, her job, our lives outside of our apartment. Daphne and I share everything—the good, the bad, and the boring." He laughed softly and said, "She's so supportive. She tried to brainstorm horror stories with me even though the mere thought of them terrifies her. The point is, we already care about each other. I'm starting to think Daphne and I were meant to meet."

"Oh, Jack." Jules reached across the table and put her hand over his. "I'm thrilled for you."

"Thanks. Me too, and I kind of can't believe I just told *you* all of that."

She pretended to lock her mouth shut and throw away the key. "You should bring her home and let everyone be happy for you. You deserve that."

The woman at the order window called Jock's name. He pushed to his feet and said, "I'll get the food, and you *forget* everything you just heard."

When he returned with the pizza, he served them each a piece and said, "Can we change the subject now?"

"Yes, and I promise I won't say a word to anyone, but just keep this in mind. You always say you're staying away because the island is Archer's home. But, Jack, it's *mine*, too, and it's Mom's and Dad's, and many of your friends'." She took a bite of pizza and said, "You belong there as much as Archer does."

He'd been thinking about that a lot more lately. "I'll keep that in mind. Now fill me in. How are Mom and Dad?"

"As ridiculous as ever. I swear every time I go to their house, Dad is grabbing Mom's butt or they're making out in the kitchen."

Jock laughed. "Good for them. We're lucky, you know. Look at the Silvers. They can't even live in the same house." Their friends' parents, Alexander and Margot Silver, ran the Silver House. They were best friends and they were married, but they had lived in separate houses for as long as Jock could remember. They acted more like friends with benefits than a true couple.

"True," she said. "Did Levi tell you about Archer's latest prank?"

"No. What did he do?"

Jules giggled and said, "He met a woman at the vineyard who had just bought a house in Harborside and was looking for a handyman. She was complaining to Archer that between work and whatever else she did, she had a hard time meeting eligible bachelors. I think she was hitting on Archer, but he told her that Husbands for Hire was a front for a high-class *escort* service and to ask for *Levi*." Levi owned one of many branches of Husbands for Hire, which was *not* an escort service. They handled handyman work, renovations, mechanics, and other odd jobs.

"No shit? That's classic."

"*Yes*, and according to Levi, she did *not* want to take no for an answer. But Archer warned her that Levi would pretend not to offer that kind of service in case she was an undercover policewoman." She laughed and said, "You guys always think up the best pranks."

They enjoyed many more laughs as they finished lunch. She caught him up on each of his siblings, and when they got back to the resort, Jock showed her his cottage, which she absolutely loved, except she said it was missing one thing. She pulled a framed family photograph out of her bag and put it on a bookshelf, just like she had when he'd lived at Harvey's.

He draped an arm around her shoulder and walked her to her car, which was still by the office. "I'm really glad you came, sis."

"I know," she said sassily. "You can't go too long without seeing me or you'll have withdrawals. I almost forgot to tell you—Grant is back, and *boy* does he need you."

Grant Silver had been one of Jock's closest friends when they were growing up. When Jock went to college, Grant had joined the military, and then he'd gone to work for Darkbird, a civilian company that carried out covert missions for the military. Grant had lost a leg during a mission almost a year ago, and he hadn't been back to the island since.

"I'm glad he's back. After what he's been through, it's good for him to be near family. Why does he need me? I've barely seen him since I moved away."

"Because you were one of his closest friends. Belly feels like she lost the brother she's known for all these years. He puts Archer's broodiness to shame." Grant's younger sister Bellamy, who Jules called *Belly*, worked for her at the gift shop.

"Sounds like Bellamy needs you more than Grant needs me.

I'm still working out my own shit. But Grant's been through hell—cut him some slack. I'm sure he'll come around."

"That's what everyone said about you." She rested her head on his shoulder and said, "Promise me you'll think about coming to the party? You know more than anyone that there's no guarantee of tomorrow. Grandma's getting old."

Jock gritted his teeth. "That was low."

"At least I didn't pull the cancer card," she teased.

She'd pulled the stress-causes-cancer card on him many times during the first year he'd lived with Harvey. It had almost worked, but Archer's hatred had overshadowed her pleas.

"I promise," he said.

"*Yay!*" She hugged him and headed up the office steps. "I want to say goodbye to Daphne."

"She's *working*," he reminded her, following her to the office.

"I'll be quick." Jules darted inside and gave Daphne a hug. She said she hoped to see her at the party and whispered something Jock couldn't hear. Whatever she'd said made Daphne laugh.

Jock had never brought a girl home from college to meet his family, and they'd already known Kayla. It was strange, and nice, to see Daphne and Jules forging a friendship.

He embraced Jules, thanked her for coming, and held the door open for her. She strutted down to her Jeep and waved as she drove away. Jock closed the distance between him and Daphne, glad she was alone in the office.

"She's so nice," she said as he drew her into his arms.

"Yeah, she's a good egg. See you tonight? Should I bring anything?"

"Just yourself. Thank you for lunch. I put your sandwich in

the fridge. Mine was delicious."

He kissed her, letting his lips linger on hers. His hands slid down to her ass, giving it a little squeeze, and heat sparked in her eyes. "You can thank me properly later."

Her cheeks pinked up, and she whispered, "I bought new lingerie. I hope you like black lace."

He touched his forehead to hers, holding her tighter. She'd been coming out of her shell these last few days, touching him more openly. He loved seeing her confidence blossom. "How am I supposed to write for the rest of the day with that image in my mind?"

She rubbed against his erection and said, "I think you have bigger problems than that to worry about right now."

He kissed her again and stepped back, tugging his shirt down. "You're a dangerous woman, Daphne Zablonski." *Dangerous to my body and my heart.*

# Chapter Fifteen

"DON'T EAT IT." Hadley thrust her hand toward Jock with a palm full of peas and a scowl on her face.

Jock eyed Daphne with a coy smile, and she melted for the hundredth time since he'd come over. They were eating dinner, and when Hadley had refused to eat her peas, Jock had made a game out of it.

He moved his mouth toward Hadley's hand and exclaimed, "My peas!"

She squealed and threw the peas into her mouth, giggling as she gobbled them down, making them all laugh.

Daphne couldn't remember ever having so much fun during dinner. Just like at the pier when Jock had traded ice cream cones with Hadley, Daphne imagined how easily being with children probably would have been for him had he not lost Liam. She was sad for the son he'd missed out on raising and for the imprint it had left behind. But Jock was proving to be one of the strongest men she'd ever known.

"*You* do it," Hadley said.

Jock dutifully put peas in his hand.

"Mine!" Hadley shouted, leaning forward.

Jock threw the peas into his mouth, making growling and

chewing noises behind his hand. Hadley cracked up, and they continued playing until Hadley had finished all of her peas and asked for more. Daphne had never heard Hadley laugh so hard, and it filled her with joy. She loved having this time with the three of them, talking about their days and sharing laughs. She and Jock had talked about his writing, and she'd enjoyed learning about his writing process. He still wasn't divulging story line specifics, but his enthusiasm bled into everything he said and did. Except, she'd noticed, for his lunch with Jules, which he'd been tight-lipped about.

As Daphne dished more peas onto Hadley's plate, she said, "I really liked Jules."

"Jules is pretty great."

"She seems to really want you to go to your grandmother's party."

"I know she does. It's a complicated situation."

"All of life is complicated," Daphne said. "Look what it takes to make Hadley eat peas."

He gave her one of those wanting smiles that sent prickles over her skin and played another round of the pea game with Hadley.

Daphne knew this was a touchy subject, but now that she'd met Jules, his family no longer felt like faceless strangers in the way that people she'd heard about but had not met sometimes did. Seeing Jules light up at the sight of him and hearing her begging him to go to the party made Daphne think about her relationships with her own siblings. She took their closeness for granted, and now she realized how lucky she was to be able to do that. She had so many questions. What was the rest of his family like? Had they taken sides between him and Archer? Did they all accept the distance Jock put between them, or were some of them actively trying to get him to go the party, too?

Choosing her words carefully, she said, "I can't imagine what it would have been like if my brother wouldn't come to see me when I lived in North Carolina. Even if I knew he wasn't staying away because of me, I would have been sad. Heartbroken, really."

Jock's expression turned serious. "She said as much to me today."

"I know it's none of my business, and I'm not saying this because Jules asked me to help her get you to the island, but I think you should consider going."

"You and Hadley are in my life, babe. That makes it your business." He sat back and said, "I'm thinking about it. I might go for an hour or two. Make an appearance, then take off."

"Down," Hadley said as she climbed out of her chair.

"Bath time, sticky-hand girl." Daphne lifted Hadley into her arms, and Jock carried their plates to the sink. "Just leave those there. I'll take care of them after I get her down."

"You cooked. The least I can do is a few dishes." He eyed the peas on the floor around Hadley's chair and said, "I think you need a dog."

"I like dogs," Hadley chimed in.

Daphne touched Hadley's nose and said, "I have all I can handle keeping up with you." She turned to Jock, clearing the remaining dishes like he'd studied a mama-porn book and knew all the right chords to strike, and said, "Seriously, Jock. Pasta and veggies are hardly considered cooking. You don't have to do the dishes. Just relax. I won't be long."

"I hear ya," he said, and blew her a kiss.

She gave Hadley a bath and got her ready for bed.

"One. Two. Three. *Takeoff!*" Hadley's arms shot through

the sleeves of her pajamas, and then she was on her feet, running out of the bedroom.

Daphne hurried after her just in time to see Hadley fling her arms around Jock's legs as he dried a pot. She no longer felt a bloom of panic when Hadley clung to him. He was done with the cringing and bolting. The kitchen was spotless, not a pea in sight, and the cushion from Hadley's chair was on the counter beside the sink, already wiped clean. He'd told her he was raised to be a gentleman, and every day he proved it all over again. If she ever met his parents, she was going to have to thank them.

Hadley tipped her face up and said, "*Wead* a story?"

Jock hadn't read her a bedtime story yet, though he'd sat in Hadley's bedroom while Daphne had read and sang to her each night. He set down the dish towel and looked at Daphne, seeking her approval before accepting Hadley's invitation. She nodded, loving that he allowed her to continue holding the reins where Hadley was concerned.

"I'd love to read you a story." He took Hadley's hand and said, "Lead me to your bookshelf, princess."

Daphne followed them down the hall, feeling all melty inside.

Jock crouched beside Hadley as they picked out a book, and then he sat on the bed beside her and said, "Make room for Mama," as he scooted over, bringing Hadley with him.

Daphne sat on Hadley's other side, and although Jock had his arm around Hadley's waist, he hooked his index finger around Daphne's thumb. How could something so small feel so big? As he read to Hadley, it was easy to imagine spending every night like this and enjoying days when Jules showed up to visit and they *all* went to lunch or dinner. Jules was so easygoing, she wondered what the rest of his family was like. She also wondered what Jock had been like before the accident. Had he been that easygoing, too?

She could listen to Jock read for hours. He had a deep, soothing voice, and seeing her baby girl cuddled up to him did funny things to her. She thought it was easy to imagine dinners, but this was even more special. She was glad she'd never made finding a man a priority. She hadn't had to swim in a sea of wrong just to find her very own Mr. Right.

After he read, Daphne sang their good-night song, and by the time she finished, Hadley had fallen asleep. They quietly left her bedroom, and Jock drew Daphne into his arms. He lowered his lips to hers, kissing her deeply. His hard body pressed deliciously against her, trapping her against the wall as his tongue swept through her mouth like he owned it. He tasted of lust and hope and sinful pleasures she'd been thinking about all day. She didn't know how she'd earned such a *glorious* kiss, but she pressed her hands into his back, hoping it wouldn't end. They were in sync, as they always seemed to be, and their kisses went on and on, turning her legs to jelly and her body to an oven of desire. When their lips eventually parted, he kept her close, one arm around her waist, his other hand flat against the wall, as if his legs had weakened, too.

"Daphne," he whispered against her neck. He lifted his head, his brows furrowed, his eyes dark and magnetic. "I'm so damn crazy about you and Hadley."

She could barely breathe as his words burrowed into her chest, freeing her own. "We're crazy about you, too."

The air rushed from his lungs in one fast burst, his lips curving into a relieved smile. "Yeah?"

"God, *yes*," she said, pulling his mouth to hers again in another earth-shattering kiss that had her clinging to him just to remain standing. He'd worshipped her body every night, and she'd spent the last two days gathering her courage to seduce *him*. Foreplay had never been Tim's favorite thing, and with him, it hadn't been hers, either. She'd never wanted to give back the way she did with Jock. She'd never known what she'd been missing until Jock had shown her the power of her own body, the incredible sensations she was capable of feeling. She hoped to bring him the same overwhelming pleasures.

Her cravings with Jock were so intense, she didn't recognize the brazen, confident woman taking his hand and leading him into her bedroom. The desirous look in his eyes emboldened her as she closed and locked the door and turned on the baby monitor.

Jock reached for her, but she wanted to take the lead, and in that moment, as heady anticipation met reality, her entire body trembled. She said, "It's my turn to show you how much I want you."

Flames shimmered in his eyes, making her even more confident. She lifted his shirt, and he pulled it off, dropping it to the floor beside them. Her hands went to his chest like metal to magnet, touching his heated flesh. She'd gone over this so many times in her head, she tried to remember how she had planned to play it out. But she was already too lost in him to think straight. He put his hand on her hip, drawing her close again, and she remembered her plan.

She stepped back, holding his gaze as she unbuttoned her shirt and let it fall to the floor, revealing her new black lace bra.

"Gorgeous," he said huskily, reaching for her.

She shook her head and shimmied out of her shorts, standing before him in only her new black silk panties with lace trim and matching bra. His chest heaved as he tugged her into his arms, taking her in a rough kiss. It took all of her will to press her hand to his chest and break their connection.

"I had a plan," she panted out. "Just let me try."

"*Try?*" he said incredulously, touching her hand. "Woman, you do me in every time you *smile*. You don't have to *try*."

There went her weak knees again…

But his words also gave her an unexpected jolt of confidence. She flipped her hair over her shoulder, holding his gaze like she'd been practicing in the mirror—and she couldn't believe she'd actually done it! She hoped she looked seductive and not as nervous as she felt and said, "Maybe I want to turn you inside out and not just do you in."

He uttered a curse.

She was shocked *and* proud of herself for coming up with something so clever and sexy on the fly, and his response sent thrills darting through her. He gritted his teeth as she fumbled with the button and zipper on his jeans and yanked them down to his ankles, freeing his erection. He stepped out of his jeans, looking like he wanted to tackle her to the bed and devour her. He reached for her again, but she bypassed his hands, putting both of hers on his chest, and pressed her lips to his warm flesh, kissing her way over and down his pecs. She'd stolen a few ideas from her erotic romance novels, and she licked his nipples, earning sharp inhalations with every slick of her tongue. She continued her exploration, enjoying every hard plane, every dip and curve of his chest and abs, until she was eye to eye with the object of her obsession.

She lowered herself to her knees, wrapping her hand around his shaft. Her heart was beating so fast, she was shaking. He caressed her cheek, bringing her eyes to his as she licked around the broad head, and the devilish eyes blazing down at her sent her body into a frenzy of need. She closed her eyes, trying to focus on something other than the pulsing heat between her legs, and licked him from base to tip. He moaned and threaded his fingers into her hair, holding tight as she lowered her mouth over his cock.

"Christ, Daphne," he gritted out.

The desire in his voice emboldened her. Silently cheering herself on, she focused on the feel of his thickness sliding through her lips, the taste of his salty skin, and the appreciative sounds he was making. She sucked harder, squeezed him tighter, loving the way his hips thrust as she dragged her tongue over the head, slowing them down between strokes.

"*God*, your mouth," he said, rough and breathy. "It's fucking *magic*."

Her eyes flicked up to his. She'd never seen him look so predatory, and she freaking loved it! She stroked faster, earning a long, torturous groan.

"Tighter," he said.

She tightened her fist, and he grabbed her head with his other hand, holding both sides as he fucked her mouth, but he let her set their pace.

"That's it," he panted out. "Aw, *fuck*, baby. So, so good."

She wanted to *taste* his arousal, to feel him lose control, but she wasn't done exploring this powerful feeling. She slowed her efforts, earning another long, agonizing moan. She dragged her tongue along the edge of the broad head. His chin fell to his chest with a *hiss* as she kissed her way up his body, nudging him backward until he was standing beside the bed, and then she pushed him down on his back, and a laugh tumbled from his lips.

"You're a fucking goddess, baby," he said as she stripped off her panties. "Come here, gorgeous."

She kissed his thighs, the muscles flexing against her lips as she crawled up his body, kissing and licking. Every press of her lips made his cock twitch. She'd never been on top of a man before. She'd always been too embarrassed to let anyone see her in that position, but everything was different with Jock. He made her feel womanly and wanted, and as she straddled his hips, she reveled in the safety of him.

He clutched her waist, visually devouring her as she took off her bra. "You're absolutely stunning." The adoration in his eyes underscored his praise. "Ride me, baby. *Claim* me as yours."

He made the act of claiming him sound visceral and raw, and that's how she felt as she sank down, burying him to the root. Electricity arced through her as they began to move. His fingers dug into her hips, his jaw went rigid, and his eyes drilled into her. She reached behind her, using his thighs for leverage, riding him faster, *harder*, adjusting her angle until he stroked over that magical spot with his every thrust.

"Touch me," she panted out, guiding his hand between her legs. "*Yesss*." Pleasures spread through her like wildfire, and she slowed her efforts.

"Don't slow down, baby. I want you wild and breathless."

Just hearing him say it made her *feel* wild and breathless. She moved quicker, losing herself in the sounds of his moans, the feel of his cock filling her so completely. He did something with his fingers, setting off sparks beneath her skin. She clenched her teeth to keep from crying out, and he sat up and sealed his mouth over her breast, sucking so hard she felt him *everywhere*, turning those sparks into spirals of ecstasy. Her body clenched around him, his entire body flexed and then shuddered with his release. He clung to her, gritting out her name like a prayer.

MOONLIGHT STREAMED IN through the balcony doors, shining across Jock's and Daphne's naked bodies as they lay in each other's arms. Daphne buried her face in his chest, probably a little embarrassed after taking control. Jock kissed her forehead and said, "Hey, let me see those angel eyes."

She tilted her face up, and his chest constricted at her reddened cheeks.

"You okay?"

She nodded and hid her face again.

"Where's all that confidence I just ate up like a starving puppy?"

She looked at him again, smiling shyly.

"Daphne, you are *everything* I could ever want in a woman and so much more. I'm as intrigued by your blushing as I am by your desire to take control. I don't *ever* want you to feel embarrassed about the things we do."

"That's easy for you to say. You've probably always been as confident as a lion. This is new for me. You've turned me into someone I don't recognize—don't get me wrong; I *love* it." She kissed his chest and lowered her voice to say, "But it's embarrassing after the fact, when that confidence is gone and all that's left is knowing that you just saw me on my knees, unsure if I was even touching you right, and then on top of you with all my stark-white nakedness on display, making you touch me in certain places. I've never been like that with anyone."

"Baby, first of all, when you touch me, you light me on fire.

There is no wrong way, because what we feel for each other makes it phenomenal. Sex without emotion is an act. It's a game, a hookup. You and I are *not* that, and your body is the *only* body I have fantasized about since the day I met you. And I'm talking dirty, *filthy* fantasies." He pressed his smiling lips to hers and said, "Don't ever be embarrassed about being naked in front of me. You couldn't be unattractive if you tried." He kissed her again and said, "When I see you, naked, clothed, or in my fantasies, you're *my* angel. You're as gorgeous as gorgeous can be. You know I love seeing you blush, but not at the expense of you believing even for a second that you're not the most beautiful creature on this planet."

She buried her face in his chest again and said, "Who *are* you?"

He touched her chin, tipping her face up, and kissed her. "I'm your man, and when we're intimate, the only thing I'm thinking about is how much I want you, how much I care about you, and how lucky I am that you *choose* to share your beautiful self with me. Okay?"

She nodded and whispered, "Okay."

"Good. Now let me straighten you out about that other thing you mentioned. I've been embarrassed plenty of times."

She scoff-laughed. "Uh-huh."

He pushed up on one elbow and said, "You want examples? Here you go. In tenth grade Archer stole my clothes and *every* towel in the locker room after gym class. I had to walk down the hall with my boxing glove over my privates and a basketball covering my ass."

She laughed.

"Oh, you like that? Here's another classic example of embarrassment. The first time I had sex, I tore two condoms trying to put them on and snapped the third on my dick."

She snort-laughed and covered her face.

"And then there was the time that Archer and Levi and I snuck out to go skinny-dipping in the pool at the Silver House. We thought we were so cool. But remember how I said that everyone knows everything on the island? We stripped naked, and then the *spotlights* turned on. We had an audience of my grandmother and all of her friends."

Tears streamed down Daphne's face, she was laughing so hard. "Who turned on the lights?"

"My *grandmother*."

She fell onto her back in hysterics. "I love her already!"

Jock laughed and leaned over her, glad she was no longer embarrassed. "See? I've been embarrassed plenty of times." His thoughts turned to more recent events, and he said, "Daph, those are nothing compared to how embarrassed I was every time I reacted poorly to Hadley, and that's the honest-to-God truth."

Her laughter quieted, and she said, "I know."

"And this whole thing with Archer has me embarrassed, too."

She reached up and caressed his cheek. "I'm sorry."

"I want to fix things with him, but I'm not sure how."

"Have you ever really tried?" She wriggled out from under him and sat up, covering herself with the sheet.

He sat up, too. "As I said, it's complicated."

"Then maybe it's time to uncomplicate it." She said it as if it were easy to do. "Jules would obviously support you. Would your other brother and sisters?"

"It's not that easy."

"Of course not. If it were easy, I doubt you would have gone to live with Harvey. Or maybe you would have, given everything you'd been through. But at least you would have probably tried to fix things with Archer."

"I blame myself," he admitted. "I know you don't want to hear that, but when Archer looks at me, he sees the guy who facilitated his best friend's death. And that's how I feel."

"I know you do, and maybe you always will, although I hope not." She took his hand in hers, the forgotten sheet bunched around her waist. "Jock, I won't judge you no matter what your answer is, but do you truly want to make up with Archer?"

Emotions burned through him. "Yes. I miss him. I miss everyone. But I don't even think he'll talk to me. He does his best to avoid me when I'm there."

"Then I'll go with you," she offered. "I'll ask my mom to keep Hadley, and we'll go together. I'm great moral support."

"No way. The last thing you need is to be stressed out because of my shit."

"You just said you're my man, didn't you?"

"Yes, but that has nothing to do with this. This only affects me."

She raised her brows and deepened her voice, mimicking his as she said, "'You and Hadley are in my life, babe. That makes it your business.'"

He laughed softly. "Smart-ass."

"You're a writer, Jock. You create backstories and weave lives together out of thin air. You *know* how every little thing your characters go through bleeds into other aspects of their lives."

"I don't want you seeing all this. It's ugly."

"But that's just it. I already see it. I see it in your eyes when you talk about the island and I hear it in your voice when you speak of your family." She scooted a little closer and said, "Look how far you've come with Hadley in such a short period of time. You didn't know you could overcome so much so fast until you opened that door and tried. And taking that chance enabled you to write again. You can't know if this rift between you and Archer affects your relationships with me, Hadley, or anyone else. How do you know it's not blocking your creativity and hindering your writing? You and I both saw how it's affected Jules. You've lost more than *ten years* with your family. Isn't that enough?"

"Yes, it's enough," he said a little sharply. "But I don't want my family caught in the middle of me and my brother. The island is Archer's home."

"They're already caught in the middle, Jock. How can they not be? And wasn't the island *your* home, too?" she said softly.

He knew she was right, despite how often he told himself it wasn't true.

"The way I see it," she said with a sweet tilt of her head, "Archer lost his best friend and you lost the woman you cared about and your baby. And you lost each other. It's all horrible. But this isn't about *just* the two of you. You have family there, and every day you miss with them is another day you'll never get back." She sat up a little straighter, as if what she was about to say required courage. "I'd like to think you and I could really be something together, and I know I'm jumping way ahead, but with Hadley I have to think ahead. Let's say we stay together. How would you explain that situation to her when she's older and wants to know about your family?"

"I'd figure it out."

"I'm sure you would. But it makes me sad to think you'd

have this hanging over you for all that time. What if we stay together and have more children? I don't want to scare you off. I'm not pushing or assuming, but these are the things a single mom thinks about. I don't think you'd want to tell Hadley that you don't speak to your brother, would you? What kind of example would you be setting? I *know* you. I watched you eat my daughter's slobbery ice cream. I've seen you go from being a guy who ran at the first blow of anxiety to a man who explained that anxiety to my little girl in such a way that it helped you both. Your heart is huge, Jock. I don't believe for a second that you'd want her, or if we have children together, then our kids, thinking that's okay."

Just the thought of that scenario playing out was more than he could take. His throat thickened with emotions.

She squeezed his hand and said, "Seeing Jules today really showed me what you're missing out on. Think about your parents. Remember when we were talking about music and I said one of my favorite artists is Blue Foster?"

"I remember."

"He sings this song, 'Dog East West,' and in it he says, *We owe it to our parents to tell them what dreams we'll be chasing and how long we'll be gone.* Think about that, Jock. You're not chasing a dream, but the idea is the same. Our parents took care of us day in and day out. I know from being a mom that nothing is harder than when your child is hurting, and I also know that it won't matter if Hadley is two, ten, thirty, or older. I'll *always* hurt when she does. Don't we owe our parents peace of mind? Your parents are probably *still* grieving for their sons' broken hearts and broken relationship. I don't think they can fully heal when you and Archer are still at odds."

He swallowed hard, her words hitting like arrows to his

chest.

"Family is so important, Jock. I know Harvey became your family. But he's gone, and you still have a family out there. All families go through rough times. But what if, God forbid, someone in your family falls ill and is confined to the hospital? Would you go for an hour because you're afraid of how difficult it would be with Archer, or would you want to sit vigil?"

He thought about Jules and knew she was right.

"What happens when your brothers or sisters get married? Will you go?" she asked with a tortured look in her eyes. She paused, sitting up a little straighter and gathering the sheet in her hand, pulling it up to her chest. "I'm sorry. I'm being way too pushy and nosy."

She was being far more assertive than usual. In fact, he realized she was as assertive as she'd been when she'd said she wouldn't be with a man who couldn't be around her daughter.

"I was wrong to think the situation with Archer didn't affect you and Hadley. This is important to you, isn't it?" he asked.

"Yes, because *you're* important to me. You're important to *us.*"

Guilt wound through him, and he knew what he had to do. "I need to tell you something. When I was telling Jules about us at lunch, I didn't tell her about Hadley. I didn't want to dredge up the past with her, but it's not because I don't care about Hadley. I care about her every bit as much as I care for you. It's just that—"

"You don't have to explain. I *know* how you feel about *both* of us. I understand why you didn't want to bring up Hadley, and just because I'm bringing all of this up doesn't mean I'll judge you, or feel differently about you, if you decide to only make an appearance at the party or not go at all. You're doing so much to be good for me and Hadley. I just want to make sure you're doing just as much to be good for yourself, too. And I want you to know that I'm willing to go, to do this with you. We're a team, and I'd totally have your back. I might get embarrassed easily, but I have mama-bear claws that come out to protect the people I care about."

"I've seen those claws." He pressed his lips to hers and said, "Thanks, babe. Let me think about it."

"Okay, you think. I'm going to use the bathroom. Be right back."

She walked bare-ass naked to the bathroom, and he loved it. He had no idea how a woman who blushed about being sexy could put him in his place like no other, but *damn...*

She came out of the bathroom with a bounce in her step and picked up his T-shirt on the way to the bed. "It's still early. Care to lose in a game of Scrabble?" she asked as she put on his shirt and grabbed a clean pair of underwear from a drawer.

"What are the stakes?" he asked, closing the distance between them as she put them on. "And don't say if I lose we have to go to the party, because I've already made up my mind."

"You have?"

The hope in her eyes told him he'd made the right decision. "Yes. We're going. It's time for me to get this shit under control. But are you sure your parents won't mind watching Hadley? I don't know how Archer will react, so it'll probably be easier if she's not with us. But don't worry, I don't intend on keeping her a secret. I will tell my family about her while we're there. I want you with me, and I'm pretty sure if I show up without you, if Archer doesn't kill me, Jules will. But are you *sure* you want to go? I don't want you to feel caught in the middle or like you *have* to go."

"I'm so proud of you!" She threw her arms around him. "I'm sure my parents won't mind watching Hadley, and I definitely want to go. I will have your back one hundred percent. You can count on me! I'll even take scowling lessons from Hadley so I can give anyone who looks at you sideways a harsh look of my own."

He put his arms around her and said, "You Zablonski girls have got me under your spell. My family has been harping on me for years to try to work things out with Archer, and in one evening, you wrangled me into trying."

"Oh, come on," she said teasingly. "We both know you only decided to go because you can't wait to get me alone on the island. Look at the woman you bring out in me when Hadley's right in the *next room*." She went up on her toes and kissed him. "I hope wherever we stay has soundproof walls, because I have no idea what vixen will come out when we have a whole night to ourselves."

# Chapter Sixteen

"I THINK SHE should go sexier and pull out all the stops." Chloe held up a glittery silver dress and said, "Let that brother of his see how good Jock has it."

Daphne had taken a *real* lunch break to shop for a dress at Renee's boutique with Tegan and Chloe. She could hardly believe two weeks had passed since Jock had made the decision to go to his grandmother's birthday party. He hadn't changed his mind, though there were moments when Daphne had seen shadows of doubt in his eyes. But with all he was facing, that was to be expected.

"That's gorgeous," Daphne said. "But I'm less worried about one-upping his brother than I am about being there for Jock this weekend. Do they have it in my size?"

"You know I always try to have your size on hand, Dee," Renee said, giving Daphne a sideways look. "Chloe, look on the other side of that rack."

"Give her a break, Renee," Tegan chimed in. "She and Jock are in that playing-house stage. She's allowed to be in la-la land."

It was true. Their lives were falling into sync without any mountains to climb or valleys to contend with. They'd come across a few bumps and potholes, which they were navigating together. Jock was still finding ways around holding Hadley, but the two had become so close, it was hard to remember when he hadn't been able to spend time with her. Daphne was feeling high on a daily basis, even when they didn't make love. Just being together made her and Hadley's life better, and she wasn't about to deny it. This was her first visit to la-la land, and she never wanted to leave.

"My sister's not playing house with anyone until Sean and I put him through the ringer," Renee insisted.

"Too late," Chloe teased.

"You haven't met him?" Tegan asked.

"Not yet. My schedule is crazy," Renee said. "But Hadley's birthday is next weekend, after they get back from the island, and I'm going to be ready to interrogate."

"Thanks for the warning," Daphne said. "I'm not intentionally keeping him from our family. We've all been *busy*. I finally finished the book for the book club and the questions for the meeting next week, and Jock is writing every day, sometimes into the evenings."

"That's fantastic," Tegan said.

"I know. He's found his muse!" Daphne exclaimed excitedly. "He's secretive about what he's writing, but you should see him when he's in the zone. I've woken up twice in the middle of the night and found him sitting on the chair typing in the dark. He gets so into it, it's like he has blinders on."

"I know you guys are banging like bunnies because of that new-moisturizer *glow* you're sporting," Renee teased. "But do you get much time together other than midnight mattress games?"

"Of course. We have lunch together most days." Daphne

loved that time alone with Jock. Although saying goodbye after lunch was just as hard as saying goodbye in the wee hours of the morning after lying in each other's arms. "And we see each other in the evenings with Hadley and all weekend. Last weekend was the *best*, and we didn't even do that much. We took walks on the beach with Hadley, collected shells, and spent an afternoon at the Eastham lighthouse. I can't believe I'd never taken her into one. Hadley had a long discussion with the guy who runs it, and she must have climbed those old narrow steps inside ten times. We brought lunch and had a picnic on the green, and then just ran around playing with Hadley. We cooked hot dogs and hamburgers on the grill and watched *Frozen* with Hadley. I'm sure to you guys our simple lives seem boring. But walks on the beach, homemade lunches and dinners, and nights spent in each other's arms are just..." She shrugged and said, "Perfect. I can't imagine being happier."

"I think it sounds great," Tegan said. "Jett and I don't go out much, and I don't miss it one bit."

"That's because when it's right, all you need is each other," Chloe said. "But you can't go to the party naked, because that won't feel right at all. So how about this dress?" She held up the glittery dress again. "Yay or nay?"

"Do you think it's too flashy?" Daphne could wear some-thing she already owned. She'd tried on several of her dresses, and Jock had raved about how great she looked in each one. Especially the last one, which she'd let him peel off before taking her to bed last night. But she wanted to look extra special for him and his family. "Jock and Jules both said the dinner was fancy, but I don't want to overdo it. Tegan, you've met his family. What do you think?"

"Oh, that's right! Have you met *Archer*?" Renee said *Archer* like it was a bad word.

"No, but I've met everyone else," Tegan explained. "When I lived in Maryland, I visited my uncle every summer. That's how Jock and I became friends. I met his family when they'd come to see him, but Archer was never with any of them. As for how to dress, I think anything goes with them. His sisters are pretty fashionable. In fact, Sutton was a fashion magazine editor before becoming a reporter, so you know she'll be dressed in something trendy. Jules is like an uncorked bottle of bubbly, so she'll probably be dressed young and flirty, and I would not put sequins past her. She could totally pull that off, and so could you, Daph. And Leni is more of a chardonnay; she is easygoing, not as flashy as Jules, and super cute."

"I guess that makes Daph a wine cooler," Chloe teased. "She's sweet, bubbly, and hard to resist."

They all laughed.

"While I agree with that assessment, and I'm all for showing off my gorgeous sister, I'm not sure full-on sexy is the way to go when you meet a guy's parents for the first time." Renee held up a short pale-green dress that had a crossover bodice, a pretty sweetheart neckline, and a chiffon skirt. "What about something like this? A little low-key, a little fancy, and classy. You could pair it with gold heels and dangling earrings. I have the perfect heels in the back. Teg, can you grab them?"

"Sure!" Tegan hurried off.

Daphne ran her hand along the skirt. "It's beautiful."

"Are you nervous about going?" Renee asked.

"Wouldn't I be crazy not to be? I'm meeting his family and I want to make a good impression, and then there's the whole Archer thing. We have no idea what to expect with him. I'm so proud of Jock for taking this step, you guys. I want so much for their relationship to heal because of how heavily the rift weighs on Jock. But I'm in this with him for the long haul, regardless of how this turns out."

"Listen to you," Renee teased.

"I know I sound all swoony. I can't even begin to describe how much I like him. I get all shivery just thinking about how happy we are. Hadley is bonkers over him. She smiles a lot more these days, and I know that's because of him and because I'm a lot happier, too. He always makes us feel special, and I want him to know how special *he* is to *us*. I want him to know that I see beyond the trouble between him and Archer. I see the wonderful man he is." She looked at her sister's and her friends' supportive faces and said, "*Aaand* I'm rambling again."

"Your rambling is very informative. Jock is a lucky man," Renee said with a wink.

"Thank you." Daphne reveled in her sister's praise. "As for the dress, I want something sexy, *yes*, bring it on—but not slutty. I want to be Jock's rock, his safe harbor, someone he can count on and be proud of. Honestly, I want to be whatever he needs this weekend."

"Honey, you're clearly what Jock needs regardless of what you wear. He's like a whole different man these days," Tegan said, holding the pretty gold heels in one hand and a gorgeous cream cocktail dress with gold flecks on the bodice in the other. "He stopped by on his way home from the gym yesterday morning, and he went on and on about you and Hadley. I asked about his writing, and he gushed for another fifteen minutes about how *you* had opened a vein to his creativity. So whatever you're doing, keep it up."

"I don't think she's having any trouble keeping *it* up," Chloe said with a chuckle. "And in case I haven't said it enough yet, Daph, you deserve this—being with a man who sees how fabulous you and Hadley are."

"Me too," Renee said. "It's about time a good man recognized my badass sister."

Daphne laughed. "Badass? I'm about as far from badass as a girl can get. You're the badass one."

Renee gave her a deadpan look. "Daph, I'd give anything to be like you. I'm tough, but trust me, tough is not an easy way to be. You're the total package. You *always* have your shit together, you're a kickass mother, and you're gorgeous." She hugged Daphne and said, "Get that mushy look off your face and get going before you have to get back to work. These dresses are not going to try themselves on."

The girls ushered her into a dressing room with their selections, and Renee said, "What other outfits do you need? We can grab some choices while you're trying those on."

"I don't need anything else. We're taking the ferry to the island Saturday morning, and if all goes well, we'll stay at his parents' house and then come home Sunday. If it doesn't go well, we'll be home Saturday night."

"You're going away alone with a man for the first time in three years, Mama," Chloe said. "If there is ever a time for new clothes, it's now. You need clothes for the ferry ride—"

"*No*, I don't." Daphne shook her head. "Besides, I think the rest of Saturday is casual. His family plays touch football before the party, and they help get the winery ready for the event, which I'm looking forward to."

"Those Steeles better watch out," Tegan said. "Do they know you're having withdrawals from event planning?"

"It's not like I'll take over or anything." Although even the idea of helping to set up for the event had her a little giddy.

"No, you're far too proper for that." Renee closed the dressing room curtain and said, "We want to see each of those dresses *on* your body. Come on, girls; let's find a cute touch-football outfit."

Forty minutes later, Daphne had more new clothes than she could wear in a week, much less a weekend. Renee handed her the last shopping bag and said, "Look at my baby sister, all grown up and ready to take on the world to help her man find his way."

Daphne hugged her and said, "Thank you for everything."

"Don't be nervous. From what you've said, you guys are really good together. There's nothing you can't handle." Renee wagged her finger and said, "But you better bring his ass over to meet me when you get back."

"I promise," Daphne said. "We're just always so busy."

"That's code for *not willing to give up a second of their time together for anyone outside their little family*," Chloe said.

As they left the store, Tegan said, "You and Jock have both been through so much, it's like you two were made for each other."

"*He's* been through so much." Daphne hoped this weekend wouldn't be overwhelming for him.

"But he's strong," Tegan said.

"Sometimes the hardest things in life lead us to the best things," Chloe added.

"And the best things are sometimes the hardest," Daphne said.

Chloe and Tegan laughed.

Daphne realized how they'd taken what she'd said and exclaimed, "*Ohmygod*, you guys! I didn't mean *that*!"

Chloe and Tegan looked at each other and said, "Peach!" in unison, then burst into hysterics.

# Chapter Seventeen

JOCK LAY IN Daphne's bed Saturday morning watching the dawn of a new day through the crack in the curtains. Hadley had slept at Daphne's parents' house last night, and he and Daphne had joined their friends for a bonfire on the beach. Daphne hadn't been kidding about not knowing what wildness might appear when Hadley wasn't in the other room. They'd barely made it in the front door after the bonfire before ripping off each other's clothes and christening the foyer, the couch, and the kitchen counter before finally falling into bed too spent to move. He'd slept fitfully, nervous about what the day would hold, but also looking forward to introducing Daphne to his family and showing her the island. His mother had been ecstatic when he'd called the other day to say he was bringing Daphne home with him. *Home.* The island hadn't felt like home in a long time, but Daphne, his *hopeful realist,* refused to let him forget that it wasn't just Archer's home; it had once been his home, too.

In the past, when Harvey or Jock's family had encouraged him to confront Archer, their well-intentioned nudges had never given much weight to how badly things could go. Daphne didn't gloss over how difficult it might be. She agreed with his concerns, and over the past two and a half weeks since he'd decided to go, she'd even said it might be worse than he imagined. But she'd urged him to do it anyway.

He glanced at her, sleeping naked on her belly beside him, a lock of hair lying across her cheek, one arm beneath the pillow, the other dangling off the bed. One of her feet was tucked under the blanket at the bottom of the bed. He would do anything for her. She was his beautiful, hopeful girl, and she believed things would work out between him and Archer because she believed in the strength of family, and she believed in *him*. She'd helped him to rediscover the man he'd once been, and because of her, he was becoming an even better man. A man he could be proud of. The man she and Hadley deserved. It was her steadfast belief and contagious hope that were driving him to finally take action to get out of this self-imposed exile and start enjoying his family again. That was why he knew that no matter how hard things got, he *would* get through this.

He was ready to face the ghosts of his past head-on.

*After* he thanked his precious angel for standing by his side. That was what she'd become to him. His angel, and he was pretty sure she was heaven sent—directly from Harvey, who seemed to always know exactly what he needed.

Jock moved down the bed and kissed his way up the back of her legs. She made sleepy, appreciative sounds as he loved his way up her body, trailing kisses along her hamstring, over the curve of her luscious derriere, and up her spine. He was so glad she'd stopped trying to cover up and let him enjoy all of her. He perched above her and brushed her hair off her cheek, his hips resting against her bottom.

He kissed her neck and said, "'Morning, angel."

"Don't you know the number-one single-mom rule? Never

wake her when there's nobody under four feet tall in the next room."

She turned over beneath him, and he was surprised to see a fierce scowl on her beautiful face.

"Aw, hell. I'm sorry, Daph."

He started to move away, but she grabbed his arms, her scowl morphing into a giggle.

"I've been working on my *Hadley scowl* in case I need it today. I guess it worked."

"I seriously thought I messed up." He tickled her, and she squealed, curling away from him, but he pinned her to the bed, eating up her giggles and wiggles. "You're a cruel woman, Zablonski."

"I just wanted to be sure my scowl was strong enough to have your back," she said through her laughter.

His heart turned over in his chest at her endless support. "I want you by my side, babe, not at my back."

"What if I want you on my *inside*?" Her hips rose, her legs parting as she brushed against his hard length, and she whispered, "I promise not to scowl."

"*God, Daph*, I'm so caught up in you."

He lowered his lips to hers as their bodies came together, and he reveled in the feel of her tight heat and her warm, willing mouth. She felt too good to go slow. He took the kiss deeper, thrusting faster. They moved in perfect harmony, taking and giving in equal measure. He'd thought kissing Daphne was overwhelming, but making love to her took him to new heights. Her head fell back with a gasp, her fingernails marking him. That was her *tell*, the way he knew she was close to losing control. He lifted her leg beside his hip, taking her deeper.

"*Jock*," she pleaded.

He felt her thighs tense. Her hands slid lower, pushing against his hips, and he quickened his pace. Heat skated down his spine as he thrust harder, dove *deeper*, struggling to hold back his own climax. She cried out his name, her inner muscles tightening exquisitely around his cock, and the world fell away. They spiraled over the edge together in a rush of needy moans and urgent thrusts. He clutched her shoulders, gritting out her name through every mind-blowing pulse. When the last shock rumbled through his body, he bowed his head beside hers, trying to remember how to breathe.

"I could stay right here forever," he panted against her neck.

"Sounds perfect."

She sighed dreamily, and *man*, he loved that satisfied sound.

Her cell phone rang on the nightstand. He rose onto his elbows, gazing down at her smiling eyes, and said, "So much for forever." He pressed his lips to hers and grabbed her cell phone, handing it to her as he shifted beside her.

"Hi, Mom," she said as she sat up. "Oh no. Of course. No, it's fine. Let me just get showered and I'll be right there."

"Is Hadley okay?" he asked as she set her phone on the nightstand.

"Yes, but my mom is sick. She has a fever and chills, and my father got called into work. There goes our sexy weekend." She flopped onto her back with a disappointed sigh that made his chest ache. "I wanted to be there for you so badly. I'm sorry. Will you be okay going by yourself?"

He leaned over her, her sad eyes slaying him. "Daph, it was never about a sexy weekend. We'll have plenty of those, I promise." He leaned in for a kiss and said, "Let's pack Hadley's bag and take her with us."

"Are you sure that won't be too stressful?"

"The three of us have been together every day for nearly three weeks. I can't imagine a day without the two of you by my side. You're my girls, and I want you both with me. I'm done letting the past keep me from living the life I want with you and Hadley." The happiness in her eyes brought his lips to hers again. "I've got this, Daph. I promise. I would *never* let anything happen to either of you."

"I know you wouldn't. I knew that the second you ran down to the water and crouched in your catcher's stance the first time we were at the beach together." She sat up and said, "You really don't mind if she comes? This isn't going to be an easy weekend for you. I don't want to make it any harder."

He stood, bringing her up with him and into his arms. "You and Hadley *center* me. You make everything better. You don't have to go if it makes you uncomfortable, but I'd be happier if you were both with me."

"We'd be happier with you, too."

"Good, then I'll have *two* expert scowlers by my side." He took her hand, leading her into the bathroom, and turned on the shower.

"Are you hijacking my shower?"

"I thought we'd shower together to save time."

They stepped into the shower, and he gathered her slick body against his. A sexy sigh slipped through her lips and she said, "It feels like this might take twice as long."

"I'm glad you noticed." As he lowered his lips to hers, he said, "I'll try to be quick."

DAPHNE ADDED *CO-SHOWERING* to her long list of things she wanted to do more of with Jock. She hadn't expected it to be so exhilarating and fun. But they needed a *lot* more time in the morning if that was going to ever happen again. They got to her parents' house to pick up Hadley with just enough time to get to the ferry—if she was fast.

"Is this where you grew up?" he asked.

"Yes," she said as they climbed out of his SUV. "You should stay out here. My mom is a real baby about people seeing her when she's sick."

"Okay. I'll call Levi and make sure he's picking us up at the ferry."

She ran inside, almost tripping over Hadley's backpack, and found her mother and Hadley in the kitchen. Hadley was coloring at the table, and her mother was making tea, wearing a fluffy blue robe and fuzzy slippers. Her hair was a mess, her cheeks were pink with fever, and she had dark circles under her eyes.

"Hi, baby." Daphne kissed the top of Hadley's head and said, "Mom, you look awful. Why didn't you call me last night? I would have gotten Hadley."

"She was asleep by the time I realized I wasn't just tired but sick. Besides, you never get time alone with your beau." Her mother sounded utterly exhausted. "Don't worry, we've kept our distance, right sugarplum?"

Hadley was on her knees on the chair peeking out the window, too sidetracked to respond. "*Dock!* Dock's here!"

As she scrambled off the chair, Daphne said, "Get Owly, please."

Daphne's mother went to the window and peered out. "My goodness, honey. That Jock is one fine-looking young man."

"Do you want to meet him quick?"

"Goodness, no. Not when I look like *this*. But I think your little lady is anxious to see him." She pointed to Hadley tugging open the front door, holding Owly in one hand.

"I see Dock!" Hadley ran outside.

"Guess we're off. Love you, Mom. Hope you feel better." Daphne picked up the backpack and ran after Hadley, getting outside just in time to see her daughter run around Jock, whose back was facing the house, and attach herself to his legs.

Jock lifted Hadley up over his head, stopping Daphne in her tracks. Hadley was beaming at him. Tears slipped down Daphne's cheeks as he turned with her daughter in his arms. Hadley put her hands on his cheeks and kissed him smack on his lips; then she wrapped her arms around his neck, hugging him tight.

Jock raised his brows, his smiling eyes locked on Daphne as he said, "I told you I've got this." He put a hand on Hadley's back and said, "We'd better get Mommy in the car before she melts."

"Mommies don't melt," Hadley said.

Jock winked at Daphne, snapping her out of her stupor, and said, "Coming, angel?" as if by picking up her daughter he hadn't just sent her world spinning.

# Chapter Eighteen

JOCK STOOD AT the railing of the ferry, the cool salty air brushing over his skin. His nerves were strung as tight as guitar strings as they neared the island. Colorful cottages and cedar-sided homes decorated the lush landscape. Silver Monument stood sentinel over the island, and just to the north, his parents' winery flags waved in the morning breeze. Some people preferred the neighboring islands of Nantucket and Martha's Vineyard, but Jock had always loved the diversity of Silver Island, with its varying boroughs—ritzy Silver Haven, artistic Chaffee, and old-school New England fishing towns, Rock Harbor and Seaport. Even as a kid he'd been taken with the beauty of the island when they'd come home on the ferry from a trip to Boston or the Cape. Now harsh memories hovered over his beautiful island like storm clouds. He hoped he wasn't making a mistake bringing Daphne and Hadley with him.

He felt a tiny arm circle the back of his leg as Hadley and Daphne came to his side. He glanced at their bags and the car seat they'd brought and realized they'd been in such a hurry, he'd forgotten to mention to Levi that Hadley was with them. He ran a hand over Hadley's head, thinking about how right it had felt when he'd picked her up at Daphne's parents' house. As he'd lifted her up, he'd felt like Superman finally overcoming his kryptonite, and Hadley had felt like she *belonged* in his arms, where she was protected and loved. He'd wondered if his little princess had known it all along, the way she'd stuck to him like glue and had sought him out.

She'd been thrilled with riding on the ferry for the first half hour, and then she'd gotten busy playing with Owly. She couldn't be cuter in her little pink top and white shorts, and Daphne took his breath away in a white ribbed blouse and blue shorts that had white blossoms on them. Her hair lifted off her shoulders with the breeze, and her contented smile told him he'd definitely done the right thing by bringing them along. He'd have felt their absence like a missing limb if he hadn't. She must have sensed him looking at her, because she turned that killer smile on him.

"Hey, angel."

"Are you okay?"

"Yeah. A little nervous about how things will go with Archer, but I'm good. I'm glad you're both here. I just realized I forgot to mention to Levi that we were bringing this little princess." He lifted Hadley into his arms and said, "My family is going to love both of you."

"I'm sure we'll love them, too," Daphne said.

"Flags, Mama!" Hadley pointed to the colorful flags strung across the dock. "*Pwetty.*"

"They are pretty. Is that a restaurant on the other side of the marina?" Daphne asked.

"Yeah. Rock Bottom Bar and Grill. It's owned by a guy I grew up with, Wells Silver. I stopped in to say hello to him during one of my last trips. It's a nice place. Wells added that deck a few years ago for outdoor seating and hired dockside waitstaff so boaters could dock and order without ever coming ashore."

"That's so cool. This looks different from when we took the ferry for Gavin and Harper's wedding. Where's the Silver House resort?" Daphne asked.

"On the other side of the island. There are two marinas, the one on the Silver Harbor side and this one. This is Rock Harbor Marina, and it's run by Roddy Remington, Rowan's father."

"It's beautiful." Daphne smiled into the wind and said, "I can't imagine wanting to leave this place. I'm such a small-town girl at heart. To me it looks like paradise. Even better than the Cape because it's an island."

He hoped Archer wouldn't pop his starry-eyed angel's bubble.

"I want to take her to the bathroom one last time." She reached for Hadley.

Daphne took Hadley to the bathroom and returned as the ferry was docking. Hadley reached for Jock, and he lifted her into his arms, pressing a kiss to her cheek.

"See that flag at the top of the island, Had?" Jock pointed. "That's where we're going. That's where my mommy and daddy live."

Daphne grabbed his arm, looking warily over her shoulders at the other people on the ferry. "*Jock*. Is the island safe? We're on the ferry with a *criminal*." She pointed farther down the dock and said, "Look."

Jock followed her gaze—to Levi standing holding an enormous sign over his head that read:

WELCOME HOME, BRO!
CONGRATS ON YOUR PAROLE!

REMEMBER, YOU CAN'T GO WITHIN 100 YARDS OF
THE PETTING ZOO.

Beneath the words was a picture of a goat with a red slash
through it. Roddy Remington, a younger version of Jeff Bridges,
with thick gray-brown hair that brushed the collar of his
vibrantly colored shirt opened three buttons deep, stood beside
Levi.

"That's Levi, and I'm going to *kill* him," Jock said.

"Levi?" Her eyes bloomed wide. "You're on *parole?*"

"*No,* I'm not on parole. Did you read the rest of the sign?"
As she squinted in Levi's direction, he said, "Don't you think I
would have told you if I'd been in jail? He's *pranking* me, the
jackass."

"*Dackass,*" Hadley mimicked.

Daphne giggled. "*Oops.*"

"Sorry." Jock put on a serious face and softened his tone for
Hadley. "Hey, princess, we shouldn't use that word, okay? It's
not nice."

Hadley nodded and rested her head on his shoulder.

"You weren't kidding about pranking each other," Daphne
said. "Look at the other passengers; they're scrutinizing each
other, searching for the parolee."

"Great," Jock mumbled.

Holding Hadley in one arm, Jock slung his backpack over
his shoulder and carried the car seat with his free hand, while
Daphne pulled her suitcase as they disembarked. Levi and
Roddy were looking curiously at Jock and Hadley, and the rest
of the passengers were watching Jock cautiously as he headed for
the guy with the shit-eating grin holding the sign. Just what he
needed.

Like Jock and Archer, Levi was tall and broad shouldered with short brown hair and dark eyes. He had tattoos down one arm and more tattoos hidden beneath his T-shirt. Levi and two of their cousins who also lived in Harborside were members of the Dark Knights motorcycle club.

"There's our favorite *parolee*," Roddy said loudly.

"Some role model you are," Jock teased as he set down the car seat and embraced Roddy with one arm, meeting Levi's curious gaze over Roddy's shoulder. Levi gave an almost imperceptible nod, as if to say not to worry; he'd be cool about Hadley.

"Life would get mighty boring if we didn't have a little fun around here," Roddy said.

Jock narrowed his eyes at Levi and said, "If little ears weren't listening…"

"Good to see you, too, bro." Levi pulled him into a manly embrace and whispered, "Does she know about you and Archer? Liam?"

"Yes," Jock said as they stepped back. He put a hand on Daphne's back and said, "Daphne Zablonski, this is Roddy Remington and my younger brother, Levi. Guys, this is my girlfriend, Daphne, and her daughter, Hadley." Damn, he liked the way *girlfriend* rolled off his tongue, and by the look on everyone else's faces, they did, too.

"Hi. It's so nice to meet you both," Daphne said. "Mr. Remington, I know your son Rowan and his daughter, Joni."

"You do? Then maybe you can drag his hippie butt back here sometime." Roddy opened his arms and said, "Bring it on in and let me welcome you to the island properly." As she stepped into his embrace, he said, "Any friend of Jack's is a friend of mine."

"That goes for me, too," Levi said. "But I have just one question. What's a gorgeous woman like you doing with this *schlump*?"

"I can see you're just as charming as your brother," she said as Levi hugged her.

Levi tickled Hadley's chin, but she didn't crack a smile. He raised his brows and said, "Looks like I'm already on the naughty list."

"Don't take it personally," Daphne said. "She doesn't smile for many people. Although she took a liking to Jock from the moment she first saw him, just like her mama."

Jock put his arm around her and kissed her temple, sure he was beaming like a braggart.

"You're still going by *Jock*, huh?" Roddy asked.

Jock nodded. "Yes, sir. Honoring Harvey's memory."

"Okay, then." Roddy clapped a hand on Levi's shoulder and said, "I'll see you kids tonight at Lenore's birthday shindig. Daphne, don't forget to send Rowan back here so I can give my granddaughter a squeeze. I'll even sweeten the pot. You get my boy here, and I'll let you and Jack—*Jock*—take my yacht out for a spin."

Levi chuckled.

"You don't need to do that," Daphne said. "I'll mention it the next time I see him."

"Still calling that fishing boat a yacht?" Jock asked.

Roddy winked and said, "One man's fishing boat…" He waved and headed down the dock.

"Ready to blow this taco stand?" Levi asked as he picked up the car seat and grabbed the handle to the suitcase.

They piled into Levi's Durango. As Daphne strapped Hadley into her car seat, Levi said, "Boy, I remember those contraptions. What a pain in the rear."

"Jock told me about your daughter, Joey." Daphne settled into her seat and said, "You must have been a very young father,"

As Levi drove out of the parking lot, he said, "I was twenty when she was born, and I fumbled through every aspect of fatherhood."

Jock turned in the front passenger seat and said, "Don't believe him. He was a natural from day one. He even built Joey her own bassinet."

"Aw, that's so sweet," Daphne said.

"Dude, you were hardly ever around. How would you know?" Levi asked.

Guilt gnawed at Jock. "Mom told me. She said you never complained about getting up a hundred times a night or changing diapers. She and Dad were really proud of you."

Levi looked at him and said, "They're proud of all of us."

They had told Jock as much, but when he thought about the feud between him and Archer, he didn't know how they could be.

Levi turned onto Ocean View Road toward the center of town. Ocean View was a residential street lined with quaint cottages, white picket fences, and colorful gardens.

"It's so pretty here," Daphne said.

Jock was excited to show her around the island tomorrow before they returned to the Cape. "Wait until you see our parents' place. On a day like today, you can see clear across the island, and at night the lighthouse is gorgeous."

"You almost sound like you miss it," Levi said. "Why don't we give Daphne a quick tour on the way."

"*Birds! Balloons!*" Hadley pointed out the window at birds

drinking from a birdbath in the park on the corner of Main and Ocean View. In the distance, balloons danced from long strings tied to strollers and the railings on the gazebo. Children played on swings and jungle gyms as groups of adults watched over them.

Levi stopped so Hadley could take it all in. "Life on the island is not as harried as other places. Even the birds take the time to enjoy sunny afternoons. We have several birdbaths at our place in Harborside. Joey loves them."

"It looks like there's a birthday party or something going on in the park," Daphne pointed out.

"Probably, but gatherings like that are a regular occurrence on the weekends," Levi said. "Those are the Venting Vixens."

"The what?" Daphne asked.

"That's what I call the mom groups that get together on the weekends to commiserate and hang out. They saved me the first year Joey was born," Levi said. "Joey and I still get together with some of them and their kids when we come back to town."

"It sounds like such a great place to live. Why did you move away?" Daphne asked.

"More job opportunities, better pay," Levi explained. "I work construction, and at the time there wasn't much going on here. But one of our grandmother's childhood friends, Metty Barrington, lived in Harborside. They were doing major reconstruction in the area and she offered to let me and Joey stay with her until we got on our feet. Metty is great. She really helped us out." He glanced at Hadley and said, "Ready to see what else we can find, Hadley?"

"Yeah!" she cheered.

When Jock visited, he always took the fastest route to his parents' or Jules's house and followed the same route back to the ferry. He didn't meander or give his mind time to linger on the past. But as Levi turned onto the main drag—a two-lane road lined by cute shops with colorful awnings, window boxes overflowing with flowers, and enough memories to make Jock's chest ache—Daphne's and Hadley's eyes danced with excitement, and he *wanted* to linger. He wanted to share the good memories with them and make new memories to overshadow the ones he wished he could forget.

"That's Jules's gift shop." Jock pointed to the Happy End gift shop, with its red-framed picture windows and balloons bobbing from strings tied around the necks of the iron giraffes out front.

"That's so cute," Daphne exclaimed. "Is she working today?"

"No, Bellamy Silver is. She's worked with Jules for a few years. You'll meet her tonight at the party." Levi pointed to the candy store two doors down from Jules's shop and said, "See that c-a-n-d-y shop? That's the place Jock and Archer took me to when I was eight and told me it was free Snickers day. As I filled my pockets, those two jokers took off and I got caught for shoplifting."

"Oh man." Jock laughed. "That was hilarious."

Levi scoffed. "Not as hilarious as when you and Archer made those homemade flight suits and jumped off the church roof."

"You didn't tell me you *actually* jumped off a roof!" Daphne exclaimed.

Jock laughed. "We did, but only because Fitz and Wells Silver dared us to."

Levi hiked a thumb at Jock and said, "This guy sprained his ankle and Archer broke his clavicle."

"You were wild back then," Daphne said. "I'm sure it was fun, but I feel bad for your parents. They must have been worried sick all the time."

Levi went on sharing childhood memories Jock had long ago stopped thinking about. Hearing them again was bittersweet, but as they made their way up the hilly streets and turned onto the road that led to their parents' house, his nerves caught fire. They passed the entrance to Top of the Island Vineyard and turned down their parents' driveway. The vineyard spanned sixty acres to the west of their parents' house. The cedar and brick winery and outbuildings—*Archer's domain*—brought a foreboding sensation. Their mother's great-great-grandparents had built their home and established the vineyard. Jock assumed that when his parents eventually stepped down, Archer would inherit the house and vineyard and carry on the family legacy.

Levi parked in front of the house, a rambling two-story with weathered cedar-shingle siding, a mix of gambrel and peaked roofs, and a built-in gazebo anchoring the right side of the wide porch. Their grandmother lived in the carriage house around back. Their mother's car and Jules's Jeep were the only vehicles in the driveway. Jock wondered where everyone else was.

"Wow. This is beautiful. I can't believe you grew up here," Daphne said.

Jock pointed to the left side of the house and said, "My bedroom was behind that tree on the second floor."

"He used to sneak out by climbing out his window, sliding down the roof, jumping to the tree, and then climbing down to the ground." Levi opened his door and said, "Bet you didn't know your boyfriend was a parkour guy."

"I definitely did not. That's insane. It's so high up," Daphne said.

"That's why Jack was my hero when I was growing up," Levi boasted. "Nothing scared him."

Jock shook his head, sure Levi was just blowing smoke to build him up. "Where is everyone?"

"Joey went with Tara to pick up Sutton, Leni, and Leni's friend Indi from the airport, and then they were going to stop and pick up a few things for the party. Dad and Archer were heading to the winery to start setting up when I left to pick you up."

At least that gave Jock a little time before facing Archer.

Daphne unhooked Hadley from her car seat and said, "Are you ready to meet Jock's family?"

Hadley nodded as Jock climbed out and opened her door. She thrust out her arms, clutching Owly in one hand, and said, "*Cawwy* me."

"Sure thing, princess." He lifted her into his arms and reached in to touch Daphne's hand. "Ready for this?"

Her eyes brightened. "I can't wait to meet your family. Don't worry about us. Your scowling girls will be fine."

He chuckled and carried Hadley around to help Daphne out on her side. Levi stopped him at the tailgate and said, "Before the craziness starts, I want you to know I've got your back. Daphne seems like a doll."

"Thanks, man, she is. I appreciate that."

"I'll grab your bags. You're going to need both hands." He nodded toward the house as the front door swung open. "Mom's going to go apeshit over both of them."

"As well she should," Jock said.

As Jock helped Daphne out, Jules ran down the front steps and squealed, "I'm so excited you're here!"

Jock turned with Hadley in his arms just as his mother

stepped outside. Shelley Steele was a big, beautiful woman with a zest for life and a heart of gold. She was a few years younger than their father and had looked the same forever, with long auburn hair, bangs, and an ever-present smile. She looked at Jock and a surprised O formed on her lips as she headed for them.

Jules gasped at the sight of Hadley, grinning from ear to ear. "Who is *this*?" She tickled Hadley's belly. "Aren't you just adorable?"

Hadley hid her face in Jock's neck.

"This is Hadley, Daphne's daughter," Jock said, rubbing Hadley's back.

"Well, you are just *full* of surprises!" Jules hugged Daphne and said, "I'm so glad you came! I can't wait for you to meet everyone."

"Me too. I'm excited," Daphne said.

"*Jackie.*" His mother sounded on the verge of tears.

"Hi, Mom." He gave her a one-armed hug, but she hugged him for all she was worth, and he soaked up her love. "Mom, this is my girlfriend, Daphne, and her daughter, Hadley."

"Hi, Daphne. I'm Shelley. It is *such* a pleasure to meet you." She wrapped Daphne in a warm embrace.

"What *other* secrets are you keeping?" Jules whispered.

"Wouldn't you like to know?" Jock teased.

"I've heard so much about you," Daphne said. "Thank you for letting us join you. I hope you don't mind that I brought Hadley. My parents were going to watch her, but my mom got sick. I promise I'll keep an eye on her so she doesn't interfere with the party."

"I'm sorry your mom isn't well, but, honey, I'm *thrilled* that you brought Hadley. The more the merrier," his mother said.

"And don't you worry for a minute about her interfering with the party. I raised six children. I can handle a…three-year-old?"

"Almost," Daphne said. "She'll be three next weekend."

"Then I haven't lost my touch," Shelley joked, eyeing Jules. Some sort of secret message passed between them.

Jock and Daphne had plans to shop for birthday presents for Hadley when they got back from the island. He was excited to spoil his littlest girl.

"Where's Grandma? Champagne brunch with the Bra Brigade?" Jock asked.

"Of course, and their special *bingo* game." Amusement rose in Shelley's eyes, and she said, "My mother thinks I don't know about her secret trips to Pythons with her lady friends. As if I don't notice that every year she has a purse full of one-dollar bills when she leaves."

"Pythons? Isn't that a club on the Cape that has male dancers?" Daphne asked.

"It sure is," Jules said, earning glares from Levi and Jock. She rolled her eyes. "I mean, that's what I've *heard*."

"In my day we called them strippers," Shelley said. "Mark my word, when Grandma comes back to get ready for the party, she and all of her Bra Brigaders will have ink stains on the backs of their left hands where they've scrubbed off the entry stamp."

"Your mother sounds like she's a lot of fun. Not that I go to strip clubs." Daphne blushed.

"My mother will *never* stop carousing," Shelley said. "She's the one who started the Bra Brigade, which is what my mother and her friends call themselves because they like to sunbathe in their bras. They've been doing it since they were teenagers, and to this day, they still get together every summer, pick a spot, and do their thing."

"I stumbled upon them once up on the cliffs by Fortune's Landing. I'm still scarred from that." Jock put his arm around Daphne and said, "My grandmother will try to recruit you into the Brigade."

"Yes, she will and, Daphne, you'll love every second of it," Shelley said. "Why don't we go inside so you can get settled. I made up your old room, Jackie. We'll put Hadley in Archer's old room since your room and his have the adjoining bathroom."

As they headed inside, Shelley and Jules flanked Daphne, chatting animatedly, and led her inside ahead of Jock and Levi.

"You're outnumbered now, dude," Levi teased.

Jock kissed Hadley's forehead and said, "I was already outnumbered, and I freaking love it."

# Chapter Nineteen

JOCK STEPPED INTO the foyer of his childhood home, enveloped by the delicious aroma of his mother's baking and happy echoes of the past. He could still hear the sounds of him and his siblings racing up the stairs, through the center hall, blazing a path to the patio doors, laughing and egging each other on. He could still smell his father's spicy cologne as he walked into a room, still see his work boots among the pile of children's shoes by the door. Even the anxiety of seeing Archer later today didn't take away from the overwhelmingly peaceful sensation of being within these love-drenched walls.

Levi put their suitcase and backpack by the stairs and said, "I'm going to get the golf carts ready and drive them around back."

"Thank you, lovey," Shelley said.

"Golf carts?" Daphne asked.

"We use them to drive to and from the winery," Shelley explained. "Why don't Jules and I take Hadley into the kitchen for a cookie and you two can take your things upstairs to get settled?"

"It's okay. We can take Hadley with us," Daphne offered.

"I want cookie." Hadley wriggled from Jock's arms and

toddled over to Shelley, taking her hand.

Jock's heart felt like it might explode, and from the look on Daphne's face as he reached for her hand, hers did as well.

"You mean, if I had offered her a cookie, she wouldn't have hidden in Jack's neck?" Jules smirked. "I won't make *that* mistake again."

"Is this okay, Mom?" Shelley asked Daphne.

"Of course. Thank you," Daphne said.

When Shelley and Hadley headed into the kitchen, Jock pressed his lips to Daphne's and said, "You okay?"

"I *love* them. Did you see Hadley walk right over to her and take her hand? Oh my gosh. She never does that. Your mom is *so* nice, and every bit as beautiful as you said. You have her smile and her eyes. Levi is awesome, and he obviously thinks the world of you, and you already know I love Jules. I just don't want Hadley to be a bother to anyone."

"Everyone who is coming tonight knows kids get cranky when they're tired and are shy around new people. It'll be fine, and I'll stick close to both of you—don't worry."

They went up to his room, and he set their things inside the bedroom door. His parents had kept all of their bedrooms the same when they'd moved out, though they'd replaced the blankets on the beds. Jock's old desk sat beneath the window. His bookshelves were filled with horror novels and littered with sports trophies. His old boxing gloves hung from a hook on the wall beside a picture of him and Archer, lanky, sweaty, and smirking, after a boxing tournament in which he'd taken first place and Archer had taken second. He glanced through the open bathroom door into Archer's room and got a funky feeling in his gut.

"So, this is where the midnight prowler *slash* troublemaker slept." Daphne ran her hand along his bed and then peered out the window. "And this is where you snuck out."

She turned around, smiling as she came to him, turning the discomfort in his gut to determination.

"So, *Jackie*, have you deflowered any girls in this bed?" she teased.

He chuckled. "Absolutely not, but I will hopefully be *devouring* a very special woman in that bed tonight." He lowered his lips to hers in a tender kiss. "Thank you for being here."

"You're welcome. I'm glad I'm here, and I'm looking forward to you meeting my family next weekend at Hadley's party."

"Me too."

"I know I said this in the car before we left, but I still can't get over that you're okay holding Hadley. She's so happy when you hold her," she said. "What changed?"

He gathered her in his arms and said, "*Everything*. I'm moving forward. You and Hadley ground me in the present, and that's where I want to stay. I *want* to hold her, to be the man you both feel safe with. I'm going to try to work things out with Archer, and I know he'll drag me back into the nightmare of our pasts, but I promise you, I'm not going to let that ruin our time here, or take away any of the changes I've made."

"You're amazing. I just want you to know that."

He pressed his lips to hers and said, "No, angel. You are the amazing one."

"I guess that means we're an amazing couple." She wound her arms around his neck and said, "Did you see how thrilled your mom was when she saw you? *I* wanted to cry. It makes me so happy that you're *here* and you're willing to try to make things better. Levi said you were his hero. You're ours, too,

Jock. We believe in you."

Gratitude swelled inside him. He brushed his lips over hers and said, "It's all because of you, angel, you and your little princess." He lowered his mouth to hers, taking her in a sweet, slow kiss, as he'd been waiting to do all morning.

"*Oops*," his mother said. "Sorry, honey."

They parted on a giggle and a blush and found his mother turning to leave the room.

"It's okay, Mom."

"Is Hadley okay?" Daphne asked, slipping into mommy mode despite the blush on her cheeks.

"She's fine, darlin'. She and Jules are having a discussion about *Dock*. She is the cutest thing. I just want to eat up those little cheeks."

"Thank you," Daphne said. "Why don't I go downstairs and give you two time to catch up."

Jock watched her leave the room, and his mother watched him. Her eyes became glassy as she touched his face and said, "I can't believe you're home for a whole night."

"It's been a long time since I've been in this room." He put his arms around her, hugging her too long and too tight, but that didn't stop him from holding on a little longer, because he'd missed her so damn much.

When he finally let her go, she said, "It's been a long time for a lot of things, Jackie. I've been so worried about you since Harvey died. This past year without him has been very difficult for all of us."

"What do you mean? Why did Harvey's death affect you and Dad so much?"

"Oh, honey." She looked a little pensive. "Harvey loved you so much. He would have done anything for you, and he did. He knew you wanted to keep your distance from home, and he allowed you the space to do it. But it was torture for us to let you have that space, and Harvey knew that. He kept in touch with me and your father and let us know how you were doing. Harvey was the reason I wasn't on your doorstep every week. He didn't only help you through your grief; he helped us through ours."

A lump formed in Jock's throat. "He did that?"

"Yes. He loved you like a son, and he wanted you to heal so you could eventually move on and have a full, happy life. Like I said, he would have done anything for you. I know he's smiling down on you right now. I can feel it. He would be so pleased with how happy you appear to be."

"I am happy, Mom. I didn't think it was possible to feel this much for someone. For both of them. I never understood what you and Dad really felt for each other until now."

"My baby's falling in love," she said, her eyes tearing again.

"*Mom.*" He pulled her into another hug, giving them both a moment to recover from the emotions filling up the room, and kissed the top of her head.

She wiped her eyes and fanned her face. "I'm sorry, Jack. All a mother wants is for her kids to be happy, and I didn't know if you'd ever let yourself get close to another woman, much less a woman with a child."

"I didn't either," he said honestly. Daphne's voice whispered through his mind. *Don't we owe our parents peace of mind? Your parents are probably still grieving for their sons' broken hearts and broken relationship.* Damn right he owed it to them. "Mom, I'm done running from the past. I don't know what will happen between me and Archer, but it's time to figure it out."

She huffed out a breath, swiping at a tear sliding down her

cheek, and said, "You'd better get it all out now, so I'm not a crying mess at Grandma's party."

"Aw, Mom. I love you."

"Now you're just making it worse," she said, wiping her eyes.

He laughed. "Sorry. There is one more thing I need to talk to you about."

She planted a hand on her hip and said, "If you're going to tell me that Hadley is yours and you've been hiding her and Daphne from us for three years, I'm not going to be happy that you've kept that beautiful little girl and her mama a secret. A mother has her limits, you know."

*I wish she were mine.* "It's not that," he said with a chuckle. "It's my name. I know when I'm home I'm *Jack*, but for the last decade I've been *Jock*. If you don't mind, I'd like to honor Harvey by using the nickname he gave me."

"Oh, baby. I don't care if I have to call you *Snoopy* as long as I get to see you, hug you, and know that you're okay."

"And Dad? Do you think he'll mind?" Jock asked.

Her gaze softened, and she said, "No. I'll let him know. Harvey came into your life at a time when we couldn't have given you what you needed. Dad and I are forever grateful to him for that."

"Thank you. I'm glad you're okay with it. I'll let everyone else know tonight at the party. I should probably get downstairs and make sure Daph is doing all right."

"I have a feeling she's a tough cookie."

"She is a hell of a woman."

"Okay, Jackie." She shook her head and said, "*Jockey.* Oh goodness, now you sound like you need a horse."

They both laughed.

"Why don't you and the others take everything to the winery and get started while I make up Archer's room for Hadley?"

"Do you want some help?"

"No thanks, sweetheart. I haven't gotten a room ready for a little girl in a long time. I keep waiting for Joey to outgrow her tomboy stage, but I'm not holding my breath. I'm going to enjoy this."

"Don't go to too much trouble. Hadley won't care if there are football sheets."

"You've got a lot to learn, mister," she said as she headed for Archer's room. "Maybe Levi can clue you in. Joey wasn't always a tomboy."

He hurried down to the kitchen and found Jules, Daphne, and Hadley sitting on stools at the counter watching Levi on the opposite side, making faces and jumping around like a monkey. Hadley was nibbling on a cookie, completely unaffected by Levi's antics.

"This explains why you don't have a girlfriend," Jules teased. "Hey, Jack. He's trying to get Hadley to smile."

"I figured." Jock put one hand on Daphne's shoulder, his other on Hadley's. "Looking pretty cool there, Levi."

"Dude, she's a hard nut to crack. Kids usually love me. What'd you do? Pay her off?" He looked at Hadley and said, "Come on, Hadley. Just one smile for Uncle Levi?"

Hadley looked flatly at him and bit into her cookie. Then she looked at Jock and a wide, cookie-crumble smile lit up her face, making the girls laugh and Levi mutter under his breath.

"Attagirl." Jock kissed the top of her head. "Give it up, Levi."

Levi shook his head. "No way, man. I'm going to get a smile out of that cute little face before the day's done."

"Have it your way," Jock said. "Mom wants us to head over to the winery and get started."

"I already put everything in the hauler. We're good to go," Levi said. "Is Mom coming?"

"No. She's fixing up Archer's room for Hadley."

"She doesn't have to go to any trouble," Daphne said. "Hadley can sleep with us."

Levi arched a brow.

Jock ran a hand down Hadley's back and said, "I think she'll be more comfortable in her own bed."

"Should I stay and help your mom?" Daphne asked.

"I offered. She's fine."

Jules climbed off her stool and said, "She'll have that room transformed into some kind of toddler haven by the time we get back."

"Okay, then I should run Hadley to the bathroom first," Daphne said. "I want to grab the toy bag for her, too."

"Levi, why don't you and Jules go ahead, and we'll catch up," Jock suggested, picking up Owly from the counter so they didn't forget him. They'd gone for a walk on the beach the other night and had forgotten to bring it. He'd had to run back to Daphne's apartment to get it.

Levi snagged the golf cart keys from the counter, and Jules said, "Hey, I want to drive."

"And I want to get there in one piece," Levi said on the way out the kitchen door.

"Come on, babe. I'll show you where the bathroom is." As they went down the hall, Jock said, "I have a feeling everyone is going to try to get Hadley to smile."

"That's okay," Daphne said.

"I know they mean well, but I worry about her. She's just a

little girl, and we don't want her to feel pressured, do we? I mean, we have no idea what she's thinking. Maybe it's good that she's discerning." He turned on the bathroom light for her and realized Daphne was looking at him funny. "What did I say?"

"You said *we*."

"Sorry. I didn't realize—"

She silenced him with a soft press of her lips and said, "I liked it. Thank you for putting her first. I understand what you're saying, but since this is the first time your family is meeting us, and she seems to be doing well with them, maybe we should just let it go."

"Okay. You know her best."

After Hadley used the bathroom, they grabbed the toy bag and drove one of the golf carts to the winery.

"This is so fun," Daphne said. "You're lucky to have such a close family. Levi told me all about Harborside. Did you know that he and two of your cousins—Jesse and Brent—are in the same motorcycle club as Chloe's fiancé, Justin? Justin is a member of the Bayside chapter of the Dark Knights."

"Yeah, I know."

"Levi said his Dark Knights brothers are like uncles to Joey, who sounds incredible, by the way. Levi and Jules raved about her. I can't wait to meet her. Jules said the same thing you did about growing up on the island, that everyone watched out for everyone else's kids. You guys were so lucky. It sounds like another fairy tale. I can't imagine Hadley growing up with that many people watching out for her. What a great life."

"Hadley's lucky, too. She's got you, your family, your friends at Bayside, and she's got *me*."

"You're right. We're both lucky."

Jock parked beside the other golf carts near the patio behind the winery. The building was U-shaped, with a courtyard nestled in the back and a covered pavilion just across the lawn. The courtyard had a built-in bar and fire pit. It bled into lush green lawn and was separated from the vineyard by a stone knee wall. All those rows of vines, between which Jock and his siblings used to race, was a glorious, comforting sight. But today he had bigger things on his mind than childhood games. He scanned the grounds for Archer, but all was quiet. His gaze swept over stacks of folded wooden chairs lying in the courtyard to the open double doors of the winery, and his nerves prickled.

"You were right about the view. You can see *everything*. I bet the lights on the island are gorgeous at night," Daphne said as they climbed out of the cart. "I can't believe you live next door to a winery. This is so cool. Do you ever regret not becoming part of your family's business?"

"Down," Hadley said, trying to wriggle free. Daphne set her down, and she ran to Jock, arms up, clutching her owl. "Up!"

Jock picked her up and said, "No. I wanted to get out in the world and become a great screenwriter."

"You became a great author instead."

"With a great girlfriend," he said, and leaned in for a kiss. "Who has an equally great little princess." He kissed Hadley's cheek, earning one of her special smiles.

"You gweat!" Hadley said.

Holding Hadley, with Daphne looking at him like he was pretty damn special, he sure felt great.

"There you are," Jules said as she came out of the winery with an armful of string lights.

Levi and their father followed her out, each carrying a long wooden table. Steve Steele was thick-chested, with short silver-

and-black hair and a neatly trimmed beard. He was Jock's soft-spoken pillar of strength. He believed in hard work, family, and taking care of those around him, which was why they had very little turnover of staff at the vineyard.

"That has to be your father. Wow. I thought you looked like your mom, but you look *just* like him, without the salt-and-pepper hair," Daphne said.

"Yeah, that's my old man," he said proudly, although Archer looked more like him than Jock did. "Come on. I'll introduce you."

His father laid the table he was carrying down on the patio, studying Jock with a mischievous grin. "If I'd known all it would take was a pretty woman and an adorable little girl to get you here, I would have started recruiting years ago." He put his arms around Jock and Hadley, embracing them warmly, and said, "I've missed you, son. Missed you so damn much."

"I missed you too, Dad." Jock breathed deeply, trying to ease the emotions clogging his chest. "Dad, this is my girlfriend, Daphne, and her daughter, Hadley. Daph, this is my dad, Steve."

"Hi, darlin'." He embraced her and kissed her cheek. "Thank you for bringing my boy home."

"I didn't do anything," she said.

"I think we both know better." His father put his hands on his hips, and his face turned serious as he looked at Hadley, who was staring stoically back at him. "So, you're Hadley?"

Hadley's expression didn't change.

He clapped a hand on Jock's shoulder and said, "You take good care of my son, you hear me, sweet one?"

Hadley put her arms around Jock's neck and said, "*My* Dock."

His father laughed and said, "Oh my goodness, son. Your mother is going to eat this one up."

"She already has." Jock put an arm around Daphne and said, "Hadley and her mama have that effect on people."

He pressed a kiss to Daphne's temple as Archer strode around the corner of the building, scowling like he was full of piss and vinegar. Jock held Daphne a little tighter, his nerves knotting as his brother stopped cold several yards away, staring him down. Archer had military-short dark hair and a short beard, which made him look a bit menacing. He was beefier than Jock, with a thick neck, barrel chest, bulging biceps, and about a thousand pounds of hatred aimed right at him.

Jock lifted his chin and squared his shoulders. "Archer."

Archer scoffed and strode back the way he came.

*Motherfucker.* Jock handed Hadley to Daphne, and as calmly as he was able, he said, "Be right back, angel." He eyed Levi. "You got them?"

"I've got *you*," Levi said, holding his gaze. "Jules—"

"We're good. I've got them," Jules said cheerily, and she went to Daphne's side.

"*Jackson.*" His father gave him a warning look.

"I've got this, Dad. It's time." As he and Levi went after Archer, Jock sure as hell hoped he was right. "Give us some space, okay?" he said to Levi as they strode across the lawn.

Levi held his hands up and stopped walking, planting his feet firmly in the grass, and said, "You got it."

As Jock closed the distance between him and Archer, his skin felt too tight, his veins constricting. He gritted out, "*Archer.*"

Archer slowed to a stop, his shoulders rising as he turned. "What the hell do you want?"

Jock stopped a foot from him, hurt and anger rushing through him like a tsunami held back by the gigantic force of sadness. "Don't you think it's time we talked?"

Archer gritted his teeth, hands fisting, eyes narrowing.

"I know I fucked up, Archer, and I haven't tried hard enough to fix things between us, but come on, man. I'm standing here looking at you, and I see my old best friend. I want to fix this and get back to that."

"That's what you see?" Archer's chest expanded. He took a step forward, getting right in Jock's face, and said, "When I look at you, I see the guy who *killed* my best friend."

He turned to walk away, and Jock grabbed his arm. Archer spun around with fire in his eyes, yanking his arm free. Jock stood his ground and bit out, "You don't have to like *me*, but you sure as hell are going to respect Daphne and Hadley."

"Oh yeah?" Archer scoffed. "Respect your fucking *replacements?*"

His words hit like a knife to the chest, and it took all of Jock's control to curl his hands into fists and channel all of his energy to them instead of pounding the hell out of Archer. "There's no replacing Kayla or Liam," he seethed. "I lost them, too, Archer. And *then* I lost you. I've given you space. I stayed away so you wouldn't have to see me, but I'm *done* with that. I'm here for Grandma, for Jules, for Mom and Dad. I'm here for *myself*, and you're just going to have to deal with it."

Archer's nostrils flared. He lifted his chin, his eyes shooting daggers. Baring his teeth like a rabid dog, he said, "Stay the fuck out of my way, and I'll stay out of yours."

Archer stalked away, leaving Jock reeling with anger, disappointment, and everything in between. They weren't done with that conversation.

Not even close.

DAPHNE FELT LIKE her heart was going to climb out of her chest to get to Jock as he stood with his hands fisted, staring after Archer. She *had* to go to him.

His father touched her arm, stopping her, and said, "It's best to give him a minute."

"He's right," Jules said. "Let him calm down."

Daphne's heart raced, and she didn't know if she was making a monumental mistake that his family might never understand or forgive, but she knew one thing for sure. Jock needed her.

She put her hand on Hadley's back, speaking as calmly as she could, and said, "I appreciate where you're coming from, but I told Jock he wasn't alone in this, and I meant it. If you'll excuse me."

She hurried toward Jock, hoping he wouldn't send her away. He was standing with his back to them, head bowed. He turned as she approached, sadness brimming in his eyes, and her heart sank.

"Jock," she said, reaching for him.

He shrugged and shook his head, and then his strong arms circled her and Hadley. He held her without saying a word for a long moment. Daphne felt his heart racing. He tightened his hold on them, and she ached for him.

"I'm sorry," she said.

He drew back, gazing down at her with determination in his eyes, and said, "I'm not done trying."

"*Dock* sad?" Hadley reached for him.

The edges of his lips tipped up as he lifted Hadley into his arms and said, "A little sad, princess, but don't you worry. It just makes me more determined to fix things and be happy."

A hint of a smile lifted Hadley's cheeks. She held out Owly, offering it to him, and said, "Be *happy*."

Tears stung Daphne's eyes.

Jock kissed Hadley's cheek and put an arm around Daphne. "I've got all I need, Had. You keep Owly."

Hadley clutched the stuffed animal to her chest.

Daphne loved that he was putting up a strong front for Hadley, but as much as she appreciated it, she needed him to know she was there for him through the good and the bad. "Are you okay, Jock? Do you want to go someplace to talk?"

"I'm still processing what just happened." He kissed her temple and said, "He's still filled with hate, but I'm not giving up. It might not be fixable this trip, or next, but I realized something when I was with him. I miss the friendship we had more than I let myself know, and I'll fight tooth and nail to get that back, even if it takes years. But as I said, I'm not going to let it ruin our time here."

"I'm glad you want to make it better, but if you need time alone to be sad or to process this, it's okay. Hadley and I will be fine."

"I've been alone for so long. I never want to be alone again."

# Chapter Twenty

JOCK REASSURED DAPHNE that he was okay, and after he did the same with his father, Levi, and Jules, there was a flurry of activity as they joined the others in setting up for the party. Hadley played in the grass with her toys while Jock and Levi carried out more long wooden tables and Jules and Daphne draped them with table runners. When Archer showed up, he and Steve strung lights in the trees surrounding the courtyard. The tension between Jock and Archer was as inescapable as a cage riddled with rusty nails and topped with barbed wire. Daphne had no idea how Jock was able to carry on with that type of tension, but he seemed to be having a good time with Levi, while Archer didn't say much to anyone.

"It's weird, isn't it? Seeing my brothers ignore each other?" Jules asked as they spread a runner along another table.

"I just feel bad for them. You can see they're both hurting."

"Yup," Jules said. "We should lock them in a room together and make them duke it out. That's what they used to do. They'd get mad at each other and roll around on the grass wrestling. My father would pry them apart and haul their butts into the garage to fight it out in the boxing ring."

"You had a boxing ring in your garage?"

"Yup. My dad boxed in college, and he taught my brothers and their friends to box, too. You'll meet some of their friends tonight. Brant Remington and the Silver brothers, Grant, Fitz, and Wells. Everyone used to call Brant and Grant the *Bee Gees* just to piss them off. It was hilarious. You'll meet my friends, too. You're going to have so much fun."

The sounds of horns honking drew their attention to two golf carts cruising across the grass. Shelley was in the driver's seat of the leading cart, with a cute little cinnamon-haired girl in her lap. The girl was steering, and the pretty blonde in the passenger seat was waving to Levi. The other cart was a bit farther out, but Daphne could see a blonde and an auburn-haired woman in the front, and another blonde in the back.

"The troops have arrived!" Jules exclaimed. "Come on. I'll introduce you."

"Is that Joey with your mom?" Daphne asked.

"Yes, and the blonde with them is Tara Osten. She's Joey's aunt. She's one of my closest friends, and she spends a lot of time with us, especially when Levi and Joey are in town."

"Will Joey's mom be here tonight?"

"No. Amelia is a travel writer, and her schedule is crazy."

"Let me grab Hadley." Daphne turned to get her, but Jock was one step ahead and had already scooped Hadley into his arms. "I was just coming for her."

Jock flashed one of his devastating grins. "You've got to be quicker than that."

As everyone climbed out of the carts, Tara headed for Levi, and Joey ran to Jock. "Uncle Jack's here!"

"Give me Had so you can say hi." Daphne reached for her daughter, and Joey jumped into Jock's arms, hugging him tight.

"*My Dock! My Dock!*" Hadley cried, thrusting her body

toward Jock.

"No, honey. Jock needs to visit with his niece. He can hug you in a minute," Daphne said, rubbing Hadley's back.

"*Dock, cawwy me!*" Hadley pleaded.

"Who's that?" Joey asked, with one arm hooked around Jock's neck.

"Joey, this is Hadley, my girlfriend's daughter." He lifted Hadley into his other arm and said, "And this is my girlfriend, Daphne."

"Hi, Joey. I'm sorry about Hadley." Daphne looked at Jock and said, "Are you sure you can handle both? I can take Hadley someplace else."

He gave her a *get real* look as Hadley put both arms around his neck and scowled at Joey.

"She *really* likes Uncle Jack." Joey waved at Hadley and said, "Hi, Hadley. I'm Joey."

Hadley buried her face in Jock's neck, clinging tighter.

"*Hadley*, be nice," Daphne chided her softly. "I'm sorry, Joey. She doesn't smile often."

Shelley joined them and said, "Now, that's a sight I'll never get tired of seeing." She put out her arms and said, "Who wants to come to Grandma Shelley?"

"Me!" Joey yelled. Steve intercepted her, and she yelled, "Grandpa!"

"Grandma Shelley is *my* wife. I get the first kiss." Holding Joey on one hip, Steve put his other arm around Shelley and kissed her right on the lips. "Missed you, gorgeous."

Shelley glowed with love as the other cart parked, and the auburn-haired woman hollered, "Get a room!"

Jock leaned closer to Daphne and said, "That's Leni, Levi's twin."

The three women climbed out of the cart, and Jules said, "The tall blonde is our sister Sutton, and the petite blonde is Leni's friend Indi."

Daphne noticed that all three of Jock's sisters had dainty features. Leni and Sutton had porcelain skin, while Jules sported a golden tan.

Sutton looked chic in a pair of navy capris and a white flowy tank top. She eyed Jock curiously and said, "First you're a caretaker; now you're a *manny*? Wait a second. You couldn't go near Joey when she was little. How is this happening?"

Before Jock could respond, Indi said, "It looks like there *are* benefits to having children."

"Back off, Indi," Jules warned. "That's my brother Jack, and he's holding Hadley, his *girlfriend* Daphne's daughter."

"Hi." Daphne lifted her hand and wiggled her fingers as the girls hugged their parents.

Indi's eyes widened, and she said, "I'm *so* sorry. I'm really not a man stealer. It was just a joke."

"I'm not worried," Daphne said.

"Hi, Daphne. I'm Leni, Jack's sister. Sorry about Indi. I can't take her anywhere." Leni opened her arms to embrace Daphne and said. "It's really nice to meet you."

"It's nice to meet all of you, too," Daphne said as she hugged her. "But I think I'm going to need you to wear name tags."

"I'll wear a name tag if you can tell me how you got my brother near your adorable little girl." Sutton reached out to tickle Hadley.

Hadley pushed closer to Jock and said, "*Dock…?*"

The women *aww*ed in unison.

"It's okay, Had, I've got you," Jock said, rubbing Hadley's

back. "These are my sisters and their friend Indi. They're nice people." He introduced Hadley to each of the women by name and gave her a clue she could remember. "Sutton is really tall with blond hair like Mommy, and Leni has reddish hair. Indi is Leni's friend, and she's—"

"Little wif yellow hair," Hadley said, making them all laugh.

Daphne was touched that he thought to take extra time to make sure Hadley knew who everyone was.

Jock met his sisters' curious gazes and put his arm around Daphne, pulling her closer as he said, "To answer your question about how I'm able to hold Hadley, these two beautiful girls came into my life, and I knew I had to get a handle on my past or I'd lose them."

Daphne smiled up at him, floored by his honesty, and he pressed his lips to hers.

"Why can't I find a guy like him?" Indi said.

Jock chuckled and said, "Archer and Levi are single."

Indi scoffed. "*Archer?* He's the grumpiest man I know."

"That's because you haven't met Grant Silver yet," Jules said.

"Hey, girls, let's be nice, huh?" Shelley said as Tara squealed and ran past them with Levi chasing after her.

"Daddy!" Joey pushed out of Steve's arms and took off after them.

Levi picked up Tara and slung her over his shoulder, grinning like a Cheshire cat.

"Do me, Daddy! Do me!" Joey yelled.

"I bet Tara's thinking the same thing," Leni said quietly, making her sisters laugh.

"*Jules! Mrs. S! Help!*" Tara hollered as she smacked Levi's butt.

"Quiet down back there," Levi said, winking at the girls. He turned his back to them, over which Tara was hanging upside down, and said, "Daphne, say hi to Tara."

"Hi," Daphne said.

Tara twisted, lifting her smiling face to say, "Hi. I'm Tara. Some of these crazies still call me Mouse. I'll answer to either."

"Say goodbye, ladies," Levi said.

Daphne and Tara said, "Bye," in unison, and Levi sauntered off like he carried Tara around every day.

"Guys like that do *not* exist in New York City," Indi said.

"No kidding," Leni and Sutton said in unison.

"All three of you live in the city?" Daphne asked.

"No, just Indi and I do," Leni said. "I work for my cousin Shea's PR firm, and Indi is a hair and makeup artist. Sutton is a reporter for the *Discovery Hour* show, which is part of Ladies Who Write Enterprises. She lives in Port Hudson, New York, near their headquarters. But she's only about an hour away. You and Jack should come visit us sometime. We'll make a weekend of it and show you around the city."

Thinking that the city would hold sad memories for Jock, she said, "I'm more of a small-town girl, but thank you."

"A girl after my own heart," Shelley said. "And for you single big-city girls, if you're really looking for love, all you have to do is come work at the winery." She snuggled up to Steve. "That's how I met Steve, and it's how my mother met my father."

"No, thank you," Sutton and Leni said.

"Hey, if you need a hair and makeup artist for tastings, then sign me up," Indi said cheerily. "I love the city, but this island snagged my heart the first time Leni brought me here."

"You're going to have your hands full tonight with these

ladies, Indi," Steve said.

"I almost forgot," Jules exclaimed. "Daphne, we're all getting ready together before the party, and Indi is going to do our hair and makeup. You *have* to join us."

"Indi really knows her stuff," Leni said.

"Thank you, but I have Hadley. I don't want to ruin your fun," Daphne said.

"Don't be silly," Shelley said. "She needs to get ready, too. Joey has been getting ready with us for Grandma's birthday parties since she was a tiny baby. It's what we do, honey. I hope you'll both join us."

Excitement bubbled up inside Daphne. "Okay, thank you."

Steve clapped his hands and said, "Now that everyone has been introduced, can we *please* get to work so we can eat lunch and play touch football?"

Jock's family cheered, and then Shelley said, "Okay, ladies, you know the drill. Let's get movin'. Daph, you and Hadley are with me."

"You heard the boss, Had. I have to get to work." Jock kissed Hadley's cheek and set her on her feet.

Hadley looked up at him and said, "I help you?"

"No, honey. You're going to help Mommy," Daphne said.

"Help *Dock*," she pleaded. "*Please?* I be good!"

Hoping Hadley wouldn't have a meltdown, Daphne said, "Jock has to—"

Jock whispered in Daphne's ear, "She can hang with me if it's okay with you."

She filled with gratitude, but before she could respond, Joey ran over carrying a backpack and said, "Can I play with Hadley? I have toys." She unzipped the backpack and tugged it open, showing Hadley all the colorful toys.

"Had, do you want to play with Joey?" Daphne asked.

Hadley nodded.

"Okay. Joey, I'll be with Shelley if you need me, all right?"

"Uh-huh, but I won't. I play with little kids all the time." Joey offered her hand to Hadley. Hadley took it, and Joey led her over to the grass, chattering about her toys.

"Wow, that seemed too easy." Daphne looked up at Jock and said, "Thank you for saying she could go with you. You can't imagine how much it means to me."

"I think I can," he said as he lowered his lips to hers.

"Let's go, lovebirds!" Leni said as she and Sutton sidled up to Daphne. "We need to get to know this wizard of a woman who captured our brother's heart."

They took Daphne by the arms and led her away, rattling off questions about her and Jock. Archer streamed music through outdoor speakers, and over the next couple of hours, Daphne got a tour of the winery, which was warm and inviting with a mix of rich wood tones and stone, and she got to know Jock's siblings as they set up tables and chairs, strung lights above the patio, hung candle lanterns from trees, and tied pretty purple ribbons—Grandma Lenore's favorite color—onto each of the chairs. Every time Jock walked past, he stole a kiss, winked, or touched her hand or shoulder, and he kept an eagle eye on Hadley and Joey. Daphne had never felt so taken care of and loved.

As she and Shelley tied ribbons on the chairs, Daphne thought about her earlier conversation with Shelley and the girls. She'd told them about her divorce, her job at the resort, and how she and Jock had met. She'd also told them about her family, and they had been thrilled to hear that she, too, was a twin. They'd joked about her and Jock getting married and having lots of twin babies. Daphne had tucked that enticing idea away beside her overzealous heart.

"I love when all of my kids are here," Shelley said as she picked up another ribbon. "Did you know this is the first time since Jock left the island that he's stayed overnight?"

"Yes, he told me. He misses coming here."

Shelley gazed at Jock across the courtyard and said, "We miss him, too. I bet you wonder why Steve and I haven't intervened between him and Archer."

"I don't really. I know it's hard for everyone, and they're adults."

Shelley glanced at Archer and said, "They were barely adults when the accident happened." She came to Daphne's side and said, "We probably should have done more back then, but they were so hurt and angry. Our efforts just made it worse. When it comes to their relationship, they've always had this bubble around them that nobody could penetrate. I used to think they'd be one of those twin sets who developed their own language, but they never did. They just had their own secrets." Her lips curved into a smile. "But one day things will get better. Jock seems determined about that now that a certain someone and her little lady have opened up his heart again."

Shelley turned back to the ribbons. Daphne thought about what Archer had said to Jock in the hospital and wondered if it wasn't such a big secret after all.

When they finished with the chairs, they stood back to take it all in. Each table had white and lavender silk table runners, complemented by the purple bows on the chairs. The girls were putting out china place settings, decorative crystal candle holders, and elegant wineglasses with swirly designs on them on the tables. Daphne tried to imagine the floral centerpieces on the tables and the cloth napkins folded prettily and set in place.

Shelley put her hands on her hips and said, "Jock said you were an event planner at your last job. Want to give me your professional opinion?"

"I'm hardly a professional, but I do love event planning and I miss doing it. The closest I come to it these days is planning the monthly meeting for my book club, which I mentioned to you and the girls earlier. Thank you for letting me be part of this. It's all beautiful. The china and crystal make the wooden tables country chic, which is all the rage right now. Once the centerpieces are put in place, they'll tie it all together beautifully and really bring the setting to life, with the lights in the trees and strung over the patio"—as if on cue, the lights in the trees lit up, and Daphne's breath caught. "Oh, Shelley. It's magical."

"Let's hope it stays that way. Two years ago, half of the lights went out during the party."

"That's not an event planner's *worst* nightmare, but it's definitely a big one. I noticed you're using holiday lights. They make heartier industrial string lights. Have you ever tried them?"

"I didn't even know they made them. Our lights are so old, it's a wonder they work at all. We've been using the same lights and everything forever. My father used to throw my mom her birthday parties just like this. He passed away about fifteen years ago, and Steve and I took over. We thought it was best to keep things the way they were."

"I'm so sorry for your loss."

"Thank you. It was a long time ago. Tell me about those lights."

"They're *great*. Since they're commercial grade and made for outdoor use, you don't have to take them down between events.

They use bigger bulbs, and they're not as finicky as holiday lights, so if you lose one bulb, you don't lose the entire string." She looked at the stone knee wall, her creative mind ticking into gear, and said, "I was thinking about the stone wall. It's so unique. Have you thought about stringing blue lights along it? That would extend the party area for your larger events and give you a gorgeous backdrop for pictures for evening weddings or anniversary parties."

"We don't do those types of events here," Shelley said. "We do tastings, of course, and we hold my mother's birthday party and the Halloween gathering, Field of Screams."

"Jock told me about that. It sounds fabulous."

"It's a great gathering of friends. It's funny how much you'll do for your kids. But other than that, events are my friend Margot's territory. She and her husband run the Silver House resort with their son Fitz. Silver House is the island's premier event venue."

"Our friends were married there in the spring. It's gorgeous."

"You were at the wedding with Jack—Jock?"

"Not as a couple, but yes, Hadley and I, and all of our friends were there. But destination weddings are huge right now. Surely there's enough event business for the Silver House *and* the winery. When I worked at the resort in North Carolina, people were always looking for unique venues. We were booked all year long and had to refer customers to other resorts." She looked out at the vineyards and said, "This view is breathtaking. It's a shame not to give it the exposure it deserves. Have you thought about working *with* Margot? I bet you could host bridal showers, weddings, anniversary parties, just about anything, and you could recommend Silver House as the lodging, or have them cater the event. That would give your friends new business. Or you could hold the rehearsal dinners and they hold the wedding, or vice versa."

"Those are great ideas, but between tastings and tours, I don't have time to think about one more thing."

"Maybe you could hire someone to help you," Daphne suggested.

"Yes, if we were that kind of business. But we've always been primarily a family-run business. We have other help, of course, but they're from families we've known forever. And unfortunately, none of my kids besides Archer, who is knee-deep in operations, wants anything to do with the vineyard or the winery."

"I understand," she said, but ideas continued sprouting in her mind like spring flowers. "If the Silvers have an event planner, maybe you could work with them and rent out this space for weddings. Then you'd just need a point person to coordinate with them."

"Now, that's thinking creatively. If only I could steal you away from Bayside," Shelley said with a wink.

"If only..." Daphne said it casually, but that seed of longing inside her dug a little deeper. "In any case, you did a magnificent job with this entire setup. I can't wait to see it all come together tonight. The cookies were so good, I can only imagine how tasty the pies and cakes you made for dessert are going to be. Are you having the dinner catered?"

"I have to. I can't cook for forty people *and* fit in time for our traditional touch-football game. My friend Ava de Messieres is catering for me. She owns a little bistro by the beach."

"A bistro? That sounds fancy."

Shelley shook her head. "It used to be quite nice, but Ava's a bit too fond of the bottle, if you know what I mean. She has two beautiful daughters that are Leni's and Sutton's age, Abigail and Dierdra. The poor girls did the best they could by her, but they needed to get on with their own lives and have moved off the island. They're doing well, but Ava's bistro has been floundering for a while now. When our kids were younger, they'd help out at the bistro, waiting and busing tables sometimes, and we have always tried to give her business when we can."

The lights on some of the trees went out, and Archer cursed.

Shelley winced. "Uh-oh. I think I'd better get that lighting information before Grandma's next birthday party. Actually, you haven't been properly introduced to Archer yet, have you?"

Daphne tried to hide her nervousness with a smile. "Not yet."

"Are you feeling strong?" Shelley asked with a flicker of amusement in her eyes.

"Strong enough," she said, hoping it was true.

Shelley gave her hand a supportive squeeze and said, "Good. Let me introduce you to my beautiful disgruntled boy."

As they walked across the patio, Daphne looked for Jock, but he must have gone into the building. Archer stood on a ladder fiddling with a string of lights.

"Archer, honey?" Shelley said.

"Yeah?" he said gruffly, and peered down at her.

His dark eyes shifted to Daphne, brows slanted, making him look more like Jock. But while Jock's eyes had been shadowed with hurt and anger when he'd told Daphne about the accident and the showdown with Archer, Archer's blazed with ire. He had his father's sharp jawline. He was a beast of a man and looked rock hard, with muscles upon muscles and tree-trunk legs. Daphne hoped his heart hadn't become impenetrable, too.

"I don't think you've met Jock's lovely girlfriend, Daphne," Shelley said.

"Nice to meet you," he said curtly, and returned his attention to the lights.

Daphne gathered her courage and said, "Hi. I understand you and Jock are having a hard time, but I hope one day Hadley and I can get to know you better."

He glowered down at her. "A *hard time*?" He scoffed.

Daphne was shaking a little, but she wanted to be strong for Jock, so she didn't give up trying to chip away at Archer's walls. "I'm sorry for your loss, Archer. Jock said Kayla was very special to you, and I can't imagine how hard it was to lose her."

"You're right, you can't," he said gruffly. "I've got to get these lights fixed."

Shelley pursed her lips. "Archer Steele, I raised you to be kinder than that."

"Yes, you did," he said through gritted teeth. "But sometimes life beats the kindness out of a person."

"I know something about being beaten down by life," Daphne said carefully. "And about finding a way not to hate when you feel like your insides are made of shattered glass. You don't have to like me or my daughter, Archer, but that doesn't mean I'll dislike you."

Archer's brows knitted, but he didn't say a word.

Shelley studied Daphne for a moment with an empathetic and appreciative expression. "Well, then," she said, cutting through the tension. "Just one more thing, Archer. Daphne has a background in event planning, and she has some interesting ideas. She was telling me about industrial lights that we can use to cut down on frustrations like these."

"These lights are fine," he said sharply.

"For now, yes, but maybe for next year we should look into them," Shelley said.

Having used up her courage and hoping to avoid any further conversation with Archer, Daphne said, "Shelley, why don't I get your number and text you a link for the lights?"

"Good idea. Archer, honey, what do you think about holding events here? Maybe working with the Silvers? It might be worth thinking about."

Without looking at them, he said, "I think that's a family decision, and not one to be made on Grandma's birthday."

"That's a shame, honey," Shelley said a little sarcastically as Jock came out of the winery. "I was hoping to get your two cents before I got my lips on your father and convinced him to take my side."

Jock's brows slanted and his jaw clenched. He strode toward them, his every determined step making Daphne's heart race. The last thing she wanted was to cause a confrontation. Thinking fast, she said, "It was nice to meet you, Archer. The lights are gorgeous. Thank you for introducing us, Shelley." She hurried over to Jock, catching him a few yards from Archer, and took his arm, dragging him away.

"What the hell just happened? What did he say to you?" Jock seethed.

"Your mom was just introducing me. It was fine, and now we've met, so it's done."

He stared as Archer climbed down from the ladder. Their eyes connected, both of their jaws clenching.

Daphne touched Jock's cheek, drawing his eyes to her. She desperately wanted to soothe the tension vibrating off him. She went up on her toes and pressed her lips to his. "All those bad feelings between you two have the power to make or break today for everyone. I know you worry about me, but I'm fine. And I know you want to fix things, but he's obviously not on the same page yet. So why don't we focus on the *good*, spend time with your family, and enjoy this gorgeous day."

He rolled his shoulders back as if they pained him and said, "Yeah, okay."

"Jock!" His father waved him over as Archer stalked into the winery.

"Are *you* okay, babe?" Jock asked.

"Yes. I'm fine. I'm glad your mom introduced us. Now Hadley and I are *people* in Archer's mind, instead of villains."

"Did he say that?" Jock snapped.

"*No.* I just meant it might help to have met me. I'm fine, Jock. Go help your dad." She nudged him away, loving his protective side as much as she adored the rest of him.

By the time they finished setting up, Joey and Hadley were thick as thieves, and Hadley was calling Shelley and Steve *Gwama* and *Gwampa*. Daphne felt like she'd known Jock's family forever, with the exception of Archer, who had pointedly kept his distance from both her and Jock. True to his word, Jock wasn't letting Archer ruin his day. After a few minutes of stewing, he'd begun joking around and enjoying his family.

As everyone else piled into the golf carts to head to the house for the touch-football game, Jock put his arm around Daphne, and together they watched Hadley settle in on Shelley's lap and Joey climb onto Steve's beside them.

"What do you think, angel? Can you handle my family?"

"Handle them? I love them, and it's obvious how much they enjoy having you home. I can't believe how well everyone worked together to get this place ready for the party. I had no idea your family didn't host events here. They should. What a gorgeous venue. Your mom and I were talking about it, but I don't think Archer is very keen on the idea."

"You talked with him about it?"

"Your mom mentioned it to him. It was just a quick chat, nothing really. I hope you and Archer can eventually find your way back into each other's good graces. It would be nice to spend more time with your family in the future."

He gathered her against him, grinning as he said, "I said *we* earlier, and you said *future*...I see a pattern forming."

As he pressed his lips to hers, Leni hollered, "Get a room!"

Heat sparked in Jock's eyes, and he said, "Now, there's a *great* idea."

LUNCH WAS LOUD and chaotic, as per usual at the Steele house. Jock's mother had prepared her famous chicken-parmesan sliders, macaroni and cheese, homemade potato salad, and fruit salad. Everyone helped set the table, and as they ate, their parents told stories about when Jock and his siblings were young. Daphne laughed so hard she had tears in her eyes, and even Archer and Hadley cracked smiles. Jock was glad his parents embarrassed everyone in equal measure, because Levi and the girls took their best cracks at embarrassing him. Joey was treating Hadley like a beloved little sister, which spurred comments about Levi giving Joey a sibling. Levi just shook his head and said it was someone else's turn to deal with sleepless nights and dirty diapers. He said it like it was a bad thing, but to a guy who hadn't seen a family in his future, it sounded like heaven.

As they headed outside to play touch football, Joey and Hadley carried their toys to the shade beneath a tree. The girls huddled together, giggling and talking, and Daphne was right in the middle of it all. Archer and Levi went to get flags to mark the field, and Jock finally took a moment to breathe. He hated the tension between him and Archer, but Daphne's continuous encouragement made him want to try even harder to find a way to fix their relationship. He was starting to think he might need a sledgehammer to break down Archer's walls.

His father sidled up to him and said, "Feeling the need to bolt yet?"

"Not this time," Jock said, watching the girls. "I never felt like it was right to make Archer more uncomfortable by being here. But then Daphne came into my life, and I want her and Hadley to know you guys. She makes me see everything differently, including all that I've been missing here, and I've got to tell you, Dad. I miss this a hell of a lot."

"We've missed it, too. I haven't seen your mother this happy in years." His tone turned serious, and he said, "What's your plan with Archer?"

"I don't know. I don't really have a plan beyond continuing to try to talk it out. Do you have any advice?"

"Yeah, watch yourself around him. He's like a volcano ready to explode. He keeps it under wraps pretty well until he hears you're stopping by, and then there's no hiding his animosity."

Jock knew that, and yet it still hurt to hear his father say it so easily. "I'm sorry to put you and Mom through this for so long. I'm not sure he'll ever get past it, and that's on me. I should have tried harder ages ago."

"This isn't your fault. You were both devastated by what happened. We all were. I'm going to tell you something that I tried to tell you years ago, but you didn't want to hear it then."

"You sure I want to hear it now?" Jock was only half-teasing.

"No, but you need to hear it. When you kids were little, you'd come home from school whiny and argumentative. As a first-time father, I thought I needed to take control of the situation. Not that I could, of course. Tired kids have powers no one else in this world possesses, because they own pieces of their parents' hearts, which makes it hard to do anything other than try to make things better. Anyway, I told your mother I felt like I was failing you and Archer by not teaching you boys to buck up. But she told me that every time we sent you off to school or to friends' houses, we told you to behave, and the *only* place you could be tired and whiny was with us. We were your safe haven, and you knew we would love you no matter what. But you and Archer used to take everything out on each other, and that was another bone of contention for me, because it was one thing to accept it as a parent, but I couldn't just watch you hurt each other. As you got older, we realized that with you and Archer, and eventually with Levi and Leni, we *weren't* always your safe haven. Twins share a womb, and there is no stronger bond than that. You and Archer were a learning experience for us, and I don't know if we did things right or wrong, but we did the best we could."

"You should have named us Trial and Error." Jock watched Archer and Levi marking the field, remembering a few knock-down, drag-out fights with Archer that he thought they'd never recover from. But nothing compared to the pain of silence.

"I guess so. As you two came into your own, we began to

understand that you were each other's safe havens. You would tear each other apart and test that bond with everything you had, but you were always the first to back each other up."

"That didn't happen this time, Dad. When Archer cut me out of his life, I think he meant it."

"Unfortunately, so do I."

Jock felt gutted all over again.

His father held his gaze and said, "I think he meant it *at the time*. We all say things we don't mean, and you know Archer is fierce. He loves as hard as he hates. But I know my son, and he does not hate you. He's lost, Jock. Lost in years of anger and pain, and he can't find his way out. He sees you, and it's a reminder of what he can't do."

"Come on, Dad. You can't believe that."

"I do believe it. The only way you two will get out of this storm is on each other's backs. He needs you more than ever, and I know that's a lot of pressure to put on you, son, so just take it for what it's worth. I'd fix it if I could."

"You ladies going to chat all day?" Levi called over to them. "Or are you going to play?"

His father put a hand on Jock's back and said, "You ready to lose in football?"

Jock scoffed, still processing what his father had said. "Not a chance, old man."

"Hurry up, you guys." Jules waved them over to where everyone had gathered. "We're divvying up teams."

They joined the others, and Levi said, "It's me, Jock, Daphne, Jules, Joey, and Indi versus Dad, Archer, Tara, Leni, Mom, and Sutton." He leaned closer to Jock and said, "*I'll* block Archer."

Shelley was holding Hadley, and she said, "This little lady is playing for *both* teams, so watch your feet people."

"I don't need to play. I'll sit out with Hadley," Daphne offered.

"No, babe. This is what we do." Jock took her hand and said, "Everyone plays—big or little. Joey's been playing since she was younger than Hadley."

"Are you *sure* it's okay?" Daphne asked worriedly. "Hadley might get in the way or get hurt. We've never played this before. Leni explained the rules, but Hadley—"

"We'll all watch out for her, I promise. Don't worry." Jock pressed his lips to hers.

"Are we going to play or what?" Archer snapped.

Jock glowered at him. "Chill out. It's just a game."

Archer grumbled something indiscernible as everyone took their positions.

Daphne took Hadley's hand, falling in line beside Jock, and said, "We're playing a big game of tag. Stay close to Mommy."

As Sutton prepared to hike the ball to Archer, Archer set a threatening gaze on Jock.

"Down. Set," Archer called out. "*Hike!*"

Sutton hiked the ball, and Archer scanned the field as Levi ran toward him. Jock blocked their father, and everyone else scrambled to cover their counterparts. The girls laughed and cheered, and Hadley was right there with them, running after everyone and giggling up a storm as Archer threw the ball to Leni. Indi intercepted, causing an uproar of commotion as she ran toward the goal, dodging their mother and Tara. Archer plowed past everyone and swatted Indi's ass, causing her to shriek and spin around, scowling at his laughter.

Indi lifted her chin and said, "That's probably the most tail you've gotten in years." She strutted off, giving high-fives to all the girls, leaving Archer fuming.

Archer stalked back to his side of the field, knocking into Jock's shoulder as he passed.

"Chill out, bro," Levi called after him.

Archer kept an angry stare locked on Jock over the next few plays. When Shelley scored a touchdown, their father smothered her face with kisses. Tara ran the ball and Levi picked her up as he had earlier, carrying her to the opposite goal, earning cheers and *whoops*. When Jock intercepted a pass, he scooped up Hadley and let her carry the ball into the endzone, where he lifted her over his head, cheering her on along with everyone else. He'd never seen Hadley or Daphne smile so bright—or Archer's glare so dark.

As the afternoon wore on, Archer made snide comments, but Jock let them roll off his back. He didn't need to be dragged into his brother's darkness. Not when everyone else was having so much fun. Their father lifted Joey up to catch a pass despite her being on the opposing team, and they both ran to the endzone, cheered on by everyone else. Joey spiked the ball like a pro, and she and their father went up on their toes in their wacky touchdown dance—knees waggling, fists pumping toward the sky. In the middle of the field, Hadley was trying to mimic the dance, which made everyone else, except Archer, crack up.

Jock wished Archer would lighten up, but all the joking and laughing just seemed to add weight to the chip on his shoulder. In the next play, Jock covered their mother, shuffling to the right, then left, hands up, ready to intercept as she tried to distract him by tickling him from behind. He turned to tickle her, and the ball slammed into his back. Jock's breath flew from his lungs.

"*Archer!*" Jules and their mother yelled at once.

Jock spun around, catching Archer's vindictive grin as Daphne ran to Jock's side. Jock gritted his teeth, hands fisting. "Dude, *really?*"

Archer put his palms to the sky and said, "Sorry, man. It slipped."

"Slipped, my ass," his father said. "Watch it, Archer."

"Are you okay?" Daphne asked.

"*Fine*, but I'm putting a stop to this." He strode toward Archer, but noticed Hadley scowling at his twin, and it stopped him cold. He didn't want her to hate Archer, and he didn't want her to witness the ugliness brewing inside him.

Daphne touched his arm and said, "What are you going to do?"

"Nothing. Not here, at least."

# Chapter Twenty-One

AFTER THE GAME, everyone seemed to have something to do or someplace to be. Archer headed to his boat at Rock Bottom Marina, which, Daphne learned, was where he lived until winter. Tara went home, and Shelley and Sutton took Joey to pick up centerpieces for the party. Leni retreated to her old bedroom to get some work done, and Jules had to go check on her shop. Hadley was exhausted, so while Jock was talking with Levi and their father, Daphne carried her upstairs for a nap. She couldn't remember the last time she and Hadley had enjoyed themselves so much. Jock's family was having a big effect on both of them. Daphne wished the day could go on forever, and her little girl was smiling as much as she did with Daphne's family. Although Daphne had noticed her scowling at Archer a few times. She didn't blame her daughter. Throwing that ball at Jock had been outright mean, and she'd been surprised that Jock hadn't clobbered him. Then again, she was proud of Jock for showing great restraint since they'd arrived.

She carried Hadley into Archer's room, shocked to find the masculine room looking quite feminine. A frilly pink bedspread and princess pillowcases decorated the bed, and a pink lamp with stars dangling from the shade sat on the nightstand. The curtains had been swapped to pink and white instead of blue, and there was even a pretty pink throw rug on the floor. She couldn't believe Shelley had gone to so much trouble for Hadley, whom she'd only just met.

"My mother doesn't do anything halfway," Jock said as he came into the room and put his arm around her.

She loved that he was always touching her, holding her, watching out for her and Hadley. She'd noticed his parents had kissed or touched every time they were near each other, and she took comfort knowing that Jock had grown up in such a loving house.

"Where did she get all of this?" Daphne whispered, so as not to wake Hadley.

"My mom made Levi's old room into a nursery when Joey was born, and it became Joey's room for when she and Levi come visit. Before Joey got into her tomboy stage, she was all about princesses. This was her stuff."

"Your mother is amazing to do all of this for one night."

Jock pulled back the bedspread, and Daphne laid Hadley down on the princess sheets, tucking Owly beside her. She kissed Hadley's forehead, and she and Jock slipped quietly out of the room. Daphne got the baby monitor from her suitcase and put it in the room with Hadley, then joined Jock in his bedroom, pulling Hadley's bathroom door closed behind her.

"Think she'll sleep long?" Jock asked.

"Probably. She was so wiped out. I'm hoping I'll have time for a shower before she wakes up." She lifted his shirt and said, "Let me see your back."

"It's fine."

"That ball hit you hard. We all heard it." She pushed his shirt up again and he reached over his back, tugging it off. He tossed it on the dresser and turned around. "Jock, there's a big purplish-red mark. It's probably going to bruise. Why didn't you say something to Archer?"

He drew her into his arms and said, "Because I didn't want Hadley to see me arguing with him."

"Oh, Jock," she said, filling up with love for him. "You're always thinking of her."

"You're my girls." He kissed her softly. "I'm sorry about Archer's attitude."

"I'm sorry for both of you. He's so angry. Are you going to try to talk to him again?"

"At some point. I don't want to ruin everyone's weekend by having it out with him. But I'm not giving up. If we don't talk it out this visit, then next time, or the next, because you were right. This is my home, too, and I want to be here, enjoying my family. I want to show you and Hadley the town before we head home tomorrow, and leave knowing my guilt won't keep us from coming back."

"Do you think that's possible? To alleviate your guilt if you and Archer don't work things out?"

"Alleviate it? No," he said. "I'll have guilt until the day I die, but I'm no longer willing to let it rule my life. I'm pursue-and-conquer guy again, remember?" He pressed his lips to hers in a deliciously sensual kiss, rousing her passion. "And right now, I want to pursue and conquer my sexy girlfriend." He closed the door to the hall and locked it.

"Jock," she whispered. "What about Levi and your father?"

He gathered the hem of her shirt in his hands, and as he lifted it over her head, he said, "I'm not into foursomes."

"*Seriously*," she whispered as he unbuttoned her shorts.

"They went to the winery." He pulled down her shorts and

underwear.

"Leni's in her room," she whispered as she stepped out of them, her body already vibrating with desire.

"We'll be quiet. I checked on her. She's got hours of calls to make."

"But your mom and sisters might come back, and I'm yucky from playing football."

"We'll be fast, and I'm just going to get you dirtier."

He stripped naked as she took off her bra, and her body ignited at the sight of his arousal. He pulled her closer, his hard length eager and enticing against her belly. She squeezed her thighs together at the heat pooling between them.

"I have been waiting to make love to you all day, watching you prance around in those sexy shorts, flashing your beautiful smile," he whispered against her lips. "I need to be inside you."

Shivers of heat rippled down her body. He laid her on the bed and came down over her, entering her in one *hard* thrust. Electricity arced through her, stealing her breath. She bowed beneath him, reveling in the weight of his body, the girth of him filling her so perfectly. She said, "I feel you *everywhere*."

His mouth came down hungrily over hers, rough and sweet at once. He pushed his hands beneath her, clutching her ass and angling her hips so he could take her deeper. The angle forced him to stroke that special hidden spot inside her with every thrust as their bodies pounded together. He devoured her with delicious kisses, his every thrust sending lightning searing through her core. She clung to him, cocooned by his rugged, masculine scent, savoring his strength and love. She felt the tease of an orgasm prickling her limbs, climbing over her skin like a thousand claws. She tore her mouth away with an urgent whisper. "Come with me."

"*Fuck*," he growled, his eyes ablaze. "I love when you tell me what you want."

He crushed his mouth to hers, thrusting impossibly deeper, holding her excruciatingly tighter, loving her so exquisitely she lost all control. She cried into their kisses, and his body went rigid, then exploded into turbulent thrusts and pleasure-filled groans as they chased their highest peaks. Their bodies bucked and shuddered as they rode the waves of their passion and hung on for dear life as aftershocks rumbled through them in short, hard jerks. When their lips finally parted, breathless and unwilling to be done, they both went back for more sensual kisses.

As the fog of lust began to clear, reality came sprinkling in, reminding her that they didn't know how much time they had. "Jock, we need to hurry before someone comes home or Hadley wakes up."

He kissed her cheek, his whiskers tickling her skin. "When we get back to Bayside, I'm going to make love to you *all* night long. No rushing, no phone calls, nothing but you, me, and a sleeping princess in the other room."

"That sounds perfect. In case I don't say it enough, you make my heart happy."

He gave her a chaste kiss and said, "Angel, you make every part of me happy." He climbed off the bed, helped her to her feet, and led her into the bathroom. "I'm going to enjoy getting you clean." He turned on the shower and gathered her in his arms, raining kisses down her neck as he said, "And then I'm going to enjoy getting you dirty all over again."

He took her hand, leading her into the shower. He was fast, but oh so thorough, greedily washing *all* of her best parts. She felt pampered and sexy and desperate for more. But when he put his hands beneath her to lift her up, she grabbed his arms and hissed, "Don't you dare! You'll drop me, wake my baby girl, and your family will find us *naked* in a very precarious position."

He laughed, and she covered his mouth, shushing him. "Shh!"

He kissed her palm, moved her hand, whisper-laughing, "God, I love you."

She stilled, her heart thundering. He didn't mean it that way, did he? Could he possibly feel the same way she did?

He touched his forehead to hers and said, "I do, Daph. I love you and Hadley more than I ever thought possible."

She. Couldn't. Breathe.

Tears burned her eyes.

"I know it's fast," he said. "And this is probably not the most romantic place to say it, but I can't hold back any longer. I love who you are and who I am with you. I love being *Dock*, and I really love being *us*."

He didn't give her time to respond as his mouth covered hers in a sweet, passionate kiss. He was hard, and she was wet—and he *loved* her! Lord have mercy, she couldn't speak, could barely think past the happiness and desire consuming her. She needed him inside her again. She spread her legs and he lowered his hips, aligning with her entrance. As their bodies came together, their lips parted, and he cradled her face, whispering against her cheek, "I love you, baby. I love you so damn much."

Consumed with emotions, she could barely breathe, but when his loving eyes met hers, air filled her lungs and her heart poured out. "I love you, too."

# Chapter Twenty-Two

DAPHNE WAS STILL on cloud nine from her and Jock's confessions when she joined the girls to get ready for the party. The air buzzed with excitement as Indi did everyone's hair and makeup in Jules and Leni's childhood bedroom. Daphne was bursting to say, *I love Jock! I love him for the man he is and for the man he is becoming. I love him for the way he loves me and Hadley and the way he loves each of you. I love him for trying to work things out with Archer and for his thoughtfulness and his sense of humor. I truly, deeply love him with all of my heart and soul.* But she kept those thoughts to herself, reveling in the incredible feeling of loving and being loved so completely, letting it drench her soul, as she soaked in the excitement of being included in the girls' pre-party fun.

Her worries about Hadley getting in the way had disappeared within minutes. Joey, adorable in a peach summer dress with a sleeveless denim vest and cute white tennis shoes, had been anxiously awaiting Hadley's arrival. She'd set up everything they needed to make birthday cards for Lenore on the desk in the corner of the room.

"When is Grandma going to get here?" Jules asked as Indi began working on Jules's hair. Jules looked gorgeous in a sparkling champagne halter dress with a plunging neckline. She wore large sparkling earrings and a choker that had a trail of diamonds dangling down the center of her chest.

"I saw her car pull around back about half an hour ago," Sutton said, giving herself a once-over in the full-length mirror. Her skintight black sleeveless dress hugged her lean frame, its fringed hem giving it a flirty vibe. Her sky-high heels made her legs look a mile long. Indi had left Sutton's long blond hair loose and had given her a little extra bounce of curls at the ends.

"Daphne, honey, look." Shelley pointed to Hadley, sitting on Joey's lap as Joey read her a book. Indi had put the cutest bow in Hadley's hair, but Hadley had immediately ripped it out. Shelley lowered her voice to a whisper and said, "I think these girls are going to miss each other when you leave."

"I know. Hadley's having so much fun. My friends have just started having kids, so she doesn't have any friends her age where we live."

"If you lived here, she'd have loads of friends," Shelley said. "So many of our children's friends who grew up here have remained on the island and have started families of their own."

"It's true," Jules said as Indi twisted her hair into a cute updo. "Lots of the girls Leni and Sutton went to school with have children Hadley's age and are in mom groups."

"The Venting Vixens," Leni chimed in.

"Levi told me about them," Daphne said.

"Sometimes it feels like Tara and Bellamy and I are the last single women on the island," Jules said. "I'm kidding. You'll meet our other single girlfriends tonight at the party."

Shelley said, "I'm working on changing their single status."

Jules rolled her eyes. "We are *not* interested in your matchmaking, Mom. Start working on Leni or Sutton, please."

"No thank you," Leni said.

Sutton shook her head and said, "Count me out. I have no time in my life for an *island boy*. Daphne, how do you like living at the resort? Is it weird being in such a transient place? Are there guys hitting on you all the time?"

"Not really, although your brother thinks I'm oblivious to guys hitting on me."

"He'd know. He never takes his eyes off you," Jules said, and the other girls agreed, which made Daphne feel good all over.

"Maybe, but the only one I'm interested in is Jock. You asked if I like living there. I do. We have a lot of return customers, and I get to know them pretty well. The guys I work for are great, although the job is a bit limiting. I would eventually like to get a place of my own with kids Hadley's age nearby. Especially after seeing how much fun she and Joey are having. I love entertaining my daughter, but friends make everything better."

"Do you have friends who live at the resort?" Jules asked.

She told them about her friends, their new relationships, and their busy lives. "They're all living their dreams. I'm sure Jock has told you that Tegan and Harper's production company is taking off."

"It's so nice when your life begins to take the shape of what you've been working toward or hoping for," Shelley said.

"I'm finally working at my dream job," Sutton said. "I have a double major in journalism and English, but when I got out of college, I couldn't find a job as a reporter, so I took a job working with my sorority sisters at LWW as a fashion editor. I loved it, but when a reporter position opened up with one of their streaming channels, everyone encouraged me to take it even though I didn't have any real experience, and I'm so glad they did. Sometimes I have no idea what I'm doing, but you know what they say: Fake it until you make it. Not that my boss is convinced."

Leni smirked. "There would be no faking it with that sexy boss of yours. Flynn Braden is super yummy."

"Yes, he is," Jules agreed.

Sutton rolled her eyes. "Let's not go there. Daphne, you said your job was limiting. What's your dream job?"

"Change the subject much?" Jules teased.

Sutton nodded. "Yes I am. Now stop calling me out and let me hear what Daph has to say."

"Event planning. But my bosses aren't open to the idea right now, and I have a feeling the way their lives are going, a year or two down the line they're only going to be busier with their families and events will be pushed off again."

"You should get out there and find the job you want," Indi said as she put the finishing touches on Jules's hair. She looked hot in a short pale-blue dress with cutouts around her middle. "Nothing is worse than watching everyone else's career take off and being stagnated by a glass ceiling or too small of a business."

"She's right," Jules said.

"I know. But it's scary," Daphne confided.

"So what?" Sutton asked. "Everything is scary. You're with a guy who couldn't be around kids, but you took him on."

"That's different. When he told me about the accident, everything fell into place. If you could have seen how hard he tried to be okay around..." She glanced at Hadley. "I knew his heart was in the right place. But a job? Moving? It feels scarier."

"Do you believe in yourself?" Sutton asked.

"Yes. Absolutely. I'm an excellent event planner," Daphne

said confidently.

"Then it's not really that different, is it?" Sutton pointed out.

"Good point, Sut," Shelley said.

"You should do it. Life is way too short not to be totally and completely happy," Jules said.

"You do have a point. So you all think I should throw caution to the wind and do it?" Daphne was getting excited. She was moving forward in her personal life. Maybe it was time to start building the career she wanted, to find her own place, and build a fuller life for Hadley.

"Yes!" they said in unison.

Their energy was contagious. "Jock and my family have been encouraging me to follow my dreams, too." Her pulse quickened. "I think I'll take the plunge and start looking for a new job when I get back. No time like the present."

"Yay!" Jules cheered, and all the girls joined in, telling Daphne she was doing the right thing.

"I get first dibs if you're really going to look for a job," Shelley said.

Leni rolled her eyes. "Mom, we don't even do events at the winery. Daphne, I have clients who rave about Ocean Edge Resort on the Cape. You could look there."

"I actually used to work there. I loved the event planning aspect, but the resort is huge, and I like a more intimate setting. My mom always says I've got a small-town heart. I like to get to know everyone by name. I'm so nervous and excited now. Thank you for your support. But that's enough about me. Let's talk about you. I want to know more about you guys. It must have been great growing up with such a big family."

The girls exchanged knowing glances and laughed.

"You've opened a can of worms with that statement," Shelley said.

"It has its perks *and* it's downfalls," Leni said.

"Brothers, brothers everywhere," Sutton chimed in.

"On the other hand," Jules said with a waggle of her brows. "Brothers' *friends* everywhere. Nice eye candy."

Leni rolled her eyes. "Oh, *please*. Levi kept eagle eyes on you when you were younger."

"I said *eye candy*, as in *nice to look at*. I didn't say they were good in bed," Jules said.

Shelley looked in the mirror over Sutton's shoulder, primping her hair, and said, "Are we pretending that none of my precious girls has experienced a Silver boy?"

The girls said, "*Mom!*" in unison. Leni and Sutton eyed Jules.

"Don't look at *me*," Jules said. "Sutton went out with Fitz in seventh grade, and, Leni, you dated Wells in high school."

"My money's on Leni," Indi said.

Leni rolled her eyes and looked expectantly at Sutton.

"Hey, I only let Fitz go to second base," Sutton insisted.

"You let Fitz go to second base in *seventh* grade?" Jules said incredulously.

Shelley patted Jules on the shoulder and said, "Careful throwing rocks when you live in a glass house."

Leni gasped. "I *knew* you weren't as innocent as you pretend to be."

"What*ever*," Jules snapped. "I think Indi's right and it was you and Wells. You guys were always going down to the beach for a *swim*, which was probably code for sex."

"Didn't he date Abby, too?" Sutton looked at Daphne and said, "Abby de Messiéres has been Leni's best friend since they were kids."

"Yeah, until Abby and I found out he was two-timing us. Chicks before dicks," Leni said.

Jules nudged Indi and said, "I wonder if he was *swimming* with her, too."

"Way to keep it *classy* girls," Shelley teased.

"*Mom!*" all three complained.

Hadley toddled over to Shelley and tugged on her pretty floral dress, scowling at the girls, making them laugh. Shelley picked her up and said, "One day you'll be talking about boys, too."

"I a *gurl*," Hadley said.

Shelley hugged her and said, "And what a beautiful girl you are."

"Well, Jules, I didn't think it was possible. But now you're even more gorgeous." As the girls complimented Jules's hair, Indi said, "Who's my next victim?"

Jules hopped to her feet and said, "Do Daphne next!"

"Let's get her all sexed up for Jack," Sutton said, guiding Daphne by the shoulders to the chair.

Indi ran her hands through Daphne's hair and said, "I bet Jack likes running his hands through these silky locks."

Daphne blushed.

"What do you usually do with your hair and makeup?" Indi asked.

"Not much. I feel lucky when I get to actually dry my hair or put on eyeliner," Daphne answered. "Our mornings are usually a mad dash."

"That seems to be a common theme among moms. Let's consider this *your* special night. What would you like me to do? Play up your eyes? Lip color? Add some soft waves to your hair?"

"I don't know." Daphne shrugged. "I just want to look pretty for Jock."

"*Girl*, my brother thinks you're gorgeous," Leni said. "We all saw him salivating over you this afternoon, and when he sees you in that dress, he's going to lose his mind."

Daphne sure hoped so. She'd decided to wear the pale-green dress. The crossover bodice and sweetheart neckline accentuated her *assets* and the A-line chiffon skirt gave the appearance of a cinched waist.

"You should have heard Jack gushing about her over lunch when I saw him at the Cape." Jules's expression turned thoughtful, and she said, "Thank you for bringing back the brother I've missed."

"I didn't do anything," Daphne said as Indi brushed her hair.

"I don't believe that for a second," Jules said. "He's a whole different person than he was just a few months ago."

"You said you met him last year?" Sutton asked. "Why did it take so long for you two to get together?"

"It's complicated," Daphne said. "You know he had trouble around little kids."

"That's putting it mildly." Leni leaned against the window-sill in her pretty olive wraparound dress, patiently waiting her turn in Indi's chair.

"With good reason," Jules said, narrowing her eyes at Leni.

Shelley set Hadley down, and she toddled off to play with Joey.

"I'm sorry I'm late!" an older woman with a blond pixie cut said as she breezed into the room waving her hands. The bell sleeves of her black-and-gold blouse flapped, and her bracelets jangled. "We got held up at bingo. You know how much Millie loves that game. But I'm here now."

"Grandma!" the girls yelled, rushing in for hugs, each of them exclaiming, "Happy birthday!" Joey joined in on the group hug, and Hadley toddled after her, saying, "Happy *bufday!*"

Shelley waited for the girls to back off, then hugged her mother and said, "Happy birthday, Mom."

"*Thank you, thank you, thank you.* Now, tell me, who had a baby when I wasn't looking?" Lenore teased, patting Hadley on the head. "I'm kidding!" She clapped her hands together, her eyes sweeping over Hadley to Daphne. "This pretty little lady in the pink dress must be Hadley."

"I Hadley!" Hadley said.

"Hello, Hadley. I'm Grandma Lenore. It's a pleasure to meet you."

"Bye!" Hadley ran back to the toys.

Lenore's amused eyes found Daphne, and she said, "You must be Daphne. Jack told me all about both of his lovely ladies. I'm Lenore, but you can call me Grandma. Everyone does."

"Hi. It's nice to meet you," Daphne said, noticing the girls checking out the red mark on Lenore's left hand.

"Not nearly as nice as it is to meet the woman who single-handedly turned our broody boy into a chatty picture of love." Lenore squeezed Daphne's hand and said, "I made you blush. Aren't you adorable?"

"It's a family curse. My mom blushes, too," Daphne said.

"Blushing is a gift, honey," Lenore said. "There's no hiding your heart."

"Gram, Daphne was just about to tell us more about her

and Jack," Jules said.

"Well, let me settle in, then. Move over, my pretty little namesake." Lenore nudged Leni over and leaned against the windowsill.

Everyone looked at Daphne expectantly.

"*Go on*, give us all the *deets* on my grandson," Lenore urged.

"Mom," Shelley chided. "Give her a moment. This is a lot of pressure. Daphne, sweetheart, you don't have to share anything you don't want to."

"I don't mind." Since Lenore hadn't been there when they were setting up, she tried to give his grandmother as complete a picture as she could without boring the rest of them. "Jock—I know him as Jock, not Jack—is an amazing man. I met him last year, as I said, and Hadley clung to him like he was *hers*."

There was a collective "*Aww.*"

"It was actually embarrassing, because as you know, he couldn't be around her at the time. A few weeks ago, she did it again, and he kind of took off, leaving her crying. I'm not sure what changed, but that night when I was sitting outside, he stopped to apologize for walking away every time she tried to get close to him."

"He's such a sweet young man," Lenore said. "He loves children, honey. He really does."

"I know that now, and he is very thoughtful. I've never gotten *apology presents* before, but Jock brought them for both me and Hadley that night. That owl she won't let go of was a gift from him. Anyway, over the next few nights we got to know each other better."

"Mm-hm. We know what *that* means," Sutton teased.

"Not like *that*," Daphne said with a laugh. "We played *games* and we talked for hours. We had an instant connection, and after a few days I realized how much I liked him." She spoke quietly, so as not to gain Hadley's attention. "I was falling for him and I knew I shouldn't because Hadley had to come first. At the time, I didn't know anything about Jock's background and all he'd been through. But as I mentioned earlier, my ex-husband hadn't wanted children, and I swore I'd never put Hadley in a situation like that again. So I told Jock that if he couldn't be near Hadley, then I couldn't be near him."

"Attagirl," Lenore said. "Many women would see a handsome, wealthy man like Jack and put their desires above their children's."

"Not me. Not ever. Not even for Jock."

"It must have been difficult for you to tell him that," Shelley said.

"It was, but when I told him, he told me everything he'd been through. My heart broke for him, for Archer, for your family, and for everyone who knew Kayla. His emotions were so raw, and he was so honest, when he said he wanted to try to get past his triggers, I knew he would find a way. He has *fought* for us, pushing past all those years of grief and guilt. I'm still in awe of how far he's come. As he was working through his triggers, all three of our worlds got better. We just feel so *right* together. It's hard to put it into words without gushing. It wasn't easy for either of us to put our hearts on the line after what we've been through, but I think that's why we have fallen so hard so fast. We understand each other, and we know how it feels to be hurt. That awareness brings a whole new level of clarity and effort into a relationship. He encourages me not to give up my dreams, and he started writing again—"

"He's writing?" everyone exclaimed, except Jules.

"That's amazing! When did he start writing again?" Leni

asked.

"*Shoot*," Jules said with a troubled expression. "I thought I told you guys after I had lunch with him."

"*No*. You just raved about how happy he was and said he forbade you from talking about his life," Leni said.

"Oh yeah," Jules said. "He did. *Sorry*."

"*How* did he start writing again?" Sutton asked. "He's been trying since Harvey died, staring at blank pages."

Shelley's eyes glistened. "Who cares about how or when? He's *writing*, girls. Your brother is *writing*." She swiped at a tear and said, "Our Jackie is back."

Lenore handed Shelley a tissue from her slacks pocket and said, "I think we're looking at the reason he's able to write again."

The love in the room enveloped Daphne like an embrace. "I think the reason he hadn't been able to write before was because he'd held in most of what he told me for so long, it was clogging up his creativity. It didn't happen all at once, and he hasn't shown me what he's written. He said it's different from anything he's written before, but he is writing every day."

"Of course it's different," Sutton said thoughtfully. "He's not the same person he was when he wrote his first book."

"He's not the same person he was a year ago, or even a few weeks ago," Daphne said. "I could talk about Jock all night long. He's loving and strong. He's determined to be good for *us*, and for himself, and to fix things with Archer, and make up for all the lost time with you guys. He is facing *all* of his demons, and none of it is easy. You should be really proud of him. Hadley and I are lucky to have him in our lives."

Jules wiped her eyes and huffed out a breath. "Great, now I'm crying."

"You're always crying," Leni teased. She went to Jules and put her arm around her.

"I can't help it," Jules said. "I like happy stories, and we're talking about *Jack*."

"It sounds like you and Jack were meant to be together," Indi said as she wound a lock of Daphne's hair around a curling iron.

"All I know is that I was with my ex for a few years, and I never felt anything like what I feel for Jock. I want him to be as happy as Hadley and I are. I hope he and Archer can work things out."

"Now, you ladies know I love all of my grandchildren. Archer is a fine, hardworking young man. He and Jack will get through this in good time." Lenore raised her brows and said, "But it wouldn't hurt to find a single lady to cast a sexy spell on him and deaden those angry brain cells."

"*Grandma*," Sutton said with a laugh.

"Honey, I was married for a hundred years," Lenore said. "I know that a little *hotsy-totsy* goes a long way to get a man off his high horse."

Indi scoffed and said, "Good luck with that. That man is drop-dead gorgeous, but he definitely needs a dominatrix to whip him into shape."

Lenore went to Indi's side and said, "Sweetheart, I've noticed you're a tough cookie, and you handle that curling iron very well. How are you at wielding a whip?"

That started a litany of jokes and laughter, which continued as Indi finished working her magic on Daphne, giving her gentle waves, smoky eyes, a hint of cheekbones, and soft-pink lips. Daphne felt like a princess in Indi's capable hands, with the girls looking on and telling her how beautiful she was.

As Indi was finishing up with Leni, the last of them who needed to be coiffed, Steve came into the room looking handsome in dark slacks and a gray button-down.

"Look at all my gorgeous ladies," Steve said.

All the girls stood and twirled, and he whistled as he reached for Shelley, planting a kiss on her lips and a pat on her butt.

"*Gwampa.*" Hadley toddled over to him, clutching Owly, and said, "Look at my *pawty dwess.*"

He lifted Hadley into his arms, and she flashed a toothy grin. "You and Joey are going to be the belles of the ball." He looked at the others and said, "Heads are going to spin tonight. Are we ready?"

There was a collective "Yes!"

"*Wait.* I want to get a picture of Jack's face when he sees Daphne." Jules hurried out of the room.

"Oh my gosh," Daphne said, turning to the others. "This is Lenore's night, not mine."

Lenore put her arm around Daphne and said, "Sweetheart, I've had seventy-eight of these nights, and the man who looked at me like I was the pie in the sky is now looking down on me *from* that sky. Soak this moment up for all its worth. Revel in those butterflies in your belly, because these are the best days of your life, only to be outdone by all of your tomorrows."

Steve carried Hadley, and Joey held Shelley's hand as they made their way down the hall, and one by one they filed down the steps. Jock and Levi were waiting at the bottom, giving them a hand off the landing.

As Shelley and Joey walked down, Levi whistled and said, "I'm going to be the luckiest man at that party." He took Joey's hand and pressed a kiss to the back of it. Then he offered her his arm. "My lady."

Joey giggled and took her father's arm as they stepped to the side.

"Go on, darlin'," Steve said to Daphne.

Daphne held on to the railing as she started down the stairs, nervous under the weight of Jock's stare as he drank her in from head to toe. His dark eyes filled with heat, love, and everything in between. She had never felt more beautiful or more loved than she did at that second. The silence that fell around them was even more powerful than the fanfare from Joey's adoring father. Daphne was vaguely aware of Jules taking pictures and the others looking on as Jock drew her into his arms and said, "My sweet love, you take my breath way."

When he pressed his lips to hers, Hadley said, "*My* Dock," and everyone laughed. Steve carried Hadley down, and she wrapped her little arms around Jock's neck. With one arm around Daphne and her baby girl clinging to him like a monkey to a tree, Jock looked at Jules and said, "Get a good one of me and my girls. This one's going on the mantel."

THE SALTY SEA air was alive with music, laughter, and the din of close friends. Lights sparkled against the clear night sky, and in the distance, the lighthouse beamed brightly over the ocean. Lenore's friends had shown up en masse, and they were huddled together chatting. Tara mingled in between taking pictures of everyone. Jock had asked her to take extras of Daphne and Hadley. He wanted to remember every minute of their first evening on the island. He'd been proud to introduce Daphne and point out Hadley, who was busy playing with other kids, to their friends. He'd received a number of surprised yet approving looks, and there were several sideways glances at Daphne's use of *Jock* rather than Jack. But as he'd expected, his friends had welcomed her with open arms. Everyone asked about his writing, and though he didn't tell them *exactly* what he was writing, it felt fantastic to finally have an active and exciting—even if different—project at his fingertips. He had forgotten how good it felt to be surrounded by caring friends and family and to be part of a community that had known him since he was a kid.

He stood by the bar sipping his drink, watching Daphne, who looked gorgeous in her fancy green dress. He hadn't even gotten a chance to dance with her before the girls had whisked her away to introduce her to their friends. Moonlight shimmered in her eyes as she talked with Leni, Indi, and Sutton and Tessa and Randi Remington. Tessa was a private pilot, and Randi was a marine archaeologist currently working on a shipwreck expedition not far off the coast of the island with the famous treasure hunter Zev Braden.

As if Daphne felt him watching her, she glanced over, sending a rush of awareness through him. How was it possible to miss her when she was standing just across the courtyard? Daphne waved and he winked. Randi gave Jock a thumbs-up, and then she touched Daphne's arm, drawing her attention away from him. A minute later his mother and Margot Silver joined the girls, talking animatedly. This was what he wanted. This life with Daphne and Hadley, surrounded by family and friends. Archer walked into his line of sight, bringing his hopeful thoughts back to reality. Jock had caught a few sneers from Archer, but they had both kept their distance, which was probably best for now, so as not to ruin the party for their grandmother.

Grant Silver sidled up to Jock with a slight limp, which Jock assumed had come from his prosthetic leg. His brown hair was long, his beard shaggy, and his eyes held the shadows of a man who had seen too much. Jock knew that look all too well.

"How's it going, Jack?" Grant's familiar baritone voice was a welcome sound.

"Not bad," Jock said, giving him a manly embrace. "Did you just get here?"

"Yeah. Bellamy and Keira texted and gave me hell for staying home." He took a drink and said, "Can't say no to them."

"Gotta love younger sisters."

Grant shook his head. "Right. Did you know Jules comes by my place all the time, trying to sprinkle her happiness around like she's a magical fairy or something? Do me a favor and run interference if she comes over. I haven't had enough alcohol for her brand of happy."

"She means well. Spreading happiness is Jules's *thing*. You know that."

"Yeah, I do. So, are the rumors true? You here with a girlfriend and a kid?"

"Yes, Daphne. She's the blonde talking with your mom over there." He pointed out Daphne and then Hadley, who was following Joey and two of Lenore's friends' grandchildren toward Steve. "That's Hadley, Daphne's daughter."

"Good for you, man. You finally turned that corner, huh?"

"Mostly. I'm a work in progress."

"How'd you do it? You were pretty fucked up."

"I know. I met Daphne, and let me tell you. When you meet *the one*, you know it, and you do whatever it takes to be the man she deserves."

"I'll take your word for it." Grant took another swig of hi
drink. "You can have *the one, two, three* and all the rest of them
I've got no need to be told what to do."

"It's not like that, Grant. But I get it. I'm sorry about every
thing you've gone through. Losing your leg had to be tough
I'm glad we didn't lose you." Jock worried about his old friend
They'd seen each other for a few minutes here and there whe
their holiday visits had coincided. But they'd lost touch this la
year, and Jock hoped to fix that, too. "I know we didn't suffe
the same losses, but grief is grief, and I know how it can fuck
person up. I'm here if you ever want to talk. You've got m
number. Use it."

Grant swirled the alcohol in his glass and said, "I appreciа
that."

"Can I give you one bit of advice?" Jock asked.

"Why not? Everyone else does."

"Talk to someone. Get that shit out of your head, and dor
push away the people you love. I lost a decade I'll never {
back."

"I'll take that under consideration." Grant gazed across
grass at his younger brothers heading their way with Levi. I
and Wells were as clean-cut as Grant was shaggy. Tension d
Grant's mouth into a fine line.

"What's up with you three?" Jock asked.

Grant shrugged. "I just don't have the patience for bul
anymore."

Jock understood that, too. Harsh realities brought e
thing into focus, including nonsense. But he knew Gı
brothers loved him and worried about him.

"Look who finally made it." Wells put an arm around (
and said, "Good to see your smiling face, bro."

Grant shrugged him off. "What are you two up to?"

"Checkin' out the ladies." Fitz pushed a hand through his sandy hair and said, "Sutton and Leni are looking *mighty* fine."

Levi glowered. "Like they'd give you the time of day?"

"Who said anything about *day*?" Fitz snickered.

Archer came through the crowd like a man on a mission, shoulders back, eyes locked on Jock. He strode up to the group and said, "The prodigal son comes home and he's the life of the party, huh?"

"Give it a rest, Archer." Jock held his gaze. "No one wants to hear that shit."

Archer scoffed. "What's wrong, golden boy? Don't want all that attention anymore?"

Levi, always the peacemaker, clapped a hand on Archer's shoulder and said, "Did you see Indi checking you out?"

"That's the sexy little blonde, right?" Wells asked. "Man, she's so frigging hot. If you don't want her, I've got an itch that needs scratching."

Archer shot him a narrow-eyed stare. "Dude, she's Leni's friend. Back off."

"She's a grown-ass woman. I bet she'd love a piece of this." Wells spread his arms out and looked down at his body.

"First she'd have to *find* it." Archer chuckled.

"All the girls grew up while I was away. Did you see Mouse in that dress?" Grant whistled and said, "*Damn.*"

Levi smacked him upside the back of his head.

Grant grinned. "Sorry, biker boy. I didn't know you were hittin' that."

"I'm *not*." Levi held his gaze. "Show her some respect."

"How do you know we're not *all* hittin' that?" Archer taunted.

Levi glowered. "Because you don't have a death wish."

Archer knew better than to mess with Levi. Archer had a size advantage, but Levi was as lethal as a grizzly. He might look like he was kicking back and enjoying himself, but fuck with the people he cared about and he'd rear up and take you out with one solid punch. There was only *one* reason Archer would mess with him.

He was looking for a fight.

*Not tonight, buddy.*

"Excuse me, but my beautiful girlfriend looks like she might want to dance." Jock finished his drink and set his glass down on the bar.

As he walked away, Archer said, "It's a good thing you're not driving."

Jock stilled. Fire seared through his veins as he turned and grabbed Archer's arm, getting right in his face, and fumed, "You got something to say to me, Archer? Say it to my face."

Archer didn't flinch. "I said, it's a good thing you're not driving. At least this one will make it home alive."

Jock saw red. He cocked his arm, but Levi shoved him back and inserted himself between them, arms outstretched. "You've got an audience. Cut the shit."

Jock looked at the crowd; all eyes were on them. *Fuck.* He glowered at Archer. "This *isn't* over." He stalked away, feeling like a grenade about to detonate and trying to tamp down his anger before reaching Daphne. Jock walked past his father, who was holding Hadley, and mouthed, *Sorry.* He tried to form a reassuring smile, but he couldn't force it.

"*Dock!*" Hadley called after him.

Jock stopped, struggling to rein in his anger. He looked at Hadley holding her owl in one hand, her other arm outstretched, her little hand opening and closing as if she could reel him in by sheer will. The rage eating him up inside was no match for the sight of her trusting eyes. He felt it crumble to pieces and fall away. He inhaled a few deep breaths, making sure he was under control, before heading for them.

"I'll take her, Dad," he said, reaching for Hadley.

"You sure?" his father asked.

"Yeah. Sorry about that. It won't happen again."

His father shook his head as he handed Hadley over. "Don't kid yourself. I ought to throw you two in the ring."

"Please *don't*," Daphne said as she came to Jock's side.

"I won't, darlin'. Don't worry," Steve reassured her.

"Are you okay?" she asked Jock. "It looked like you two were going to fight."

"I'm sorry, Daphne. He said something and I just about lost it."

"What did he say?" she asked.

"What he say?" Hadley mimicked.

He winked at Daphne indicating they could talk about it later and said, "You know what, princess? I can't remember. But they're getting ready to serve dinner, so why don't we sit down?"

His father said, "Actually, your mother and I thought you might want to announce dinner tonight."

Jock had dozens of fond memories of his parents telling funny and touching stories about their grandmother when they announced her birthday dinner. It was an honor to be asked, but he wasn't sure he deserved it. "Really? Even after *that* scene?"

"You call that a scene?" His father cocked a grin. "You have been away from the island for far too long."

Jock chuckled.

"Here, give me Hadley." Daphne reached for her.

"Baby, you okay?" Jock asked.

She caressed his arm and said, "If you are, then I am."

"Thanks, babe." He kissed her and stroked Hadley's back. "How about a kiss for good luck, princess?"

Hadley grinned and puckered up, planting a kiss on his cheek. "Luck."

"I'll have three beautiful ladies by my side tonight," Steve said, guiding Daphne toward the table.

Jock moved to the front of the crowd and said loudly, "I'd like to invite everyone to sit down for dinner." He waited while everyone took their seats.

Lenore sat at the center of one of the tables, and Jock was surprised to see his father seating Hadley between her and Daphne. Lenore took Owly and wiggled him like he was dancing in front of Hadley. Hadley was smiling, and beside her, Daphne watched with a joyous expression. A wave of guilt washed over Jock as he thought about Kayla and Liam and what might have been. He assumed his brother had been in love with Kayla and that was why he'd turned his back on Jock. If she and Liam had lived, would they be sitting with Archer tonight? Would he and Archer have remained close? Could they have co-parented Jock and Kayla's child?

For the first time, those memories and questions didn't leave a trail of anxiety. Thanks to Daphne, they no longer felt like torturous secrets trapped in a dungeon. They were no less painful, but they had a place now, an accessible place where he could think about them, or talk about them, without losing his mind.

If only he could figure out how to help Archer do the same.

He looked out at his friends and family, trying to clear his thoughts, and said, "Thank you all for coming out to celebrate our grandmother, Lenore Dawson's, seventy-eighth birthday."

A round of cheers rang out.

"I think most of you call her *Grandma*, like we do, so I'm rolling with it. I have a lot of good memories about both of my grandparents—family dinners, riding on the tractor with Grandpa, stumbling upon Grandma and her fellow Bra Brigaders." Laughter rumbled around him. "I'm still trying to recover from that. Not that you ladies aren't beautiful, but there are some sights young boys shouldn't see. I think I avoided Grandma Osten for two full years after that eye-opener." More laughter rang out. "I have lots of other crystal-clear memories, and then I have some that are not so clear, which I'm pretty sure is because when Grandma and Grandpa babysat, they swapped mine and Archer's juice in our sippy cups for wine."

Another round of laughter sounded.

"That's right. Remember that, Archer?" He looked at his brother, hoping to break the ice, but Archer looked away. Jock tried not to let his disappointment show and said, "We'd conk out right after dark and wake up in the morning without a single memory of what had happened the night before. Funny enough, when we'd turn on cartoons in the morning, the television was always on that adults-only channel."

Everyone cracked up, including his grandmother. Archer cracked a smile, but he quickly schooled his expression.

"Gotta love Grandma," Jock said with a nod. "She didn't believe in punishing in the conventional sense, as many of you probably remember from our night of attempted skinny-dipping in the resort pool."

"We were blinded by the light of the full moon that night!"

his grandmother shouted, earning another round of laughter *and* applause.

"By the way, Gram, you're not babysitting Hadley," he said, earning more chuckles. "Daph, check her sippy cup, will you, please?"

Lenore winked at Daphne and said, "Don't you dare. Grannies are allowed their secrets."

"In all seriousness, I couldn't have asked for a better grandmother. Here's to the reigning queen of the Bra Brigade. If only we could convince them to put up warning signs before taking off their shirts." Everyone laughed, and Jock said, "Thank you all for joining us tonight. I love you, Grandma. Happy birthday."

Cheers and applause rang out again.

Jock waited for a moment, giving his grandmother her due, and then he raised his hands, and when the din of his family and friends quieted, he said, "Just a quick side note, which is not about Grandma or her birthday. I think you're all aware that I lost a very good friend last year, Harvey Fine. He saved my life. He was family to me, and one hell of a jokester. Most of you have heard Daphne call me *Jock*, and many of you have asked about it, while others have looked at her like she didn't know my name, which I assure you, she *does*."

More chuckles ensued.

"Harvey coined the nickname Jock for me as a joke, but it stuck. Over the many years that I worked with him, I healed and I grew as a person. I *became* Jock, and honestly, it felt good to leave that other guy who made some big mistakes behind." The lump in his throat threatened to steal his voice, and he looked at Archer. Archer blinked several times, his jaw tight, as if he were just as affected by Jock's words as Jock was. His eyes remained trained on Jock as Jock said, "I know now that there is no leaving Jack or the mistakes I made behind. I can't change the past, but I can and will continue to make better decisions in the future. I'd like to honor the man who saved my life by using the name he bestowed on me. I know it'll take some getting used to, but I hope you will join me in honoring Harvey Fine by accepting this change and calling me *Jock*."

Applause rang out. Jock was acutely aware of Archer still watching him as he said, "Thank you. That's all I've got. Enjoy your dinner."

As he made his way toward Daphne, Archer yelled, "*Jock-strap!*" causing an uproar of laughter.

"*Jockhole!*" Wells called out.

And so began the start of many nicknames Jock hoped would *not* stick, and a crack in his brother's armor he hoped would set them both free.

# Chapter Twenty-Three

DINNER WAS DELICIOUS, and the company could not have been better. With a cool ocean breeze sweeping over the hills, the festive, twinkling lights, and Jock's family and friends telling funny tales of their younger days and filling Daphne in on all the sights they thought she should see tomorrow before heading home, Daphne couldn't imagine a more perfect evening. Even Archer had kept his attitude under control.

As the table was cleared, Jock put his arm around her and said, "In case I haven't told you lately, I *love* you, beautiful."

"I will never tire of hearing that."

He had been whispering sweet, sexy things and holding her hand throughout dinner, and when Hadley had gotten whiny, before Daphne could pick her up, he'd settled her on his lap. Hadley's head rested on his chest, a small smile gracing her tiny lips. It had been a big day for her, and she'd held up like a champ. It had also been a big, trying day for Jock, and he, too, had held up like a champ.

"That's good, because now that I've uncorked that bottle, there's no stopping my love for you." He kissed Hadley's head and said, "For both of you."

Daphne was wrong. The evening just got even more perfect.

Lenore began telling a story about Archer, and everyone quieted to listen. "It was the Easter parade, and Archer had begged his parents to let him be the Easter bunny on the winery float." Lenore looked at Archer and said, "We all know our Archer is always prepared for anything, and even as a little boy he was one step ahead of the rest of us. He asked his mother to sew a fly into the suit in case he had to use the bathroom, and of course Shelley was happy to oblige. Little did she know that while everyone else was waving to the crowd, Archer was peeing off the back of the float in front of the whole town *and* waving like a king as he did it."

Laughter filled the air.

"I was *five*," Archer said loudly.

"You were *six*," Lenore corrected him. "I remember because that was also the year you came home from school and announced that Grant Silver had told you where babies came from."

"Someone had to do it," Grant shouted from the other table.

Lenore pointed a finger at Grant and said, "I sure hope you've learned the *right* way to make babies by now, Mr. Silver. I'm sure anyone who was pregnant on this island at that time remembers Archer pointing and shouting, 'She got a back rub, too!'"

Daphne laughed along with everyone else. She could listen to their stories all night.

Shelley stood up and said, "Okay, kids, let's get dessert."

As all of Jock's siblings got up to help, Jock tried to hand Hadley to Daphne, but Hadley shook her head, clinging to him.

"It's okay. I'll go help." Daphne stood.

"Sit, sweetie." Lenore took her hand and pulled her back down to her seat. "You're a guest. You get to relax."

"I don't mind helping," Daphne said.

"And we appreciate that, but as a mother, I remember what it was like, never having a minute that wasn't spent working or taking care of someone." Lenore looked at Jock and said, "What did your grandfather always tell us?"

Jock cocked a grin. "Enjoy each and every day. No one else can do it for you."

"Your grandfather would be mighty proud of who you are, honey. I want you to know that."

"Because I remembered what he said?" Jock teased.

"Smart-aleck. You know what I mean." Lenore looked at Daphne and said, "Know what else my once-in-a-lifetime love said?"

"What?" Daphne asked.

Lenore glanced at Jock, and they both said, "'Why pussy-foot around when you can jump in with both feet?'" They cracked up.

"I want you two to promise me that you will embrace Grandpa's words from this day forward," Lenore said with a serious lilt to her voice.

Jock gazed at Daphne, and she knew he was thinking the same thing she was as she said, "That's easy. We already have; we just didn't realize it."

"Love you, baby," Jock said loud enough for others to hear. As he touched his lips to Daphne's, Hadley said, "Love you, Mama."

"I love you, too. Both of you," Daphne said as Jock's siblings filed out of the winery with the desserts and set them on the table by the bar.

Shelley reached for Steve's hand and said, "Tonight we have the honor of singing 'Happy Birthday' to two very special ladies. My mother and our new little friend Hadley."

Daphne's pulse skyrocketed. She looked at Jock, who was grinning, and said, "Did you…?"

Jock shook his head. "My mom and Jules."

"Hadley can't hijack Lenore's birthday," Daphne said.

"Oh yes she can," Lenore said. "You're with my grandson, which makes you family, and we celebrate family."

Daphne was so deeply touched, she could do little more than listen as Shelley said, "Hadley will be three years old next week, and we are thrilled to share in this special moment with her. Shall we?"

Shelley and Steve began singing "Happy Birthday," and everyone joined in as they carried two cakes—one big and one small—to Lenore and Hadley. Levi lit the candles on each, three for Hadley and several for Lenore. Steve set the larger cake in front of Lenore and Shelley placed the smaller one in front of Hadley as they finished singing.

Hadley sat up, her eyes bright and wide. "*Mine?*"

Laughter filled the air, and Shelley said, "A girl after my own heart."

"Yes, it's yours, princess," Jock said. "Ready to blow out the candles with Grandma Lenore?"

Hadley nodded.

Everyone counted. "One. Two. *Three!*"

Hadley and Lenore blew out their candles, and applause rang out. Jock took the candles out of Hadley's cake. Hadley thrust her hand into the frosting, grabbing a fistful of cake, and held it up to Jock's mouth. "For *Dock*."

As laughter and cheers rang out, Jock stole another piece of

Daphne's heart, by letting her little girl feed him her cake.

Daphne held her breath, feeling like she might cry she was so happy. She pushed to her feet and ran to Shelley, hugging her tight. "Thank you so much for including Hadley. You didn't have to do this."

Shelley didn't let go. She held her tighter and said, "Thank *you*, Daphne. I hope we can celebrate many more birthdays together." When they ended their embrace, Shelley was teary-eyed again. She tugged Daphne into another hug and said, "Sorry. Just go with it."

AFTER THE LONG fun-filled day and too much cake, Hadley fell asleep on Jock's shoulder while he and Daphne enjoyed a few stolen kisses and mingled with his family and friends. But Daphne was nowhere ready to go inside and call it a night. She loved seeing this lighter side of Jock with the people he'd grown up with. It seemed to her that *this* was where he belonged. Even with the tension between him and Archer, over the course of the day, Jock had flourished. He seemed more at ease, and at the same time, he stood taller and his eyes sparkled brighter, as if connecting with everyone had breathed new life into him. He and Archer were still giving each other a wide breadth, but even if this wasn't the trip to heal their wounds, it was definitely a move in the right direction.

Jock took Daphne's hand and said, "Come with me, my love."

*My love.* She adored that! "Where are we going?"

"To ask my mom to hold Hadley so we can dance."

He led her to Shelley, sitting with Margot Silver and Gail Remington, whispering behind their hands. They looked like they belonged on a postcard about friendship. Shelley, with her easy floral style and voluptuous curves, radiating warmth and joy, and Margot, tall and lean with perfectly coiffed hair cut just below her ears, exuded an air of elegance in flared black slacks and an expensive silk blouse. Gail was a Glenn Close lookalike with a pointy nose and sharp chin, trusting eyes, and dressed in an earthy fashion. Her patchwork skirt brushed the tops of her Birkenstocks, and her batik blouse might look casual on someone else, but she pulled it off as though it were a designer piece made just for her. Daphne had spent a long time talking with Shelley's closest friends, and she'd found Margot to be anything but pretentious and Gail to be sharp-minded and curious, although very laid-back.

"Excuse me, ladies," Jock said.

"I'm glad you're here," Shelley said. "I need to talk to Daphne. Margot was just telling me that she was going to turn away a bridal shower because the resort is booked, so I told her I'd take it!"

"You did? That's fabulous!" Daphne bounced on her toes. "I bet you'll be swamped with business once you get started."

"If I had known that Shelley would even *consider* taking on events, I'd have been sending her business ages ago," Margot said.

"Hold on. You're doing events now, Mom?" Jock asked. "I thought Archer wasn't okay with that."

"I'll deal with Archer, and it's only *one* event. I just want to see how it goes." Shelley looked at Daphne and said, "It's a fall shower, which means we don't have much time to prepare. I was thinking we could talk about it at breakfast tomorrow."

"With Archer?" Jock scoffed. "Good luck with that."

Shelley shook her head. "Not with Archer—with Daphne. I need her help."

"I'd love to help," Daphne said, wondering how she could help enough over breakfast to make a difference.

"Mom, we're leaving tomorrow afternoon, and I was hoping to show Daph the island before we catch the ferry," Jock said.

"Of course. How else will she get island fever?" Gail teased, trading secretive looks with Shelley and Margot.

"I'd love to talk over breakfast," Daphne said. "I have some ideas. And once we're back on the Cape, we can email, text, or talk on the phone."

Shelley breathed a big sigh of relief. "Perfect."

"I look forward to it," Daphne said.

Jock put a hand on Daphne's back and said, "Mom, I don't want Daphne put in the middle of anything with Archer."

"Don't you worry, honey. I talked with your father about this, and he's all for it. We'll talk to Archer tomorrow and make sure there's no trouble."

"It worries me, but I trust you to handle it." He kissed Hadley's forehead and said, "Would you mind holding Hadley while I dance with my beautiful date?"

"My pleasure. Give me that sleeping beauty," Shelley said as she reached for Hadley.

"You two are adorable together," Margot said, looking at them with an endearingly soft gaze.

"Thank you." Jock put his arm around Daphne. "Daph could make anyone look good."

"You're not too shabby, either, Jack—*Jock*. I'll get used to that, I promise," Margot said. "Maybe you two could drop a few hints to my kids about how wonderful it is to have Hadley around. I swear kids these days have an aversion to marriage or something. I have *five* children and not one grandbaby yet. Did I tell you that Keira said she's sworn off dating?" She looked at Daphne and said, "Keira is my beautiful daughter who, unfortunately, puts more energy into her bakery than she does her personal life."

"Jules mentioned that," Shelley said. "Keira told her that cupcakes were sweeter than men."

Jock scoffed. "That seems a little harsh."

Gail gave him a discerning look. "I love my Roddy, but there are definitely times when I'd gladly take a cupcake over him." She leaned forward in her chair and said, "Maybe we could set up one of my boys with Keira and change her mind."

"I don't think so," Margot said. "She dated Jamison in high school, remember? That did *not* end well."

"How did I forget that?" Gail settled back in her chair and crossed her legs. "My Jamie has his head in the stars. *Literally*."

"Jamison is an astrophysicist," Jock explained.

"Wow. I've never met an astrophysicist. I didn't meet him tonight, did I?"

"No, he's traveling. He can go on forever about planets and galaxies," Gail said with a wave of her hand. "But he is *clueless* when it comes to women. Now, my boy Rowan? He's going to make a fine husband one day."

"I know Rowan and Joni," Daphne said. "They're really nice."

"Daphne, did you have a chance to meet Fitz yet?" Margot asked.

"Yes, Jock introduced me. He was lovely."

"On that note, I think I'd better get my girl out of here and onto the dance floor before Mrs. S and Mrs. R marry her off.

Thanks for watching Hadley, Mom. We won't be long."

"Take your time." Shelley rubbed Hadley's back and said, "I love baby-girl snuggles."

As Jock led Daphne toward the dance floor, he said, "I doubt anyone has ever described Fitz Silver as *lovely*."

"What did you want me to say? That he struck me as the kind of guy who knew all the right things to say to make a good impression but I'm pretty sure that when he cuts loose, there are no holds barred?"

"That would be accurate."

Jock's sisters and their friends were dirty dancing, and the Silver brothers were practically salivating over them. "Really, guys?" he said as they walked by.

"It's a small island," Fitz said.

Jock shot them a harsh stare and led Daphne away from them. He gathered her close, swaying sensually to the fast song. It felt so good to be in his arms, she didn't want to think about Fitz or anyone else, but she was too excited at the idea of helping his mother to hold it in.

"I can't believe your mom is going to do an event. I'm so excited to help her."

He held Daphne a little tighter and said, "Yeah, that was unexpected."

"This place is gorgeous and lends itself perfectly to formal affairs and casual celebrations."

He trailed feathery kisses across her cheek, heating her up with every touch of his lips. "Mm-hm." He pressed a kiss beside her ear and nipped at her lobe, sending pangs of lust darting through her. "How about we have our own private celebration?"

She wound her arms around his neck, loving the seductive look in his eyes, and said, "Everyone is going to know what you're doing to me if you keep this up."

The song changed to a slower one, and they watched with amusement as Levi pulled Tara out of Fitz's clutches to dance with her and Wells claimed Leni, who tried—and *failed*—to wriggle out of his arms. Steve brought Joey out for a dance, and Lenore grabbed Margot's husband. Jules tried to coax Grant into joining her, but Grant stalked off toward the bar, so she snagged Archer instead, her voice carrying in the night. "Get your butt up here or I'm never talking to you again!" Archer relented, and they joined Brant and Sutton a few feet away from Daphne and Jock. When Fitz and Indi joined them, Jules called "Swap!" and pushed her way in to dance with Fitz, leaving Indi to dance with Archer.

"It's like musical arms," Daphne said.

"As long as you're in mine, I don't care what they do. I have wanted to dance with you since Gavin and Harper's wedding, which is weird, because I've never been a dancer. But that night I had the overwhelming urge to take you in my arms."

She'd wanted that, too. "You did?"

"Hell yes. I wanted to know how you'd feel pressed against me, how our bodies would fit together." He brushed his lips over hers and said, "*Perfect.*" He kissed her softly. "It was hell keeping my distance from you. You were so gorgeous in that blue dress, and all those guys were checking you out, but I didn't want to complicate your life." He gazed deeply into her eyes, causing butterflies to swarm in her belly, and said, "I wish I hadn't wasted so much time."

Did he have any idea how romantic he was? "I have to believe that everything in life happens for a reason. I wish I had never married Tim, but if I hadn't, I wouldn't have Hadley. If I didn't have Hadley, I couldn't have helped you find your way past your triggers. And if we hadn't gone through that, I wouldn't be here dancing with you beneath the stars on this beautiful island on what has turned out to be one of the best nights of my entire life."

"God, angel, how did I get so lucky to find you?" He lowered his lips to hers, taking her in a knee-weakening kiss that sang through her like a symphony.

"Get a room!" three female voices called out.

Their lips parted on a laugh. They looked over and were met with cheesy grins by Jules, Indi, and Leni.

Jock's dark eyes found Daphne's, and he said, "A room sounds good to me."

That sounded great to her, too. But most of the guests were still there, so she said, "We can't leave yet. Everyone will know *why* we're leaving." She lowered her voice to a whisper and said, "But we can dance, and kiss."

"You're killing me softly, baby."

They continued dancing, kissing, and whispering their desires. When a new slow song came on, Steve cut in to dance with Daphne, and Joey was excited to dance with Uncle Jock.

"Do you mind, son?" he asked.

"Yes." Jock laughed and kissed Daphne one last time before handing her over to his father and sweeping Joey into his arms.

"Are you ready to run for the hills yet?" Steve asked.

"Why would I run for another hill when I'm already on the one with the best people and the best view?"

"Sounds like someone is catching island fever," he said warmly. "It happens, you know. The sea air, the views, the romantic nights. Shelley and I fell in love on a night just like this."

"All in one night?"

"I fell in love with Shelley the first second I met her. She was the most spectacular girl I had ever met. She was beyond confident, and over that first summer she put me through the ringer. Have you heard this story?"

"No, but I'd like to."

"I grew up in Trusty, Colorado, and when I went away to college, I met Alexander Silver and Roddy Remington. We did everything together. We caused trouble, but we studied hard— you know, college days. The summer after our freshman year, Alexander and Roddy came home to work with their families, and they invited me along. I got a job working with Shelley's father here at the winery. I didn't know squat about vineyards or wines, but I wanted to be close to my buddies. Shelley was sixteen at the time. She strutted into the office one day when I was talking with her father, and she said, 'Excuse me, college guy, but I need to speak with my father *alone.*'" He chuckled. "She still calls me that sometimes. Anyway, her father didn't appreciate the interruption, and he told her as much. She said she didn't think he wanted me to hear that she had just decked his new vine guy for groping her butt and that her father needed to fire him. The vine guy was a seventeen-year-old kid who her father had taken on to help his buddy out."

"I cannot see Shelley punching anyone, but good for her."

"My wife is fierce, stubborn, *and* the happiest, warmest woman I have ever met. Where do you think Archer gets his stubbornness from?" He glanced at Archer, deep in conversation with Grant, and said, "It's a shame that you've only seen this side of him. He's a genuinely wonderful man, a gifted vintner, and yes, I'm biased, but all these people here are his friends, too. That should tell you something."

"I don't think Archer is a bad guy. People lash out when

they're hurt. If he and Jock didn't care about each other, they wouldn't fight."

"You're a wise woman. It's no wonder Jock is turning his life around."

"I think he's been trying to find a way back here for a while. I just offered a little support."

"You did more than that. I bet you didn't know that he inherited his mother's gift of happiness. Jock was a cocky kid, but he was a *happy* kid. Before the accident, he had this energy that drew people in. He was the guy who never let anything stand in his way. He lost that light, and that belief in himself, for a very long time. It's nice to see it coming back. And you've sparked something wild in my wife, too, with your idea of hosting events here. You're a whirlwind, Daphne. You and Hadley are changing lives and taking names, and I feel lucky that our family has come into your path."

"We're lucky, too. But you should know that even before Jock found those hidden parts of himself again, he drew people in. Hadley saw something special in him, and she was not going to let go until she held it in the palm of her hand. He drew *me* in, too, and I'm so glad he did, because what Hadley saw is the most loving heart either of us has ever known."

WHEN JOCK FINALLY got Daphne back in his arms, he kept her there. They danced and kissed, gazing into each other's eyes like lovers who had been together for months rather than weeks, which was exactly how he felt. When guests began leaving, they said goodbye to friends with promises of future visits, and to his grandmother, whom they would see in the morning at breakfast. His parents offered to put Hadley to bed and keep the baby monitor with them, allowing Jock and Daphne a little adult time, and he wasn't about to complain.

After helping his siblings clean up from the party, Jock drew Daphne into his arms and said, "Is it crazy that I missed that, too? Cleaning up?"

"Yes," Leni said as she walked by with Sutton and Jules. They plopped into chairs, took off their heels, kicked their feet up on the edges of each other's seats, and started gabbing.

Jock wanted to visit with his family, but he also wanted to take a walk with Daphne. He pressed his lips to hers and said, "Is it okay if we hang out with them for a minute?"

"Of course. This is your only night with your family. Enjoy it."

They joined the others as Levi came out of the winery. Jock kept his eyes on the doors, watching for Archer.

"Where's Indi?" Daphne asked.

"She went for a drink with Wells." Leni rolled her eyes and said, "I told her not to, but that woman is stubborn as a mule."

"Jealous?" Jules teased.

Leni scoffed. "Hardly. But I think Archer was. He basically threatened Wells. But Indi can take care of herself."

Levi sank down in a chair beside Jock and said, "Damn, what a night. It was nice that you were here, Jock. Everyone is talking about how glad they were to see you and to meet Daphne and Hadley."

"Mom and Grandma are so in love with both of you," Sutton said to Daphne.

"That makes three of us." Even in the moonlight Jock could see Daphne's cheeks pinking up. He pulled her closer and kissed her.

"Told you!" Jules jumped up and ran over to hug each of them. She pulled Levi to his feet and said, "I love you, but please swap seats with me." As Levi went to her seat, she sat down and snuggled up to Jock, lifting his arm and putting it around her. "This has been the best visit *ever*. You two are in love, and you're here, and you're staying overnight!"

"What are we—chopped liver?" Levi teased.

"No, but you guys visit all the time. Did you see how happy Mom and Dad and Grandma were tonight?" Jules asked.

"We had a great time, too, and I'm glad we came," Jock said. "But where's Archer?"

"He took off." Levi shrugged.

Jock sat back and said, "That sucks."

"I thought you'd be glad," Levi said.

"No, man. I'm not glad. I want to fix things between us. I hate that I'm here with you guys and he took off. I stayed away from the island so nobody would have to take sides, and look at this shit."

"We're used to it," Levi said reassuringly.

Jock gritted his teeth. "That's another problem."

Daphne put her hand over his and said, "Maybe it's just too much, and you should try coming home by yourself so he doesn't feel like he's outnumbered."

"Maybe," Jock said. "Or maybe I should go over to his boat and *make* him talk to me."

Jules shook her head. "I wouldn't do that. He said he was heading home, but I bet he's at Rock Bottom having drinks with Grant and the guys."

"Or keeping Wells away from Indi," Leni said. "Is it just me, or are the guys in the city less overt with their sluttery?"

They all chuckled.

"I love being home with everyone—don't get me wrong," Leni said. "But I'll be glad to hit the mainland tomorrow. What time are you guys leaving?"

"I'm leaving with you right after breakfast," Sutton answered.

"We're heading out after breakfast, too," Levi said. "Joey's got a playdate tomorrow, and I'm going to meet up with a few buddies for a motorcycle ride."

"Jock?" Leni asked, looking at Jock and Daphne.

"Afternoon sometime. I'm going to show Daphne around the island."

Jules, Leni, and Sutton said, "Island fever!"

Daphne giggled. "If there's such thing as island fever, then why do two of you live in New York?"

"Because they already burned through all the eligible bachelors here," Jules joked.

"Ha ha," Leni said. "I travel all the time. It's easier to get to clients from New York than it is from here."

"What about you, Sutton?" Daphne asked.

"Because the only thing to edit on the island is the local newspaper, which has been owned by the same family for a hundred years." Sutton looked at Jock and said, "By the way, why did we all have to hear secondhand that you're writing again, Jock? That's front-page news."

"It's group-text worthy, too, but he forbade me to share," Jules chimed in.

Jock shrugged. "I've been a little busy trying to write *and* start living my life again."

He leaned in to kiss Daphne, and Levi said, "Hey, man, I'm just glad you're here and an active part of the family again."

"*I love my fam-i-ly,*" Jules sang to the tune of "We Are Family."

"Oh boy, here she goes," Sutton said with a laugh.

Jules popped to her feet and started dancing and singing to the same tune. "*I love my fam-i-ly. I got Levi, Leni, Sutton, Jock, and Daph-e-nee. They're my fam-i-ly.* Get up and sing with me!"

Leni laughed and said, "No. Just no."

Jules shimmied her shoulders as she sang the chorus again, and Levi jumped up and shimmied with her, singing, "*Look at us back together.*"

"*As we hang outside!*" Jules sang, reaching for Jock's hand. "*Get up now!*"

Jock pulled Daphne up with him and sang, "*And we bicker like brothers and sisters. That's who we are!*" He twirled Daphne around, and they laughed and kissed as Leni and Sutton joined in, making up their own lyrics. Jock put his arms around Daphne, and they moved to their own private beat.

Levi put his face beside them and sang, "*Welcome to our fam-i-ly!*"

Jules popped up on the other side, singing, "*Hey, girl!*" and Daphne joined in with her own lyrics. "*You got all your siblings with you! I love your fam-i-ly.*"

As Levi and Jules twirled away, singing their hearts out, Jock dirty danced with Daphne, singing, "*Our life together has just beg-un.*"

"*It's al-ways just begun,*" Jules shout-sang to the tune of "It's Only Just Begun."

"No!" Leni and Sutton said through hysterical laughter.

Levi hauled Jules over his shoulder as his sisters cheered him on, and Jock drew Daphne into his arms again. "Damn, baby. I could use a hell of a lot more nights like this, with you and

Hadley, my family…"

Her eyes lit up, and she said, "I'm *in* Jock, ready to enjoy each and every day, just like we promised your grandmother."

"Me too, angel, with both feet." And on their perfect night, with his siblings causing a ruckus and his heart beating out a love song, he sealed their promises, dipping her over his arm and kissing her breathless.

# Chapter Twenty-Four

SHELLEY AND STEVE were early risers. By the time everyone came down for breakfast, there were fresh-baked banana-nut and apple-crumble muffins—*Thank you, best boyfriend in the world, for cluing in your parents to my favorite type.* The kitchen smelled heavenly and vibrated with sibling banter and laughter as everyone pitched in to prepare the rest of the meal. Archer hadn't made an appearance yet. Jock had said he wouldn't be surprised if Archer didn't show up this morning, but Daphne hoped he would. It would be a shame for him to miss such a wonderful family gathering.

"Okay, what else do we need to know?" Shelley asked, pulling Daphne from her thoughts. Lenore had joined them for breakfast, and the three of them had commandeered one end of the large farmhouse-style table to begin planning the wedding shower while Sutton and Indi finished setting it for breakfast.

"You'll need to talk to the bride-to-be and find out how many guests she expects, the atmosphere she's hoping for—festive, classy, low-key, youthful. The time of day, which will determine the meal—brunch, lunch, dinner, just appetizers."

"Excuse me, ladies," Indi said as she finished setting out the plates and utensils by them. "Remember, I'm your hair and makeup girl for events. I love this island, and I'd come back in a heartbeat to help with anything you need."

"*Great* idea," Daphne said excitedly. "Having a hair and makeup person on site would be a fantastic selling point for weddings and bigger events."

"There's an empty retail space a few doors down from me, Indi," Jules said as she set a bowl of fruit she'd cut up on the table. "You could have your own shop."

"And you could bring your whip," Lenore said with a wink. "Solve two problems at once."

"*Mother*," Shelley said with a shake of her head. "That is something to think about—the on-site hair and makeup, *not* the whip. If we do decide to go big and handle more events, and you moved here, maybe you could get Leni here, too."

Indi glanced at Leni, who was talking on her cell phone to her cousin Shea in the living room, and said, "While I would *love* to live on the island, that girl in there has been *citified*. You might never get her back here full-time."

"But you keep dreaming, Mom," Sutton said as she set down the last glass and kissed her mother's cheek.

Indi and Sutton headed into the kitchen with Jules, and Shelley said, "Okay, what else do we need to know?"

Daphne glanced at Shelley's list to see where they'd left off and said, "See if she has a type of food in mind, and if not, then we have to look into catering options. The food from the Bistro was amazing, and it'd be nice to use your friend, but do you have other restaurants in mind just in case she wants something different?"

"*Plenty* of them," Lenore said. "We've got deep roots on this island, honey."

"I love that." Daphne quickly realized she sounded a little

dreamy, so in a more professional voice, she said, "We'll also need to know what type of cake the bride is interested in, if she has a theme in mind, and if not, maybe you can suggest a few. We'll need to prepare decorations and maybe music. You should ask her about that. You can do almost anything with the space, and the outdoor pavilion is great to block the sun or a light rain. The tasting rooms are perfect for smaller gatherings, and the larger area you showed me off the lobby would be ideal for larger events. If you do them, we'll need to think about marketing, too."

"I have a granddaughter who is very experienced in marketing and public relations." Lenore nodded toward Leni in the other room.

"I'm sure Leni would squeeze us in. But I'm going to need Daphne's help coming up with themes and decorations," Shelley said. "With *everything* really. Tastings are so simple compared to this. Plus I've been doing them forever, so they're second nature to me. This is all new and exciting. I couldn't sleep last night, I was so revved up about hosting bigger events, especially since Margot is all for it."

"I'm excited, too. Jock and I are thinking about coming back the weekend after Hadley's birthday so you and I can make more plans and get things in order. If that works with your schedule, of course."

"You're coming back?" Shelley said softly, her eyes misting over. She gazed lovingly at Jock, standing at the stove making animal pancakes with Hadley.

"Bigger *eahs*," Hadley said from her perch on a chair beside Jock. "*Mawshall* has big eahs."

"Bigger ears coming up, princess." Jock poured more batter into the pan and said, "I think I need to start watching *PAW*

*Patrol.*"

"I'll get you a *PAW Patrol* gym bag." Levi chuckled and cracked more eggs into the pan for the scrambled eggs he and Joey were making. He was wearing a black leather vest like Justin's with the Dark Knights emblem on the back. It made him look even tougher.

"My kitchen is full again." Shelley put one hand over Daphne's and the other on Lenore's, but she didn't say a word as she watched her children working together.

Daphne thought about last night. After everyone else had gone inside, she and Jock had taken a walk through the vineyard. They'd talked about how nice it would be to spend more time on the island, how being there had made Jock long for the years he'd lost with his family, and how spending time with them had given him even more inspiration for his book. They both wished they could stay longer so he could have more time to try to get through to Archer and so they could visit with his parents and Jules without the commotion of the party. Watching Jock with his arm around Hadley, making her and Joey giggle at his comments, she was overcome with wanting more of this—for him, for them as a couple with Hadley, and for his family.

Levi looked over his shoulder at no one in particular and said, "The bacon and sausages are done."

"I've got them." Sutton came around the counter in her cute summer dress and grabbed the platter. "But first I need to taste-test the bacon." She plucked a piece of bacon from the plate and bit into it. "Pretty darn good."

Steve snagged a piece of bacon as Sutton walked by, then followed her to the table. He'd been smiling all morning as he talked with everyone, putting a hand on his sons' shoulders or around his daughters' waists. He'd kissed Hadley good morning and she'd put her little arms around his neck and said, "*Mownin'*, Grwampa." Steve had scooped her up and planted a kiss on her cheek, earning a big grin and making Daphne's heart even fuller.

"Better hurry, Leni," Sutton called into the living room. "Dad's going to eat all the bacon."

"Save some for my girls," Jock said over his shoulder.

Shelley squeezed Daphne's hand.

Indi peered around Hadley and said, "Those pancakes look great. You should make a snake for Archer. He's a snake in the grass if I've ever met one."

"Make snake, Dock," Hadley said.

Jock arched a brow at Levi, who handed him something from a cabinet and said, "Go for it."

The kitchen door opened, and Archer walked in. Shelley squeezed Daphne's hand again, this time a little harder.

Archer's hair was wet, his shirt stretched tight over his biceps and chest. His dark eyes swept over the kitchen, slowing on Jock, who managed a smile and a nod. Archer's gaze paused on Indi, who crossed her arms and lifted her chin in defiance. Daphne wondered if they'd gone head to head last night, although Jock had wondered if Indi had ended up going *hip to hip* with Archer or Wells because she'd gotten in as late as Jock and Daphne had.

"Hi, Uncle Archer!" Joey ran over and hugged him around the waist. "You smell good."

"Finally," Sutton said. "You're like a teenager, you sleep so late."

"Or like a thirtysomething guy with a life," Archer said stoically.

"Good morning, son," Steve said. "Late night?"

"Little bit." Archer strode over to Shelley and Daphne, and Jock watched his every step. Archer seemed even bigger looming behind them, scanning their notes. "What's all this?"

"We're hosting a bridal shower at the winery in a few weeks. Daphne is helping me plan for it. You can discuss it with your father and me later."

Daphne held her breath, hoping he wouldn't start an argument.

He eyed Daphne, and she managed a nervous smile. He looked at the notes again and said, "Do whatever you want— just don't ruin my vines."

"Really?" Jules said, sharing a disbelieving glance with Sutton as Leni walked into the kitchen. "Archer, you must have gotten lucky last night not to put up a fight."

Archer smirked, his eyes drifting to Indi. "Making waves and taking *no* names."

"*No* freaking way." Leni glared at Indi.

"Don't look at me! He's *your* brother." Indi turned angry eyes on Archer, who was chuckling, and said, "And, *you*, do not look at me like that. 'Making waves and taking no names.' How old are you? Sixteen?"

Archer's eyes narrowed. "Baby, I go twice as long as a sixteen-year-old and three times as often."

"Archer!" Shelley snapped. "That's *enough*."

Archer scoffed. "Just stating the facts, Mom."

"Gets that from his grandfather," Lenore said under her breath.

Steve clapped a hand on Archer's shoulder and said, "How about we get breakfast on the table."

There was a flurry of commotion as Shelley and Daphne put

their papers away and the others carried the rest of the food and drinks to the table.

Hadley turned on her chair by the stove, holding a plate, and said, "*Awcher*, your pancake is *weady*."

Jock put his arm around Hadley, chuckling with Levi and Indi as Archer took the plate, eyeing the snake pancake, his jaw clenching.

"Like it?" Hadley asked.

"Yeah," Archer grumbled.

"Indi, he likes the snake in the *gwass*!" Hadley announced as she scrambled off the chair and ran to the table.

Archer looked like he was chewing on nails as he carried his plate over.

"It's so nice to have everyone under one roof," Shelley said as the girls gathered around the table.

Jock and Levi were whispering to each other as they put the pans in the sink, troublemaking grins on their faces. Daphne wondered what they were up to.

Archer picked up the snake pancake with his fingers and ate half of it in one bite. His eyes watered, his face turned beet red, and he coughed and choked. He flew to his feet and grabbed the carafe of milk, guzzling it down.

"Are you choking?" Shelley got up and started patting his back, but he pulled away, still guzzling the milk between coughs.

"What's happening?" Jules asked frantically.

"What did you two do?" Leni glowered at Jock and Levi, who were laughing hysterically in the kitchen.

"It was just a little ghost-pepper extract," Levi said through his laughter.

Steve pinned a dark stare on them. "Seriously?"

When Archer finally put the carafe down, chest heaving, hands fisting, he locked eyes with Jock and Levi, who were still cracking up, and gritted out, "You're *dead*."

"Tell me something I don't know," Jock said as he and Levi bolted out the back door with Archer on their heels.

Panic exploded in Daphne's chest.

Hadley screamed, "Dock!" and scrambled off her chair. At the same time, Joey yelled, "Daddy!" and Jules ran for the door. Daphne scooped up a crying Hadley, and Steve caught Jules and demanded they stay inside. As Steve took off after the guys, Shelley comforted Joey, and with her heart in her throat, Daphne said to Hadley, "*Shh*, honey. They're just playing tag," wishing she could believe it, too.

JOCK HEARD HIS brothers' thundering footfalls behind him as they tore through the yard, Levi's laughter joining his own. He hoped the prank would break the ice, and he couldn't help grinning like a fool when Archer hollered at him. He spun around laughing, and Archer's fist connected with his jaw, blindsiding him, sending him careening to the ground. He caught himself with one hand, his head spinning. *Holy fuck. Guess we're doing this now.*

Jock spit out a mouthful of blood and pushed to his feet. "That all you got?" He plowed forward as Archer came at him. "Come on. Get it all out."

Archer clocked him again, but Jock was ready this time. He stumbled, but remained standing. Levi grabbed Archer from behind.

"I'll fucking kill you, too, Levi." Archer seethed, struggling to get free.

"Let him go," Jock commanded, putting his hands up and wiggling his fingers. "Come on, Archer. Give me all you got." It was time for this shit to end.

Archer sprinted forward, plowing his shoulder into Jock's sternum, taking them both to the ground. But Jock was quick to get on his feet.

"Go on," Jock panted out. "It's not going to bring her back."

"You fucking killed her!" Archer fumed, fists flying.

Jock dodged the hit, and Levi stepped up, but Jock waved him off, never taking his eyes off Archer. "It should've been me driving. We *both* know that."

Archer swung again, and Jock blocked his punch, but he didn't hit back. He *wouldn't*. "Keep going. At least you fucking *see* me now."

"I *hate* you," Archer spat. He came at Jock, head down, and Jock burst forward. They slammed into each other like linebackers, legs planted in the ground, two immovable mountains.

"I lost her, too, man," Jock gritted out. "I despise myself for it."

"You promised to look after her!" Archer punched him in the ribs. Jock reeled sideways, and Archer hit him again. "You didn't even respect her enough to marry her!"

Jock stumbled back and shouted, "Because she loved *you*, man. She didn't *want* me."

"Bullshit." Archer came at him, fists flying again.

Jock blocked a hit and had to swing back, connecting with Archer's jaw, sending his brother stumbling backward. Jock closed the distance between them, shouting, "She was in love with *you*!"

Archer bared his teeth. "Liar!"

He ran toward Jock, and Jock shouted, "*Think*, Archer! She texted *you* morning, noon, and night." Archer's shoulder slammed into him again, knocking the wind out of him. But Jock was not backing down. He dragged air into his lungs and said, "She hung out with *you* at the marina when we came to visit. It was always *you*! She *loved you*!"

Archer froze, nostrils flaring, hands fisted.

"It's true, man. We were going to come home and tell you the next day. I was going to back off, let you two raise my son if you were in love with her." Tears burned Jock's eyes, memories pummeling him.

Archer looked away, shaking his head. "*No*. She loved *you*."

"She loved *the baby*. We both did. Think about it, man. We were just having fun when she got pregnant," Jock said, moving into Archer's line of sight. He leaned his hands on his thighs, sucking air into his lungs. "Were you in love with her?"

Archer closed his eyes, teeth gritted.

"Archer, get that shit out of your head. We *both* lost her. I lost my baby, man. I know how much it hurts. I know how hate eats us alive and makes us want to hate everything around us. I couldn't fucking stand to look at myself in the mirror for a year, and for years after that, I hated the person I saw in that mirror. But we've already lost a decade. It's time to get it all out on the table." Holding his brother's confused and angry stare, he said, "Did you love her?"

Archer looked down, shaking his head. "As a *friend*. A fucking best friend. Not as…*No*." He turned sorrowful eyes on Jock and said, "I didn't *know*."

"That's on me. I should have told you sooner, but you wouldn't even look at me." Jock felt like his heart was being torn out all over again, but they had to get this out, so he forced the words, and they tore from his lungs like shards of glass. "When you said I was dead to you, I didn't blame you for it. *I* wished it had been *me* driving that fucking car."

Archer stared him down, chest heaving. "I hated you, but I hated myself even more." His fists opened and closed as he paced. "I missed her so damn much. I missed her laugh, her bullshit texts at three in the morning when she couldn't sleep. She was always there, from the time we were kids, and then she was gone. I hated myself for wanting her to live because that would mean I'd have lost you. But I didn't *want* that, either. I wanted you *all* to have never gotten into that fucking car."

"I know," Jock said.

"Do you?" Archer challenged. "How can you fucking know how guilty I've felt for all these years? You're my brother, my blood. My fucking *twin*. I can't..." He turned away.

"That's how I know. Because you're my twin. I didn't let myself know that until yesterday. Dad said something and it made me realize that maybe you don't really want me dead. But don't turn it inward, Archer," Jock demanded. "Hit *me*. Get it out of your system before it kills the best part of you."

Archer shook his fist at him and shouted, "You should have just married her."

"I *couldn't* marry her, and she couldn't marry me."

"But I didn't love her like that," Archer said, angry and pleading at once, his shoulders slumped in defeat. "If she'd told me, maybe then you two could have—"

"No, Archer. The feelings weren't there. We *tried*. We thought they'd develop, but they didn't. And then, at the restaurant that last night, she told me she was in love with *you* and she thought she always had been."

"Well, *fuck!*" His face contorted. "So what was the plan? She'd come here and tell me, and I'd be a dick and not love her back? Then what would she be left with?"

Jock softened his tone and said, "Two guys who would've stood by her and loved her like family. We would have raised Liam together, not as husband and wife, but as two people who had created a child together. I respected the hell out of her, Archer. She could have aborted the baby and I would have never known. But she didn't, because she respected me, too."

Tears slipped down Archer's cheeks. "Why did she have to love *me?* I'm a dick. I couldn't even be there for you when you lost your *baby.* I fucking hate myself for that, too."

"Don't hate yourself, Archer. You were grieving the woman you knew. You had no room to grieve the nephew you'd never met. You're not a dick. You're pissed off. And you weren't a dick before she died. You were a twenty-two-year-old guy having fun, just like I was, and she was the same way. We were all young. We didn't even know what love was."

"But she *did,*" he said firmly. "She loved *me.* And what'd she get back?"

"I get it, Archer. But you can't allow her feelings for you to ruin the rest of your life. I know this is a lot to handle, but you can't change how you felt about her, any more than I could. Or for that matter, any more than she could have changed how she felt about us."

Archer stared at him, his emotions storming around him. "I can't..." He shook his head and stalked toward the winery.

Jock gritted out a curse and hollered after him, "I'm not going to let you hate me anymore, Archer. I love you too damn much to lose more time with you."

Archer continued walking, raised his right hand, and flipped him off.

"I'd say that's a good sign," Levi said as he and their father approached.

Jock huffed out a laugh. He had forgotten Levi was there, and he didn't know his father had been watching them. "How long have you been standing there, Dad?"

"Long enough to say I'm proud of both of you." He pulled Jock into an embrace, and Jock winced. "Let's go put some ice on that, Rocky."

"Nah, I'm good."

"Are you?" Levi asked.

"Yeah, man, I am. We needed that." He glanced at the house and said, "Please tell me my girls didn't see us going at it."

"Jules sent a group text," Levi said. "All the girls are with the kids in the rec room. Joey and Hadley are playing. Daphne's probably a mess, though Jules says Mom is sidetracking her with event talk."

All their phones vibrated at once.

"Probably Jules again," Levi said, and they pulled out their phones, exchanging confused glances at Archer's name on the message bubble.

They opened the texts and laughed at Archer's message—
*Stop talking about me, Jockstrap. You're still an asshole.*

# Chapter Twenty-Five

DAPHNE WALKED INTO the bedroom looking for Jock. He'd seemed a little *too* fine when he'd told everyone what had happened between him and Archer. She knew Jock well enough to realize there was much more to it than *We broke the ice.* She found him washing his face in the bathroom and leaned against the doorframe, aching at the angry purple bruises forming on his rib cage and the same coloring peeking out from beneath the scruff on his jaw.

He lifted his face and smiled. "Hi, angel." He reached for a towel and patted his face dry.

"Hey." She was relieved to see he'd lost some of the shadows that had haunted him. She went to him, trying to read his beautiful, complicated mind. She touched his waist, needing to feel closer. "Are you okay? Do you want to talk?"

He put his arms around her and pressed his lips to hers. "What I want is to take you and Hadley to see the island, like we planned."

"Jock, I know what you said downstairs, but this is just *us.* What does breaking the ice really mean? Did you bruise his face and ribs, too? Does it mean more fights? Did you talk about anything real? Is anything going to change?"

"It's a start, baby. It's exactly like you said when my mom introduced you to Archer. He *sees* me now, whereas before he only saw hate—toward me and toward himself. We talked about everything, or at least touched on it. We opened doors that I worried might never open again, and I'm sure we'll be working through it for a long time. He has a lot of guilt about what he said to me, and that fueled his hatred of himself. That's a lot to live with, and if anyone understands what that feels like, it's me. Unfortunately, telling him Kayla was in love with him added to his guilt. He wasn't in love with her, and he didn't want to believe it at first. It's a lot to take in. But now he knows, and he does believe it. The ties that bound years of hurt, anger, and guilt are unraveling, and that's a lot to process for both of us."

"You seem better, but I want you to know you can talk to me, and if you'd rather stay home and go see Archer, or just be with your family this morning, that's totally fine."

Leni, Sutton, Indi, Levi, and Joey had left for the ferry after talking with Jock. His grandmother and his mother were downstairs with Hadley. His father had gone to the winery to see if Archer was there, and Jules had gone to work. Jules made Jock promise they'd stop by to see her before they left on the five o'clock ferry.

Jock drew Daphne closer, kissing her softly. "Talking with you is what made this possible. I feel freer, and I think Archer does, too. I'd say he and I will probably take baby steps toward a better relationship, but you know I suck at going slow, and Archer is my twin, so…"

"Does that mean we have more bruises to look forward to, but they'll happen fast and furious?"

He grinned. "I have no clue, but I do know it's a good

thing, however it happens. Now, let's get the heck out of here before I tear off those sexy striped shorts and that tight tank top and show you what island fever is really all about."

HALF AN HOUR later, Jock borrowed his parents' car and took Daphne and Hadley to see Silver Monument, located in the center of the island, with incredible views in every direction. The stately monument resembled a turret from a castle, surrounded by a brick-paved courtyard with iron benches and beautiful trees. A line of people waited to enter and climb to the top of the massive monument.

Jock held Hadley's hand and pointed to a park just beyond the monument, saying, "The island Christmas tree is located in Majestic Park, right over there, and the annual holiday festival takes place there a few weeks before Christmas. There's a Christmas tree lighting and people gather around singing and hanging ornaments on the tree. If the weather cooperates, kids sled ride, and everyone hangs out drinking hot chocolate and eating roasted chestnuts and other treats. It's really fun. Then every weekend leading up to Christmas, there's something going on. The marinas have the flotillas, where boaters and fishermen decorate their boats for the Island of Lights Holiday Flotilla and they cruise along the harbor competing for the best decorations. There are horse-drawn sleigh rides down Main Street, and the Silver House has caroling and a big holiday dance."

"That sounds *wonderful*." Daphne got goose bumps thinking about enjoying all of those things with Jock and Hadley and his family and friends. Maybe they could even have Christmas dinner with both of their families this year. Her heart fluttered at the thought. She was getting ahead of herself, but she could see it all so clearly, it felt *real*, and she wanted it more than she wanted anything—other than for Jock and Archer's relationship to continue to heal.

"It's really special. I haven't been since I left for college." He lifted Hadley into his arms and put his other arm around Daphne, hugging her to his side. "We should come this year. What do you think?"

"I'd *love* that." Daphne gazed up at him.

"I want this with you and Hadley, Daph. I want to come to the parades and see Hadley on the winery float dressed up as a little bunny." He kissed Hadley's cheek and said, "Would you like that, princess? To be in a fancy parade?"

Hadley nodded.

"I want that, too," Daphne said, and this time she didn't even try to tamp down her imagination as it skipped ahead to seeing Hadley on that float with *Gwama* and *Gwampa*, and she even let herself think about bigger dreams. *A winery wedding. A sister or brother for Hadley...*

"Want to see where I went to school?" Jock asked, leading them around the monument. "We have three schools that are K through eight on the island, and they all feed into Silver Island High." He pointed down a road and said, "The high school is five minutes that way. That's one reason kids here get to know each other so well. It doesn't matter if you're from a wealthy family or a family that's making it paycheck to paycheck. You all end up at the same high school." He took Daphne's hand and said, "Come on, I'll show you."

They got back in the car and Jock drove by his high school, showing them where he played sports and telling them about pranks and things he'd done with his friends. There was a new spark in him again, just like there had been last night at the party. Only this time it was even brighter, as if the crack in the ice with Archer had helped him shed more monkeys from his back.

A little while later, they parked in the center of town and strolled down Main Street, lined with colorful shops and bustling with tourists. OPEN flags waved in the ocean breeze announcing shop entrances, and painted wooden benches offered places to sit and enjoy the sunny day. Window boxes overflowed with summer blooms, and picture windows boasted enticing displays, drawing them in to meander through one cute shop after another. Daphne collected cards and contacts from shop owners so she could more efficiently help Shelley plan the bridal shower. Hadley walked down the sidewalks, but inside the stores, she lifted her arms for Jock to carry her. Daphne worried about his bruised ribs, but he assured her that *his* little princess would never be too much for him.

"I want to grab a card from here, too," Daphne said as she walked into the flower shop.

"You do realize my mother grew up here and knows every-one, right?" Jock teased.

Daphne snagged a business card. As they walked out of the shop, she said, "Yes, but *I* don't. I want to surprise your mom and put together a helpful list of local shops in case she decides to go bigger and do more events. If she becomes a destination wedding venue, she'll need these things handy for her event planner to use and to give out to clients. Everyone thinks a venue is just four walls or the property, but it's so much more than that. She'll be relied on for everything, and even though she knows the island inside and out and backward, your mom is busy running the winery. A list is something she can give out to alleviate a million questions."

He hooked an arm around her as they walked down the sidewalk and kissed her temple. "You're really something. You know that?"

"I'm yours. I know *that*." She looked at her little girl holding his hand, and a gust of happiness swept through her. "We both are."

"Damn right you are." He leaned in for a kiss, and they continued window-shopping.

"My house!" Hadley ran to the window of a real estate company and pointed to a picture of a cute two-story cedar-sided house with a white picket fence out front and a deep front porch. Planters overflowing with vibrant pink flowers hung from the porch roof between each of the columns.

"That's pretty isn't it, baby?" Daphne said.

"*Mine*," Hadley said as if it were a fact, blinking innocently up at them.

"That's not ours, honey. We live on Cape Cod, not Silver Island." A pang of longing struck Daphne, and she tucked it away. "Maybe one day we'll find something just as cute."

"*Mine*," Hadley said adamantly. She pressed her tiny hand to the window and grabbed Jock's hand, putting it on the window, too. "*Mine*, Dock."

"I think she knows who the softy is," Daphne said.

Jock laughed.

"Your daughter has good taste," a tall brunette said as she came up the sidewalk. "That house is over in the Bluffs. It's a relatively new and very sought-after development. There are lots of young families there, a great view of the water, and a small park, too. Would you like to come in to get more information about it?"

"No, thank you," Daphne said. "We're just visiting."

"Just out of curiosity, what town is that in?" Jock asked.

"Here. It's five minutes away," she said cheerily. "I'm Charmaine Luxe. I work here." She reached into her purse and handed him a business card.

"Jock Steele. This is my girlfriend, Daphne." He put his hand on Hadley's shoulder and said, "And this is Hadley."

"Related to the Top of the Island Steeles?" Charmaine asked.

"Yes. They're my parents."

"It's nice to meet you. I'm relatively new to the island, but I know your parents, and of course Jules and Archer." Charmaine pulled the door open and said, "If you change your mind, give me a call. I'd love to show you around."

As the door closed behind Charmaine, Daphne said, "She was nice. Come on, Had, let's keep walking."

Hadley shook her head. "My house!"

"I have an idea." Jock went inside and came out with a for-sale flyer for the house. He scooped up Hadley and gave it to her.

She beamed up at him. "My house is *pwetty*."

"You spoil her, you know," Daphne said as they passed a boutique.

"It's a picture. I didn't buy the house. *That* would be spoiling her." He kissed Daphne, and they continued window-shopping.

They walked through a bookstore and passed a restaurant. When they came to a jewelry shop, they admired the pieces in the window. Hadley dropped Owly, and Jock picked it up and said, "How about I hold on to him for a little while?"

"Okay," Hadley said, and rested her head on his shoulder.

"I want to grab a card," Daphne said as she opened the door.

Jock went to say hello to the person behind the counter, and Daphne snagged a business card, taking her time admiring the sparkling jewelry displays.

After the jewelry store, they crossed the street to visit Jules in her shop before stopping for lunch. Color burst from every shelf and tabletop in the cheery gift shop. There were so many things to look at—candles, mugs, stuffed animals, toys, greeting cards, jewelry, and beachy signs and pillows emblazoned with cute sayings about love and sunshine. Dream catchers hung from the ceiling, and cool scarves were draped over displays of shirts and totes.

"You came!" Jules squealed as she rushed toward them. The ponytail on top of her head spread out like a fountain over the rest of her long tresses. She hugged Daphne and Jock and tickled Hadley's belly. "Great timing. Tara's on her way here with pictures from last night. How do you like our island?"

"I am so in love with this island, it's ridiculous," Daphne said. "I can't wait to come back."

"My house!" Hadley thrust the flyer toward Jules.

"That's *your* house?" Jules eyed Daphne and Jock curiously.

"Not really. She saw it in the window at the real estate office and *spoiler* over here got her the picture." Daphne touched Jock's arm and said, "I have to teach him the value of saying no sometimes."

Jock flashed a panty-melting smile and said, "But, angel, you *love* saying yes."

"I don't think I want to know this about you two," Jules whispered.

Hadley tried to wriggle out of Jock's hands, and he said, "There's a lot of breakable stuff in here, princess. I should probably carry you."

"She's *fine*. Let her down," Jules urged. "We have kids in here all the time." She pointed to the other side of the store, where two young families were hovering around displays of stuffed animals and pillows.

Jock put Hadley down and said, "How about I hold your picture?"

Hadley gave him the flyer. "No lose it."

"I wouldn't dare," he promised.

"Stay with me, Had," Daphne said.

Jock patted his pockets, his brow furrowed. "*Shoot.* I think I left O-W-L-Y in the jewelry store. I'll run and get it while you look around." He kissed Daphne's cheek and touched Hadley's head lovingly. "Be right back, princess."

Daphne sighed as he headed for the door.

"Girl, you are *so* in love with my brother," Jules teased.

"Yes, I am," Daphne admitted, earning another squeal and a hug from Jules.

The door to the shop opened, and Tara breezed in, carrying a large messenger bag. "I'm so glad you're still here," Tara said. "I can show you the pictures I took. I got some great ones."

"Mommy, look." Hadley toddled toward a display of colorful wands with fuzzy stars on the top.

"Don't touch," Daphne said. "I'd better follow her."

Jules and Tara walked with them. Tara took a folder out of her bag and said, "Jules, look at this picture of your parents." She handed her a picture of Steve and Shelley embracing. Steve's hand was low on her back, fingers spread, like he wanted to hold as much of her as he possibly could. His eyes were closed, but his expression conveyed that everything he ever wanted was right there in his arms.

"This is so *them*. I want to be that happy one day," Jules said.

Tara rolled her eyes. "If you were any happier, you'd explode."

Jules giggled. "I mean with a guy. I want to be loved like my mom is loved, with *everything* a man has. I want be looked at the way Jock looks at Daphne and feel like Daphne did when he walked out of here."

"I highly recommend finding the person who will make you feel all of that," Daphne said. "Can I tell you guys a secret?"

"You don't have to ask. The girl code is always in effect on the island," Tara said as they followed Hadley to a display of plush children's blankets.

Daphne whisper-gushed, "It's scary to be this happy, to see my little girl so in love with Jock. A good kind of scared. Sometimes when it's just the three of us, there are these moments when everything feels so intense and our love feels so big—when he's holding Hadley, or we're just sitting together, or putting her to bed, or when it's just me and him and he looks at me *that* way. I hold my breath sometimes because I'm afraid if I breathe, I might wake up and find out it was all a dream."

"I want *that*," Jules said breathily.

"We *all* want that," Tara said. "I have good news for you, Daphne. You will never have to worry that it's just a dream again, because I caught your reality in two perfect pictures. I have a ton of pictures that you'll love." She flipped through the folder. "But these two are magical."

She handed Daphne a picture of Hadley sitting on Jock's lap, stuffing cake into his mouth. They were both smiling so big, it brought tears to Daphne's eyes.

"If you think that's good, look at this one." Tara handed her another picture, in which Daphne was nestled in Jock's arms as they danced. He was holding her protectively, like he'd give his life for hers and never wanted to let her go. Their faces were a whisper apart and they were gazing into each other's eyes.

Everything she felt was right there—the intensity, the love, the *hope*.

Jules put her arm around Daphne and said, "I think Tara's right. No more holding your breath."

Tara showed them more fun pictures of everyone. She'd even caught Archer smiling during Jock's speech, with Jock watching him from where he stood. Daphne asked for copies of many of the pictures, including that one. "We'll be back in two weeks. Is that long enough to get them done?"

"Definitely. I'll have them ready," Tara promised.

"And I'll have our girls' day all planned!" Jules said. "The three of us—and I'll see if Belly wants to come. If so, I'll schedule Noelle to fill in. She works on an as-needed basis for me. Maybe Mom and Grandma will want to come. We can do the Bra Brigade! I wonder if I can get Leni and Sutton to join us. We'll take my parents' boat to Bellamy Island. Or as Belly calls it, *her* island since she's named after it." Jules pulled her phone from her pocket and began texting.

Tara nudged Daphne and said, "See how she did that? Get used to it. She just makes plans and we all go along with them."

"I love it, but shouldn't I make sure Jock doesn't mind?" Daphne asked.

Jules slanted her brows, like she was thinking about it, and then she waved her hand dismissively and said, "Nah. He'll love that we're hanging out. Wait! I have a better idea. Let's do half of a girls' day; then later in the afternoon we'll go on the boat and bring Jock and Dad. Maybe by then Archer will even come."

"Can I ask Levi and Joey to come?" Tara asked. "Joey loves girls' days."

"I've already got them covered. Group text," Jules said, her thumbs flying over her phone's screen.

Hadley toddled by dragging a pink blanket with a princess on it. "Hadley," Daphne called after her. Hadley turned around, and Daphne said, "We have to put the blanket back, baby, so it doesn't get dirty."

Hadley clutched it to her chest and shook her head. "*Pwincess.*"

"Guess you're taking that home." Tara laughed.

"That can be my birthday present to her," Jules said excitedly. She crouched in front of Hadley and said, "Do you like that blanky?"

"I *love* it." Hadley clutched the blanket with all her might. "I'm Dock's *pwincess.*"

"Yes, you are." Jules gathered the bottom of the blanket in her hands and said, "Let me tell you something special about this blanket." She moved Hadley's free hand around the bundled blanket. "It has magic powers. It can make you smile and feel better when you're sad. It can even help make *all* of your dreams come true. But you have to take really good care of it. Do you think you can do that?"

Hadley nodded, eyes wide.

"Okay, then it can be your birthday present from Auntie Jules."

"Thank you!" Hadley ran to Daphne and said, "It's mine. It's *magic!*"

Daphne admired the blanket and said, "I think Auntie Jules is going to make a great mommy one day." She looked at Jules. "Thank you."

Jock came through the door carrying a bag, and Hadley shouted, "Dock!" She ran to him and showed off her new blanket.

"Where did you get such a special blanket?" he asked, winking at Daphne.

"Auntie Jules. You have my house?"

"Of course." He handed her the flyer and glanced at Daphne. "She's so smart. She never forgets anything."

"Owly?" Hadley asked.

He pulled the stuffed toy from his pocket and handed it to her. Hadley snuggled it against her cheek, and Jock said, "How's it going, Tara?"

"Great. I'm glad I got a chance to see you guys before you left," Tara said.

"Wait until you see the pictures Tara took last night," Daphne said.

As Tara showed him the pictures, he studied the ones of them and of Archer for so long, Tara said, "Keep them. They're just proofs. I'll give you better copies when you come back."

"Thank you," he said. "I appreciate that."

"What's in the bag?" Daphne asked.

"I stopped in at the café and got sandwiches for lunch. I thought we'd take Hadley to the park around the corner and eat there."

"You went to Trista's and didn't bring me anything?" Jules teased.

Jock opened the large bag and pulled out a smaller one. "Do you really think I'd go to your favorite café and not bring you something? You can share it with Tara."

"I knew I loved you." Jules hugged him. "Thank you."

"It's all yours, Jules," Tara said. "I have to head out to Fortune's Landing. I'm doing an engagement photo shoot with a couple from the Cape."

"Tara, can I get your number?" Daphne asked. "Jules, you, too? I'm putting together a list of contacts for Shelley's event clients. It would be great to have a local photographer on it, and we can pimp out Jules's shop as the perfect place to find unique bridesmaid gifts."

"*Yesss!* I am so adding you to our group texts!" Jules exclaimed, and the girls exchanged numbers.

Jock laughed. "And so it begins…"

AFTER LOTS OF goodbye hugs and promises about an upcoming girls' day that Jock was happy to hear would include Daphne and Hadley, they left Jules's shop and headed down to the park to have lunch. Hadley ran for the swings, and as Jock pushed her, Hadley pleaded, "*Higher!*" He worried about pushing her higher, and though Daphne said Hadley could handle it, he couldn't escape the new sensations of worry tightening inside his chest. The thing was, he didn't want to escape it. He loved that little girl as if she were his own.

When they finally settled in for lunch beneath the shade of a giant oak tree, Hadley made a bed for Owly with her new blanket, set the picture of her house beside him, and planted herself in Jock's lap as she ate her peanut butter and jelly sandwich.

"You have a new bestie," Daphne teased, glancing at Hadley.

Jock kissed the top of Hadley's head and said, "It's nice. Unless it bothers you?"

"It doesn't. All I've ever wanted was for her to be loved." She bit into her sandwich and said, "This is delicious. There's cranberry and nuts in the chicken salad. Yum! We'll have to stop by the café and get a menu for Shelley."

Jock pulled a menu out of his back pocket.

"You're the *best*." Daphne leaned forward and kissed him. Then she kissed Hadley's head. "I love it here. The island is so close to home, but it feels like we're worlds away. It's hard to believe such a great day started with a fight. How's your jaw and your ribs?"

He'd forgotten he'd been hit. Something happened to him when he was around Daphne and Hadley—nothing else registered, or mattered. "They're fine."

Daphne was about to take a bite of her sandwich, when she stopped, lowering her hand as she said, "Why are you looking at me like that?"

"Like what?" he asked, though he knew the answer. There was no hiding how he felt.

Her cheeks pinked up, and that sweet and sexy smile he adored appeared. She lowered her eyes and said, "Never mind."

"Like you're the most beautiful woman I've ever seen?" he asked, and she lifted her eyes to his. "The most incredible friend I've ever known? The perfect mother?"

"Jock...?" she whispered.

"Like I want to wake up next to you every day for the rest of my life?"

She inhaled shakily.

He kissed the top of Hadley's head and said, "Like I want to be there for Hadley when she starts first grade? When she has her first boyfriend? When she graduates from college?"

Daphne's eyes teared up.

"Because that's what I feel when I look at you. I have a confession to make. Leaving you-know-who at the jewelry store wasn't an accident. I wish I had been there when Hadley was born so you could have had this the whole time." He reached into the lunch bag and pulled out a velvet bag from the jewelry store. He shook out the gold charm bracelet he'd bought, and as he put it on her wrist, he said, "The little-girl charm is for Hadley."

"Me?" Hadley leaned forward to inspect the charm.

"That's right, princess. That little-girl charm is you."

"Pwetty," she said, and took a bite of her sandwich.

His and Daphne's eyes connected. He touched the book charm and said, "This charm is because you are my muse, angel. I wouldn't be writing if not for you. And the muffin…well, that was where we started, wasn't it? And you know how much I *love* your muffins."

She lifted her wrist to look at the charms, and a tear slipped down her cheek.

He pulled her into a one-armed hug, his other arm circling Hadley. "I love you, sweetheart, and this is just the beginning."

"I love you, too, so, *so* much. It's beautiful. Thank you."

"Mommy *cwying*?" Hadley put her hand on Daphne's arm.

"Happy tears, baby," she said, wiping her eyes.

"I have something for you, too, princess." Jock withdrew Hadley's charm bracelet with the tiny crown charm from the bag, drawing more tears from Daphne. He took Hadley's sandwich and put it on a napkin. As he put the bracelet around her wrist, he said, "This is yours, because every princess needs a crown."

"Look, Mommy, a *cwown*!" She thrust her little hand toward Daphne.

"It's beautiful, honey." Daphne sniffled and wiped her eyes. "What do you say to Jock?"

Hadley threw her arms around Jock's neck and said, "I love you, Dock!"

Jock hugged her tight and said, "That's even better than a thank-you."

# Chapter Twenty-Six

DAPHNE HADN'T STOPPED looking at her bracelet since Jock had given it to her. He'd been *this close* to proposing. The urge had pounded inside him like a second heart, but he'd worried it might be too fast for Daphne, so he'd held back. They were sitting on opposite sides of the couch in the living room, playing footsie. Jock's parents were outside with his grandmother, and Jock was supposed to be writing while Hadley was napping, but he was watching Daphne pluck away at his mother's laptop, creating the lists she'd been talking about all day.

She ran her toes along the arch of his foot, and her eyes flicked up to his as she said, "I don't hear magic happening over there."

"I'll show you magic." He set the laptop on the floor and scooted forward, lifting her legs over his so they would straddle his waist when he got closer. She set the laptop on the floor as he moved forward. He put his arms around her and pulled her into a kiss. "Mm. Now, *that's* magic."

"You think? I'm not so sure." She brushed her fingers lightly along the back of his neck and said, "Maybe we should try again."

"God, I love you." His mouth descended over hers devouringly despite the twinge in his jaw. *Oh yeah, we're magic all right.*

Hadley whimpered through the baby monitor, and their lips parted. "Sorry," Daphne whispered.

"Don't be." He pressed his lips to hers and said, "I'll get her."

"We'll both go. I bet she's excited to ride the ferry again."

Jock grabbed her butt on the way up the stairs and stole a kiss on the landing. They held hands on the way into Hadley's room. Hadley looked pale, but the apples of her cheeks were pink. *Too* pink. The hair on the back of Jock's neck stood on end.

"Mama," Hadley said weakly. "My Dock."

"We're here, baby." Daphne reached for her, and Hadley whimpered. Daphne touched her cheek, then put the back of her hand on Hadley's forehead. "She's burning up. Do you know if your mom has a thermometer and children's Tylenol? I didn't bring either."

"I don't know," he said. "I can look. If not, I'll run to the store and get some."

When he turned to leave, Hadley cried, "*Dock.*" Tears streamed down her cheeks, one little hand reaching for him, the other clutching Owly. "Want *my Dock.*"

"Would you mind staying with her and I'll go ask your mom?" Daphne asked.

"Of course not. I've got you, princess." He lifted Hadley into his arms, and she slumped against his chest. Her skin wasn't just hot. It was *boiling*. Panic flared inside him. "Daphne, she's too hot." He pulled his phone from his pocket.

"Who are you calling?"

"The doctor."

"Jock, she's *fine*. She just has a fever. Your mom is right out back. Let me see if she has what we need. If she doesn't, I can ask your mom to run me to the store and get it. I should pick up Pedialyte, juice boxes, and a few other things, too. I don't think we should take her on the ferry. Do you think your parents will mind if we stay another night?"

"Of course not." He paced, rubbing Hadley's back. "I want the doctor to check her out."

"Just let me take her temperature. Little kids run high fevers."

"Daphne, *please?*"

Her brows knitted, and then understanding showed in her eyes. "Oh, Jock. This is scary for you, isn't it?"

*More than you realize.* "Bet you didn't know there were two girls who could bring me to my knees."

"Actually, I did." She went up on her toes to kiss him. "Thank you for loving her. She's going to be fine, I promise. She probably just has what my mom had. My mom texted earlier and said she's feeling better. But you can call the doctor if it'll give you peace of mind. I'm going to check on the thermometer and Tylenol. I'll call Rick and let him know I won't be in tomorrow."

He pressed a kiss to Hadley's cheek and said, "I'm going to call the doctor, but what else can I do for her?"

"I don't think she'll put up with you wiping her with a wet washcloth to try to bring her temperature down, or even putting one on her forehead, but if she will, it would help until we can get medicine in her."

"I'll try."

As Daphne went downstairs, Jock called the doctor. Dr.

Fletcher was on his way back from the Cape and had just gotten on the ferry. He told Jock that Daphne was right: Try the wet washcloth, make sure she was drinking plenty of fluids, give her Tylenol, and he'd be there as soon as he could. Jock was filling Hadley's sippy cup with water when Daphne and his mother came into the room. His mother fawned over Hadley and reassured Jock she'd be okay.

"Your father went to the winery, and Lenore went to a friend's house. I'm going to take Daphne to the store, but we won't be long." His mother rubbed Hadley's back and said, "Are you okay, honey?"

"Yeah," he lied, but he didn't want to thrust his worries on them.

"Want me to stay with her?" Daphne asked.

Hadley clung to him. "No, we're okay. I've got her."

"Okay. We'll hurry back."

After they left, Jock sat on the edge of the bed, but Hadley whimpered, so he got up and paced again. "How about we try that washcloth?" He carried her into the bathroom and held his hand under the water until it was warm, then worried that maybe it should be cooler. But how cool was too cold? He pulled out his phone and said, "Siri, what temperature should a wet washcloth be to help reduce a fever?"

Siri said, "Here's what I found," and a list of websites appeared on his screen. He navigated to the first and scanned the information, gritting his teeth at the mention of febrile seizures. He went back to the list and clicked on the next site and once again found a reference to seizures. He clicked on the link for seizures. *High fevers can cause convulsions in young kids without a history of neurologic symptoms? Holy fucking hell.* He shoved his phone in his pocket, pacing again, silently cursing Siri for being no damn help at all.

"We have to do this, princess. We can't let you have a seizure." He wrung out the washcloth, hoping he got the temperature right, and felt like a villain as he said, "I'm sorry about this, but I have to try to get your fever down."

He ran the washcloth down her arm. She cried and pulled her knees up to her chest against his body, like she wanted to burrow inside it.

"*Sorrysorrysorry.*" *Shit.* "We need to cool you down, baby."

She shook her head, whimpering.

"Will you take a drink of water for me? *Please?*" He set the washcloth down on the sink and handed her the sippy cup.

She buried her face in his neck and cried. "*No.*"

"Look, Had. I'll drink it." He pretended to take a sip, and she shook her head, her lower lip trembling. "Okay, no drink, no drink," he said quickly, and set down the cup. He picked up the washcloth again and paced, bouncing her a little, worrying about her blazing skin. A few minutes later, he said, "Can we try the washcloth one more time?"

"*Mm-mm.*" A definite *no.*

He tried again to get her to take a drink, to lie down, and to allow him to cool her off with the washcloth, but she didn't want anything except to be held while he paced the floor.

"'Eyes on You,'" she said in a voice as thin as air.

Her weak voice cut straight to his heart. Thank goodness he'd sung her version of the song with Daphne enough times to know it by heart. He began singing and continued pacing, rubbing gentle circles on her back. "We've been to North Carolina, seen the big blue sky. Driven down the coast a time or two. Brewster, Eastham, Wellfl—"

"What the hell song is that?"

Jock turned at the sound of Archer's voice. His brother stood in the doorway, brows knitted, a bruise peeking out from beneath his beard.

"It's her song, and she's sick," Jock said sharply. "Did you know kids can have seizures from high fevers? She can't have a seizure. Doc Fletcher is on his way back from the Cape, and Daph went to get medicine. I'm supposed to wash Hadley down with this." He shook the washcloth. "But she won't let me. She won't drink, either."

Archer looked at him like he was nuts. "*Jesus Christ.* Give me that." He tore the washcloth from Jock's hand and disappeared into the bathroom. When he walked into the bedroom, he said, "Lie on your back on the fucking bed."

"Why?"

Archer scowled. "For the *kid*. And put her next to you."

"She doesn't want to lie down." Jock toed off his shoes and lay on his back, shifting Hadley to the bed beside him. Hadley whined and curled against him. He put his arm around her and said, "See?"

Archer uttered a curse, unlaced his work boots, and lay down on Hadley's other side. He put a wet washcloth on Jock's forehead; then he lay flat on his back and put one on his own forehead.

"Do *me*," Hadley said, settling onto her back between them.

"Seriously?" Jock said. The three of them lay on their backs staring up at the ceiling with wet washcloths on their foreheads. "How'd you know to do this?"

"I don't know. Watching Levi, I guess. If you're going to have kids, you can't be a pussy. You have to know how to do this shit."

"Don't curse around her."

"What the hell *can* I say?" Archer asked.

"I don't know. Nothing…*Poop.*"

"I'm not saying *poop.*"

"Well, you're not saying *shit,* either." Jock winced. "Sorry, Hadley."

"What's wrong with you?"

"I *love* her, man. She hurts, *I* hurt. Is that so hard to understand?"

"You're the adult. You gotta figure this shi—*poop*—out. She's counting on you."

"No shi—*poop*—genius," Jock snapped, tucking Hadley closer to his side. "It freaks me out a little, okay?"

"Why?"

"Because."

"*Why?* She's a kid. She's got a fever. She'll be fine."

"Because it stirred the memories, okay?" Jock barked.

"What memories?"

"Of *Liam,* you idiot. I know she's not him, but I…" His throat thickened, the rest of his confession vying for release. *Fuck it.* He had to let it out. "I held him at the end, and the memories are pretty tough."

Archer looked at Jock. "Oh man, I'm sorry. Was he…?"

Struggling against the sadness clawing at his chest, he met Archer's gaze and said, "I held him as he…*went.*"

"Aw, *fuck.*" Archer sounded as tortured as Jock felt. His eyes darted to Hadley, and he said, "Shit…Aw, he—heck!"

Jock gritted his teeth, but Hadley had gone soft against him. "She's sleeping. Just keep it down," he said quietly. "I *can't* let anything happen to her. I wouldn't survive it. Daph wouldn't survive it."

"She's *not* gonna die, dude. She's not him. She just has a

fever. She's going to be fine, but I'm *really* sorry, Jock. I had no idea that you held Liam in the end."

"Yeah, I know."

Archer swallowed hard and said, "I never should have said that stuff to you at the hospital. I'm sorry."

"We're past that. Just don't do it again or I'll knock you on your ass."

"*Butt*," Archer said, and they both chuckled.

Jock pressed a kiss to Hadley's head and said, "Thanks for doing this for her. She's a special girl. I'm pretty sure there's a little magic inside this one." He looked at Archer and said, "Or a future therapist."

"Are you guys sick, too?" Daphne startled them as she came into the room with their mother.

"No. Had wouldn't let me do the washcloth thing. Archer got her to do it," Jock explained.

"Aw, look, Daphne," their mother said. "Your baby is lying with my babies, and mine aren't killing each other."

"I'm out." Archer swung his legs off the bed.

Jock grabbed his wrist. When Archer looked over, he said, "Thanks, Archer. I mean it."

Archer nodded curtly. His eyes shifted to Hadley, lingering for a moment before he pushed to his feet and headed for the door. When he walked past Daphne, he stopped and said, "He's really good with her. He was singing to her when I came in."

"He was?" she asked dreamily.

"Yes, but if writing doesn't work out, singing should *not* be considered an option." He grinned and said, "I'm sorry I was an asshole." He glanced at Hadley. "I mean a *poophole.*"

"It's okay," she said sweetly. "Thank you for helping with Hadley."

He nodded again, eyes serious, and headed for the door.

"Oh, no you don't," their mother said as she grabbed his hand and hauled him into her arms, squeezing him tight. "I love you, and I'm so very proud of you, you grumpy poop."

As Archer stepped out of her embrace, she took his hand, unwilling to let him escape. Her loving eyes moved over each of their faces, and she said, "It takes a village to raise a child, but it takes an even stronger one to bring peace. I'm so glad we're all part of the same village."

"Yeah, yeah," Archer said. "My job here is done. Just don't expect me to babysit."

He walked out the door, and their mother said, "Are things okay here?"

"They will be," Jock said, and he believed with his whole heart it was true.

# Chapter Twenty-Seven

DAPHNE FINISHED BRUSHING her teeth and looked at herself in the mirror. Her hair was damp on the ends from her shower, her cheeks had a little color from their afternoon in the sun, and her eyes held the unmistakable sheen of a woman in love. She'd seen the look on the faces of each of her girlfriends, on her mother, and on Shelley. She'd seen a similar look on herself after Hadley was born, and she remembered the shock of seeing that deep-seated emotion in the mirror for the very first time. She'd nurtured her baby inside her own body, her feelings for her daughter growing with every kick, every thought of what would be, and still she'd been bowled over the second she'd heard Hadley's first cry. She looked down at her bracelet, soaking in the shivers of love spreading through her chest. How did she get so lucky to have found a man who loved Hadley like his own? A man who fought with everything he had to be theirs? An honest man who valued family and was selfless enough to have put his twin's happiness above his own?

Clutching her braceleted wrist to her chest, she threw a silent thank-you out to the universe and opened the bathroom door to Hadley's bedroom. Her heart stumbled once again. Jock was reclining against the headboard with Hadley draped over his chest. His eyes were closed, and he had one hand on her back. His laptop lay open beside him. He'd hovered over the doctor earlier, rattling off questions about dehydration and seizures, as nervous as Daphne had been the first few times Hadley was sick. They'd gotten her fever under control, and the doctor had reassured Jock that she probably just had a twenty-four-hour bug. Jock had stayed with Hadley all day, making sure she drank plenty of fluids and took medicine at the appropriate times. When she'd refused to take it, he'd come up with the best parental hack of all. He'd cut open one side of a juice box and put the medicine cup inside it, tricking Hadley into drinking it through the straw. Was there anything he couldn't figure out how to do?

Her gaze moved to the *Parenting* and *Highlights* magazines on the nightstand beside Hadley's house flyer. Archer had brought the magazines up a few hours ago when he'd said he was checking on Hadley, but Daphne had gotten the distinct impression he'd really been checking on Jock.

Jock's eyes opened as she came into the room. "Hey, angel."

"You're going to completely unFerberize my little girl," she teased. She lowered herself to the edge of the bed and touched Hadley's back, glad she was still cool.

"She was squirming in her sleep. I just wanted to comfort her." He pressed a kiss to Hadley's head.

How could Daphne do anything but smile? Her little girl had gone from having a daddy who had never wanted her to being loved by a man who couldn't help but love her.

He patted the space beside him and said, "Sit with us."

"We should put her to bed, let her sleep."

"We will soon, I promise. I need a little more time."

"You're both spoiled." She leaned in and kissed him. She

moved his laptop and settled in beside them. He'd been writing on and off all day while Hadley slept. "Are you going to let Sutton read what you've written? She asked me to try to get you to send her your manuscript."

"At some point. It's not finished, and I want you to be the first person to read it."

"Really?"

"You're the reason I'm writing again. Your love for Hadley is what inspired the story."

"It did?" She thought about the first time he'd come into Hadley's bedroom when she'd been putting Hadley to bed, when he'd gotten so inspired he'd written until the wee hours of the morning. Her body heated thinking of their intimate celebration that had followed.

"Do you want to read it?" he asked.

"Of course. Now?"

"Why not?"

Reaching for his laptop, she said, "Is it scary?"

"Not *horror* scary. I'd give you a warning if I thought you needed it. It's intense, but nothing you can't handle."

Excitement bubbled up inside her. "Are you sure? I feel like I'm peeking into your private world."

"You are, but I want you to."

She glanced at the screen and read the cover page: *Eyes on You*, by Jock Steele. "You're using our good-night song? And Jock instead of Jack?"

"I'd like to use your song, if you don't mind. But I can change the title to *What He Sees* if you'd rather I didn't."

"No, it's totally fine as long as the heroine doesn't get killed."

"She doesn't, and yes, I want to use Jock."

"Won't your publisher want you to use the same name as before?"

The edges of his lips tipped up. "That brain of yours is always thinking. Normally, yes, but I actually sent the editor who bought my last book a synopsis of this one, and he said the genre is different enough that it would be a good thing to use a slightly different name, so as not to confuse readers. But who knows if it'll even get published. Now, stop procrastinating and read."

"My, aren't we pushy tonight?"

"Just excited."

She loved knowing he was excited, too, so she dove into the story. Within the first few sentences she was riveted to the world he'd created and the tale he'd spun about a single mother hunted by a deranged killer. Her heart raced as several near captures played out like a movie on the page. Her pulse raced for a whole different reason as she became infatuated with the detective who had lost his family years earlier and was slowly falling in love with the killer's prey. Jock's writing was fluid and mesmerizing, sprinkling in just enough intrigue about the romance without overshadowing the intensity of the central plot. Daphne held her breath when the killer got so close, she could feel his heartbeat jumping off the pages. She cried when the overwhelmed heroine sank down to the floor of her pantry sobbing while her little girl watched television in the other room, and several chapters later, she lost her breath when the detective took the heroine in his arms and held her while she cried.

By the time she looked up from the story, Hadley was fast asleep in her bed and Jock was wrapping a towel around his waist after a shower. She hadn't even realized he'd gotten up.

She stood up and wiped her tears, too distracted with the story to let the tingles in her belly take over, and said, "What happens next? I need to know."

"You and me, both," he whispered, reaching for the laptop.

She clung to it. "What do you mean? I *need* to read it," she said quietly. "You can't just leave me hanging."

He turned on the baby monitor and said, "Babe, it's not on purpose. That's all I've written."

"*What?*" She whispered, "How do you sleep at night?"

He took her hand, leading her through the bathroom into his bedroom, and closed the door behind them.

"How can you leave it unfinished and still *function?*" she asked as he set the laptop on the chair and turned on the monitor. "I'd be writing twenty-four-seven if I were you."

He locked the door to the hall, turning a seductive gaze full of sinful promises on her. He cut the lights, and moonlight spilled in through the curtains, illuminating his path as he strode toward her. Desire gusted off him like the wind, engulfing her like a lasso and drawing her in. His gaze slid down to her mouth, lingering there so long her thoughts fractured. He drew her into his arms, holding her against his damp, hot, and deliciously hard body. Her fingers trailed up his back, then down to the edge of the towel, and his hips pressed forward. The desire tingling and burning inside her radiated outward, to the very edges of her being.

He cradled her face in his hands, gazing deeply into her eyes, and said, "Why don't I write twenty-four-seven?"

His voice was so low and gravelly, it took her a second to make sense of what he'd said. She'd forgotten she'd asked the question.

He lowered his lips so close, his breath became hers as he

said, "Because I have people in my life who I want to spend time with, and because sometimes…" He kissed down her neck, and it was all she could do to remain standing. "My sexy muse is busy inspiring me in *other* ways."

He sank his teeth into her neck, giving one long suck, sending rivers of pleasure slicing through her. A moan escaped before she could stop it, and he crashed his mouth over hers, swallowing her sounds. His fingers dove into her hair as he intensified their kisses, demanding and loving at once. She tugged at his towel and felt him smile against her lips as it fell to the floor. He pulled off her nightie, and she shimmied out of her panties. He made a growling sound and hauled her against him, one hand on her ass, the other on her jaw, holding her there as he devoured her. She loved when he took control. It made her feel sexier, even more feminine, and somehow it also made her feel *bolder*. She clung to that confidence, wanting to take as well as give, and pushed a hand between them, fisting his cock.

He tore his mouth away, and "*Fuuck*" fell from his lips.

The greedy sound spurred her on. She stroked him as she stumbled backward toward the bed and sat down on the edge, guiding his thick cock into her mouth.

"Christ, baby," he gritted out as she took him to the back of her throat.

He tangled his hands in her hair as she worked him with her hands and mouth. She *loved* pleasuring him, feeling his restraint, hearing the lustful sounds streaming from his lips. "*So good…oh yeah…just like that…*" Every word made her hotter, *needier*. Wanting everything he had to give, she put her arms around him, clutching his ass as he thrust fast and deep, then slow, loving her mouth like she knew he'd soon love her body.

His thighs flexed, and she felt him withdrawing, but she held him there, urging him on.

"Baby, I'm going to come. You feel too good."

She pulled him in deeper, and he uttered a curse, but he didn't hold back. Every thrust made her wetter, *hotter*. His fingers tightened in her hair, and his legs went rigid. Knowing he was close, she moved quicker, sucked harder. His thrusts turned to powerful jerks as his climax claimed him. He chanted her name like a prayer, and she stayed with him, loving every shudder, every groan, as ecstasy ravaged him, leaving him panting and dropping to his knees before her.

He touched his forehead to hers, running his fingers through her hair, and said, "*My God*, angel. You do me in."

He kissed her lips, her cheek, and then his mouth found hers in a tender kiss. *So tender...*

He whispered, "My turn," and loved his way down her body in a series of openmouthed kisses, tantalizing sucks, and slicks of his tongue. "I love your curves." He kissed along her belly and teased between her legs. When he spread his hands on her inner thighs, pushing her legs open wider, she lay back, giving herself over to him. His talented mouth drove her out of her mind. She clawed at the blanket, her hips rising to meet his efforts, and then his fingers entered her, and he did something incredible with his tongue, sending an orgasm crashing over her. She clamped her mouth shut to keep from crying out as she shattered into a million little pieces.

When the world started to filter back in, he kissed his way up her body, every touch of his lips rekindling her desire.

"Still with me, angel?"

"Always," she said.

He shifted beside her, dragging his fingers through her sex

as he circled her nipple with his tongue. She moaned, pleasure radiating from her core. He lowered his mouth over her breast, and his hand circled his cock, giving it a few tight strokes. Holy cow that was *hot*. She couldn't look away from his hand moving along his shaft. Her sex clenched greedily. He lifted his face, catching her staring, and she felt her cheeks burn.

He pressed his smiling lips to hers and said, "I'm going to enjoy discovering everything you like."

"Yes, please," she whispered.

"God, you're incredible." He took her in a slow, sensual kiss as he moved over her, aligning their bodies. He brushed his lips over hers, gazing into her eyes, and said, "I'll never get enough of you."

The raw passion in his voice swamped her. As their bodies came together, her eyes fluttered closed, and she reveled in the feel of him, the piece of herself she'd never known was missing.

He cradled her beneath him, holding her so close they felt like one being, and he whispered in her ear, "One day we're going to give Hadley brothers and sisters, and I'm going to show you how beautiful you are every step of the way."

When he'd first spoken of love so confidently, it had sounded like a fairy tale, but he was as real as the bed they were lying on. She blinked her damp eyes dry, trying to come up with big enough words to convey everything she felt. But as his handsome face came into focus, the emotions in his eyes mirrored the soul-deep love in her heart better than words ever could.

# Chapter Twenty-Eight

MONDAY MORNING JOCK stood in his parents' kitchen talking with his father while Daphne finished getting ready and his mother and Hadley packed snacks for the ferry ride. Hadley's fever had broken in the middle of the night, and she'd rebounded to her energetic self by morning. There was no better sight than his little princess standing on a chair at the counter chatting happily with his mother.

His father sipped his coffee and said, "Your mother kept me up half the night talking about getting into the event business."

"How do you feel about that?"

"When have I ever denied your mother anything?" His father grinned and said, "Besides, with all this renewed excitement, I'm reaping the benefits."

"*Dad*, I don't want to hear that."

His father laughed as he walked around the counter and swatted his mother's butt. She turned with a big smile and kissed him. His father put an arm around Hadley and said, "I'm going to miss you, peanut."

"I miss you, Gwampa. Wanna bluebewwy?" Hadley held up a blueberry, and when his father opened his mouth, she popped it in.

Jock's heart thumped a little harder.

The kitchen door opened, and Archer strolled in. Gone was the tension that had accompanied him like Pig-Pen's dirt. He lifted his chin in Jock's direction and said, "Hey, Jockstrap."

"How's it going, butthole?"

"I'm glad to see things are getting back to normal, but did you two revert to elementary school?" his father teased.

Archer nudged his father's arm and nodded toward Hadley. "No cursing."

"*Ah*, right," his father said.

Jock swore his parents looked ten years younger than they had when he'd arrived.

"I'm glad Squirt's feeling better," Archer said, stealing a blueberry.

"*Mowah?*" Hadley held up a handful of blueberries.

Archer put out his hand, and Hadley dumped them into it. "Thanks, Squirt."

Daphne screamed upstairs, and Jock's gut seized. He tore out of the kitchen, taking the stairs two at a time, and flew into the bedroom. She was sitting on the floor, her hand on her chest, tears streaming down her cheeks—and she was *laughing*.

He fell to his knees beside her. "What happened?"

She picked up a long rubber snake. "*This* happened."

That's when he heard Archer's laughter floating up from downstairs. "I'm going to kill him," he said, half laughing as he pushed to his feet.

"No, you're not." Daphne stood, looking excruciatingly sexy in a white sleeveless top and jeans, and wrapped her arms around him, smiling sweetly, and said, "It's a rite of passage. That means he doesn't hate me."

"Nobody could ever hate you." He kissed her softly and

said, "Come on, we've got to get going or we'll miss the ferry. My mom and Hadley packed twelve days' worth of snacks."

"I love your mom. She knows Hadley will make up for not eating last night by eating everything in sight today." She looked at the snake and said, "You know this means that we need to come up with an even better prank for our next visit, right?"

"Absofrickinglutely. He must have done it when he brought those magazines last night." He gathered their bags, and they headed downstairs. "Did you remember Had's house flyer and Owly?"

"Of course," Daphne said as they walked into the kitchen. "They're in the outside pocket of her toy bag."

Archer was leaning against the counter with a shit-eating grin. "What was all the commotion about?"

"I ought to tear you apart," Jock said as he set their bags down.

Daphne dropped the snake on the counter and said, "You're in for it, buddy. Just you wait."

"Archer, you *didn't*?" their mother said incredulously.

"You'd better watch it," their father warned. "Daphne's no wallflower."

"I'm counting on that. Liven things up around here." Archer sipped his coffee, watching Jock as he put a muffin on a plate for Daphne and helped Hadley down from the chair.

"Your sandals are by the door, princess," Jock said. "Why don't you go get them on?"

"You're quite the caretaker," Archer said.

"I'm not *caretaking*. I'm being nice." Jock hoped his brother wasn't going to turn into a dick.

"You've always been *nice*. This is different." Archer took

another sip of his coffee and said, "Whatever it is, it looks good on you."

"It's called being a thoughtful boyfriend." Daphne leaned closer to Archer and said, "Pay attention. Your grandmother's trying to find you a woman."

Archer scoffed. "I have plenty of women. Where is Grandma? I figured she'd be all over saying goodbye to the golden boy."

Jock gave him a sideways look. "She said goodbye last night."

"Grandma went to watch the sunrise with her Bra Brigaders, and then they're going down to Chaffee to go shopping." Their mother handed Daphne the bag of snacks and said, "Hadley and I put together extra juice boxes, fruit, a sandwich, a granola bar, and a few other little things, just in case."

"Thank you, Shelley." Daphne hugged her. "We had such a good time. I appreciate you including Hadley in the birthday celebration and for letting us stay here and taking such good care of us."

"Darlin', I'd give my left arm for you to move right in upstairs," Shelley said. "You have got my mind going a hundred miles an hour about hosting events. Steve and I talked at length about it last night. It would take an investment of time and money, but we think it would pay off and even help the island economy. But we can't make any decisions until we see how this event goes. Are you sure you can find time to answer my questions and help me along once you're back at work?"

"Yes. I'm excited to help. Last night I made a list of local shops and restaurants and categorized them under *food*, *gifts*, *decorations*, and a few other things. It's on your laptop in a folder called Winery Events. There are two lists. One is for you, labeled as the *Master*, and the other is for you to give to clients. On the client copy, I included a brief description of what's offered at each place, type of food if it's a restaurant, type of gifts or clothing. You get the idea. I found a master directory of each town on the island and pulled the local shops from those, too. But please be sure to look them over carefully. I'd hate to include someplace that isn't reputable. I tried to be specific in the descriptions to save you from answering dozens of customer questions. If you like it and think it's useful, I can help you put together whatever else you need. And if it isn't something you want to use, that's totally fine. My feelings won't be hurt or anything."

"You're a godsend." Shelley hugged her again. "I'm sure it will be exactly what we need." They continued talking as Daphne finished eating.

"Dad, if you're driving us to the ferry, we'd better get moving," Jock said.

"I'll take you over," Archer offered. "I'm heading to Seaport anyway."

Jock was filled with so many emotions, he had to work hard to tamp them down as he said, "Great. I'll grab Hadley's car seat out of Mom's car."

He moved the car seat and put their bags in Archer's truck, and then they said goodbye to his parents, who hugged them forever, thanked them profusely, and loved up Hadley like she truly was their grandchild. For the first time since the accident, Jock didn't want to leave. He was so happy, it felt surreal. A month ago, he was trying to make it from one day to the next. Now he was planning a future he'd never expected, rebuilding a relationship with his brother, and he had the two most beautiful girls in the world by his side.

As they drove away from the house, Hadley clung to Owly, waving and shouting out the window, "Love you! Bye! See soon!"

He reached over the seat for Daphne's hand. She smiled, but it was a bittersweet smile, not her bright-eyed heading-for-a-home-run smile he was used to. "I know," he said softly.

"You don't know shit," Archer said. "*Squat!* Sorry. You don't know *squat*."

That earned a brighter smile, and she said, "You're wrong, Archer. Jock *definitely* knows."

They bantered all the way to the ferry. The parking lot wasn't as busy as it was on the weekends, but there was a fair amount of people milling about. Daphne held Hadley's hand as Jock grabbed their bags and the car seat and set them on the pavement.

Archer crouched in front of Hadley and said, "Are you going to make me pancakes when you come back?"

She nodded and said, "A snake."

Archer cocked his head, looking at Jock. "Yeah, a snake works. Think you can give Uncle Archer a hug?"

She wrapped her arms around him and kissed his cheek. "Love you, Unca *Awcher*."

Daphne leaned against Jock's side and said, "Why does that make me want to cry?"

"Because you care." He put his arm around her.

"I hate leaving. You and Archer are finally talking again, and we've had such a good time." She sighed. "Have you ever felt like everything you could ever want was right there in front of you and wished you had the courage to throw caution to the wind and capture it all?"

*Yes, at the park, but I thought you needed more time.*

Before he could decide if he should reveal that, she reached for Hadley's hand, and Archer said, "Guess this is it. Sorry about the rubber snake, Daphne. You were a good sport." He hugged her and said, "Take care of Jockstrap for me."

"I will," she said, gazing affectionately at Jock.

"We'll see you in two weeks," Jock said, embracing Archer. He closed his eyes, soaking in the feel of the brother he needed to relearn by heart.

"Puppy!" Hadley yelled.

"*Hadley!*" Daphne screamed.

Jock broke away from Archer and saw Daphne sprinting after Hadley across the parking lot, and a car heading directly for Hadley. He bolted past Daphne and scooped Hadley into his arms as tires screeched behind him. Daphne's blood curdling scream tore through him, exploding like a bomb in his chest as he spun around, clinging to Hadley, and saw Daphne lying on the ground. Hadley wailed as he sprinted to Daphne and fell to his knees. Her hair was bloody, and she wasn't moving. "*Oh, baby, no, no, no.*" *God, please no. Don't take her from us.*

Archer ripped a screaming Hadley from his arms, saying something about an ambulance.

"Daphne, wake up," Jock pleaded, tears pouring from his eyes. He leaned over her, listening to see if she was breathing, and held his breath—*Breathe. Please breathe.* He heard Daphne's shallow breaths, and the air rushed from his lungs. *Thank God.* He clung to her shoulders, wanted to lift her into his arms, but he knew he shouldn't, so he stayed there, hunkered over her, listening to her breathe and trying to get a response. "I'm here baby. *Please* wake up. Come on, baby. We need you. Don't leave us. Keep breathing, angel. Come back, baby. Wake up." Hadley screaming "*Mommy! Dock!*" cut through the murmurs of the crowd gathering around them. "Archer!" he hollered without looking up. "Get Hadley *out* of here."

"I'm not leaving you," Archer snapped.

"Hang in there, Daphne. Help is on the way." Jock looked at Archer through the blur of tears and pleaded, "She can't see…" Sobs stole his voice as sirens rang out. *Thank God.* He leaned over Daphne, choking out, "I love you, baby. I need you. You're my girl. My *heart*. Don't leave us," and everything else faded away except his beautiful angel, lying lifeless in his arms.

# Chapter Twenty-Nine

JOCK PACED THE waiting room of the hospital, swamped with fear, silently making deals with the universe in exchange for Daphne's well-being and struggling to keep his horrific past from slaying him anew. He stared at the double doors keeping him from getting to Daphne as if they were villains. If only he could switch places with her, turn this fucking nightmare around. Her eyes had fluttered open briefly and disoriented in the ambulance. The paramedics had rattled off concerns about brain injuries and internal bleeding. He'd wanted to make them take it back. His head was spinning. The second they'd arrived at the hospital, they'd taken her for tests to determine the severity of her injuries. That was more than an hour ago. The waiting felt ominous. He could barely breathe, as memories of being in the hospital after his and Kayla's accident pummeled him—the look on the doctor's face when they'd told him she was gone and that Liam wasn't going to make it. The all-consuming horror of his words sinking in and sucking the life out of him. Was he fucking cursed? How could this be happening again? Not to *his* Daphne, his *love*. Not to Hadley's mommy. He put his hand on Hadley's back, feeling every breath as if it were his own. She was fast asleep on his shoulder, and still he needed to remind himself she was safe. Hadley needed her mommy to be okay even more than he did. Archer had told him Hadley had cried her little heart out when Jock had gone with Daphne in the ambulance, and she hadn't stopped until they'd found him at the hospital and she was safely in his arms once again.

"Hey, man, what can I do?" Archer asked as he and their father sidled up to him. "Do you want me to try to take Hadley?"

Before coming to the hospital, and while juggling a hysterical Hadley, Archer had found Daphne's phone in her bag and called *her* parents. He'd arranged for Tessa Remington to fly to the Cape and bring them to the island and for Jules to pick them up at the airport. He'd also been the one to call their parents and Jules, who had sent a group text, alerting the rest of their family. Archer was fielding those texts for him, too. Jock didn't know what he would have done without him.

"No. You've done more than enough. Thanks. I just…I can't lose her, and I can't fucking stop it from happening." He brushed a hand down Hadley's back, tears welling in his eyes. "*We* can't lose her. I wish they'd tell me something. *Anything.*"

He'd begged the woman at the desk to get him an update, but they wouldn't tell him a damn thing because he wasn't family. He had no idea how he'd face her family. He didn't even know them. How could he tell them he had no idea if Daphne would live or die? His chest seized just thinking about it.

"You're *not* going to lose her," his father said.

Jock whispered harshly, "They were talking about brain injuries and internal bleeding. We don't know *what* they'll find." He struggled against tears and said, "I was going to propose to her in the park yesterday, and I held back. I didn't want to rush her. I shouldn't have held back. If she doesn't make it, she'll never know how much I wanted to be a family with her and Hadley. She needs to know. She *deserves* to know."

"Dude, you are *not* going to lose her," Archer said adamantly. "She's *strong*. That woman in there looked me in the eye—*me*, the biggest asshole on the planet for the last decade—and said that I didn't have to like her or her daughter, but that didn't mean she'd dislike me. She's tough, man. She has bigger balls than we do."

Their father put his arm around Jock and said, "Archer is right. She's strong, son. Have faith. I know that's hard right now."

"I *promised* I'd never let anything happen to her, and now...It's like some kind of fucked-up punishment," Jock seethed. "Hadley and Daphne don't deserve to pay the price for my mistakes."

Archer got in his face and said, "This is *not* a punishment. What happened to Kayla and Liam was not your fault. *You* didn't run that red light, and you *didn't* cause this. And if you think Daphne doesn't know how much you love her, you've got your head up your ass. She looks at you like you're a fucking god."

Jock gritted his teeth. "If only I were a god, then I could fix this mess."

Their mother came out of the ladies' room, her face a mask of despair. She touched Jock's arm and said, "Honey, why don't you sit down for a bit?"

Jock shook his head. "I can't. I need to know she's okay, Mom. She's my world."

Her eyes teared up. "I know. Oh gosh, now I'm going to cry again."

"Come here, Shell." Their father drew her into his arms.

Jules hurried into the waiting room with a couple who looked like they'd been through war—*Daphne's parents*—and her brother, who Jock recognized from seeing him at Daphne's apartment, and…the girl from the gym who Cree had wanted to set him up with? What the hell?

"Jock!" Jules hugged him, careful not to wake Hadley, and said, "These are Daphne's parents, Ken and Diane, and her brother and sister, Sean and Renee."

"Hi." Jock shook her father's hand. "I'm so sorry."

Diane took one look at Hadley and burst into tears. Ken pulled her into his arms, comforting her. Jock ached for them. For all of them, Hadley, Daphne, and himself included. He'd give anything to be able to hold Daphne in his arms and comfort her.

"We don't know anything yet," Jock explained. "They won't tell me anything because I'm not family. Daphne woke up in the ambulance for a few seconds. She was disoriented, and they're running tests. I don't know anything else." He tried to swallow past the lump in his throat and said, "Hadley ran into the parking lot and we went after her, but—"

"It's okay, Jock," Ken said. He was a rugged-looking man with serious blue eyes and wavy brown and gray hair. The firm set of his shoulders told of his ageless strength and his comforting tone told of his experience dealing with grave circumstances. "Archer told us how it happened when he called."

"Archer, *right*. Sorry." Jock introduced Archer and his parents to the Zablonskis.

As they greeted each other, his mother embraced Diane and said, "I'm so sorry," starting a flood of tears from both of them.

"Hadley?" Diane asked through her tears. "Did she see…?"

"At first," Jock said regretfully. "But Archer took care of her. Hopefully she won't remember."

Ken held Jock's gaze and said, "I'm glad you were there. Daphne told my wife everything you've been through, and this can't be easy. We appreciate all you've done. My family tells me our little girl is crazy about you." His eyes shifted to Hadley. "She has two good reasons to fight with everything she has to get through this, and Daphne is a fighter. As a fire chief, I've seen hundreds of accidents. Usually they look worse than they are, and that's what we're praying for. I'm going to see what I can find out."

"I'll come with you," Jock's father offered.

"Why don't we sit down," his mother suggested.

"I can't," Jock said.

Archer crossed his arms and said, "I'm not leaving his side."

"I'd rather stand, Mom, thanks," Jules said.

"Sean? Renee?" Diane asked.

Sean and Renee exchanged a glance, and Sean said, "We're okay, Mom."

Their mothers went to sit down, and Sean said, "She's my twin, Jock. She's going to be okay. I can feel it."

"Thanks, man."

"My dad was right about Daphne being crazy about you," Sean said. "She saved you from getting your ass kicked the night you came by her apartment."

Archer scoffed and stepped forward. "You and what army?"

Sean threw his shoulders back, and Archer did the same.

"Would you two *stop*?" Jules put a hand on both their chests, pushing them back.

"Daphne is in there fighting for her life, and with everything Jock has been through, do you think he needs to hear you two bickering?" Renee added. "This is when we come *together*, so put your dicks away and be supportive."

Archer cocked a brow at Renee, his eyes gliding down the length of her. Jules swatted him.

"Listen, Sean. I have a shitty past, but I'd never hurt Daphne," Jock reassured him. "That night I saw you in her apartment, I told her everything I'd been through. I love her, and I'd give my life to be the one in there instead of her."

"I know. She called me yesterday and said she was madly in love with you," Sean said.

"She called *you*?" Renee asked. "Why didn't she call me?"

"You didn't share a womb with her," Sean said arrogantly.

"I feel your pain, Renee," Jules said. "I have *two* sets of twin siblings."

Jock looked at Renee and said, "We go to the same boxing club, right?"

"Yes. It was me who asked Cree about you." Renee shrugged and said, "You can't blame a girl for trying."

"Sorry to have blown you off, but—"

"I get it," Renee interrupted. "You had your eye on my gorgeous sister. You were her white knight bearing apology gifts and all the sweetness she deserves. You made the right choice. She's the best person I know. I would have just broken your heart."

Archer chuckled, and then he turned a scorching gaze on Renee, singeing the air with electricity. Sean glared at him, and Renee rolled her eyes at her brother.

Jock stepped away. He didn't want to watch Archer flirt, or see a brother protect his sister. He wanted to plow through the double doors, take Daphne in his arms, and never let her go.

AFTER WHAT FELT like forever, the doctor finally came through the double doors. Jock pushed to his feet with Hadley in his arms. Hadley had asked about Daphne when she'd woken up, and Jock had told her that the doctor was just fixing Mommy's boo-boos—then he'd prayed his fucking heart out, as he'd been doing all day.

As everyone else stood up, making a semicircle around the doctor, Jock scrutinized the doctor's face, but he was giving away nothing.

"Mr. Zablonski?" the doctor said.

Ken stepped forward, his arm around Diane. "That's me. We're Daphne's parents. Is she okay?"

"Would you like to talk in private?" he asked.

Ken glanced at the rest of them, his eyes settling on Jock. "No. We're all family. How is she?"

"She's stable, and very lucky."

The air rushed from Jock's lungs, and tears burned his eyes as murmurs of gratitude sounded around them. He kissed Hadley's cheek, finally able to breathe a little easier. Archer put a hand on his shoulder.

"She hit her head on the pavement, but there are no indications of brain injury, no swelling or bleeding," the doctor explained. "She *has* suffered a concussion, which we'll need to monitor. She has a fractured knee and ankle, which we've stabilized, and several scrapes and bruises. She's going to be sore all over for a while."

Relief consumed Jock. He hugged Hadley tighter and whispered to Archer, "I need you to do me a favor…"

As Archer headed for the elevator, the doctor said, "We're going to need to keep her here for observation for the next four or five days, but she should make a full recovery."

"Can we see her?" Jock and Daphne's parents asked at once.

"Yes. We've given her something for pain, and it's normal for her to be a bit groggy, so don't be alarmed. I would suggest not overwhelming her. Perhaps three or four of you at a time? Keep the commotion to a minimum."

As her parents thanked the doctor, Jock hugged Hadley again and said, "Mommy's okay, princess. She's okay." He kissed her cheek again and again, thanking the heavens above.

"Mommy's boo-boos fixed?" Hadley asked.

"Yes. She's going to have a special bandage on her knee and ankle for a while, but she's okay." He was sure she didn't have a clue what he meant, but she was grinning so big, it didn't matter. She'd see it for herself soon enough, as Ken and Diane had invited him to bring Hadley into Daphne's room with them.

His heart slammed against his ribs as they pushed through the double doors and the woman behind the desk told them where to find Daphne's room. "We have to be quiet in case Mommy's sleeping," he said to Hadley.

"I be quiet," she said.

He wanted to bolt ahead, but out of respect for her parents, he let her father lead them into the room. Daphne lay with her eyes closed, looking fragile and beautiful beneath the sterile sheets. Her leg was casted from her thigh down, propped on pillows, and she had an IV snaking from one arm. Her eyes opened to only half-mast, and her head lolled in their direction. The sweetest smile lifted her lips, drawing tears from Jock and her parents and an excited whisper from Hadley.

"Mommy! Your boo-boos are better."

"Almost," Daphne said groggily.

It was killing Jock to let her parents go to her bedside and hold her hands first, but as he stood beside her father while her parents talked with her, he knew it was the right thing to do. If this situation had happened to Hadley, even though he wasn't Hadley's father, he'd need to *feel* her hand in his, to talk to her, to know she was safe just as much as they did with Daphne.

Ken looked at Jock, and he must have seen the need in his eyes, because he said, "Come here, son."

"Thank you," he said as they changed places.

"Why don't you give me Hadley," Ken suggested.

Ken reached for Hadley, but she clung tighter to Jock and whined, "*My Dock, Pop Pop.*"

"It's okay. I'd feel like I was missing a limb without her." Jock took Daphne's hand and said, "Hey, angel."

Tears welled in her eyes, bringing tears to his own.

"*Mommy.*" Hadley lunged for Daphne.

Jock caught her and said, "Hadley, baby, we have to be very gentle with Mommy right now. Okay?"

"Gentle, Mama," she said as Jock leaned down so she could touch Daphne's face. Daphne kissed her little hand and held it against her cheek for a moment, bringing even more tears to all of them.

"I love you, chickadee," Daphne said.

"Love you, Mommy," Hadley said.

Daphne's teary eyes met Jock's, and she sobbed. Her eyes shot to Hadley, and she tried to hold the sobs in as she said, "I lost my bracelet."

"No, baby, you didn't. They took it off in the ambulance." He pulled it from his pocket and handed it to her father.

"Would you mind, please?"

Tears slipped down Daphne's cheeks as her father put it on her.

"Thank you." Jock got choked up as he sat on the edge of the bed with Hadley on his lap so she could hold Daphne's hand. "Angel, I'm so glad you're okay. Just the thought of something happening to you..."

He held Hadley tight and leaned closer, their temples touching, and closed his eyes, breathing her in. Her arm circled him, and neither said a word as they cried for what they'd almost lost.

"I love you," he finally managed.

"I was so scared," she said against his neck. "I didn't know if Hadley got hit."

"I got to her and the car turned to miss us. I'm so sorry, baby."

"No, it's not your fault. You saved our little girl."

*Our.* She felt it, too...

He leaned up and brushed his hand down Hadley's back, kissing her cheek. Hadley put her head on his shoulder as he gazed at Daphne and said, "Daph, everything I want is right here in front of me. I've known it since the first time I watched you put Hadley to bed. I wanted to say something at the park, but I thought you might need more time, and maybe you still do, but I don't want to wait, so here goes. I don't want to miss a single day with you and Hadley. Let's throw caution to the wind, angel. Let me be your husband instead of your boyfriend, and Daddy instead of Dock. We can move to the island and you can plan events with my mom, or we can stay on the Cape. I don't care where we live, as long as we're together. You're my other half, baby. Marry me, Daphne, and I promise to make all of yours and Hadley's dreams come true."

"Oh, Jock" came out with a sob. "*Yes*. You're everything we want, too."

His heart stumbled. "Yeah?"

"*Yes*. With all my heart and soul, *yes!*"

"She said *yes!*" he said, making her parents laugh through their tears. As he leaned down and pressed his lips to Daphne's, Hadley exclaimed, "Yes!"

Jock hugged her and lowered her to kiss her mommy's cheek.

"Do you want Jock to be your daddy?" Daphne asked.

Hadley nodded. "Daddy Dock?"

They all laughed, and Jock said, "Daddy Dock sounds perfect to me."

"I don't care what the doctor said. I'm going in that room." Archer's angry voice sailed down the hall seconds before he flew through the door. He scanned their teary eyes and said, "Those better be happy tears after what I just went through." He pushed the little black box into Jock's hand and said, "How're you doing, Daphne?"

"I'm getting married," Daphne said loudly, earning more elated laughter.

Archer slapped Jock on the back and said, "Congratulations, bro."

"Thanks. Hadley, can you go to Pop Pop for a minute, please?" Jock asked.

"Unca Awcher." She reached grabby hands for Archer.

"All the girls want *Awcher*," he said with a wink, and took her from Jock.

Jock opened the box, revealing the teardrop-shaped halo diamond engagement ring he'd bought while they were in town.

Several small marquis diamonds formed a crowned peak above the rounded end of the center diamond.

Daphne and her mother gasped.

"*Jock*," Daphne said breathlessly. "Where did *that* come from?"

"The engagement fairy." God, he loved her. "I want to do this right, baby, because you deserve the best of everything, and I plan on showing you how special marriage vows are every day for the rest of our lives." Jock got down on one knee beside the bed and took Daphne's hand as her parents watched with tears in their eyes. "My sweet Daphne, you came into my life like the most beautiful, unexpected gift, bringing light into my dark world, and in a few short weeks you showed me how to believe in myself and trust in others. You made me laugh and love and *feel* deeper than I ever thought possible. You and Hadley gave me a reason to conquer my past and believe in a future I never saw coming. And somehow your brilliant little girl knew all along that we belonged together. You have become the axis on which my world spins. I love you, Daphne Zablonski, with every iota of my being. I love the sound of your voice, the way you blush, the way you kiss, the way you touch my face, and the way you mother your baby girl. I love your big, beautiful heart, and I hope one day we have babies with your ability to see past the surface, to the heart of others."

He paused to take in the light in her eyes, the flush of her cheeks, and the hope in her heart, which he could feel beating between them, and said, "Daphne, will you do me the honor of being my wife and allow me to be Hadley's father? To love, honor, and cherish you both? To scare off boys as Hadley gets older and to love your *muffins* even when we're too old to eat them? Daphne, my angel, my love, will you marry me?"

"Absolutely, positively *yes!*"

Jock slid the ring on her finger as he rose to his feet, and with her mother crying and her father and Archer watching with approving grins, he sealed their promises with a long, sensual kiss. "I love you," he said against her lips, and then he went back for more, because he knew he'd never get enough.

"Get a room!" Jules's voice rang out, and they turned to find the rest of their families standing in the doorway with a nurse, who shrugged and winked at Archer.

Jock laughed and said, "Welcome to our new life."

"I'll take it." She pulled him into another kiss, while everyone cheered them on.

"Seriously, dude?" Archer teased. "What are you doing? Going for Man of the Year?"

Jock broke their kiss on a laugh, locked eyes with his beautiful fiancée, and said, "Not even close. My girl deserves the Man of the *Century*."

# Chapter Thirty

DAPHNE SAT ON a lounge chair in her parents' backyard with Renee and Jock's sisters, watching Hadley and Joey chase bubbles as fast as Levi and Jock could blow them. When the bubbles floated too high, Archer and Sean scooped the girls up to reach them. They were celebrating Hadley's birthday, which they'd put off for a week. Hadley had torn through all of her presents, and the minute she was done, she snagged the gift Sutton had given her—three bottles of bubbles with different-sized wands—and ran into the yard to play.

It had been twelve days since the accident, eight days since Daphne had gotten out of the hospital and she and Hadley had moved in with Jock at the cottage in Bayside. Daphne could hardly believe how helpful everyone had been. Not only had Rick, Jett, Dean, and Drake shown up to help Jock move them in, but so had Archer and Levi. They'd set up Hadley's bedroom exactly as it had been in their apartment, with the addition of a framed photo of the house she'd fallen in love with on the island. Hadley was thrilled that *Mine and Dock's house*— the Bayside cottage—had truly become *theirs*, at least temporarily. Jock had taken incredible care of both Daphne and Hadley while Daphne was in the hospital. He'd spent most days entertaining her, talking, or just lying next to her in the hospital bed, and he'd taken advantage of her naps, using the time to write. Every night like clockwork, he'd returned to his parents' house to put Hadley to bed.

Daphne looked around, feeling blessed. She couldn't imagine her life getting any better. Her father and Steve were chatting in the shade of a large tree, watching the guys play with the kids, and her mother's voice floated out the open patio door, where she and Shelley were cleaning up from lunch with Lenore. They'd become close while Daphne had been in the hospital. Though her father had needed to return to work the next day, her mother had stayed at Jock's parents' house with Hadley and Jock, and she'd even become part of the famed Bra Brigade. Daphne tried not to think about her mother parading around in her bra, but Lenore had already warned her that once her cast was off, they were indoctrinating her into the Brigade, too.

"Scoot over and stop drooling over our brother. We need to talk," Leni said as she sat beside Daphne's casted leg.

Her cast now boasted colorful get-well wishes from her and Jock's families and all of their Bayside friends. Daphne's two favorite messages were from Hadley—wild pink scribbles—and Jock, who had staked a bold claim down the side of her cast in black letters, WORLD'S HOTTEST FIANCÉE. BACK OFF, BOYS, SHE'S TAKEN. Every time she looked at her ring, and about a hundred other times during the day, she fell even deeper in love with him.

Jules waved her hand and said, "Go ahead and drool. I love seeing you two so happy."

"He is *very* drool-worthy." Daphne couldn't help teasing Renee and said, "Just ask my sister."

Renee laughed. "It's true. I will forever be known as the sister who wanted to hit on my future brother-in-law. But in all fairness, that was before I knew he was going after Daphne. If I'd known that, I would never have tried." She waved at Daphne and said, "Just look at her. Would you want to compete with *all that*?"

Daphne blushed as the girls gushed about her being sweet, pretty, and sexy. She wasn't sure she believed that she was *all that*, but she had no doubt that the man lifting a giggling Hadley onto his shoulders across the yard thought her to be all those things and a whole lot more.

"Daph, have you and Jock talked about a wedding date?" Sutton asked. "I want to be sure I arrange for time off."

"I know the perfect venue," Shelley said as she came outside with Lenore and Daphne's mother.

"It's free *and* on a beautiful island," Lenore said as she and Shelley joined the girls at the table.

Daphne's mother kissed the top of her head as she went to sit at the table and said, "I can't wait to shop for your wedding gown with you."

"There's a gorgeous dress shop on the island," Sutton said. "Maybe we can make a girls' weekend out of it and all shop together."

Emotions bubbled up inside Daphne. "I would love that."

"You'll be such a beautiful bride. Do you have a date yet?" Jules urged.

"Sort of. I'd marry him *tomorrow* if my knee and ankle weren't injured. This is my *last* wedding, and I really want to walk down the aisle to Jock and not limp down it," Daphne said a little dreamily, imagining how she'd feel at that moment and the love she'd see in his eyes. "We're thinking about a smallish winter wedding, just family and close friends. Shelley, I'm glad you offered, because we'd love to get married at the winery."

Shelley threw her hands up in the air and exclaimed, "Yes!"

Everyone laughed.

"Thank you. And, Renee, I know you're crazy busy and everything, but would you be my maid of honor?"

"Really, Dee? Not Sean or Chloe? You told Sean you loved Jock before you told me, and I know how close you and Chloe are. She arranged to have your book club meeting in the hospital for you. I'd understand if you want one of them instead."

Chloe had brought all the local girls to the island hospital for the book club meeting, and Jules had come with Tara and Bellamy. They'd had a great time.

"I love Sean and Chloe, but I want *you* by my side. You knew when I got my first *everything*, and you made sure I was okay afterward. You've always been there, taking care of me and cheering me on. You're the person who taught me to love myself for who I am. I want you by my side on my big day."

"You're going to make me cry, and I never cry." Renee got up and hugged her. "I would be honored. Thank you." She wiped her eyes, and then she stood on the edge of the patio and yelled, "Hey, Sean! I'm going to be Daphne's maid of honor!"

"Oh boy, here we go," her mother said.

"Seriously?" Sean held his palms up to the sky. "I'm your *twin*, Dee!"

"Glad it's not just my kids who do that kind of thing," Shelley said.

"Dude, you'd look awful in a dress." Archer leered at Renee and said, "But your sister? *Mm-mm.* She'll make a *fine* maid of honor."

Renee put her hand on her hip and said, "Damn right I will."

Sean stalked over to Archer and dragged him farther from the girls, his angry voice muffled by the distance.

Renee laughed. "I like a man with an attitude."

"Do you own a whip?" Lenore asked, and all the girls cracked up.

Jock's eyes locked on Daphne's, and he blew her a kiss.

She looked at him, standing there all handsome and happy, feeling grateful for a second chance. They'd both been so scared when she'd gotten hit by the car, they had a whole new appreciation for living in the *now*. They decided not to wait for some mythical *right time* to go after their dreams. With Jock's encouragement, Daphne had already put the wheels in motion toward achieving one of hers. When they'd celebrated Hadley's birthday with their friends at Bayside a few days ago, she'd told her bosses that this would probably be her last season working at the resort. She was returning to work tomorrow, and once her leg healed, she was going to start looking for a job in event planning. They hadn't been surprised, and they'd said they were her friends above all else and had known they were lucky she'd stayed for so long.

"Can I get you anything, angel?" Jock called out to her. He had been waiting on her hand and foot since she'd gotten out of the hospital.

Daphne looked around the table at the friendly faces of the women who had become her family, listening to the banter of the guys and kids in the yard, and said, "What more could I possibly want?"

Jock winked and said, "I have a few ideas, but they're a little inappropriate for our girl's birthday party."

As the girls laughed, Daphne felt her cheeks burn, and she *loved* it. She hoped Jock never stopped trying to make her blush.

Sean glowered at Jock and said, "Dude, that's my *sister*."

"Hi, Mama!" Hadley waved from her perch atop Jock's shoulders. She leaned forward, hugging his head, and rested her cheek on top of it as she said, "Got Daddy Dock!"

Her insides turned to a puddle of goo when Hadley did things like that. Her little girl had always been happy, but now she smiled almost *all* the time.

"I see that. You're a lucky girl," Daphne said. "We both are."

Sean lifted Joey onto his shoulders, and Levi and Archer started chasing him and Jock and Hadley around.

"One glance at the sexy Steele siblings tells me that you have great genes," Renee said. "So tell me. Does the ability to be such a good boyfriend run in the family, too?"

"Sure, we'll pretend that's the case," Leni said with a laugh as the guys, and their fathers, headed for the table.

Levi and Archer jogged toward the side of the house, and Leni yelled, "Where are you escaping to?"

"Be right back," they hollered, and disappeared around the corner.

"Someone wants to open her last present," Jock said as he lifted Hadley from his shoulders and set her on the ground beside Daphne's chair.

Daphne looked at him with a silent question in her eyes, and he shrugged. She touched Hadley's hand and said, "You already opened them all, sweetie."

"I got *nothah*." Hadley looked up at Dock and said, "*Wight?*"

"That's right." Jock patted her head.

Archer hollered, "Where's the birthday girl?" as he and Levi came around the house carrying a dollhouse replica of the house on the island that Hadley had fallen in love with.

Hadley's eyes widened as Levi and Archer set the house down in front of her. "My house! Mama, *my* house!"

As her daughter squatted to look inside the dollhouse, and everyone else gathered around to check it out, Daphne reached for Jock's hand and said, "Who is that from?"

He sat on the edge of her chair and said, "Me."

"Where did you get it? It's just like the house on the island."

"While you were in the hospital, I built it with my father and Archer at night after Hadley was asleep."

Her heart was going to explode. "You *built* it? I didn't even know you could build things."

He slipped his hand to the base of her neck and said, "There's nothing I can't do for you and Hadley." He leaned forward and kissed her. "Today is your special day, too, because you're the mommy who birthed our beautiful girl."

Tears welled in her eyes.

His father gave him a set of papers, and Jock set his loving eyes on Daphne as he handed them to her. She scanned them and realized it was a contract for a house with both of their names listed as the buyers. Tears slipped down her cheeks. "Jock…?"

"You said you wanted to buy a house for Hadley with a backyard she could play in and friends her age nearby. The Bluffs has all of that on an island we all love, and the house has four bedrooms. Plenty of room for more kids. You've already told the guys at Bayside that this is your last season. All you have to do is sign on the dotted line and we can close on the property and move in next month."

"That was a dream."

"That's the idea, baby. I told you I'm going to make all of yours and Hadley's dreams come true, and I meant it."

Her heart was beating so hard, her words came out rushed. "But I don't have a job there. How can I help pay the mortgage?"

"Good Lord, woman," Archer interjected. "Don't you know you're marrying Mr. Moneybags? You don't have to work another day in your life."

"*Archer*," Shelley said sharply. "Daphne is used to taking care of herself and Hadley." She turned her vivacious smile on Daphne and said, "And since we love to hire family, we're hoping our future daughter-in-law would like to join the family business as our event planner."

A sob burst from Daphne's lips, and she covered her mouth. "But you said you weren't sure if you were going to do it."

"That was before I knew of Jock's plans, honey," Shelley said.

"With you at the helm, we can't go wrong, Daphne," Steve added.

Shelley reached for Daphne's mother's hand and both of them grinned at her as Shelley said, "With you there, we're hoping our new friends will come visit a lot more often."

Daphne looked at her parents, who were both nodding their blessings.

"Maybe my butthead brother and I can pound out a few rounds in the ring again, too." Archer cocked an arrogant grin and said, "I'll whip his ass, but—*shit. Shoot.* I meant *butt.*" He scrubbed a hand down his face as everyone laughed, and he said, "This is going to be tough with Squirt around all the time."

Daphne looked at the man holding her hand, the man who

owned her daughter's heart and her own, and fresh tears slipped from her eyes as she said, "A lifetime with you in our beautiful house on the island is more than we could ever want, but just so you know, your endless love is all that Hadley and I will *ever* need."

As she put her arms around him and pressed her lips to his, Hadley crawled onto the lounge chair and put her little arms around them, too, drawing sounds of hearts melting all around them.

Their hug was interrupted by the sounds of fire engines. Hadley climbed down and ran to Daphne's father, throwing her arms up in the air. "*Fi-yah twuck*, Pop Pop! Gwampa! Come on!"

Hadley had been waiting all day for this moment. When Daphne had said she'd ride on the truck with her, her bright-eyed, newly smiling three-year-old had insisted she was a *big guul* and could ride by *huself* with *both* of her *gwampas*!

"Better get my crutches," Daphne said.

As her father scooped up Hadley, Jock lifted Daphne into his arms and kissed her, earning catcalls and *get a room*s from their siblings.

"He's like one of your romance heroes!" Renee said.

Daphne wrapped her arms around his neck and said, "He's even better, because he's *mine*."

# Chapter Thirty-One

FALL EASED GRACEFULLY onto Silver Island, bringing colorful foliage and crisp, chilly nights perfect for cuddling by a warm fire in Daphne and Jock's new home. They'd moved into their cozy four-bedroom home two weeks ago with the help of their families and friends. They adored their new community as much as they loved their new life together. Nothing compared to waking up with Daphne in his arms and Hadley's sweet voice chattering away about this or that. They'd had fun furnishing their house together, picking out things they liked as a family, making their house a *home*.

Not a day had passed when Jock didn't count his blessings. Daphne's injuries had healed, and she had dived headfirst into planning their wedding for the week after Christmas and working with his mother to coordinate events for the winery, which would begin after the New Year. Today they were decorating their front yard for Halloween, which was right around the corner. They'd gone all out for their first holiday in their new home, decorating inside and out. Jock was perched on a ladder, positioning a stuffed zombie to look like it was climbing out the window. They'd made ghosts out of torn sheets and ribbons with Hadley earlier that morning, which now dangled from limbs of trees and peeked out from thorny bushes. Joey, Levi, and Hadley were setting up a graveyard in the grass with headstones and skeletons climbing out of the graves, and Grant was hanging up spiderwebs and gigantic spiders on the porch.

Jock looked at Hadley as he climbed down the ladder. She was carrying a plastic hand with fake blood on it and chattering about how *scawy* their *gwaveyad* was going to be. She wasn't afraid of anything, which Daphne said she got from her Daddy Dock. He'd never tire of hearing his little princess call him that, just as he'd never get enough of her beautiful mommy, who was carrying a stuffed zombie out of the house, looking at him like he was the best muffin she'd ever seen and she was *ravenous*.

"Look, Mama!" Hadley waved the fake hand.

"What are you going to do with that?" Daphne asked.

"*Scawe Witchie*," Hadley said. Ritchie was the four-year-old boy who lived next door with his uncle. They were out for the afternoon, and Jock knew that the minute they returned, Hadley would make a beeline for her new best friend. She had made several friends in the neighborhood and had settled into her new preschool without any issues.

More blessings to count.

"She was meant to be yours, all right," Grant said as he hung a web between the balusters. "She's got the prank thing down pat."

Jules had been right about Grant needing him now more than ever. He was definitely struggling, blocking everyone out as best he could. But Jock wasn't going to let that happen if he could help it. He'd dragged Grant's ass out of the house to help them today, and he was glad he had. Jock was taking all that he'd learned and trying to use it to help Grant avoid the same mistakes he'd made.

"You're going to have to change her last name to Steele," Levi said as Jock moved the ladder to the next window.

"We are. Don't worry." They'd already spoken with an attorney about Jock adopting Hadley after they were married. Jock reached for Daphne's hand and said, "Right, angel?"

"We wouldn't have it any other way," she said. "Hadley Steele has a nice ring to it."

"So does Daphne Steele." He stole another kiss, took the zombie, and headed up the ladder.

When he glanced down, Daphne was admiring their work, taking in the zombies, the gauzy webs, and the enormous spiders they'd hung on the front of the house, and said, "It's really coming together. Jules called and said she and Archer will be here soon."

After Jock had finally finished reading Harvey's manual, he'd shared it with Archer. Archer had balked at first, but when Jock had gone to see him last week, he'd seen notebook number four lying open in the cabin of Archer's boat. Their relationship was a work in progress, but it was growing stronger every day.

"Are you sure you can handle all of this scary stuff?" Jock teased as he stapled the zombie's foot just below the windowsill. Daphne had tried to watch another horror movie with him, but she'd turned it off after seven minutes and said she'd try again in a few months. He didn't care if she ever watched one, but she was determined to make it happen.

"If my daughter can handle it, so can I," she insisted. "I'm learning to deal with horror one page at a time, thanks to a very talented author."

She blew him a kiss and went to help Joey with a skeleton, and Jock went to work hanging the zombie.

"Dude, did you get an offer on your new book yet?" Grant asked.

"Not yet. It's going up for auction next week." His agent had loved his final manuscript. Thanks to Daphne's influence, it had turned into a romantic suspense page-turner, and the heroine found what Daphne called *forever love* with the detective. Forever love was the perfect term for him and Daphne, too. They had both known happiness, and they'd known grief, but with each other, they found a love that was stronger and more beautiful than either of them ever imagined possible. They had already started brainstorming his next book. They usually ended up making out or laughing so hard they got tears in their eyes. He never thought he'd need a brainstorming partner, but now he couldn't imagine starting a story without first tossing ideas around with her.

Grant shielded his eyes from the sun and said, "What're you going to do with your inheritance from Harvey when your book gets published?"

Jock stapled the zombie's arm beside the window and said, "We're putting money away for Hadley's college and buying into the winery. We're also setting up a scholarship for the arts in Harvey's name at my alma mater and donating the rest to cancer research."

"No shit? You're giving up all that financial security?" Grant glanced at Daphne and said, "She doesn't mind?"

"No way. We've got each other and Hadley. That makes us the richest people around. Right, babe?" he called out to Daphne as he put the last staple in the zombie.

"Absolutely," Daphne said.

They had talked for a long time about the two-million-dollar inheritance. Family was everything to them, and Daphne was putting her heart and soul into the winery. She wanted their family—the three of them—to be a *real* part of his family's business for generations to come and to show his parents and Archer that they were not only here to stay, but that she was as committed to making the event side of the business work as they were to making a life there. Investing in the winery also took the burden of the new endeavor off his parents, which Jock felt good about since he'd caused them so much worry in the past. While the balance of the inheritance could offer them financial freedom, they both agreed that there were people who needed it far more than they did.

Daphne's cheeks pinked up as he climbed down the ladder, and she said, "I need help setting up my ladder in the backyard. Any tall, dark, and handsome volunteers?"

"I'm all over that." Jock hauled her in for a kiss and slapped her butt, earning a surprised squeak, another sound he'd never tire of hearing.

They headed into the backyard, and he kissed her as he backed her up against the house beside the ladder, which was *already* in place. She tasted of sweet happiness and sinful intent. His hands roamed over her curves. He groped her breast, earning a needful moan.

"You're a sneaky one," he panted out between kisses.

"What do you expect?" she said heatedly, pushing her hands beneath the back of his shirt. "Hadley ran into our room when we were about to…" Her cheeks flamed.

He pressed his hips forward and couldn't resist taunting her. "When we were about to…?"

"*Make love,*" she whispered sharply, like he'd made her say a dirty word.

"Was that what we were going to do?" *Kiss, kiss.* "Because as

I recall"—he grabbed her ass with both hands, lifting her higher, so his cock rubbed against her center—"I had your hands pinned to the mattress and had promised to fuck you six ways to heaven."

"Oh God, *yesss*."

Their mouths crashed together and they feasted on each other, pawing and groping, grinding and rocking.

"Unca Awcher!"

Hadley's voice cut through his reverie, and he tore his mouth away, leaving them both breathless, and ground out, "*Fuck*."

"I think we have to wait for that," she whispered, and stroked him through his jeans.

He gritted his teeth. "Daphne…"

She feigned surprise. "Oops. *Sorry*."

"No you're not," he said, taking her in another hungry kiss.

"Where's Daph?" Jules's voice broke them apart again.

He touched his forehead to hers and said, "Remind me why we thought it was a good idea to move near family."

She giggled. "Because you love them." She gave him a chaste kiss and said, "Now, if you don't mind, I have to go change my underwear."

He put his hand between her legs, rubbing as she squirmed. "Leave them on and I promise to find a way to sneak you off to someplace private and get those panties even wetter."

DAPHNE WAS GOING to lose her mind with her sinfully delicious husband-to-be, and suddenly insanity was looking mighty fine. "You'd better make good on that promise rather quickly, because paybacks are hell."

He touched her chin as he stepped back and said, "When have I ever left you hanging?" He pulled his shirt down to cover his erection and reached for her hand. As they walked toward the front yard, he whispered, "You might want to wipe that look off your face, or everyone's going to know what we've been up to."

"I can't," she teased. "I think it's permanent." She knew she looked dreamy-eyed and she didn't care who saw it. She'd seen that look of love in her eyes every morning since they'd been together. And now they were living in their own home—she still couldn't get over the fact that they had a real home for Hadley with friends and a backyard to play in. In a few weeks, when the leaves fell from the trees, they'd even have a view of the water. Jock had a home office, where he disappeared into his fictional worlds, and they'd set up one of the bedrooms as an office for Daphne, where she could work from home when Hadley was off school. Jock still went for morning runs, but now he ran with Archer or one of his friends. She and her friends from Bayside video chatted over breakfast once a week, which she and Hadley loved. They'd made a pact to get together once a month, rain or shine, for a couples' night, and they planned to alternate meeting on the island and meeting at Bayside. Between her new job, which she loved, her new friends on the island, and her incredible fiancé, she didn't feel like she was missing out on a thing.

Jules was flitting around the front yard in a cute minidress, going from decoration to decoration, touching each one and commenting on how great it looked. Hadley and Joey were holding Archer's hands, telling him all about their graveyard, and Grant stood with his arms crossed, narrow eyes locked on Jules, as he talked with Levi.

"Dude, you didn't tell me Jules was coming," Grant said as they approached.

"Is that a problem?" Daphne asked.

Grant shook his head. "Nah. I've got to take off soon anyway."

Daphne didn't know what that was all about, but she left Jock with him and Levi and went to say hi to Jules. "I love your dress."

"Thanks." Jules twirled around and said, "This is the one I bought from Renee last week, remember?"

"I forgot you went to see her when you were picking up supplies." She loved how close her family had become with Jock's. They'd all gone fishing together the weekend before they'd moved into their new house, and her parents were talking about spending their next vacation on the island.

Archer joined the guys, and it was great to see Jock laughing with his brothers and Grant. Although Grant wasn't smiling. He was staring at Jules like he was ready to bolt if she headed his way.

"Is there something going on with you and Grant?" Daphne asked. "He seems like he's trying to avoid you."

"He's trying to avoid everyone, but I won't let him," she said proudly. "The big grumpy oaf. He used to be different. When he'd come home on leave, he was the life of the party, and it kills Bellamy that he's changed so much."

"Just Bellamy, or you, too?" Daphne asked.

"Belly's one of my closest friends. I just don't want her to lose as much time with him as I did with Jock." Jules looked at Grant, watching her, and waved to him. He didn't even crack a smile, but he didn't look away, either. "Look at him, all gruff and miserable. He stares at me like a challenge, and I'm going to win. That man *will* be happy again. He just doesn't realize it yet."

"Aunt Jules! Aunt Daphne!" Joey waved them over from the other side of the yard, and they both headed over.

Jock intercepted Daphne, drawing her into his arms, and said, "I'm going back up on my ladder to hang another zombie. You okay doing your own thing?"

"I can't wait to do my *thing*, but I'm hoping I won't have to do my *own*," she teased. He might still make her blush, but that didn't stop her from exploring all the dirty things they both wanted to explore. The only problem was, the more they explored, the more she wanted him.

He gave her a chaste kiss, and as he walked away, he said, "Hey, you boys going to lollygag all day, or are you going to decorate the heck out of this house?"

"You're lucky I'm here to take these decorations to the next level," Archer said arrogantly.

As Jock and Archer tossed barbs, Daphne said, "I'm going around back to hang the lights." She walked around to the backyard, and as she headed for the back door, she heard Jock say, "Archer, can you do me a favor and hold the ladder for Daph?"

She bolted upstairs and opened the window, peeking out for Archer. As he came around the house, she dropped the mannequin they'd made to look like her off the ladder and screamed, hiding behind the curtains and peeking out.

"Oh, fuck! *Jock!*" Archer's face was a mask of terror as he ran to catch the mannequin. "*I've got you!*"

Jock ran around the side of the house just as the mannequin

landed in Archer's arms and he stumbled backward and tripped, landing on his back with the mannequin splayed over him. He frantically touched the mannequin all over, as if he couldn't make sense of what had just happened. "What the…?"

Daphne popped her head out the window and said, "Gotcha!" as everyone else came around the side of the house.

Jock, Levi, and Grant cracked up as Archer threw the mannequin and pushed to his feet, fuming.

"Sorry, Archer!" Daphne called down to him.

He glowered up at her. "Seriously? I saw you get hit by a car and you pretend to fall off a ladder?"

She laughed and said, "It's kind of a rite of passage into the *new* Steele family's inner circle."

"Oh, man, you are cruel." Archer's last words tumbled out with a laugh. He pointed at Jock and said, "You are in for big trouble."

Jock held his hands up and said, "This was all my beautiful fiancée's doing."

Hadley toddled up to Archer and said, "Like Mommy's doll, Unca?" causing even more laughter.

Jock's laughing eyes found Daphne's, and her heart beat faster.

"Hey, handsome," she called down to him. "Maybe they can watch Hadley for a few minutes while you help me with that *thing* we talked about."

Jock's eyes flamed, and even from the second-story window, Daphne felt the air heating up between them. Jock said something to Jules, then headed inside. She heard him taking the steps two at a time, her heart thundering with each footfall. He flew through the bedroom door and swept her into his arms, taking her in a long, sensual kiss, full of love, laughter, and promises of their magical happily ever after.

**Ready for more Steeles?**
Fall in love with Grant Silver and Jules Steele in *My True Love*

**Even war heroes need a little help sometimes...**

After spending years fighting for his country and too damn long learning to navigate life with a prosthetic leg, Grant Silver returns to Silver Island to figure out a future he couldn't fathom without fatigues and a gun in his hand. He'd almost forgotten how a man could suffocate from the warmth and caring community in which he'd grown up, and if that weren't bad enough, his buddies' beautiful and far-too-chipper younger sister won't stop flitting into his life, trying to sprinkle happy dust everywhere she goes.

As a cancer survivor, Jules Steele knows better than to count on seeing tomorrow. She doesn't take a single moment for granted, and she isn't about to let a man who used to be charming and full of life waste the future he's been blessed with. She's determined to get through to him, even if it takes a few steamy kisses...

**Have you met the Whiskeys?**

Get ready to fall in love with the family everyone wants to join.

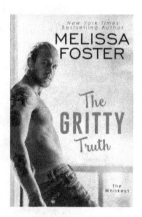

Quincy Gritt has fought his demons. He's confessed to his crimes and conquered his addictions. But when his past comes back to haunt him, can he and the woman who has captured his heart learn to live with the gritty truth, or will he spiral back into the darkness? Come along for their sexy, emotional ride.

**Curious about Daphne's Bayside friends?**

Read each of their love stories in the Bayside Summers series, starting with *Bayside Desires*. Brock and Cree's love story is told in *Seaside Serenade*, a Seaside Summers novelette.

Desiree Cleary is tricked into spending the summer on the Cape with her badass half sister and a misbehaving dog. What could go wrong? Did I mention the sparks flying every time she sees her hunky, pushy neighbor, Rick Savage? Yeah, there's that...

## About the Love in Bloom World

Love in Bloom is the overarching romance collection name for several family series whose worlds interconnect. For example: *Lovers at Heart, Reimagined* is the title of the first book in The Bradens. The Bradens are set in the Love in Bloom world, and within The Bradens, you will see characters from other Love in Bloom series, such as the Snow Sisters and the Remingtons, so you never miss an engagement, wedding, or birth.

## Where to Start

All Love in Bloom books can be enjoyed as stand-alone novels or as part of the larger series.

If you are an avid reader and enjoy long series, I'd suggest starting with the very first Love in Bloom novel, *Sisters in Love* and then reading through all of the series in the collection in publication order. However, you can start with any book or series without feeling a step behind. I offer free downloadable series checklists, publication schedules, and family trees on my website. A paperback series guide for the first thirty-six books in the series is available at most retailers and provides pertinent details for each book as well as places for you to take notes about the characters and stories.

## See the Entire Love in Bloom Collection

www.MelissaFoster.com/love-bloom-series

## Download Series Checklists, Family Trees, and Publication Schedules

www.MelissaFoster.com/reader-goodies

## Download Free First-in-Series eBooks

www.MelissaFoster.com/free-ebooks

# More Books By Melissa Foster

## LOVE IN BLOOM SERIES

### SNOW SISTERS
*Sisters in Love*
*Sisters in Bloom*
*Sisters in White*

### THE BRADENS at Weston
*Lovers at Heart, Reimagined*
*Destined for Love*
*Friendship on Fire*
*Sea of Love*
*Bursting with Love*
*Hearts at Play*

### THE BRADENS at Trusty
*Taken by Love*
*Fated for Love*
*Romancing My Love*
*Flirting with Love*
*Dreaming of Love*
*Crashing into Love*

### THE BRADENS at Peaceful Harbor
*Healed by Love*
*Surrender My Love*
*River of Love*
*Crushing on Love*
*Whisper of Love*
*Thrill of Love*

### THE BRADENS & MONTGOMERYS at Pleasant Hill – Oak Falls
*Embracing Her Heart*
*Anything For Love*

## THE WICKEDS: DARK KNIGHTS AT BAYSIDE
*A Little Bit Wicked*
*The Wicked Aftermath*

## WILD BOYS AFTER DARK
*Logan*
*Heath*
*Jackson*
*Cooper*

## BAD BOYS AFTER DARK
*Mick*
*Dylan*
*Carson*
*Brett*

## HARBORSIDE NIGHTS SERIES
Includes characters from the Love in Bloom series
*Catching Cassidy*
*Discovering Delilah*
*Tempting Tristan*

### More Books by Melissa
*Chasing Amanda* (mystery/suspense)
*Come Back to Me* (mystery/suspense)
*Have No Shame* (historical fiction/romance)
*Love, Lies & Mystery* (3-book bundle)
*Megan's Way* (literary fiction)
*Traces of Kara* (psychological thriller)
*Where Petals Fall* (suspense)

# Acknowledgments

I loved writing Jock and Daphne's story, and getting to know all of the Silver Island characters I have been thinking about for years. I hope you enjoyed getting to know them, too. Each of Jock's family members will be getting their own love stories, as will each of their friends. If you'd like to read more about Silver Island, pick up *Searching for Love*, a Bradens & Montgomerys novel featuring treasure hunter Zev Braden. A good portion of Zev's story takes place on and around the island, and includes Roddy and Randi Remington, and other Silver Island residents. My upcoming Silver Harbor series will feature Abby and Deirdra de Messiéres. Look for it summer 2021.

If this was your first introduction to my books, you have many more happily ever afters waiting for you. You can start at the very beginning of the Love in Bloom big-family romance collection with *Sisters in Love*, which is free in digital format at the time of this publication (price subject to change), or if you prefer to stick with the Cape Cod series, look for Seaside Summers and Bayside Summers. I suggest starting with *Seaside Dreams*, which is currently free in digital format (price subject to change). That series leads into the Bayside Summers series. Chloe Mallery and Justin Wicked's love story, *A Little Bit Wicked*, is the first book in the The Wickeds: Dark Knights at Bayside. I hope you'll enjoy them all.

I am blessed to have the support of many friends and family members, and though I could never name them all, special thanks go out to Sharon Martin and Lisa Posillico-Filipe, who are my right and left hands and allow me to spend my time creating our wonderful worlds. Heaps of gratitude go to Missy and Shelby DeHaven, who keep me sane here in my hometown, and have continued with safe social distancing lawn visits during the pandemic. I'd like to give a shout out to my son Jake, indie-pop musician Blue Foster, for allowing me to use his lyrics within this story.

Nothing excites me more than hearing from my fans and knowing you love my stories as much as I enjoy writing them. Thank you to all who have reached out. If you haven't joined my fan club, you can find it on Facebook. We have loads of fun, chat about books, and members get special sneak peeks of upcoming publications.
www.facebook.com/groups/MelissaFosterFans

Heaps of gratitude go out to my meticulous and talented editorial team. Thank you, Kristen, Penina, Elaini, Juliette, Lynn, and Justinn for all you do for me and for our readers. And of course, there is no thank-you big enough for my boys, who allow me to disappear into my fictional worlds and force me back to reality with their good-natured ribbing. You four and me forever.

# Meet Melissa

www.MelissaFoster.com

Melissa Foster is a *New York Times* and *USA Today* bestselling and award-winning author. Her books have been recommended by *USA Today*'s book blog, *Hagerstown* magazine, *The Patriot*, and several other print venues. Melissa has painted and donated several murals to the Hospital for Sick Children in Washington, DC.

Visit Melissa on her website or chat with her on social media. Melissa enjoys discussing her books with book clubs and reader groups and welcomes an invitation to your event. Melissa's books are available through most online retailers in paperback, digital, and audio formats.

CPSIA information can be obtained
at www.ICGtesting.com
Printed in the USA
LVHW041954061120
670968LV00004B/669